THE
DEATH
BRINGER

ALSO BY CHRISTY R. HARRILL

The Blood Vier

The King Slayer

THE DEATH BRINGER

CHRISTY R. HARRILL

Rose Hollow Press

The Death Bringer

Copyright © 2023 by Christy R. Harrill
Cover Art and Design by Franziska Stern
Map by Christy R. Harrill

Published by Rose Hollow Press, LLC
Oklahoma City, Oklahoma
christyrharrill.com

Cataloging Data
Harrill, Christy (Christy R.)
The death bringer/ Christy R. Harrill. –First edition.
p. cm. (The Blood Vier series; bk 3)

Summary: Vladimir struggles over doing what is right or what is easy for Gharridan as he navigates the political shambles of the kingdom while facing war, and Taryn is trapped in a game of riddles interwoven with her mother's past that threaten death. Loyalties are tested as destruction closes in, and for them to both win and survive will demand the greatest of sacrifices.

Library of Congress Control Number: 2023915397

ISBN 979-8-9859243-6-7 (hardback)
ISBN 979-8-9859243-7-4 (paperback)
ISBN 979-8-9859243-8-1 (e-book)
[1. Fantasy. 2. Action and Adventure—YA Fiction 3. Assassins
4. Kings, queens, rulers, etc.—YA Fiction] I. Title

First Edition, November 2023

For Donna

DELLWYN
CITY OF ISO
GAPSVAR
BRENDEN
HYTHE
PALAZAAR
ALGARAF

ADELLAIA
CARNA
THE CAPITOL
NAVARRE
GHARRIDAN
VARRA RIVER
JIDERO RIVER
THE COVEL SEA

Death knew.

Death *always* knew.

Time favored no one—except Death.

Every second, he waited for souls, waited for the moment when the *other* thing called Life would release the mortal bodies. Release them so he could touch them and catch the souls as they departed. He was nothing more than a fact whispered on the lips of those who now stood around a lifeless form. Nothing more than a means of balancing the scales against the *other*. Nothing more than a weapon wielded by those who wished harm upon people.

But still, he was something to be feared.

Something to dread.

Something to hate.

And sometimes, he took interest in those he waited for, wondering when time would finally grant him what he wanted. He knew the dark-haired girl could sense him, knew that the golden-haired boy feared him. He knew the blue-eyed man wanted to destroy him. But what he really wanted was for the redheaded visage to reach out and wield his touch.

One day. They couldn't have long.

But he was busy.

Time was running out. War was circling. The *other* was about to be eradicated.

And Death?

Death came knocking—for everyone.

CHAPTER ONE

VLADIMIR

THE BATTERED GATES of Gharridan dangled wide open and vulnerable to the world, a depiction of the kingdom itself, crumbling into dust and becoming a thing of the past. Where once stood an archway was now only jagged rocks jutting out in uneven teeth from the explosions that had mutilated them. Its vicious opening loomed above me like a guillotine ready to strike. Blood still stained the cobblestones, and ash and soot clung to the streets. The walls. The buildings.

I could still hear the ringing in my ears from when the explosion had blown me from Dante's saddle, and the pain as my body smashed against the ground, smoke clouding my vision, filling my lungs. The ghosts of the fallen soldiers haunted me, and War circled, laughing at me. I stared at the destruction around me, took everything in.

But the sight did not weigh me down with sadness.

It angered me.

Boiled the rage simmering just beneath the surface.

No military leader in their right mind would have set off explosions so close to the gates. The only entrance into the city was to be secured and protected at all costs, not blown into a million pieces. I ground my teeth together. It was purposeful. Planned. The order would have come directly from the queen, or from whomever she had paid to sabotage this kingdom. Our capital lay exposed to the vulnerability of being attacked by Brenden—or whoever else might wish to lay waste to Gharridan.

We guarded the useless gates day and night while working tirelessly to fix the damage, but it couldn't be fixed soon enough. The army I had amassed at Finnigan's bidding was spread out before me on the plain of Gharridan, growing restless with nothing to do and nowhere to go. We'd slowly begun intermingling some of them within the city walls, but tensions still blazed high. They'd come expecting a siege and had been told to stand down.

Fear and apprehension endlessly raced through me as each issue we had to resolve multiplied and built within my mind. I told myself I'd come to the gates to appear useful, but in reality I was here to distract myself, to try to forget the meeting that waited for me in the castle. The meeting that made me toss and turn all through the night, that made my skin clammy and my hands slick with sweat.

Both my fate and the fate of the Kavari had yet to be decided.

After this meeting, they would be.

Nic appeared at my side, gaze roaming over the battered structure. Wrinkles adorned his military uniform, and his dark hair was a disheveled and curly mess.

"I give it a week." He gave me a knowing eye. "If they spent less time glaring at the men camped out on the field, they could do it in half that."

I restrained an eye roll and shook my head instead. Sometimes I forgot how young he was, but leave it to him to pull humor out of this dire situation.

"Are you here to make sure they're getting the job done?" he asked.

"No."

A brief wave of confusion passed over his features before clarity dawned. "Your meeting is today, isn't it?"

I worked my jaw, my skin crawling to do something, to be anywhere but here. "I don't really know if you could classify it as a meeting."

He shrugged. "If you ask me, I think what you need to do is just go in there and show them who is boss."

I did roll my eyes this time. "Well it's a good thing I didn't ask you, because that sounds like a great way to get myself executed, or removed from power completely. Especially since I'm *not* the boss."

"And William is?"

I hesitated. "William is the king, but right now Gharridan is under the authority of the council until they decide who deserves to be in charge."

Nic cocked his head. "And you really think that William is the best choice right now?"

"What I think doesn't matter right now," I snapped.

Even after everything that happened, I could tell that William was trying, even if his mind and heart were not yet completely in it. His entire world had been turned upside down. He'd awakened a prince one morning and gone to bed a king. Everything he'd believed about his mother had been revealed to be a lie—her entire life was a fraud. His own mother had murdered his father. William hadn't fallen apart yet, a feat in and of itself, but he'd turned to the bottle. I hadn't seen him completely sober since his coronation, and war was marching toward our doorstep.

Nic ignored my sharp tone, getting in my face. "Listen to me, Vladimir. One of you is going to have to assert dominance. If there's a way for both of you to rule this country amicably as a diarchy right now, I don't see it. One of you will come out on top, and I think that I, as well as most of the people in this country, would prefer it to be you."

My conversation with Finnigan flashed in my memory.

"We're not putting William on the throne."

"Then who? Who could possibly be better?"

"You."

I'd never wanted the crown, never desired to fulfill the position of king. I'd only ever wanted what was in the best interest of Gharridan. "That ship has sailed, Nic," I growled. "I already told you that I wouldn't take the throne. Everything I did, I did to preserve this kingdom and to save William's and Taryn's lives. If I try to usurp William's authority, we will run into the same problem that I've been trying to prevent that army out there from facing this entire time."

Nic quieted before continuing. "You're right, but you're also wrong. Everyone knows that you have your head screwed on straight right now and that William doesn't. He just learned—"

I swung toward Nic, not in the mood for his antics. "All that happened to William is that his mother died, and he became king of Gharridan. That is all this country currently thinks happened, and that's the way it's going to stay until we can sort this mess out."

He stepped back at my outburst, taking the hint to keep quiet about whatever secrets he may know. Only a handful of us knew the truth of what happened in the throne room, and in that tower. It would get out eventually, but it needed to be released in a controlled manner. Having to tell your people that their queen murdered their beloved king and had been sent to destroy your kingdom by another country was no easy news to break. Especially when it had the potential to wreak complete chaos.

"I'm just asking you to not let me—*or any of us*—down, Vladimir. We've fought alongside you. Heard your wisdom. We trust you and your judgment. You always do the right thing, no matter the cost."

The right thing.

I was beginning to wonder if that even existed.

I'd tried to do the right thing by going behind Finnigan's back, rejecting his notion to amass an army to overthrow the Crown and instead amassing an army under the guise of uniting Gharridan. It seemed like it had only multiplied our problems. Every day, I questioned if that had been the right choice, but still I could find no other solution. No other way.

Nic's footsteps faded up the path, his warnings and pleas circling in my mind.

One of you is going to have to assert dominance.

And a bloody battle that would be.

I peered at the rising sun before turning on my heel, unaware of whether I approached the reestablishment of my position in the Kavari—or its imminent destruction and my pending execution.

CHAPTER TWO

TARYN

THE NEED TO flee shot through my veins like wild-fire, seared my skin, consumed my mind. I fingered the newly conditioned leather of the saddlebags, mentally checking off everything I needed and everything stashed inside for the third time. Food. Clothes. Weapons. I possessed little in this world. Fear clamped down on me, tried to swallow me whole, but I couldn't let it.

The queen's death haunted me. Everywhere I turned, every time I looked around, her vacant eyes stared back at me, and blood crusted my hands, soaked my dress. When I blinked, it all disappeared, but it never completely left me.

I'd killed her.

Killed the queen of Gharridan.

Killed William's mother.

Killed my father's murderer. A spy. A liar.

It was self-defense. It was justice. It was torment.

I couldn't take another day here.

From the moment I'd stepped foot in the capital, I'd only caused chaos, only made things worse. And even after all this time, I still held no place, no standing within the government of Gharridan.

I wasn't a royal.

Wasn't a Kavari.

I'd done enough damage, and it was time for me to leave, time for me to search out my mother's family, to heal whatever rift had been driven between them. I'd put it off for too long, been caught up in political affairs that I'd wanted no part of in the first place.

But it wasn't just that.

Vladimir was meeting with the king and the council at this very moment. While it wasn't intentional murder, I didn't have enough faith that they wouldn't charge me with something—wouldn't lock me away. Vladimir kept assuring me that nothing would happen, but after today, I questioned what authority he would still hold. A shiver caressed my spine. I could feel the heat of the councils' and courtiers' stares boring into me, judging me. Only a handful of people knew the truth, knew that I had killed the queen, but it wouldn't be long until that changed.

I would have already left days ago, but I'd only just mustered the courage, and tonight was the coronation feast. It had been postponed due to everything going on within the kingdom, but the council had insisted that it needed to go on to keep up courage and morale. I'd decided to wait to leave until after, to go in support of Gharridan, but everything within me wanted to get out of going to it altogether.

I laid my heavy cloak over the saddlebags to obscure them from view before crossing the room and sinking into the chair at my desk. I pulled out a fresh sheet of parchment and dipped the quill in the dark ink. The envelope that I'd found in my father's room with my mother's insignia hovered near the edge of the desk, taunting me with its secrets but never revealing them.

I thought I'd been so close, but I'd been wrong.

I felt farther from finding my mother's family than I ever had. I still didn't understand. The letter my father had hidden in the notebook, it said that he'd gone back for her. It appeared she'd been connected to the massacre, but how? How in the world could any of this be connected?

I bit my lip, questioning for the hundredth time if it would be better to stay, to keep turning over stones even though I'd yet to find anything. I had help here where I had none elsewhere, but I couldn't bear to stay.

I brought my focus back to the task at hand, the thoughts jumbling around in my head impossible to put into words. The blank parchment loomed before me, a splash of ink dripping from the quill and marring the surface. Vladimir would be angry when he found the letter. This was the second time I would leave him without explanation, with nothing more than a note—but I didn't know how else to say goodbye.

The tip of the quill fell to the paper, scribbling out nothing, and yet everything. I was ready to put this castle and everything that had happened in it behind me. I replaced the quill when I was finished, rereading the note again before setting it aside. It would have to do.

But another fear gnawed at the pit of my belly. Another reason why I wanted to wait until after the coronation feast.

William.

I held no doubt it would be better for me to simply walk away without ever addressing him again, but I couldn't bring myself to do that. I felt like I owed him something. The least I could do was offer him an apology, but that felt deceptive given that I wouldn't change anything even if I could. It was either my life or the queen's, and I wouldn't sacrifice my life to allow her to carry out more of her sadistic plan—but it didn't make bearing the burden of what I had done any easier. From what I'd heard, William was having a hard time even believing the truth of who his mother really was, let alone accepting it.

I expected my entire scheme to backfire, for them to drag me to the dungeons before the feast even began, but it was only one night.

One night.

One last dance of deception with the courtiers.

And then, finally, I would be gone.

CHAPTER THREE

THE SIX HOURS we endured in the previous deliberation were pesky housekeeping compared to the arguments that raged around us now—and we'd only just barely begun.

"One of the biggest issues plaguing us right now," Tanner, one of the elder councilmen, began, "is how much of the truth we want to reveal to the people. Their queen is dead, and the crown prince has taken the throne. Brenden marches at our doorstep. Rumors of the Kavari going rogue are still spreading throughout Gharridan, and an army now lies before the capital. No one knows if the army is here to overtake the throne, or to aid in the fight against Brenden. Our people are confused, scared. They want answers. Answers that I do not know if we should give them. Learning their monarch was actually an enemy, that her entire reign was built upon a lie, could be the very undoing of Gharridan."

The council remained silent, taking in the weight of his words. The truth treaded dangerous ground. Tanner spoke wisely, but concealing this would do more harm than good. The people were scared. I saw it in their hollow eyes when I passed through the town, the closing of their shutters, whispers in the alleys. I heard it in the mutterings of the soldiers we were still trying to force to get along with one another, that threw hostile looks toward the other side of the line between Crown and Kavari.

"The people of Gharridan deserve to know the truth," I answered first. "If we lie to them, and they later discover it, that will do far more damage than simply being honest with them from the beginning. They don't deserve to martyr a ruler who tricked and betrayed them from the very beginning to overthrow their kingdom."

"Or so the witnesses claim," William snapped. "None of us were actually in that room when my mother was killed."

Tension gripped the room.

"No," a councilman interjected, "but every witness testified with the same story, and every one of us present were all there when your mother ordered our deaths and the deaths of our fellow councilmen who are no longer with us today because of your mother's horrific betrayal."

William's jaw ticked.

"And do not forget, *Your Majesty*," he continued, "that it is only by *our* grace and *our* mercy that you assumed the throne. We still hold the power to remove you if we so see fit."

I watched William closely, but his expression gave nothing

away. His gaze remained locked on the table, his face carved of stone.

Tanner cleared his throat as if to dispel the unease from the room. "There is also the issue that if we tell the entire truth, will the people question William's right to rule considering that his mother was a traitor and the blood of our enemies runs through his veins?"

That was one troubling fact that had not yet crossed my mind. William's expression shifted before he could hide it, and it was clear that this idea had already occurred to him. He grabbed his half-filled glass from the table, throwing his head back as he downed the rest of the amber liquid. The alcohol had been his closest confidant since his coronation, but he had yet to learn that it would ultimately betray him. My throat bobbed, waiting for a comment from the council, but they made none.

William's voice cut through the room like steel. "Algarian blood may run in my veins, but my heart is Gharridan through and through. I have no claim to anything in Algarar, nor will I ever. My dedication lies with the people I've sworn to protect."

"But the people may not see it that way," Tanner responded. "There are very serious consequences that we must take into consideration."

"I do not think dumping the entire truth onto Gharridan at once—if ever—would be wise," another councilman said. "It would cause even more unrest than has already been created."

"If you do not wish to give them the truth, what kind of lie do you plan on concocting for them?" I asked. To think they could uphold a lie of any proportion was foolishness.

"We have been discussing that in our own meetings," Hart

said. "Someone has to take the blame, and we believe we have decided on who would best fill that role."

My throat constricted, Taryn's face flashing before my mind. "Who?"

William's eyes gleamed with interest as the council members passed secret looks with one another.

"Finnigan."

My hands curled into fists at the traitor's name. If only he'd died with the others in the throne room. The arrow that freed Taryn from his grasp had only grazed his chest, resulting in massive blood loss, but not enough to kill him. He was currently chained within the lowest dungeon, awaiting trial—or now awaiting some other misfortune, it would seem.

I mulled over the idea, not liking the taste of it. "Finnigan is not exactly innocent, but are you really going to charge him with crimes he didn't commit along with the crimes that he did?"

Hart shrugged. "He doesn't have to confess. It can be a private trial, or we could simply declare that he has already been executed."

"It wouldn't be that hard to believe," another councilman added. "Most of the soldiers already know that he was planning to overthrow the queen and put you on the throne. It's not that far-fetched that he would in turn murder the queen. It will be an easy story to weave."

"The queen has spent the last decade trying to persuade the people that Katherine was behind the king's death," I said. "She deserves to be exonerated from that accusation."

He sighed. "We've discussed that, and it will be made clear that Finnigan was behind that as well."

"And what about the soldiers who saw Finnigan go down in the throne room, that know Finnigan was never in the tower?" I asked.

"They will be made to keep their silence."

I didn't like the lies. The deception. If the true identity of the queen and everything that had transpired in that tower ever got out, it would be the final blow for Gharridan. People wouldn't trust a ruler or government that lied to them.

"You're balancing the survival of a nation on a lie. I still think the people deserve to know the full truth."

"We are making the best of a terrible situation, and that has been taken into consideration," the councilman said. "But we will leave it up to a vote. All of those in favor of charging Finnigan with the murder of the queen?"

Every hand in the room rose.

Except mine.

This was wrong.

"I need your word that you will honor this decision, Vladimir," Tanner said.

I locked my jaw. "I will not cause unnecessary turmoil, but only to keep the peace. Not because I agree with it."

I gripped the edges of the table, not wanting to ask the next question, but knowing that I needed to. "If you're pinning everything on Finnigan, what of Taryn Gallows?"

The councilmen glanced between one another before answering. "We have conducted our own investigation. We believe that she acted in self-defense and have chosen to not charge her. With anything."

William's back remained rigid, his face unreadable. As far as I knew, neither of them had spoken since Taryn killed his mother, and I didn't know if they ever would. I hadn't dared bring it up to William, but if he wasn't speaking out against her, perhaps he was not as far gone as I thought.

Several more issues of state were discussed, William's and my opinions not needed except to agree or disagree. They discussed Brenden and the mounting war, everything that we needed to prepare for. Another batch of troops was being dispatched in the morning to secure the western border. The council threw around information, but none of it was new. I'd held a briefing with the war council every morning and no further intel had been received.

"The biggest question we have right now"—Hart hesitated—"is who will ascend to the throne if anything happens to William."

His words left the room deathly silent. The crown prince had assumed the throne, leaving the position of heir vacant. This question was one that had been running through my mind over and over again.

"Much discussion could be given to the topic," Tanner said, "but the obvious choice here is Vladimir—"

"No." William's voice came out solid, definitive.

The attention of the council shot to William, whose fingers dug into the edge of the table, his downcast gaze boring into the grain of the wood.

"I understand your hesitance, Your Majesty, but given the circumstances—"

"I said *no*," William cut Tanner off again, and a dangerous tone now coated his voice. "Vladimir already tried to steal the throne from me once. If you put him in the line of succession, I have no doubt that he will try to expedite it."

I bit back the retort clambering its way up my throat. I'd already argued the fact time and time again. It would make no use to argue it now. William knew that I had no desire for the throne, that I had only done what I had to do to keep both him and Taryn alive, but he refused to see that. He chose to stay blinded to the truth, creating his own fantasy about the events. But Tanner was right. I was the obvious choice. Even if I didn't want to be. Brenden had a bounty on William's head, about that I had no doubt. They would come for him eventually, and there was no guarantee that we could hold them off. Gharridan couldn't afford to lose the royal line with no plan for succession.

"You don't exactly have an heir, William," Tanner continued. "Which is something else that we need to consider. Having you marry right away and produce an heir would be the wisest choice right now, and having an ally wouldn't hurt."

His statement caught me off guard. "What do you mean an ally?"

"Given the circumstances, William would be free to marry a noblewoman for the sake of producing an heir, but our neighbor Adellaia resides to the east, which still has an unwed princess. It would be wise to form an alliance through marriage. To have them on our side. If we could convince Adellaia that a war across the entire continent is imminent, they would be more apt to accepting us as an ally."

"I've heard that the Adellaion princess is very beautiful," one of the councilman jested, following with a crude comment.

The council stood here talking about both William and the Adellaion princess as if they were pieces of property to be bartered for and sold. Nothing more than breeding stock to suit a kingdom's needs. I knew little of the princess, but I did know that she was too young—not possibly older than fifteen—and there was no way her parents or kingdom would let her be sold into a marriage. Adellaia had no allies. They kept to themselves, nestled between the mountains and the coast. All their affairs and marriages were kept in-house, and they weren't given to enlisting in foreign aid.

Hart pulled a piece of parchment from the table. "We've already taken the liberty of drafting a proposal for an alliance by marriage. With your blessing, I feel that we should finalize it and have it sent out at first light. A delay as much as a single day would be catastrophic at this point."

"Yes, I agree with you," Tanner said. "Send out our fastest riders. The Adellaion princess would need to travel here immediately, as time will be of the essence."

"Perhaps the king should meet her halfway, and they could wed at the border of the kingdoms, shave off some traveling time."

Each of the council members piped up, talking about the alliance, the marriage, how much of a dowry the princess had, and if the Adellaions did accept, what was the timeline for the marriage, how quickly could it take place?

I listened to them in stunned silence, watching as they ran away with the idea. William said nothing, but I could see the rage slowly building in him, the red tingeing his face, the vein in his neck bulging. I knew I should speak up, speak out against the absurdity of the plan and how much they were riding on an alliance that Adellaia was not likely to accept, but I couldn't, even as the discussion grew more ludicrous.

"And then how long would it take to produce an heir?" Hart

asked.

The questions continued. Yes, how long before there would be an actual heir with a claim to the throne? How long would it take the princess to conceive an heir … could the princess even produce an heir? Was the king himself fertile? Perhaps experts would need to be hired to ensure that a pregnancy would happen immediately—

"Enough!" William slammed his fist down on the table with a finality that rang through the room. "All we have done is run in circles again and again and again, and I am done. You are done. You have fulfilled your role as mediator within the diarchy and your leadership is not needed anymore. You have blasted your opinions and asserted your power, bullying your way in as if you should continue to hold the highest authority in the land when that power does not belong to you. It belongs to the Crown and the Kavari!"

I straightened, encouraged that he'd still named both of our positions.

William glared at each of the council members. "This marriage alliance will not be going out in the morning. Or ever, because I will not submit to the wasted time of an arranged marriage for the simple sake of a woman bearing my child when Brenden is marching for war!"

"But, Your Majesty, as the only heir—"

"As the *only* heir," William interrupted and paused for emphasis. "I am still *alive*. If I die, then so be it. I won't care who sits on the throne at that point, and I highly doubt that you would honor my wishes anyway. There was a time for the council to restore the balance in the wake of my mother's death, but we are far beyond that now. We don't need any more division and quarrels over trivial matters. We need unity. Our neighboring country is marching on our borders because *I* killed their king. It doesn't matter that it was on my mother's orders. They will not stop, and we cannot allow division to hinder us. *I am the king.* I am *ruler* of this country, and I will have the final say in *all* matters."

A hushed silence descended, everyone afraid to break it. I swallowed, fearing where he was headed. He couldn't let the council run away with his kingdom, but nor could he claim sole sovereignty over the land. He would become the very thing his grandfather had created the Kavari to prevent. If he dissolved the Kavari—

"Now." William's gaze roved over each of us, landing on me. "Gharridan may have been established as a diarchy, but for the time being, I am the *only* reigning monarch. The Kavari has barely stood on its two feet since the death of their leader. If they wish to restore the government that once ruled over Gharridan, then the Kavari will prove their allegiance to their king. Once this is all over, I will decide whether they still have a place in this kingdom."

If he was rebuking my power now, there was no way he would ever hand it back to me again. His flair about the Kavari earning their place was only to appease the council, to keep them from totally rejecting his notion of power. The Kavari had only ever sworn allegiance to Gharridan—not the Crown.

"William—"

He cut me off before I could get two words out. "That is my decree, and it is final." He slammed his empty glass on the table, the sound ricocheting around the room. "All of you are to answer to me as we try to bring Gharridan back into some frayed form of unity. If any of you"—he waved his finger at us—"are in disagreement with this decree, you will be arrested and then face trial. Trial for either execution or to be exiled from Gharridan permanently."

Shock was the only word to describe the tone of the room.

"We do not have time for petty games," William continued. "Is there anyone here who wishes to disagree?"

Unease clouded the council members. If they rebuked William, they would lose him, but if they gave in to his demands, they may never be able to seize their power back. They exchanged glances with one another, hushed whispers, unaware if they should speak or not. I myself couldn't find the words to challenge him. He'd made up his mind, and he would not be swayed, even if his decision was to the detriment of Gharridan. The desire for power or peace warred within my mind, not wanting to let William do this, but not wanting to risk further confrontation.

A sarcastic smile plastered William's lips. "Well, since we all seem to now be in agreement, I'm glad we had this meeting." He strode around the table and headed for the doors, leaving his glass behind, the cup looking as empty as I felt.

"Everything will carry on as normal at the coronation feast tonight, to keep up good spirit. We will reconvene at the weekly council meeting in two days' time, and I will have picks for both my adviser and the members of my cabinet that I wish to instate. Happy feasting."

The door slammed behind him, the harsh noise echoing through the room.

So, that was it.

For now, the Kavari were done. Our fate rested solely with

William, and I'd watched like a coward as he took that power into his hands. Nic's face swam before mine, his words haunting my mind.

One of you is going to have to assert dominance.

One of us did.

And it hadn't been me.

CHAPTER FOUR

TARYN

THE MAUVE SILK caressed my body, fitting like a second skin. The metallic sheen of the elegant embroidery on the skirt caught the light and shimmered in it. I examined the dress in the mirror, the bodice pleated and covered in little crystals. I stared, not really believing that the girl looking back was me. It was the finest dress I had ever worn, and probably the finest I ever would.

"It's stunning."

Katherine's voice drifted from the doorway, startling me.

"It really compliments your skin tone."

My fingers danced over the olive skin of my arm, tracing the scar left from Queen Adamara's blade. I may have inherited my father's eyes, but my skin and hair were all my mother's. I studied myself in the mirror, imagining that it was her standing here in this dress, that I could really see her again.

But I couldn't.

She'd been gone for so long, every day I found it harder to recall her face to mind, to remember the little details about her that made her who she was. I'd written down everything I could remember shortly after she died, but words could only conjure so much. Each time I read them, more of the details had slipped away, disappearing like dandelion dust in the wind.

"You should know." I turned to Katherine. "You're the one who picked it out."

Katherine wasn't looking at me. She had crossed the room and was reading the letter still sprawled out on my desk for all the world to see. The letter meant for Vladimir.

"Were you really not going to say goodbye?" She spoke the words plainly without accusation in her voice.

I swallowed. No. I hadn't planned on it.

"It's easier," I said. "Besides, I'm sure that he'd try to talk me out of it."

A smile twitched at the corner of her mouth. "Indeed he would."

She gently placed the letter on the desk, and the silence stretched between us.

I clasped my hands in front of me, unsure of how to begin what I needed to say. "I want you to know how grateful I am, for everything. You've saved my life more than once, and I could never repay you for that."

"There is nothing to repay," Katherine said, and walked back to the door. "You will be missed, but I came to fetch you for the feast. It will be starting soon."

The dread in the pit of my stomach intensified. I plastered

a fake smile onto my face and nodded, but didn't move.

Katherine sensed my hesitation. "It's just courtiers, Taryn. You've seen all of these people before. It's not anyone new."

I nodded again, my throat constricting.

Katherine crossed back across the room, sitting on the bed. "They're not who you're worried about, though, are they?"

I shook my head.

"Are you really leaving to find your mother's family, or are you leaving for other reasons?"

I knew what her words implied. She was both right and wrong. I was leaving to find my family, I was leaving to get away from William, but I was also leaving to get away from the capital because I felt no worth in staying here.

"There's nothing left for me here, Katherine," I said.

"And you think that there's something out there waiting for you? With no leads? Not even knowing if they're still alive or even interested in repairing whatever made your mother and them part ways?"

I threw my hands in the air. "What else am I supposed to do? Spend the rest of my days aimlessly wandering these halls? I don't belong here."

"You could belong here. If you wanted to. In fact, you have the very birthright to belong here. To serve a purpose."

Her gaze bore into me, and I knew exactly what she was insinuating. I'd thought of it before, optioned it in my mind, but that life was not for me. That life would never be for me.

"I have no desire to join the Kavari, Katherine."

"Many times the very thing you do not desire is exactly what you need."

I shook my head. "Not this time. Not ever. I went down

that road once, and I don't ever want to go down it again."

Disappointment flickered across her face. "Then if that's how you feel, it's your decision. You're free to do with your life what you will." She turned to the door. "But I'm not going to lie and say that I agree with you."

She disappeared into the hall, leaving me standing there in stunned silence. It didn't matter if she didn't agree with me. It didn't matter if no one agreed with me. I'd made my choice, and nothing could sway me from it.

Hostile faces greeted me in the great hall, boring into my back and staring deep into my soul. Perhaps my imagination was amplifying my paranoia, or perhaps they all hated me as much as I feared.

Murderer. Their glares seemed to whisper, even though I tried to convince myself it was all in my head.

Dancers swirled through the center of the room, skirts flying with the movement, the rhythm dictated by the string orchestra performing by the far wall. Any food imaginable from savory meats to steamed dishes and fresh vegetables lined the tables at the edge of the room along with an abundance of sweet cakes and tarts, but I couldn't bring myself to eat it. Colors swam before me, chatter and laughter, but it was all foreign to me. Something I didn't feel part of.

For the hundredth time, my eyes traveled to where William sat on the throne atop the dais. He'd passed right by me when he entered the room, but never even acknowledged my presence. His face was constructed of stone, expression unreadable.

The fine royal apparel of dark purples and navy that draped him did not fit his mood or personality. They clashed with it. One of the servants climbed the dais, dark red wine spilling from the pitcher as they refilled the king's goblet. It was not the first time. Or the second.

I squeezed my hands into fists at my sides. Maybe it was better to not speak to William. I knew I was opting for the easy way out, but if he continued drinking at this rate, it would only end in disaster—or worse.

"His mother murdered your father, and you killed his mother. That's got to be awkward."

My back bristled at the unfamiliar voice, and I glanced around to see if anyone else had overheard the words. No one moved. I turned to the stranger, steeling myself. She was beautiful in a fierce and wild, captivating way. A red dress the color of dying embers was molded perfectly to her body, flashing in the light. Her dark skin was smooth, brown eyes sharp and penetrating. Curly hair fell down her back in torrents of ringlets with shining beads intermingled among the locks and woven braids. A silver band adorned her left arm and a silver cuff outlined her ear.

"I don't know what you're talking about," I said.

Her eyebrow cocked in question as she sipped from her drink. "I may be just a messenger, but that doesn't mean I don't know the inner workings of the court, and as a messenger I have access to otherwise unattainable intel. Especially when the powers that be deem my input and testimony necessary."

I stared at her, fitting together the pieces of everything I'd gleaned since the attack. "You're *the* messenger. The one who brought the missive from Marco to Vladimir."

She snorted *"Brought the missive?* More like became homeless traveling from town to town through every sort of unimaginable element while carrying proof of treason that people would kill to conceal. I shoveled horse dung at one of the inns for over a month waiting for Vladimir to return, all the while trying to figure out what to do with it if he turned up dead like Michael." She stopped at those words. "I am sorry about your father. I didn't know him personally, but Marco always spoke very highly of him, and losing a parent is never easy."

I nodded my thanks, somewhat taken aback by her strong personality.

"It's Taryn, isn't it?" she asked. "I'm Darya, by the way. Thought I'd introduce myself, seeing as I'm the one who helped solve your father's murder, and you are the legendary blood vier, after all. Have they not made you a Kavari yet?"

"I'm not joining the Kavari," I answered, annoyed that this had been brought up twice in one day.

She shrugged. "It would be too much politics for me. I like it every once in a while, purely for entertainment purposes, but I'd hate being tied down, tethered to one place. I like to come and go as I please." She lifted a finger. "Not that the life of a messenger is very glamorous, because I can assure you that it isn't. Especially when you're stuck sleeping outside, and it's freezing, and your toes and fingertips feel nearly frostbitten." She shivered as if picturing the idea or remembering a past instance. "It could be worse. I could have become a maid." She scrunched up her nose in disgust.

I cocked an eyebrow. Being a maid sounded far more appealing to me. "Do you anticipate staying long in the capital?"

"I don't know." She turned thoughtful. "Vladimir offered

me a position among the high messengers. There's enough uncertainty and excitement going on right now that it might be
worth it. But the new king is a lot to handle. I'd need a stipula-
tion that I didn't have to work directly with him, and the stench
of traveling soldiers who haven't had a bath in weeks might be
more than I could bear."

She looked over her shoulder and rolled her eyes. "You'll
have to excuse me, but I've just caught sight of who I was looking for and must speak with them. Pleasure meeting you."

I watched her saunter away, unsure exactly what had just
transpired and where all the conversation had stemmed from.
Her humor was so dry, her words so blunt, her tone so sarcastic,
but not in a rude way. It was actually entertaining, and I envied
her easy manner, her blatant lack of care for what others must
think of her.

A server approached me, extending the last glass on his silver tray. I frowned, but took it, downing the punch in one gulp
and then discarding it on an empty table. I was once again
alone, and I already missed Darya's carefree attitude. I didn't
know these people, nothing more than punitive interactions
and conversations. Coming here had been a mistake. If I'd left
this afternoon I'd have already been hours down the road, and
everyone would have been too busy with the feast to realize I
was missing. But I hadn't, and now I was stuck here. I drew in
a deep breath, deciphering the time and counting down the
minutes until it was appropriate to leave.

CHAPTER FIVE

❖

VLADIMIR

EVERYTHING ABOUT THE banquet hall irritated me.

The people.

The dancing.

The alcohol.

The endless tables of food.

I sat toward the back of the room, sipping my blasted drink and pushing the uneaten food I'd mutilated with my fork around on my plate.

I didn't want to be here.

Was humiliated to be here.

Didn't deserve to be here.

I'd lacked the guts to stand up to William or the council, and now I had possibly jeopardized the kingdom and the future of the Kavari because of it. William was right in one sense, that what this country needed right now was unity and not further division, but saying the Kavari held power in name only went far beyond that.

And it *wasn't* because I was trying to grasp at power or was afraid of losing it. That's what William and the others would say. I couldn't care less about the power. My only interest was Gharridan. William's actions were turning him into the very thing the Kavari were created to prevent. Monarchies succeeded well in almost all other lands, but what his grandfather had arranged was meant to keep a monarch from absolute power, from handing the fate of a nation into one man's hands.

I doubted the repercussions of that had connected in William's brain, but I also didn't trust William enough right now to entertain the idea that he could rule this kingdom sensibly by himself. His resolve was cracking, and it wouldn't take long for those fissured lines to split and burst into an explosion. He needed help but wasn't willing to admit or accept it. A dangerous place to be.

A throat cleared next to me, interrupting my thoughts, but I didn't look up.

"Are you just going to sit here brooding all night?"

I shoved a piece of cheese into my mouth and turned my attention to the dancers. "I'm not brooding."

"The definition of the word would beg to differ."

I pursed my lips, willing her to go away.

"I believe it means—"

"I'm not in the mood to be pestered, Katherine," I snapped.

"Most definitely not brooding."

She muttered the words underneath her breath, but I still heard them.

Katherine pulled out the chair next to mine and sat down. "You never told me how your meeting went today."

That's because I hadn't told anyone. I'd locked myself in my room, alone with my thoughts.

I paused mid-chew.

Perhaps I *was* brooding.

I explained to her in brief detail what had transpired but was unable to meet her eyes.

"I'm surprised the council allowed William to take control like that," she said.

"He was …" I trailed off, recalling William's demeanor. "I've never seen him that confident before. That sure. That intimidating and imposing. I think he fully embraced it because his position is the only stability he still holds in his life, and his throne isn't even secure."

"If you're brooding because you feel like a failure, you're not," she tried to reassure me.

Feeling like a failure wasn't even the half of it. She meant well, but words and assurance wouldn't get me anywhere.

"I could've done more," I said.

"Perhaps." She shrugged. "But that's in the past. All you can do now is do your best to better shape the future." She leaned in. "And that's not going to happen with you sitting back here and *brooding*."

Katherine's chastising felt like being scolded by a meddling aunt. "I'm sorry," I said. "Would you like me to go engage in fake pleasantries with the rest of the court gathered here? Pretend like I care?"

A smirk twitched at the corner of her mouth. "Not really. I actually had something better in mind."

"Like what?" I rolled my eyes as I took another swallow of my drink.

"Like why don't you go ask Taryn to dance?"

I choked on the liquid, sputtering some back into the cup. "*What?*" She had to be joking. "Why in the world would I do that?"

Katherine narrowed her eyes. "Because if you had been paying attention to what is going on tonight instead of being so absorbed with yourself and throwing your own little pity party back here, you would have noticed that Taryn has been alone nearly the entire night. Hardly anyone has approached her, and those that have glanced at her are all full of suspicion. The court knows she had something to do with what happened in that tower, they just don't know what. People are afraid of her. Give them a reason to not be afraid.

"*And,*" Katherine continued with a judgmental glare, "you shouldn't need a reason because it's the *nice* thing to do. She's too pretty to be sitting alone while there is dancing going on, and she knows hardly anyone here."

My gaze swept across the room. The nobles passing Taryn realized who she was and gave her a wide berth. Katherine was right, people were avoiding Taryn, even if they weren't quite sure why.

"She'd probably just say no." I took another sip of my drink.

"Gossip is flying around the court, Vladimir. People are afraid of her. Give them a reason not to be. And"—she wagged her finger at me—"you're also an angsty oaf who needs to learn how to lighten up every once in a while and enjoy the simple things in life."

"You're one to talk about angst," I quipped.

"Shut up." She slapped me across the shoulder. "Now get your brooding mass out of this chair and go ask her. I haven't seen you crack a smile in months."

That was an exaggeration. I smiled all the time.

I frowned. Didn't I?

Katherine disappeared into the crowd, and my gaze wandered back to Taryn, still sitting alone and very out of place, eyes darting around the room with nervousness. I took note that they drifted to the dais more than once, where William still sat drinking the night away.

I held no fondness for dancing. Had bruised the toes of everyone who tried to teach me.

Maybe Taryn hated it too and this was one grand mistake.

Nevertheless, I heaved myself out of my seat and maneuvered my way toward her. Her expression was unreadable, but I detected the apprehension simmering beneath the surface. When she'd first entered I'd had to do a double take, unaware if my eyes were deceiving me, but it really was her. Dressed like a royal and looking like a scared puppy, hands fidgeting in her lap as if desperate for a task. Her purple dress brushed against the floor, her hair elaborately braided partially up with the rest of her dark waves flowing down her back. My throat bobbed—Katherine was right.

Taryn was far too pretty to be sitting alone.

CHAPTER SIX

Katherine

I DIDN'T WANT to be here any more than Taryn or Vladimir did—but I would never tell them that.

It wasn't because my dress strangled me—the design was absolutely gorgeous. Nor was it because the pins holding my hair dug into my scalp. I loved the elaborate updo, the polished jewelry adorning my neck, the smell of the sweet perfume on my skin, the soft feel of the slippers on my feet. I loved all of it. The sparkling punch, the delicate foods, the string players' sweet melodies setting the tone of the feast.

It was the people I didn't care for.

I'd learned to ignore the disapproving looks, to pretend like I didn't hear the whispers that trailed my presence, but just because I'd learned how to deal with it didn't mean that I was immune to it. Vladimir and the council were trying to remedy the blame that had been placed on my shoulders, but even if the people believed Finnigan had orchestrated the death of Brenden's king, they still suspected me of King Roldan's death. Even if the queen's treachery one day came to light, years of despising and loathing wouldn't disappear with the snap of a finger. It would take years. Decades. The insinuations and ghosts of my past would always haunt me, hold me prisoner. People would never forget what I was associated with. The crime I was suspected of committing.

And that was just the way it was.

The way it most likely would always be.

While many avoided me, there were still those who stood behind me. Many were old friends of Michael, whom he'd persuaded of my innocence, but even in a room full of people that didn't blame me, there would still always be one that would.

A hand slid across my lower back as someone came to stand beside me. I stiffened, not uncomfortable with the touch but with the eyes that could too easily see the display.

"There are people here, Verone." I ducked my head, afraid someone might see my moving lips.

He remained silent.

The remnants of the conversation we'd shared less than an hour ago still hung between us, driving a wedge in what should have been easy conversation.

I knew he was still upset.

And I couldn't blame him—but I also couldn't change my mind.

He kept his stance open, turned out toward the crowd. "If you're afraid to even speak to me, I guess that dancing is definitely out of the question. It's a shame. I'd been looking forward to you stepping on my toes."

I couldn't prevent my lips forming into a smirk. "It was only one time, yet you still never let me live it down. Both of us know that my dancing skills are far superior to yours."

"But only because you're younger. I was a force to be reckoned with when I was your age."

I shook my head. "Heaven help us, Verone is dominating the ballroom again. There aren't enough partners for the men because all the women are standing in line to dance with him. Forget about his eligibility, fine dancemanship is the only quality needed."

He chuckled, but even with the humor a wave of sadness swept over me. "There had to have been others, Verone."

He took my meaning. "Of course there were, but that was before I met you."

I rolled my eyes. "Because you chased me down."

He lifted his eyebrows in mock surprise. "Excuse me? I objected to it. Heavily. Never sought anything more than your friendship, yet you practically threw yourself at me."

I glared up at him "I did not throw my—"

"And then it was too late for just friendship. Even when you tried to convince yourself otherwise."

I looked away, cheeks hot, knowing exactly where this was going. "You know why—"

"I do know why," he interrupted again. "And I don't care."

"But I do," I said.

I strode away before he could interrupt me again. Interrupting was my job, but I wasn't about to have a full-scale argument in front of the entire court of Gharridan. He continuously ventured to this topic, and I shut him down every time, but I knew he was finally about to push his way through the entire thing.

Cool air brushed against my cheeks as I stormed out onto the balcony. A few people mingled about near the banister, but it was mostly deserted. I leaned against the railing, looking out at the courtyard below, the hanging lights twinkling in the night.

"Katherine."

I closed my eyes at his voice behind me.

"Verone ..."

He took my hand without warning, leading me into the shadows of an alcove, away from watching eyes. His lips met mine. It had always been like this. Dark corridors, concealing shadows, brief conversations when no one else was around.

And it always would be like this.

I pulled away, knowing what was coming and wanting to free myself from it, but his hand in mine locked me in place, and he blocked my escape.

"Katherine, you've avoided this for too long—"

"I know what you're going to ask," I interrupted. I didn't like feeling vulnerable. "And the answer, as always, is no. I can't."

"You can't now or you can't ever?"

I wanted to look anywhere except his blue eyes, but they were all there was to look at.

"Not never, but—"

He pursed his lips together. "I love you, Katherine, and I'm willing to wait as long as it takes, but not if you're never going to be ready. Which is the impression you've been giving me for quite a while now. You keep insisting it's what you want, but words can only go so far without actions."

I squeezed my eyes shut. We'd been over this before. It

made perfect sense in my head. Why could it not in his?

"I love you too, but there will always be people that hate me, Verone. All of Gharridan is not privy to the secrets that we are privy to. You know how that would affect your station, how it would affect your appearance. You're too good of a man fulfilling the position to risk that. *I'm* not willing to risk that."

He shook his head. "You can't keep doing this, Katherine."

My eyes snapped up to him. "Doing what?"

"Punishing yourself."

"I'm not punishing my—"

"Yes, you are!" He stared at me. "I've seen it, ever since the queen accused you. You don't think you're good enough, that you deserve anything, but you *do*, Katherine. You say that everyone here judges you, yet you run yourself ragged for them. I want this. I've told you millions of times in millions of ways exactly how I feel, have never given you any doubt."

Tears pricked at the corners of my vision. "If I'm punishing myself it's not because I don't feel like I deserve something. It's because I'm afraid of losing it. Anything or anyone I've ever loved in this world has turned their back on me or betrayed me. I can't lose you too."

Verone's hand dropped from mine, the shine of tears glistening in his eyes. "I've proved that to you over and over again, Katherine. That I'm not going anywhere. But if you keep pushing me away instead of letting me in, if we can't ever go further than this, you will lose me. Because I would rather rip myself away from you than watch you agonizingly walk away from me one step at a time."

He held my gaze for a moment, and I knew he was waiting for me to say something, anything. But I couldn't. I didn't trust myself to.

He stepped away, into the light of the great hall, leaving me trembling in the shadows. I couldn't lose him. But I also couldn't have him. And it wasn't fair to keep him stuck in the middle with false hope. I tried to pull myself together and convince myself it was for the best, but I knew that he could only take so much, and if I wasn't willing to compromise then I would one day watch him walk away from me for the last time.

CHAPTER SEVEN

TARYN

SWEAT PEBBLED MY brow as I fiddled my fingers together, desperate to leave but also scared to. No one besides Darya had approached me all evening. Not Katherine. Not Vladimir. He'd hid in the corner all night, and while I wanted to approach him, it seemed he desired no company—which left me surprised when he rose from his seat and crossed the floor directly for where I was sitting.

Panic seized me. Only moments ago Katherine had sat by him. Had she told him that I was leaving?

My heart hammered within my chest as he approached. If he knew the truth—

"Is everything all right?" The question burst from my lips before I could stop it.

Confusion flickered in Vladimir's pale blue eyes before he

glanced around, tugging on the cuffs of his black sleeves. Whether from discomfort or nervousness I wasn't sure. A weathered uniform, unkempt hair, and scruff held the familiarity of Vladimir. None of which was presented before me. Silver buttons trailed down the front of his uniform, and his dark hair was neatly combed and untangled. His formal attire and tidied appearance left him looking unfamiliar to me.

"Everything's fine." His gaze bounced around the room as if looking for a distraction, or using it as a stall. Eventually he returned it to me. "Would you like to dance?"

The question caught me so off guard that I stared at him in stunned silence for a moment, thinking I'd heard him wrong. "What?"

Uncertainty tinged his features as he cleared his throat. "Would you … like to dance?"

My jaw slackened a little. Dancing was the last thing I could ever imagine Vladimir doing. He was too, too—I couldn't find the right word for it. And what about me, did I want to dance? Did I even know how to dance? But Vladimir was standing there, waiting for my answer while a million questions paraded across my thoughts.

"Sure." My voice sounded foreign to my own ears as I suddenly became aware of everyone around us. Watching. Their judging eyes searing fire across my back and cheeks.

Vladimir offered his hand, and I let him lead me into the midst of the rustling skirts and twirling dancers. The air warmed around me, the room shrinking as my heart beat furiously against the confines of my chest even though I could find no explanation as to why. I shook my head, trying to clear the fog that seemed to have suddenly descended on me. I didn't want to make a scene by tripping over Vladimir's feet because, for some strange reason, I'd become suddenly disoriented. Nerves had frazzled me all evening, but nothing about being on the dance floor should change that. The people could still criticize me from here as much as from sitting in a chair. Albeit I proved more visible on the dance floor.

Awkwardness overcame me as I tried to focus on the steps, Vladimir leading the dance with one hand in mine and the other at my back.

He said nothing.

"I didn't know you danced," I said, trying to start a conversation.

Vladimir's attention constantly shot around the great hall, his feet moving in time with the music, but his mind apparently somewhere completely different. "It's a rare sighting."

I cocked an eyebrow. "Did Katherine teach you?"

"No, my mother—" He cut off abruptly as if he'd said something he shouldn't have. "I—I learned when I was young."

I waited for him to continue, but he didn't, so I dropped the conversation, feeling he was fulfilling a sense of duty out of the dance and nothing more.

He still hadn't looked at me.

The blinding lights made my head ache, my muscles strangely growing heavy and tired. From the corner of my vision, I sensed the eyes of the onlookers, and I shrank further into myself.

"Don't let them get to you, Taryn."

Vladimir's piercing eyes met mine for the first time, full of guilt as if seeming to become aware of his aloofness.

I briefly squeezed mine shut, trying to block out everything trying to cram itself in. "It's like they know, Vladimir. They have to know."

"Trust me. They don't."

He spoke with such conviction that I wanted to believe him, but I couldn't bring myself to.

"They know that something is going on, but they don't know what, and I need to apologize for not being around to shield you from this."

I let out a little chuckle. "You don't need to waste your time worrying about me. I can take care of myself. You've had far bigger issues to deal with, and it's not like you've been sitting around with nothing else to do."

Vladimir leaned closer, sincerity hovering in his gaze. "You were forced to take a life in self-defense, Taryn. That's not something you handle on your own."

I swallowed, my mouth going dry as I felt the all too famil-iar pang of shame and regret pulse through me.

"But you're doing far better than anyone else I know." Vladimir spun me in a circle, and I nearly stumbled, feeling un-naturally dizzy. "You're so much like him."

I didn't have to guess who he was talking about.

"I've always found that strange," I said. "Considering that I spent more time with my mother than him. I barely knew him."

"I'm sure you possess some of her qualities as well."

For whatever reason, the topic of conversation had let Vladimir's guard down, and with the brief opportunity, I ven-tured where I knew I shouldn't. "What about you? Would you say that you're more like your father or your mother?"

The change in Vladimir was instantaneous. His lips pursed into a thin line, limbs going rigid.

"I'm sorry," I backtracked, tripping over my words. "I just meant— I've just never heard you speak about them before."

Sweat dampened my back and gathered on my forehead, and the palms of my hands turned slick with the perspiration. Why had the room grown so warm? The heat smothered me, making me feel short of breath. Dancing was definitely more exertion than sitting, but not enough to feel like this. My thoughts wandered as if locked in a fog. I was aware that I had somehow insulted Vladimir, aware that I needed to smooth this over, but I couldn't think clearly. Could hardly think at all.

"I don't think I've ever spoken of them. Not here." The muffled words slipped between his lips, and I had a feeling that he hadn't meant to release them.

"It must be heavy, to bear that burden by yourself for all these years," I said.

I stumbled, but Vladimir didn't seem to notice.

Had I drunk alcohol by mistake?

No. No, I wouldn't have missed that.

Yet whatever memories I'd had of earlier I now had trouble recalling.

Vladimir faded in and out of focus, and I watched his gaze lock on mine, heard him call my name, but it sounded so far away. It was so hot. Like a blazing furnace. All noise became distorted except for the sound of my labored breathing and pounding heart. My legs wobbled beneath me, unable to support my weight, and my head tilted backward, the lights above us turning into stars and shapes that constantly changed. I felt myself falling before losing all sense of my body, sense of time, and watched as the blackness closed in around me.

CHAPTER EIGHT

◆◇◆

Vladimir

UNEASE COILED IN my gut as I sensed confusion wafting over Taryn, felt how hot her skin had grown beneath my touch. Her words slurred. Her eyes lacked focus, and unless it was a trick of the light there seemed to be a tint to her usually green eyes. She stumbled and I navigated us out of the couples and to the edge of the dance floor. Trepidation crept up my spine as I tilted her chin up, trying to figure out what was wrong.

"Taryn?" I asked.

Her pale lips parted to form words, but little more than a moan slipped out.

"Taryn!"

Her eyes rolled back into her head, body going limp in my arms. I fell with her for a moment before hauling her back up enough to slip an arm beneath her legs and carry her off the dance floor. I glanced down at her, a million thoughts whirling in my mind. Fear racing through my veins. She'd been completely fine. What had happened?

Whispers and curious glances trailed us as I pushed my way out of the hall, the crowd parting around me. The doors swung shut behind us, muffling the noise of the feast. My arms tensed around her body. Taryn's dead weight frightened me.

I hurried to the far wall, where I laid her gently on a wooden bench. The deathlike pallor of her skin struck a chord of fear within me as I patted her cheek, calling her name, but she remained completely limp. Unresponsive. If she'd simply fainted she should've come to by now. I swallowed. Something else was going on. She hadn't just passed out.

"Boss?" Nic's apprehensive voice came from behind me.

My fingers trailed across her arm, which now burned like a blazing fireball, and stopped at her wrist where I checked for a pulse.

Nothing.

No.

Faint.

Faint, but still there.

Her chest barely rose and fell, a brief trickle of air slipping between her lips.

Panic coursed through me.

"Taryn!" I shook her shoulder, trying to wake her from whatever evil claimed her, but she didn't respond, remaining completely still before me.

"Nic, get Katherine." I spared a glance behind me at his worried face and noted the hesitation. "Now!"

I kept calling to Taryn, checking for any sign of injury, but continued to find nothing. I took her warm hand in mine, squeezing it and praying she would open her eyes. I recalled the strange tint they'd held and pulled up the lids to find that it had only amplified. The whites of her eyes had transformed into a dull yellow.

I stilled. Countless possibilities raced through my mind, and I sorted through everything I knew, any once-useless knowledge I could conjure up, but I only came up with one solution, and that solution shouldn't be possible.

Footsteps clattered across the floor, and I sensed Katherine and Nic approaching.

"Oh heavens." Katherine knelt beside me, green skirts swishing around her, her face tainted with fear. "What's wrong?"

"We were dancing and she just collapsed out of nowhere. She's been unconscious since." My fearful eyes met hers, and whatever she saw there scared her. "I think she's been poisoned."

The words tasted bitter and foreign as they fell from my tongue, but they spurred Katherine into action.

She turned Taryn's pale wrist over, fingers feeling for a pulse, checking her eyes just as I had, trying to elicit a response from her but to no avail.

"Do you have any idea what it could be?" I asked.

Katherine was well studied in poisons. I wasn't, but I did know the signs, and depending on what it was, Taryn might only have minutes to live.

"Yellow eyes, fever, slowed pulse …"

Taryn's face was nearly completely white. I brushed the

damp hair from her face, still holding her hand and giving it another squeeze. How had she been poisoned?

Katherine stood up straight on her knees, eyelids drifting shut, chin lifted as she evened out her breaths and brought her hands up to rest on Taryn's sweaty forehead. The familiar prickle as the hair on the back of my neck rose accosted me, shivers rippling down my spine as my body sensed the change in the air around us. The way that it seemed to be drawing in a breath.

I was also holding mine.

Minutes passed.

Katherine remained still, brow furrowed in concentration. Her arms locked, back rigid.

Impatience rose within me as nothing changed. As neither moved.

"Katherine?"

She didn't respond.

I glanced at Taryn, who looked even worse. I waited a moment longer but still nothing. Katherine's body seemed frozen in time, until it started to shake. It was slight at first, starting with her head, then spreading through the rest of her limbs. Her lips trembled, eyes flicking back and forth underneath her eyelids.

"Katherine!" I yelled, completely taken aback and scared. She'd never reacted like this before.

The violent convulsions shook her body so hard I didn't know how she hadn't fallen over. I reached for her hands to remove them from Taryn, but they wouldn't budge. It was like an iron grip was clamping them down. Katherine whimpered, fear etched into the strained muscles of her face, tears slipping from her closed eyes and traveling down her cheeks. Taryn stirred, crying out.

"Katherine!"

Nic knelt beside me as we shook her shoulders, tried to wake her up, but it was to no avail. What in the world was going on? We yelled her name, drawing the attention of the guards and the people still within at the feast. It was like something had taken hold of her. Held her prisoner. I slapped her cheeks but got no response.

I frantically searched for what to do, a way to pull her out of this. I rose to my feet and searched for a glass of water or some liquid to throw in her face, but I didn't get far.

Katherine screamed. A chilling, blood-curdling shriek that tore itself out of her chest like a monster.

I barely had time to register the terror on her face before an explosion bellowed from within the great hall, rattling the stone beneath my feet.

CHAPTER NINE

VLADIMIR

T HE RINGING IN my ears disoriented my hearing as the world seemed to momentarily blur. I braced against the wall for balance, trying to clear my head. The explosion pulled Katherine from her trance, leaving her gasping for air, and she gripped my arms like she needed to possess something real and solid. Tears streaked her face, pain lining her eyes as she hyperventilated, staring at the world around us as if she expected it to disappear. Screams erupted from the hall behind me, and I grabbed Katherine's face, searching for a sign that it was really her.

"Are you okay?" I asked.

She gave me a shaky nod and I rose to my feet, facing the entrance to the great hall and unsure what I was about to meet. The doors flew open and guests poured out into the corridors, screaming, running from whatever lay within its walls. Smoke drifted into the hallway; some faces were plastered with soot.

"Get Taryn somewhere safe!" I yelled to Nic before fighting against the crowd to get through the doorway. They pushed against me like a herd of stampeding cattle, no thought given to the Kavari fighting against the current. The hazy air surrounded me as I crossed the threshold but didn't completely cloud my vision. Where once sat the dais now lay a blackened hole in the earth, everything within close distance charred and flames licking at what was left.

William.

I'd last seen him perched on the throne of the now-destroyed dais. With a wild look, I searched for him in the confusion around me, smoke burning my eyes.

A coughing guard tottered past me.

I caught his arm. "Where's the king?" I demanded.

He coughed again, soot concealing his features and clothes. "The king is safe. His bodyguards rushed him out after the blast. I'm not sure where they took him, most likely to a bunker."

My gaze flew to the exit at the far end of the room, finding the door swinging ajar in the haze.

"What happened?" I asked.

The guard wheezed, pointing to the left of the dais where I noticed several guards trying to secure a screaming man with flailing arms. I jogged over, wary of any new threat. The man lashed out like a rabid animal, the four guards struggling to keep him subdued. A fifth soldier ran over to help, trying to keep the man still.

"Lord Vladimir!" one of them gasped. "He's the one—"

The soldier bellowed as the wild man raked him across the arm. "He's the one who threw the explosive."

The man took notice of me, baring his teeth, his face consumed with hatred.

Another soldier pinned him to the ground with a knee to his back, yanking the man's arm behind him and lifting it to the point of breaking.

"What happened?" I asked.

The man stopped struggling for a moment.

"A guard caught him sneaking through the crowd, found him suspicious, and ordered him to stop. At that point, this man ran for the throne shouting in Brenden, and lifted his arm to launch something. Captain Verone and the guards tore William from the throne and shielded him just before it exploded. We caught him before he tried to end himself in the flames."

I felt the blood drain from my face, unable to hide the shock ripping through my body. Assassinating William shouldn't have even been within their reach. Brenden should never have been able to get this close without us noticing.

"Were there any others?" I asked.

He shook his head. "Not that we've found."

My eyes shot to the hallway.

Taryn.

The poison.

I motioned to the doors. "I want every soldier armed and on duty. Lock the gates down. No one goes in or out without verification of who they are. Conduct a full search of the castle. Look for anyone or anything suspicious, and have someone start going over the record books, looking for anyone who slipped inside that shouldn't be here."

I turned to another guard. "Find out where William is and put him under lockdown if he isn't already. Make sure that wherever he is hiding is secure. I want a minimum of six guards with him. No one goes in or out without my permission first, not until I meet with him and we can ensure that it is safe."

I looked down at the man who still glared up at me with hatred. Where there was one, more were sure to follow. I grabbed the Brenden by his loosened collar, wrenching him to his feet and dragging him kicking and screaming to a serving room adjacent to the great hall, where I deposited him onto the stone floor. Heat built within me as I unbuttoned my jacket and threw it across a nearby table, my hands already trembling with anger knowing that this man tried to kill Taryn. Kill William. Two guards followed me into the room, watching cautiously as they stood on either side of the door.

The Brenden scrambled to his feet, showing no signs of fear. I flicked my hands at the guards.

"Restrain him."

They advanced, each grabbing one of his arms and forcing the impostor to his knees. The Brenden features of the man were undeniable. Sickness roiled in my stomach at how he managed to make it past the guards without suspicion. Without question.

"Who are you?" My voice sounded so cold, yet so calm.

He spit in my face without hesitation, a hostile smile spreading across his soot-covered cheeks.

I wiped the slippery fluid from my skin without ever taking my eyes from him.

My fist slammed into his stomach, and he doubled over. Before he had time to recover I rained down a second strike across his face then yanked his head back, nearly tearing the hair out with the force.

"I asked you a question," I growled between gritted teeth.

He released a maniacal laugh, spitting out blood, more running down his mouth and coating his teeth. He lifted a singed eyebrow. "Is your king dead?"

My next blow caught him off guard, sending his head whipping to the side as pain shot across my knuckles. I rifled through his pockets, noting that he was wearing Gharridan clothes. He would have blended in well. My hand emerged with another explosive, which I carefully set across the room. His pockets held nothing else.

"Are you an assassin?" I asked, my voice still eerily calm.

He grinned. "I am now."

My knee slammed into his groin before I jerked him from the guards' grasp and shoved him up against the wall, his head smacking hard against the stone.

"Who sent you?" I roared. "Are you from the Brenden government?"

His eyes glassed over and he pursed his lips, refusing to speak, determination set within the lines of his face.

"Are you also responsible for poisoning the woman?"

Confusion flashed across his face before I punched his abdomen and heard a crack. My arm jolted with the force. He let out a ragged gasp, his face scrunched with pain.

"Are you?"

He looked up, laughing bitterly as he struggled to talk through the pain. "If your king is still alive, he won't be for long. You can kill me, but there will always be another to take my place. You won't ever stop us. Not until your king and everyone inside your country is dead."

I jammed my fingers into his side, pressing against the broken rib. "How many more of you are here? Did you come alone?"

He didn't answer, and I dug in further, drawing a strangled cry from his throat.

"I came alone, but more will follow."

A roaring filled my ears as I hit him again, but no matter what way I phrased it, his answers remained the same and I couldn't pull any more information from him.

I shoved his bleeding body to the floor and strode to the door, jerking a thumb at him. "Question him until he gives you a useful answer."

The soldiers had extinguished the fire around the dais, but smoke still clouded the room. I scanned my surroundings, momentarily lost, unsure how to move forward.

A woman's scream reverberated through the room. Katherine's. I watched her fall to her knees next to a body on the floor.

Verone.

His burned clothing hung off him, skin puckered with burn marks and covered in soot.

He and the guards had shielded William from the blast.

Oh, dear heavens above.

Katherine's hands immediately descended on Verone to heal him. I turned away, unable to watch as I left the wreckage of the great hall behind me.

"Vladimir!"

The soldier I'd tasked with locating William ran up and verified that the king was locked and secured within one of the safe rooms. I nodded, quizzing him on the events as we strode through the castle, noting that Taryn was missing from the bench. Nic better have her somewhere safe and she better be alive—better be okay. I couldn't keep this many people safe. Not all at the same time.

Chaos reigned at the castle gates, frightened nobles and courtiers screaming and angry about not being allowed to leave. Lines had formed, guests being questioned one at a time before they could exit to the courtyard. I made my way through the crowds, questioning everyone, trying to fit all the pieces together. Most didn't see anything, had no idea something was happening before the running Brenden caused the commotion and then the dais exploded in flames. None of the guards had any recollection of the man entering or seeing anything else suspicious.

I scanned the faces around me. Maybe the Brenden was telling the truth. Maybe he *had* been acting alone, and he'd so easily infiltrated our defenses. The dust was settling, nothing was happening. Someone else should be involved here. Could he really have almost pulled off poisoning Taryn and assassinating William by himself?

I pulled one of the higher officers from the front of the crowd, still suspicious that enemies moved among us in the shadows of the evening. I couldn't keep the irritation from my voice as I spoke with him. "I want to know how a foreigner infiltrated the safety of both our city walls and castle defenses and was able to get close enough to nearly assassinate the king." Anger flared in my eyes. "I want answers. And I want answers by morning. You find anyone suspicious, you lock them up for questioning. You hear the slightest hint of any lead, you come tell me immediately. This should not have happened, should not have been even remotely possible, and it will not happen again. Are we clear?"

He nodded in salute and I surveyed the courtyard around me once more before striding back into the castle, passing by the infirmary where I ran into a distraught Katherine.

Sorrow haunted her eyes, tears staining her cheeks. She was trembling, looking haggard and worn to the point of falling over.

I caught her elbow, guiding her over to a chair. "You need to sit down, Katherine."

Perspiration dotted her pale face and I waved a servant over, instructing them to bring her a glass of water.

I turned back to her when it was just us, afraid to ask but knowing I had to. "Verone?"

She squeezed her eyes closed, shutting away tears as she bit her lip and gave a weary nod. "I—I healed him. The physician is with him right now. He should be okay, I think, but I don't know how severe the damage was on the inside, how deep the flames reached inside his body." She took a breath, meeting my gaze. "Also, I think Taryn is fine too. I don't know what happened, I—" She cut off as if seeing a horror play out before her. "I drew the poison out. I know that much. She should be safe now."

I studied her, unsure of myself. The way she reacted after laying hands on Taryn still stirred the fear simmering within me. That hadn't been normal. Hadn't been natural. "You scared me, Katherine. What happened back there?"

Her thoughts grew distant as her bottom lip trembled. She shook her head, a new fear I'd never seen in her eyes taking hold. "I don't want to talk about it. Not now."

I heard what she didn't say in those words.

Not now.

Not ever.

It only stoked my curiosity and fear even more.

"That's fair, but are you sure you're going to be fine?"

She stared down at her soot-stained hands, red hair curtaining her face. "I will be." She straightened, glancing around as if desperate for a different subject. "I've only picked up pieces. What have you picked up so far? Is William safe?"

I relayed everything I'd learned to her, voicing my concerns of how the Brenden managed to get so close to the king, how I wasn't certain he could have acted alone. There were too many questions. Too many variables.

She mused over it, that sparkle of discernment rekindling within her green eyes. We threw ideas back and forth, trying to unearth the answers that didn't seem to be there.

A soldier jogged around the corner, chest heaving and breath ragged. "Lord Vladimir, the prisoner."

I stood, fear shooting down my spine. "What is it?"

"When the prisoner learned that William was still alive, he got an arm free from one of the soldiers, and grasped hold of their dagger. He—he slit his own throat."

I stared at him, not wanting to accept the words I was hearing.

"He's dead," the soldier finished.

I swallowed before nodding. "Search and inspect him again, just in case we missed anything."

He saluted, disappearing just as quickly as he came.

Suicide.

Suicide by failure.

If the Brenden hadn't succeeded at his plan, he wouldn't allow himself to be caught. Questioned. Tortured. I never should have left him, should've stayed to get more answers.

"If he took his own life, and nothing else has happened, I think he was working alone." I mulled over the idea, chewing on my bottom lip. "I'm keeping William in lockdown for the time being. I don't like it."

Something was still off. Not right. My mind strayed back to when I'd searched the man. All he had on him was the second explosive. He'd probably planned to set it off on himself if he failed, meaning we might have had more casualties. If he'd set it off when those soldiers were still trying to hold him down—

I didn't go there, but it troubled me. He'd had no poison on him, no evidence of poison. He hadn't worn gloves, there was no scarring on his hands from the chemicals, not that it would show up there anyway. He could have disposed of the bottle, thrown it in the flames, but if he'd been so set on getting the job done, would he not have kept one for backup in case Taryn failed to ingest the first one?

"I'm not sure how we thwarted two assassination attempts tonight."

Katherine's voice sounded far away as I lost myself to my own thoughts.

Two assassination attempts.

One on Taryn.

One on William.

"The deal with the explosive was messy," I pointed out.

Katherine cocked an eyebrow. "Yes, those things do tend to be messy."

I shook my head, ignoring the sarcasm. "No, I mean it was

too messy."

I had her attention now.

"What do you mean?"

I sifted through the details in my mind, something about the entire situation making me uneasy. "The assassins of Brenden have always been obscure, meaning I don't know much about them, but I do know that they're meticulous, which has aided them in remaining so ambiguous. If they came here tonight with the intention of killing William, they would have succeeded. They would not have failed. When I interrogated the Brenden man, he resisted me, but his responses were not that of a well-trained assassin. They were that of a vengeful and devoted citizen of Brenden. Someone who was willing to do whatever it took to restore honor to their country."

The idea simmered between us.

"It was messy," Katherine repeated, catching on. "He figured out well enough how to get into the castle, but the soldiers said once he was in the great hall, he gave himself away, charging at the dais without thought for the consequences. We found no other trace, the investigation will take a while, but the evidence points to him acting alone. Nothing else has suggested otherwise."

"That man was no trained assassin," I said. "Especially not a Brenden assassin."

Katherine's eyebrows knit together. "Then how do you explain the attempt on Taryn's life?"

I couldn't. If she was poisoned, it would have to have been through the food or the drink, and if she was the only one who was poisoned, she was the only one who had been targeted. Only administering poison to one person without that individual or anyone else being suspicious or noticing something off required extraordinary talent and discretion. Someone knew what they were doing, and they had done their job well.

"If I hadn't seen the yellow in her eyes," I said, "I don't know that I would have come to the conclusion it was poison that quickly. Not until it was too late. It had to have taken effect within minutes, because she was perfectly fine when I first approached her, from what I could tell."

"But you weren't watching her for the entirety of the ball. She could have ingested it early on."

"It's possible," I agreed, "but I don't think so. If I hadn't been dancing with Taryn, she might have left when she began to feel unwell."

"And stumbled down the hall, possibly to die with no one around." Katherine's face grew serious. "Vladimir, she was at death's door when I healed her. Any longer and she would have died."

"It was meant to take effect quickly," I said. "William was drinking all night. If they managed to get around his taster, they could have easily poisoned him. What I don't understand is why Brenden would want Taryn dead, or why they would poison her. They're assassins, so it's not beneath them, but from what you and Taryn told me about what happened in the king's study in Brenden, Tristan was aware that Taryn meant to let him and his father go. Tristan knew William was the one who murdered his father. Why try two different assassination attempts, one messy and one discreet. Why even target Taryn at all?"

"Like you said," Katherine put in. "Poison is not beneath Brenden assassins, but it's not their preferred method. My knowledge of them is also little, but I do know that they have always left a trace. They always let those left behind know exactly who it was that pulled off the assassination. Brendens are a proud people, and they would never let someone else take responsibility for their achievements. It would be too disgraceful for them. I've also never seen this poison used before, and I've studied hundreds. Brenden assassins carry a different type of poison. More dramatic. This is too subtle for them."

We stared at each other, minds working through all the possibilities.

"Are you coming to the same conclusion I am?" she asked.

I stared at the far wall, recalling Taryn's unresponsive body and the charred remains of the dais in the great hall.

"I don't think these two incidents are connected." I met her eyes. "I think we're dealing with two different assassins."

CHAPTER TEN

TARYN

THE RAWNESS OF my throat nearly bled me dry. No air existed. No peace. Only screams. Darkness. Unbearable nightmares that shredded me to pieces, leaving me more damaged than I already was. The pain. The torture. I'd never felt anything like it, and no matter how hard I fought, I couldn't get away. Reality was blurred. I was back on the gallows in Gapsvar, the explosion rocking the ground beneath my feet. Beva's lifeless body was bleeding out before my helpless eyes. I was drowning. Drowning. *Drowning.* The edge of Zedekiah's blade was pressed against my throat. Queen Adamara's dagger was cutting into the flesh of my arm. Her blood soaked my dress, staining my skin.

On.

And on.

And *on*.

When I awoke from the memories intermingling into my nightmares, darkness cloaked me. A mound of blankets weighed me down, pinning me to the mattress I lay atop. A fuzzy cloud obscured my vision, but cleared as I blinked it away, taking in the room around me. My room. Moonlight whispered through the drawn curtains, a sliver traveling across the floor, shifting with each breath of air that tussled the drapes.

I grasped for clarity, but struggled to remember what had happened before the dreams came. Movement to the right caught my attention, and I turned to find someone sitting in the chair beside my bed.

"Vladimir," I croaked. It felt like sawdust was coating my mouth.

I coughed, pain slicing down my throat when I swallowed. I brought my hand from underneath the covers in search of a drink. Vladimir rose, seeming to guess what I was searching for and bringing a glass to my lips. The cool water rushing down my throat felt like heaven, and I closed my eyes in gratitude for it.

"How are you feeling?" Something hovered in Vladimir's voice. Sincerity rang in the question, but I sensed an emotion hidden beneath it.

Resentment? Disappointment?

"A bit difficult to describe," I said, weariness flooding my veins at the simple motion of drinking. "What happened? The last thing I remember is …"

I trailed off, trying to figure out exactly what that was, and I shivered at the nightmares, the horrors my mind had dragged me into. A dress of mauve silk. I'd been draped in finery.

"We were dancing." Vladimir's deep voice cut through my thoughts. "At the coronation feast in the great hall."

Flashes of swirling skirts and comforting music played out before me, Vladimir's hand in mine. The dizziness in my head, the heat, the confusion. But why?

"I must have passed out," I mumbled. "I remember being flushed, disoriented."

My eyelids drifted shut, trying to drag me back to sleep.

"Taryn." Vladimir leaned forward in the chair, his expression expectant as he seemed to choose his words with care. "Was there anyone … *unusual* that caught your attention at the feast, anyone that you talked to?"

My brow furrowed. "I met Darya, but other than her you were the only one I talked to."

"I'll bet she made an impression."

I let out a weak laugh. That she did.

"Do you remember what you ate and drank?"

I threw him a peculiar look. "What are you getting at, Vladimir?"

"Do you remember what you ate and drank?" he asked again.

"I ate a platter of food from the main table, and downed a glass of punch."

"You pulled your drink from the main drink table, and that was the only one that you had?"

I didn't like where he was going with this. "Yes, from the table with all the other—" I halted, recalling the last glass I had. "No, I had one more drink, a punch from one of the serving trays."

Vladimir grew eager. "The person serving the tray, do you

remember anything about them? What they looked like?"

I ran the event through my head, but couldn't come up with anything. "No, I was distracted. I was offered the drink and simply took it. I don't even know that I looked at the server's face. What's this about?"

Vladimir interlaced his fingers, reserved, as if he didn't want to say the next words. "You were poisoned, Taryn."

I stared, thinking I hadn't heard him right. "What?"

He dove into a lengthy explanation about my poisoning, the explosion and attack on William, the death of the assassin, his and Katherine's thoughts on the matter, the idea of two different assassins. The reality made me sick. I fought even harder to remember the server's face, but it wasn't there.

Poisoned.

I lay back, staring up at the bare ceiling.

"Someone wants me dead."

The fact circled my mind, fusing with different memories before breaking away from being disproved. There had been more attempts on my life in the past few months than in the whole entirety of my life, but all the people I knew that had wanted me gone were now dead. Vladimir didn't seem to think it was Brenden, and I agreed, but also—maybe it was. Maybe Tristan didn't care that I was never going to kill his father. I was still guilty by association with William. Maybe they wanted us both dead, no matter who had wielded the blade.

"I've been here since an emergency meeting with the council," Vladimir continued. "The castle is currently locked down, and we've heightened security as well as kept William secured in a bunker until we're sure it's safe for him to emerge. Whoever poisoned you, we're going to find them."

Whoever wanted me dead was still alive, and possibly still in the castle if everyone hadn't been permitted to leave castle grounds yet, but if they'd slipped in unnoticed, I had no doubt they'd be able to slip out. If Brenden didn't want me dead, then who did? I'd made enemies, yes, but to this extent?

"Is William all right?" I asked.

"I haven't spoken with him yet, but I was assured he sustained no major injuries."

The whole reason I'd endured the coronation feast was to talk to him one last time, clear things up, maybe say goodbye. If I'd left like I wanted to, if I hadn't needed closure, maybe this whole mess could have been avoided.

Or I could be lying dead on the side of the road.

"I found this." Vladimir's voice turned distant. "On your desk."

My gaze fell to the letter I'd penned for him, the rough parchment lying open in his hands with the seal cracked. Inwardly, I groaned.

I averted my gaze, saying nothing.

The silence stretched between us, unanswered questions and unfinished conversations lingering in the air.

"Were you just going to leave without saying goodbye? Again?" His voice was quiet, disappointed.

"I thought it would be easier," I finally managed.

"I thought I would have deserved more than that."

His words pierced through me. It was the second time I would have left him without explanation, because technically, I didn't have one.

Didn't have one, or didn't want one?

"There's nothing for me here, Vladimir. I have no place in

the politics of Gharridan, no standing in the court. I came here to solve my father's murder, and I have. I have no reasons left to stay."

Vladimir was silent for a moment before continuing. "You have me, and Katherine. Your birthright basically grants you a position in court."

I shook my head. "I'm an outsider to them. I always have been, and I always will be. I have no desire to wedge myself into a life I was not made for, and you and Katherine have your own lives, your own responsibilities that I will never be a part of."

Vladimir caught my eyes. "But what if you could be?"

I stared at him, afraid that I understood what he was trying to say. "What do you mean?"

He cocked his head. "There are two gaping holes in the Kavari, Taryn, and last I checked, you were still a blood vier."

First Katherine, now him.

A blood vier.

From the moment I'd first heard those words, my life had never been the same. I'd been thrown into a political game that I never wanted to take part in, and my entire world had been turned upside down. I'd never thought I would have to go through with becoming a Kavari after agreeing to Vladimir's bargain, and when I realized that I might have to, I'd made peace about it, willing to sacrifice my desires to stop my father's killer. Even after everything that had happened, I'd still considered it, dwelled on the idea, but every time I kept coming back to the same conclusion.

"No," I said. "I have no interest in joining the Kavari. I never did."

Vladimir's jaw ticked, his face betraying nothing else as he simply nodded and accepted my decision. "I understand, just know that if you ever choose to walk through it, that door will always be open."

I suspected I'd spend the rest of my life trying to slam that door shut.

I leaned my head into the pillow, eyes drifting shut. "I'm sorry, but I can barely keep my eyes open, and I would like to get some sleep."

Guilt withered through me at my attempt to end the conversation, but the sudden darkness of my eyelids pulled me under its influence, faster than I thought possible. As sleep took me, I felt callused fingers brush across my forehead, sweeping the hair away from my face while a gentle voice whispered something near my ear—but I was already lost to the dreams.

CHAPTER ELEVEN

TARYN'S BREATHING EVENED out, and I carried my chair to the shadowed corner of the far wall. It offered a better view of the room and kept me out of the illuminating moonlight. I knew I should go. I still had to brief William, and there were a million other tasks waiting for me, but I couldn't bring myself to leave, even though guards were posted outside the door. Someone that meticulous wouldn't give up easily if they were trying to assassinate Taryn. I trusted no one as much as I trusted myself, and staying here presented me with the opportunity to sit and think alone in the darkness.

When I'd first walked through her door, I'd taken my time to inspect and survey the room—which was how I'd found it. A folded letter, sealed in red wax. My name scrawled across the top, calling out to me. Taryn had still been asleep, so why not open it? It wasn't like it had been left for someone else.

After reading it, I don't know why I'd been so surprised. I shouldn't have been. She'd already done this once before, left without saying goodbye, and I'd had an inclination that she wouldn't remain in the castle forever. But I *had* hoped … well I don't know *what* I had hoped for. Taryn had just become such a crucial part of my life that it seemed cruel and painful for her to go.

More than that, the idea of her leaving felt, felt *wrong*. Like the world around us protested against it. I couldn't explain it, but the only thing that made sense, the only space she seemed to fill or the piece that she could fit was the very one she wanted nothing to do with.

The Kavari.

I'd refrained from mentioning it to her, but I had to bring it up. It was like something in me needed to, a force outside of my control. Michael had briefly explained it to me once before, barely more than a statement thrown over his shoulder.

"How do you choose the right person to join the Kavari?" I'd asked.

"When you lead the Kavari one day, Vladimir, you won't have to choose. You'll have a certainty, a sense. Like a whisper in your ear, a solid truth within your heart. You'll know."

What he hadn't told me was how to suppress that sense— that call—when the candidate had no intention of answering it. The finality in her words when she'd outright rejected the idea of being a Kavari *was* what I had expected. She'd nearly been forced into it against her will when she'd faced off with Mordakai, but I wished that she would have given it at least a little consideration.

Because she could be a Kavari.

And she could be a good one.

My eyes slipped open. Confusion wafted over me at my surroundings, but then I grasped my bearings—I was in Taryn's room. I must have dozed off. Her steady breathing was the only noise disturbing the quietness of the night.

I frowned. Then why had I woken up?

Calm permeated the room, but the hair on the back of my neck prickled, rising on my arms, sensing something that my sight could not.

We were not alone.

I remained completely still, my wandering eyes the only movement I allowed, searching for the sound that had roused me from sleep. Hidden beneath my folded arms, my right hand strayed to the dagger strapped to my hip, grasping the hilt. My sword belt lay useless by the door, and I cursed myself for taking it off.

A flicker of movement caught my attention, the curtains flowing out farther than before. The window hung open, latch swinging freely. The latch. That was what I had heard. I forced myself to stay seated, to not give away my form concealed within the shadows, partially hidden behind the wardrobe.

I watched a figure materialize from the darkness, lurking at the foot of the bed. Moonlight glinted off the steel of a dagger, the perpetrator's gloved fingers grasping the hilt. They were cloaked in black from head to toe, making them one with the darkness. The figure cocked its head, staring at Taryn before stepping around to the side of the bed, lifting the dagger in its hand.

I flew from the chair, disrupting the silence as I tackled the man to the ground, wrenching the dagger from his grasp.

"Guards!" I bellowed as we rolled on the rug. I struggled with the man as he somehow slipped out of my grasp.

A knee crashed into my face, sending me sprawling to the right as the door burst open, flooding the room with torchlight. Head pounding, I leapt after the man as he raced for the window, yanking him back. His hand shot out. A knife. It sank into my leg and I roared with pain. Another knife flashed from the corner of my vision and I jumped back, on the defense. I blocked his blow, retaliating as I tried to take the man alive and incapacitate him. I never figured out exactly what happened in the next moments, how fate got so twisted, but the next thing I knew the man was lying on the ground with a knife embedded in his throat, the moonlight no longer reflected in his lifeless eyes staring up at the ceiling.

I heaved to my feet, stumbling back in shock and horrified over the scene before me, over what had just happened. Adrenaline pumped through my veins, and the warmth of blood slid down my leg, the knife still embedded in my skin. The guards rushed forward, weapons raised as if afraid the man would rise from the dead.

They'd come back. They'd come back to kill Taryn, and if I hadn't been here—

"What happened?" They all looked stunned.

"Assassin," I gasped, sweat dripping from my brow.

My gaze found Taryn, swaying at the edge of the bed, trying to walk but not appearing to have regained enough strength to do so.

I limped back to the man, kneeling beside him as I rolled

him over and started searching him. Every single layer of his clothing, even the stitching, was pitch-black. Secured around him in hidden compartments were various weapons, a rope dyed the color of coal. I didn't recognize some of the sharp contraptions. He had at least a dozen different knives on his person. I discovered a pouch and rolled it out to reveal multiple vials stashed inside. One was empty. The poison that was used on Taryn, no doubt.

"Help me." I motioned to the men, grimacing in pain as we undressed the assassin, searching for any kind of tattoo, any kind of markings on the man to identify where he was from, who had sent him.

We found nothing.

Something about him seemed oddly familiar for a moment, but then vanished.

"He's no Brenden," I deduced. "But I have no earthly idea where he's from."

"The skin tone is different," one of the men observed. "Gharridans have many faces, but I can't quite say that I've seen one like that before. I know a Gharridan when I see one, and he's not one of us."

Taryn padded around the side of the bed, coming to stand beside us where she had a better view. Her face blanched.

"What is it?" I asked.

Unease and fear littered her green eyes, as if she'd seen a ghost. She didn't answer, didn't move, her gaze locked on the dead man marring her bedroom floor.

I stood, shuffling closer. "Taryn, are you all right? Do you recognize him?"

She shook her head, never taking her eyes from the man,

and swallowed hard.

"I think I know where he's from."

I stilled at her response. Stunned. "What? How? Where?"

She turned to me with more fear than I had ever seen, some unknown expression flashing across her features.

"Because," she hesitated, as if she didn't want it to be true. "Because he looks exactly like my mother."

CHAPTER TWELVE

◆◇◆

TARYN

THE MOMENT I saw the dead man's face, it was like seeing a ghost, and time turned back. I was with my mother in our little cottage, burrowing under knitted blankets before a fire as we tried to stay warm in the winter, sweat pouring down my brow and between my shoulder blades while picking blueberries and wildflowers in the summer, the autumn breeze caressing my skin, the familiarity of my mother's hand in mine, the warmth of her dark olive skin, the curve of her thick brows. I'd never seen anyone like my mother. She was so unique from everyone else, almost otherworldly. Like a rare and brilliant gem in a mine full of dull rocks. My skin had never been as dark as hers, bearing the resemblance of both hers and my father's, but it still carried the olive complexion. Still carried the memory of her.

"Taryn?"

Vladimir's expectant voice brought me back. Back to my room. Back to the dead assassin sprawled across my floor with blood pooling around his head. Vladimir was staring at me, clearly bewildered by my previous statement.

"Not—" I said. "Not exactly like her, like as in a relation, but it's the same skin tone, the same features. The same look."

I had no doubt this man also came from wherever my mother was from. From whatever life she had run from—whatever life she had never told me about.

And whoever he was, he had tried to kill me.

Twice.

The thought defeated me, shattered the remnants of hope that still dwelled within me. My mother had always spoken of hoping to reconcile with her family, but I never imagined that whatever wound severed them had sliced this deep. Deep enough for them to want me dead.

I turned away from the sickening sight of the dead man plastered to the floor. My head spun, the fading adrenaline leaving me struggling to stay upright.

"Did you know he would be here?" I asked Vladimir.

"I had a hunch," he said. "He was messy this time. After the Brenden's assassination attempt on William, he probably thought we would shift the blame to them without any question. Which confirms that there's no way the poisoning and this incident weren't connected."

Vladimir hobbled over to a chair, and I caught sight of the dagger still embedded in his thigh and the blood saturating the leg of his pants. "Do you have a strip of cloth, anything I can tie this off with?"

He winced as he lowered himself into the seat. I maneuvered over to the wardrobe and dug out a sash, handing it to him. Vladimir ripped the sash in half and motioned to one of the guards. They stepped over, wrapping the sash around his leg and fastening it into a tourniquet. Without warning, Vladimir ripped the dagger from his leg with a pained grunt and the guard immediately wrapped the other end of the sash tightly around the injury. Without so much as a blink, Vladimir returned to his feet, speaking to the men.

"I want to know how he got in here, even though he was dressed and moved like a wraith. Once it's daylight, get someone up on the outer wall and figure out how he managed to climb through the window."

He turned to me. "Grab whatever you need. I'm moving you to another room. You can't stay here now."

I nodded without question, relieved that I wouldn't have to spend the rest of the night in here knowing what had just happened. I doubted sleep would come anyway. I snatched up a few items before following Vladimir out into the hall, watching his lilting steps. "You need to get that leg looked at."

"It's fine."

It was not fine.

I lifted my gaze to his face, where a dark bruise was forming on his forehead and cheekbone. He'd have a black eye by morning. Vladimir sent one of the guards to find Katherine and the others flanked us as we made our way through the corridors and climbed up and down stairwells. I felt faint, though I was trying to remain strong and keep going. Even if Katherine had drawn the poison out, whatever it had done to me was continuing to drain my energy, but Vladimir's determination and talent of hiding the excruciating pain he must be in kept my mouth shut and my feet moving.

When I realized where we were headed, I balked, not wanting to go in, but then relented as Vladimir stepped inside. He lit a candle and scoured my father's room, checking underneath the bed, in the wardrobe, behind the chair, places that even a child's body would never fit. His gaze briefly strayed to the skylight before darting away.

"There's no latch for that. If someone tried to drop in, you and everyone within a hundred feet would hear it. You should be safe here."

I nodded, but memories of my father haunted me no matter where I looked in the room. I threw the skylight a suspicious look, but the glass was thick and dirty. You'd need a ridiculous amount of force to even think about crashing through it.

"I'll leave several guards stationed outside the door and be back as soon as I can." He hesitated. "Will you be okay in here by yourself?"

I swallowed. Did I want to be left by myself? Absolutely not. There were too many thoughts rumbling through my mind, too many fears slithering down my spine, but I didn't have a choice. He had more important things to do.

I nodded, agreeing despite my apprehension.

He handed me the candle. "Lock the door behind you, and do not let anyone in unless you can verify for certain who is on the other side of the door."

"Do you think there's more of them, that they'll try again?"

I wished I knew who *they* were.

He stopped in the doorway, uneasiness wavering in his pale blue eyes. "I don't know, but I'm not willing to risk it."

He left me holding the candle in the darkness, and the silence became deafening. I tried to move, but my feet did not obey. All I could feel was the tiny heat of the candle. The cold stone beneath my bare feet. The loneliness surrounding me. I was alone. Again.

Alone.

These walls once again trapped me, and I was unable to leave because leaving surely meant certain death. Out there in the world, there was no one to protect me.

Out there in the world—I suddenly had no one.

Because I'd only ever wanted to find my mother's family.

The family that apparently wanted me dead.

If they'd waited one more day to try to attack me, I would have already been by myself, on my own. Vulnerable. And with that, I realized the assassin may have inadvertently saved my life.

CHAPTER THIRTEEN

VLADIMIR

MY LEG STILL tingled from the knife wound, but the skin was now colored light pink with a puckered scar. I didn't know what I would do without Katherine, and I knew that I tended to take her healing touch too much for granted. The memory of the sting of the blade in my flesh made me grind my teeth—that wound would have left me limping for weeks.

In total the palace had three different safe rooms, all easily accessed by the secret tunnels, but they'd sat vacant since the first day I'd come here. The one William occupied wasn't hard to find, especially with the eight guards standing vigil outside.

They allowed me to pass by them, and I gave one long rap on the door followed by three short ones.

"Where does the sparrow fly in the face of death?" asked a

voice from the inside.

"Out of the jaws of the enemy, but never out of the fight," I answered.

The scraping sound of a bolt being removed came from inside, and then the door swung inward.

The room hovelled deep into the earth, lit only by the torches set into sconces along the wall and a lone candle flickering on a primitive desk. A dreary carpet lined the chilly floor next to a rickety bed with blankets that looked older than the establishment of Gharridan. The air smelled of mildew and other dank substances I didn't care to think about.

The two guards in the room saluted me, but my gaze fell to William. He was lounging in the only chair in the room, balancing it on its two hind legs as he leaned back, both feet propped up on the desk. I didn't miss the apple in his right hand, or the flask cradled in his left.

"Well, well, look who it is!" William threw me his most sarcastic smile. "So nice of you to finally join us, Vladimir. I just love sitting down here. In the dark. With no earthly—pun intended—idea of what's going on in my kingdom. It's not like I'm, you know, the king or anything."

The storm billowing beneath his words tottered on the verge of exploding.

Oh.

This was going to be fun.

I shrugged and crossed my arms. "I mean, if you'd rather have stayed up there and been assassinated, I'm sure we could've worked something out, but I also, you know, didn't want to lead them straight to you or anything by rushing down to this bunker."

William flipped the withering apple in his hand into the air before catching it again. "I can't exactly see daylight down here, Vladimir, but surprisingly, I do know that it has been hours, and, interestingly enough, I have not received a single word as to what is transpiring in the world above. Are you trying to make an incapable fool of me or is this another ploy for you to steal the throne?"

I bit back the retort warring to leave the tip of my tongue, shoving it back down into silence. He sounded just like his mother. "William, if I wanted to be king do you really think you would have left the great hall alive?"

His expression soured as he returned the two front legs of the chair to the floor and stood, walking toward me. I could see the glaze coating his eyes, the redness staining them.

"Although it seems coming to get you out of here was premature," I added. "You may want to stay down here for a while. Sunlight might be too much for you right now."

His hands clenched into fists. "Do not forget it is only by my mercy and grace that you have not been exiled or executed, Vladimir. I would tread carefully lest you should succumb to one of those two fates."

I took the necessary steps forward until we stood nose to nose. "And do not forget it is only by my mercy and grace that I did not bar you from the throne and string your mother's body up from the highest gallows."

I moved away before he could consider hitting me. "Now focus. We have matters of state to discuss. The man who tried to kill you last night was no assassin. We interrogated him. He was an extremist, but no one who possessed actual discipline. He killed himself the first chance he got, but I believe that he was acting alone."

"So what you came here to tell me is that after an overnight investigation, you still don't know anything?"

I rolled my eyes right along with William's.

"How can you be certain he was working alone?" he asked.

"Because I am, but that's not the biggest issue we have on our hands."

William threw me a disapproving frown. "What could possibly be a bigger issue than someone trying to assassinate me?"

"Someone also tried to assassinate Taryn. Twice."

Seriousness momentarily overcame William's face before he wiped it away. "You just said you believed this man to be acting alone."

"And I still believe that."

"Then how—"

"I'm not done," I interrupted. "Someone spiked Taryn's drink at the ball. She almost died, William. Would have, if Katherine hadn't drawn the poison out of her."

William averted his gaze as I searched for any kind of reaction, but he offered none.

I continued, "Whoever spiked her drink broke into her room a few hours ago to finish the job."

William's face snapped up. "Is she—"

"She's fine. For now. But the assassin is also dead. I wasn't able to take him alive."

He quirked an eyebrow at me. "Do you just really not like to keep prisoners alive for questioning?"

I gritted my teeth as my fingernails dug into my palms. "What's disturbing is where the assassin was from—"

"Brenden thinks that Taryn was involved with their king's

assassination." William brushed me off. "It's no surprise that they'd want both of us dead."

Sometimes I really wanted to punch William's mouth shut, and I would wholeheartedly do so if I didn't know that it would just make the entire situation worse.

"First of all," I started again, "you were the one that assassinated the king of Brenden, not Taryn. Second of all, this was no Brenden poison, and no Brenden assassin."

The words snapped William out of his foolishness. "What? Who else would want Taryn dead?"

"Apparently someone in her family. Taryn said the assassin looked like her mother, like he came from wherever she did."

William cocked his head. "But Taryn doesn't have any idea about where her family came from. Before we found out the massacre at Northunder was referring to—" He paused. "Referring to my mother, Taryn thought that was where her mother was from. All she was told was that they were in the north."

"Navarre is so south that technically everything is north. If north is even referring to a direction and not something else entirely," I said.

William shrugged. "Gharridan is north. So is Adellaia. Gapsvar. Any one of the villages in the mountains. She referred to it once as Dalendria, but I don't recall any place with that name."

His words stopped me. "Dalendria?"

"Yes."

The word pricked at a memory buried deep in the back of my mind, like I'd heard it before, but the thought could bring forth no solid connotation. I would have to do some digging on my own.

"Is it safe for me to come back to the surface, or are you going to keep me stuffed down here like a mole?"

"I'd prefer if you wait until we had a better understanding of what is going on, but if you insist, I want a minimum of six guards with you at all times and surveillance sweeps of every room before you enter."

He practically raced me to the door, turning back once we entered the hallway and meeting me with a knowing gaze. "There is one person who could tell you what the poison is. He trained in them for an entire year."

The thought had already crossed my mind, but I didn't like it. Didn't like him. Wanted nothing to do with him or to ever see his face again.

"I know who."

The admission left a bad taste in my mouth.

CHAPTER FOURTEEN

◆◇◆

KATHERINE

THE WARM AIR in the infirmary smothered me like a flaming blanket. Sweat gathered on my brow, threatening to slide down my face. I swept it away with the back of my hand, leaning forward in my chair and placing a hand on the bed where Verone slept. Faint scarring lined his face, but the severe damage was forgotten. He was lucky. I was lucky. A few more minutes and I might not have reached him in time. His chest rose and fell in even breaths, his body trying to recover from the traumatic ordeal it had been through. My own body protested staying awake, fighting the exhaustion of bringing Verone back nearly from the dead.

But I couldn't sleep.

Couldn't even close my eyes.

The infirmary around me lay quiet now that everyone had

been taken care of, but inside my mind roared the hum of a thousand voices. No matter what wall I shielded my mind behind or thoughts I pushed to the forefront, the voices played what I'd seen when I healed Taryn over and over in my head. My hands trembled at the memories and my skin crawled from fear. When I could no longer ignore them, could no longer forget them, I finally had to succumb to them.

Taryn's still body had scared me into a panic, but the moment my hand had touched her forehead, darkness swallowed my world and transported me into an abyss. The new ground beneath my feet was cool, its surface black and polished like obsidian. A dark mist swirled around me, distorting my vision, but off in the distance I saw a twinge of yellow, drifting up and becoming one with the mist. I stepped forward, confused, glancing around for any kind of familiarity as I made my way toward the color. The yellow disturbance hovered over Taryn, who lay pale and lifeless on the ground. I rushed to her, the black fog stinging at my cheeks with a chill like formless ice. Cold pressed against me, like I was inside a cavern buried deep underground and encased in snow.

I placed my hands on Taryn, closing my eyes to the strange world around me and focusing on the poison pulsing through her veins. I could see it, even beneath the darkness of my eyelids. The florescent yellow glowed inside her veins as it circulated through her body. My touch called it out of her, and as I pulled it toward me until it was no longer touching her, the yellow lines swirled across my own arms like fluorescent vines traveling across my skin.

A hint of rose colored her cheeks, and then Taryn's form vanished, leaving only an empty space before being quickly claimed by the mist. I whirled around, looking for where she could have disappeared to, but her body was nowhere to be found. Every hair on my body stood on end as if preparing for a lightning strike as I sensed a presence morph behind me. A chill made the air even more frigid than before. I turned. And I stared.

The being had no definite shape, no definite description, but I knew exactly who it was.

He cocked his misty head, studying me with curiosity. "You're not supposed to be here."

Death's voice shuddered through me as fear slithered down my spine.

He inched closer. "Now you'll see things you were never supposed to see."

The world transformed around me. I looked to the right, and I saw Gharridan engulfed in flames, dead comrades bathed in blood sprawled on the field of battle. Dread choked me as I stumbled through the carnage, screaming as I searched for a way out, searched for a way to end the nightmare. The world transformed again until a king stood on a hill above another massacre, a young girl by his side. At his feet lay the bodies of a man and woman, their lifeless eyes staring into the abyss.

My body revolted, twisting until I was running in the opposite direction before careening into a decaying house where a woman lay in a bed, suffering the travails of childbirth. She was dying. Someone by a side table crushed a red flower to dust, mixed it with other herbs into a concoction, and gave it to the woman, who whispered, "Take care of her."

The woman screamed as she delivered the child, a babe with blood-red hair, and I watched the mother hold the baby in her arms for the first time outside the womb before she closed her eyes for the last time.

The house disappeared, and a black lion roared before my eyes. Teardrop diamonds arranged in a unique design spread out before me. A finger pointed to a spot on a map. Then I saw myself covered in blood and standing with a bow in my hand, staring at something. I stepped closer to the apparition of me, trying to find out what she was looking at. I looked down and my eyes landed on William, crumpled on the floor with the shattered pieces of his crown spread around him. An arrow had pierced his chest. His body was limp. Dead. William was dead.

I screamed and ran again, charging through the mist, trying to find a way out of this nightmare, unable to rid myself of the scenes playing out before me. I scrambled and stumbled, tears slipping down my face, trying to escape, and then an earthquake rocked the ground beneath me, bringing me out of whatever dark place had taken me captive.

I blinked away the nightmarish visions, Verone still asleep. Sense concerning the visions hadn't come to me. I squeezed my eyes shut, plagued by the presence of Death and haunted by what he had shown me. The symbolism continued ricocheting in my mind, trying to tell me something, warn me of something, but I couldn't figure out what. Except for one thing that clung to me more than all the others: I had been warned that William was going to die. I didn't know how, and I didn't know when, but William's demise approached.

Callused fingers grazed across my skin, taking my hand.

I opened my eyes. Verone was watching me, a calm expression resting on his face.

"You look more coherent than the last time you woke," I

said.

"Last time I didn't want to be coherent. I'm not sure I do this time either, but your face does make it more bearable." He studied me closely. "Are you all right?"

I forced a smile onto my lips, the terrifying visions clawing at my mind and trying to squeeze out everything sane within me. "I am now."

But I was not.

Something had changed.

Something had been set in motion that I needed to stop.

"And," I hesitated. "I'm sorry for arguing."

A swathe of memories flashed across Verone's face, but he remained silent.

That conversation had haunted me as I'd healed each and every wound on his body, taken away the burns. Begged for him to come through it, to not leave me. Almost losing him had changed things.

"I think," I squeezed his hand gently. "I think we need to talk about it again."

CHAPTER FIFTEEN

VLADIMIR

WATER DRIPPED FROM the ceiling, coating the stone walls and floor with a dampness that smelled of freshly growing mildew. The plinks of the droplets orchestrated a haunting rhythm that followed me down the staircase and the long dungeon hallway. Pale faces stared at me like vipers waiting to strike, but I ignored them as I passed them by, going deeper than I had ever ventured before into the depths of the dungeon.

My boots slid across the dingy ground, my eyes squinting against the dim torchlight that barely lit the way, shadows dancing up and down the walls like ghosts at a banquet. I stopped before the rusty bars of a cell, dropping the torch into a sconce. It illuminated the legs of a prisoner dangling over the edge of a cot in the far-right corner of the cell, the upper half of their body encased in shadows.

"I need to speak with you." My voice fell flat in the emptiness around us, in the depths of the earth.

Something scattered in the darkness, the sound of tiny claws tapping against the wet stone floor.

"And why would Vladimir, *leader of the Kavari*, contender for the throne, need to speak with *me?*"

Despite being imprisoned in these conditions for over a week, his voice betrayed no weakness.

I cleared my throat. "Because if you ever want any hope of getting out of this dungeon and living long enough aboveground to see another sunrise, you will answer my questions."

He mulled over my words before his legs drew together and he pushed himself to his feet. His stride was slow, lazy, as the shaft of the light from the torches moved up his body, revealing the dirty clothes he wore, then his face.

"From your expression, I'd say you're disappointed I'm still alive."

That was an understatement.

"You threatened the lives of people I care about, and threatened the stability of Gharridan. By any means, you shouldn't be alive. One more centimeter, and that arrow would have done far more damage than simply graze across your chest. Broken skin and lots of blood, but nothing permanent. Nowhere near what you deserved for your betrayal."

Finnigan smiled, his scraggly beard scrunching up with the movement. "I never betrayed Gharridan, Vladimir. I tried to preserve it. You're just so set in your ways, so stubborn and steady, that you're not willing to do what needs to be done. To take the actions that need to be taken. Unity is not accomplished by playing justly and fairly. Sometimes, for the greater good and to make things right, you have to get your hands dirty."

My lips pursed into a thin line, my anger barely controlled. "Considering you're the one behind bars and I'm the one bringing unity to the Gharridan above our heads that you will never lay eyes on again, I'd have to disagree."

He laughed. "One day, Vladimir. One day you won't have a choice, and you will learn."

I pulled the empty vial from my jacket, handing it to him through the bars. "You worked in foreign affairs. You know poisons, choice assassination drugs. What is this?"

Finnigan stared at the glass vial in his hands. "Who tried to kill who?"

"That's not exactly your concern."

"It is if you want an answer."

I weighed my options, but decided the information was of no use to him down here. "Someone tried to poison Taryn."

He cocked an eyebrow, a curious look on his face. "I'd thought that someone would have been more likely to try to kill William. Or you."

He uncorked the bottle, leaning down for a sniff then turning it this way and that in the dim light, looking for any remnants. "What were the symptoms?"

I listed the effects to him, watching his expression carefully.

"Yellow eyes?"

I nodded.

"That seems quite rare. And you have no idea who did it or where they were from?"

I shook my head.

He shrugged. "This doesn't look like Brenden's work."

I hesitated, unsure how much was wise to share, but unwilling to hide information that might prove useful. "We caught the assassin, but he died during the capture. He bore no identification, nothing to figure out where he was from, but …" I trailed off.

He leaned forward, eager. "But what?"

"When Taryn saw him, she said that he looked like her mother."

Something sparkled in Finnigan's eyes. A greedy glisten that he quickly tried to hide, but not before I picked up on it. He shrugged, acting disinterested and like my words were of no consequence. "Where did you say Taryn's mother was from again?"

"I didn't." I stared him down, trying to read the thoughts he was masking. He was digging for something. "Taryn has no idea where her mother was from. All I know is that her family name is Illdalore."

Finnigan considered the information, rolling the empty vial back and forth in his hands.

He was stalling.

"It's obvious you know something," I said.

His calculating gaze met mine. "Maybe I do know something. Maybe I don't. But I'm not saying another word until you find me a way out of this cell that doesn't lead to the gallows. If you want me to talk, you're going to have to use other means to get the information—you've done it before. You might think Michael was the only one who knew the darkness of your past, but when you've traveled half the continent like me, you learn things. You discover things about people that you never would have imagined. I know that side of you still exists, Vladimir." He leaned forward. "I just want you to let it out."

My hands curled into fists at my sides, long-repressed memories suddenly pervading my thoughts, crippling me. My chest constricted, squeezing the air from my lungs. Fear. Hurt. Pain—

I forced a breath out, composing myself. He was bluffing. He couldn't know. Michael had done everything within his power to keep my past exactly where it needed to be—buried. Coming here had been stupid, but I wouldn't have come unless I thought Finnigan could help. Now it was clear that he could, but his willingness was another matter entirely. Frustration boiled like a billowing storm beneath my skin, but I kept my voice calm and even.

"Maybe you give me the information, or maybe you don't, but there is only one fact I know for certain, Finnigan. You will rot in this cell until disease or old age takes you first."

I pivoted back the way I had come, still unsettled by his words. The click of my boots was the only sound echoing off the halls as I left him imprisoned in the darkness.

CHAPTER SIXTEEN

TARYN

DEATH CLAWED AT my throat, his spindly fingers formed of twisting darkness choking me, trying to take me with him into the blackness. I couldn't breathe. Couldn't think. My fist slammed into his head again and again only for his skull to keep reforming in the swirling darkness. His grin was evil, his intent and want raw. I'd thought he was finally gone. Wanted him to be gone. Forever.

I writhed beneath him, desperately trying to break free until I found myself twisting in damp sheets and lying on a soft mattress. Above me, light streamed in from the skylight, signaling daytime.

I scrambled to my feet, wiping at the sweat coating my brow, taking in the feel of the cool stone beneath my feet, the familiarity of the room around me. I sat back on the bed, feeling dizzy from the sudden motion. My wrist ached, and I stared down at it, seeing several black spots. I rubbed my eyes, thinking they caused what I was seeing on my skin, but the black spots remained. I shook my head. Maybe it was a side effect.

The poison.

I shouldn't complain—I should be dead.

Someone had tried to kill me—twice in one night. Tried to remove me from this world. I squeezed my eyes shut, wishing I could discard it as a dream, but I knew it was real. The picture of the dead assassin on my floor swam before my eyes, the haunting familiarity of his appearance striking me straight to my core.

My family in the north.

My mother's words echoed within me. I leaned back onto the bed, sinking into the blankets, recalling the lyrical sound of my mother's voice, the gentle touch of her hands. Perhaps this was the reason we'd always hidden away. Why no one could know where we were. Who my father was. Any mention of her family was brief and far between, but it was always with sorrow, conveyed with a deep longing. She'd spoken of reconciliation, of mending what had been broken. I'd thought it had been a mere falling out, but if an assassin had been dispatched to kill me, it was obviously far more. Keeping our lives so secret and hiding away all my life no longer seemed so preposterous to me, but why here, why now, and why me?

What could my mother have possibly done to warrant my death sentence?

She'd kept more from me than I'd ever imagined. As if the secrets I'd known about weren't already enough. I stared at my father's room around me, questioning how he'd come into this and how he had met my mother. He'd grown up in the capital, grown up beneath Gabriel.

Or so I'd been told.

My head lolled to the side, and a rectangle of white resting on the stone just inside the door caught my attention. I hurried to retrieve it. Vladimir must not have had time to see me himself, and I was desperate for any news. I pulled open the parchment, going still as I read the words.

we thought to kill you swiftly, but now you shall die slowly with anticipated dread.

we wait in the shadows, ever present but never seen. you will first hear my voice when you are given a riddle, but you will first see my face when I am killing the last scion of Illdalore.

you cannot hide. Rest well, for your calamity is coming, and the nightmares have only just begun.

CHAPTER SEVENTEEN

"WOULD SOMEONE LIKE to explain to me how this"—I held up the note slipped underneath Taryn's door—"was able to get past six guards, without any of you noticing?"

My chest heaved. The anger within me needed to calm down, but I wasn't quite sure how to stop it. It felt like I was going mad. How many times could the enemy slip by our defenses? Invade us in our most vulnerable states? I couldn't be everywhere, and anytime I turned by back for the briefest moment, we were attacked.

Taryn stood off to the side, still looking exhausted from the poison and, no doubt, paranoia.

My head spun. Maybe I couldn't trust these men. Maybe the division between Crown and Kavari was buried deeper than I thought. Did traitors still walk among us?

"Did any of you leave guard duty?" I asked. "Were you sleeping?"

I was grasping for an explanation, but at the same time, if someone had managed to get past six guards, why not break into her room and finish the job instead of slipping a note underneath her door?

"Sir," one of the younger guards spoke up, his voice shaking. "We stood out here all night. We never closed an eye. I cannot explain the presence of that letter, but I swear it. We took this very seriously. We never once let down our guard."

While fear and bewilderment was scrawled across their faces, truth hovered in each of their expressions, making me feel guilty for my outburst, but there was still no explanation for the mysterious note. We'd moved Taryn to a different room in a completely separate part of the castle, yet whoever wanted Taryn dead had still found her. My gaze flit up to the ceiling, looking for any way an intruder could have planted that note without the guards noticing, but the amount of skill it would take to accomplish something like that was otherworldly.

"Did you notice anything suspicious of the people who passed in this corridor?" I asked.

They glanced between themselves as if hoping one of them might come up with an answer.

The younger one spoke again. "Nothing out of the ordinary, sir."

"Nothing?" I pressed.

"The only thing I recall was the one man who tripped when he passed us," the guard said. "But he came nowhere near the door."

"Did you see his face?"

The guard shook his head. "It was the middle of the night. I think he was dressed in servant's clothes? I didn't think much of it, and it was too dark to define his features anyway."

I wracked my brain and questioned them till we were going in circles, but I came up with no additional information to go off. This assassin was good. Very good. But if he knew how to move through the castle undetected, if he knew where to look, where certain rooms for—

"Vladimir." Taryn's demanding expression indicated she wanted to speak with me in private.

Exhaustion rippled from the guards' demeanor. "Thank you for your honesty, men. As soon as your replacements arrive, please head back to your quarters to get some rest. It's been a long night for all of us."

They strode out of the door, and once we were finally alone I turned back to Taryn. "Gather your things. You're not staying here tonight."

I surveyed the room again, running possibilities through my mind for a few moments. We could hide her in a bunker. It wouldn't be fun, but it would be safe. Hopefully. No doubt this assassin would find some way around it. I glanced back at Taryn, confused as I noticed she hadn't yet moved.

She crossed her arms.

"If you don't want me in my old room because of the windows, that's understandable, but I'm not moving again. I'm going to stay here."

I stared at her. "The assassin managed to slip a note underneath your door without the guards noticing anything. And you want to stay here? Where he knows exactly where you are?"

She rolled her eyes. "He'll always know exactly where I am when there's six guards flanking the door. It's not very subtle."

I pursed my lips.

"Besides, they're not going to kill me." She fidgeted. "Yet."

"And why is that?" I asked, not following.

"Read the note again."

I did.

We thought to kill you swiftly, but now you shall die slowly with antic-ipated dread. We wait in the shadows, ever present but never seen. You will first hear my voice when you are given a riddle, but you will first see my face when I am killing the last scion of Illdalore. You cannot hide. Rest well, for your calamity is coming, and the nightmares have only just begun.

"'Slowly with anticipated dread.' 'Rest well.' 'You will first see my face.' Those all indicate events in the future."

"Tomorrow is the future, Taryn."

"If he wanted me dead, I would be dead."

I met her determined eyes. They were so much like Michael's. "Why try twice in one night and then leave you well alone?"

I watched the thought work its way through her mind.

She turned away, worrying at her lower lip. "That's what I've been trying to figure out. I think that when you killed the other assassin, something changed."

"Like what?"

She shook her head. "I don't know, but whatever their plans were, they changed them, and the note implies that something bigger is coming. What, I don't know."

"It still doesn't make sense for them to drag this out instead of getting it over with," I said.

"That's another thing I don't understand. The longer they're here, the more risk they have of being caught."

"We can't protect you from an enemy we don't understand," I said. "What if it's someone on the inside?"

She rubbed her forehead. "Isn't it always?"

Her words bit through me.

Zedekiah. Finnigan. Adamara.

Gharridan bred more corruption than it bred honesty.

"I don't think this was Gharridan, Vladimir. That note confirmed that either my family—or someone who knows my family—wants me dead. Wants the line erased, which means ..." she trailed off.

The last scion of Illdalore.

The unsaid hovered between us. I didn't want to voice it, and I don't think she wanted to hear it, didn't want it to be true. All she'd ever wanted was to find her mother's family, but if they'd called her the last scion there might not be any family left to find.

"I really don't need six guards."

I cocked an eyebrow. "Then at least four."

"Four?" Her face turned incredulous.

"Four."

"If they're determined to kill me, I don't think a hundred guards would stop them. I'll stay here, in my father's room, but I refuse to be a prisoner within these walls. I've been a prisoner for long enough and I will not live in a state of constant fear, because it seems like that's exactly what they want me to do."

"You also can't make yourself an open target," I protested. "I still don't think it's a good idea for you to leave the castle."

I gauged her reaction. I didn't think she was stupid enough to traipse out on her own with a bounty on her head, but her stubbornness tended to outrun her reason.

She looked down. "I'm not going anywhere. For now. I may not even have to look for my family. It appears they've come for me, just not in the way that I expected."

If these assassins tried to drag this out, we would catch them. They couldn't stay invisible behind our walls.

I glanced at the note again. "Do you have any idea what he meant by the line with the riddle?"

She shook her head, and I frowned. It could just be non-sense.

"What are you going to do?" I was afraid to hear what she might have up her sleeve.

She snorted. "I'm going to find out why someone wants me dead, that's what, and stop them before they're given a chance to finish the job."

CHAPTER EIGHTEEN

TARYN

S HADOWS FRIGHTENED ME, even as I tried to push the paranoia away. I imagined dark figures within their depths, waiting for the moment they could spring from the blackness and kill me with one stroke. The four guards stepped in unison around me as I walked in the midst of them. My gaze darted at every noise, every inconsistency, looking for an attack. But there was none. Whatever had changed the assassin's original plan, I was sure their new one was intended to drive me mad.

But even with all the uneasiness, something in my heart told me that I was safe. For now. Maybe for a few days, though my mind still roared that every corner held imminent danger. Held an assassin. I'd been smothered all day, feeling like I couldn't ever fully breathe with the guards never more than a few steps behind me.

I swallowed, the weight of the thoughts that had been burdening me suddenly crashing down on me.

What if I had no family?

The last scion of Illdalore.

The idea hadn't ever planted itself in my mind. My mother's family had always been this distant but living, breathing thing within me. Now it was like the hope fluttering inside of me for all these years had been ripped from my chest.

I tried to convince myself it wasn't true, that what I was seeking had never existed, but something was off. I knew the rift with my mother's family was strong, but strong enough to want her only descendant dead? I ran my fingers through my dark hair, my mother's hair. The disgrace tunneled deep. What if she wasn't even from this continent? No one recognized her surname, no one had heard of Dalendria. Maybe she had come from somewhere across the sea. The thought nearly brought me to my knees.

All those years hiding in Navarre, waiting for my father's blessing to leave. The idea that there was someone or something out there I was connected to. That I could belong to. That might want me. Something that I could be a part of—that's what had kept me going.

And without that, if there was no one waiting for me …

Then I had nothing.

I blinked away tears. I couldn't think like that, needed a strand of hope to hold on to that would keep me tethered to sanity.

I'd been digging in the library for something. Anything. Nothing had turned up yet, but there had to be *something* buried within those thousands of pages. I'd keep looking.

First I just needed to do what I'd put off for far too long.

The daunting doors to the study stared back at me. They swung inward, and it was like a massive beast opening its jaws and threatening to swallow me whole.

I stepped inside the room. My personal bodyguards did not.

"I told you I didn't wish to be disturbed."

William's wavy golden hair spilled across his forehead as he leaned over the desk, shuffling through the mess of documents scattered across it. He picked up a glass full of amber liquid and threw his head back, downing the rest in one gulp.

When I remained silent, he raised his head to look at me, hazel eyes locking with mine. I couldn't even remember the last time I had met his gaze, but his look stopped me in my thoughts, brought back so many memories. Him freeing me from the guards after his mother ordered my death sentence, the touch of his lips against mine, fingers woven into my hair, his hand pressed against my back—but then came the memory of him ripping his sword out of King Arguis, the cold expression on his face, his decisions and the path he had chosen to take.

My palms turned slick, pulse racing. We remained fixed on each other. I tried to decipher the emotions burning behind his eyes, what lay hidden beneath his hard exterior.

"Why are you here?" His voice fell flat, emotionless.

My mouth went dry, and I struggled to find the words I needed to form "I—"

I cut off.

This was going to be harder than expected.

Much harder.

"I wondered if we could talk," I finally managed.

He stared at me for a moment before lifting an eyebrow, his tone tinged with mockery. "You wondered if we could *talk.*"

"It's just that I haven't spoken to you since—"

William let out a bitter laugh. "You mean since you killed my mother?"

I went rigid, the crackle of flames in the hearth filling the tense air.

"I'm sorry," I let out.

"That's the thing." William shook his head. "I don't really think you are."

This wasn't the most drunk I'd ever seen him, but the alcohol had possessed him enough to loosen his tongue. Red rimmed his eyes, exhaustion marring his features.

"I am," I croaked out. "I've avoided you because I didn't think you wanted to see me, but I've seen your pain. I wish there was something to do to ease it, but I can't. And I just wanted you to know that I was sorry for what I've put you through and wish that it didn't have to be this way."

He ignored my plea, leaning back over the papers before him.

I closed my eyes, praying for mercy as I strode up to the desk, not allowing him to ignore me. He'd been through far worse than I had, and even if I didn't want to remain in his presence, I needed to know that he would accept the apology.

"William—"

"Did you not already say what you came to tell me?" he asked. "Try again when you actually mean it."

My temper flared unbidden, and I slammed my palms down on the desk. "I'm not denying that this is a mess, William, but you can't play the only victim when your mother was the one who ordered the death of my father."

William stalked around to the front of the desk, standing too close. He was looking for a fight, and I couldn't stop myself from giving it to him.

"Now you want to be upset about that?" he asked. "Because if I recall correctly, you were the one who was glad that he died."

Anger and shame ignited my cheeks, my hands tightening into fists.

William poured more of the amber liquid into the glass.

"Can you not even get through one conversation now without enslaving yourself to the alcohol?"

William let out a venomous laugh. "You always have to comment on that, don't you?"

He lifted the glass to his lips, but I snatched it from him before he could taste a drop, hurling it into the flames in the hearth. They enlarged and devoured it like an angry wolf.

"At least my mother didn't *murder my own father*, killing countless innocents in the process and trying to annihilate an entire kingdom."

Fury raged across William's face as he grit out, "She was *still* my mother and the queen, and she deserves the proper respect."

"No murderer deserves respect."

He stepped closer and I backed away, kept backing away as he followed until my back pressed against the wall and all I could see was the rage exploding in his eyes, his face mere inches from mine. My breath hitched in my throat.

"I never should have saved you from the guards when they

were leading you to the dungeon." His voice was low. "Maybe I shouldn't have sided with Vladimir in the throne room. My mother would still be alive if I hadn't."

"And all of us would be dead. You would still be left at the mercy of a mother you could never please. You've done her bidding before. I have no doubt that you would've done it again."

William's hand slammed against the wall to the right of my head. "All we ever do is argue. Why are you here, Taryn? I know that you don't care about me."

So many moments and experiences shared, but now it seemed that only heated discussions and words said too late were all that was left between us. Even through the anger, tears pricked at my eyes. "Because I need you to know that I'm sorry."

"That you're *sorry*? And you expect me to *forgive* you?" The hurt in his eyes welled deep, unfathomable, and in that brief glimpse of raw vulnerability, I saw not a king, but a boy who had lost everything. Everyone. Who didn't know how to keep going. Didn't know what to believe. Looked as if he was drowning beneath the weight of it all. His life, will, resolve had fractured, and he was crumbling from the inside out.

His voice broke on his next words. "Maybe there was something between us before, Taryn, but every time I look at you, all I hear is your confession in your room when I was drunk on the anniversary of my sister's death. Your hatred of me. How you lied to me for so long, pretending like you still cared when you didn't. Was any of that even true?"

I wished that it wasn't but it had been. And I couldn't lie to him. Not now. He'd been lied to enough in his life. "It was." I tried to keep my own voice from breaking. "Until I saw your true character. How much you would sacrifice others, and how much you were like your mother."

He stared at me, looking as if he was trying to hold back a wall of resolve that threatened to crack. "Tell me, do you regret what you did?" His voice rasped. "To my mother? Do you wish that you could take it back?"

I met his gaze.

I didn't.

It was written all over my face.

"Because I can't help but think that you wanted to kill her," he went on. "I know how angry you were about your father's death. I think that you took the first chance you had to take her life. Don't think I've forgotten how vengeance-driven you were in Gapsvar. You very nearly got us both killed. Every time I look at your face, I see you pulling that dagger out of my mother's gut, I see your deceiving and conniving eyes lying to me, and I picture a smile on your face as you kill my mother. Villain or not, I don't think I could ever forgive you for that, because I can never trust you again. I can never trust you to tell the truth."

"I don't regret it," I shot back. I would not let him attack me like this, shift all the blame to me. "But that doesn't mean I enjoyed it, and if you think your mother deserved more than what she received, then you are just as bad as she was. I thought maybe with your new responsibility you would have changed, but you're still the coward who doesn't know how to grow or stand up for himself." I took a deep breath. "And you're right. If I could go back I wouldn't change anything, wouldn't undo what I have done, because I would never sacrifice my life over the vile life of a creature as foul as your mother. Death was too merciful for one such as her."

The words were too harsh. They tasted foreign and bitter on my tongue. This wasn't what I had come here to say, but William had a way of drawing out the worst in me, bringing out a side of me that everyone else seemed to suppress, and it wasn't a side that I was proud of, wasn't a side that I wanted to admit even existed.

Resolve formed in his eyes, the coldness of his gaze chilling me to the bone, his face inches from mine.

"You're done here." William took a step back, morphing into someone that I didn't know, concealing the hurt he'd vulnerably displayed. "I want you out of the castle by dawn, and I don't ever want to see your face again."

I stared at him, waiting for him to take back the words, to say it was just the anger, but he didn't. I pushed past him, suppressing the tears until I made it back to my father's room. William was no longer the cocky prince I'd met so many months ago, exuding so much confidence but also lacking it. No. William was now a king. A king I didn't know and would never know. A king who trusted no one, because he'd had everyone and everything taken away from him.

CHAPTER NINETEEN

TARYN

IF WILLIAM WANTED me thrown out of the castle, he would have to do it himself.

I barricaded myself in my father's room, trying to ease the anger burning so hot within me. I should have kept my temper in check, but just as usual, when I was around William and his digging comments, I was unable to.

I didn't think there would be any way to come back from this. I doubted it was even possible for us to stay friends, which was—well, maybe it was for the best. More than anything, I was angry at myself. I'd gone there to fix things, to smooth them over, but in the end I'd only made them worse—which seemed impossible given the circumstances.

I pored through more history books until my eyes were crossing then snapped them shut, venturing out into the hall, trying to ignore the tramp of the guards around me. After offering only a brief knock, I barged into Katherine's room. She turned to stare at me, brush halfway through her blood-red hair. When I started to pace, she cocked an eyebrow.

I waited a moment to gather my thoughts before blurting out, "He can't just throw me out of the castle."

Her expression remained stoic. "I'm running through a list of names in my head, mentally checking them off. The one that keeps resurfacing is the only one who sounds arrogant and stupid enough to do that. Are we speaking about William?"

"Yes!" I threw my hands in the air. "All I tried to do was apologize, smooth everything over, and it all went horribly and destructively wrong. Now he wants me out. By dawn."

"Did you talk to Vladimir?" she asked.

I crossed my arms with a sigh. "I'm tired of asking him to fix my problems."

"I will, then. If William hasn't already tried to shove orders down Vladimir's throat."

"He was angry this time." My voice fell quiet. "Really angry."

Katherine set her hairbrush down. "William's position may seem daunting, but he doesn't hold as much power as you think he does. If it came down to it, the council would choose Vladimir over him, but to avoid any more conflict they're trying to keep the peace among themselves and make this transition as peaceful as possible. Don't worry, I'm sure you're safe."

"From William," I muttered.

"Vladimir told me about the assassins. The note. If you need it, I'd like to help you look for information about your family, where your mother was from."

I met her eyes, which were genuine. "Thank you."

I noticed her dress, more extravagant than usual. A small portion of hair encircled her head in a crown, the rest falling down around her. "Are you going somewhere?"

She looked down, seeming to realize what I had noticed, and for the first time since meeting her I saw what looked like a flustered expression cross her face.

I cocked my head.

Her gaze shot back to me before regaining control and avoiding me. "I have some things that I need to take care of."

Katherine, hiding something? She wasn't exactly an open book, but this wasn't like her either.

A blush crept up her neck, and I recognized the look on her face.

"Does this 'something' have to do with the captain of the guard?" I asked.

Her reaction confirmed my suspicions, gaze accusatory. "How did you know? People I've lived with in this castle for years don't even know."

"I spent my entire childhood watching my mother pine after someone she couldn't be with. At least, not for more than a few days at a time. Verone's reactions concerning your safety have always been strong, and Vladimir may have let something slip."

She didn't appear angry, but I could tell it bothered her that I knew.

"How did you two even …" I trailed off, suddenly feeling awkward asking.

She smirked. "When I shadowed Michael on one of their meetings, he completely ignored my existence. Whether intentional or not, I tormented him after that. The poor officers were blamed for the snow in his bed, and the maids were blamed for the salt stuffed inside his pastries.

"When he received his promotion for captain of the guard I stepped on his foot during our dance. Twice—not by accident either. However, afterward I spilled an entire glass of raspberry punch down the front of his new uniform."

I lifted my eyebrows. "On purpose?"

She cringed. "That *was* actually an accident. I'm sure I looked horrified as I profusely apologized, unsuccessfully trying to wipe the stain off. My erratic behavior was so out of character for me that it drove him to laughter. I'd never seen him laugh like that before. I offered to walk with him in the gardens to give him an excuse to not go back to the party in his soiled uniform, and that's … that's where it began."

"But even after all this time," a question hung in my words.

She looked toward the window. "The way I was viewed by this country, the way I was raised, always by myself, I didn't want him to suffer the same scorn I did, and it has taken me a very long time to accept it."

What the queen had done to her had affected not only her life, but the lives of everyone around her.

"I hear that your family is trying to kill you," she said, changing the subject.

"The dead assassin in my room had the same features as my mother."

"But why would they want to murder you?" she asked.

"That's what I've been trying to figure out. Had you ever come across that poison that they used on me before?"

She shook her head, but something strange passed across

her face.

"What is it?"

"I'm not ready to talk about it yet." She hesitated. "But something very strange happened when I tried to heal you. It was like the poison was combating my powers, and it was winning. I've felt the effects of injuries, infections, and diseases, but none have ever felt anything like what it did in that moment. It—it took me into some kind of trance."

I cocked my head. "Trance?"

I could tell that she was going to a very dark place.

"I don't know how to explain it, but there are things about me, Taryn, things that would scare you if you knew. I think there's more to the Radonaya than I ever could have guessed."

"What are you saying?" I wasn't quite sure where she was going with this.

Debate warred in her eyes, the challenge over whether to tell me what was really going on. "When I was out visiting the villages, I met another Radonaya for the very first time. Her name was Colleen."

Katherine dove into her recounting of the events, about what it was like to meet another one of her kind, the City of Iso where they supposedly came from, the blood-red hair, the truth of her mother, the touch of death. She stared at me expectantly once she finished, as if waiting for me to grow frightened, but I didn't.

"And you think this vision was somehow connected to the Radonaya?" I asked.

She nodded.

"Then I think we need to figure out how they're connected."

I left Katherine to whatever she and Verone were up to and stopped by my old room to pick up a few books and an extra dress. One of the guards inspected the room before allowing me to enter. He made as if to stay, but I shooed him out. I was grateful for their protection, but it was too much, and I would be fine by myself for a few moments.

I picked through my small stack of books, but realized if I wanted to find something about the Radonaya, I would have more luck in the library or from the shelves in my father's room. I popped open the wardrobe, fingering through the dresses and trying to decide what I needed. Something clicked behind me, and I jumped, turning only to see that it was just the door that had slid shut.

"Miss Gallows?" one of the guards called, knocking.

I pushed the hair from my eyes, and leaned back into the wardrobe, pulling out a simple brown dress. "I'll be right out."

I pushed the cupboard shut, slinging the dress over my left arm.

A gloved hand clamped over my mouth.

I screamed, but little more than a muted muffle escaped my mouth.

Another arm clamped around my middle like an iron cage as I fought to get away. The tip of a knife pressed against my side.

I stilled.

"It's time for your first riddle, *Miss Gallows*." The man's voice was hushed, low.

My heart smashed against my chest, fear pumping through

me.

"We're going to play a game. If you win, you have a small chance of surviving. If you lose, you're guaranteed certain death. I have three riddles for you—but you'll need to answer them before time runs out. Before *your* time runs out."

A lilting accent possessed his words.

The guard knocked again, rattling the locked door handle, then pounded harder. I struggled to inhale through my nose, terrified to move with the knife pressed against me.

"Listen closely," he instructed, tightening his grip. "What is red as blood, bitter as wormwood, and holds the keys to both life and death?"

Someone kicked at the door, trying to break in.

He shoved me forward and I crashed into the floor. I rolled over, turning to see his dark form bound out the window just as the door burst open from the outside force. The guards rushed over to me, glancing at the window hanging ajar.

"It's him," I gasped out, rising to my feet. "He was here."

CHAPTER TWENTY

THE COUNCIL SPENT hours deliberating over the assassination attempts. The rising unrest in the camps of soldiers outside the city. The impending threat of Brenden. The fear that the Brenden government would send an *actual* assassin to take William out. And the threat of an assassin still lurking within the city walls, trying to take out Taryn.

Each issue weighed on me in different ways. Everything needed to be dealt with all at once, but that was impossible. None of this information was new to me. We were running in circles when there was actual work that needed to be done. Council meetings had always been a headache, but now they loomed before me like a dreaded death sentence. William was in an exceptionally foul mood today, even for him, and his drunkenness, evidenced in the looseness of his tongue, wasn't helping matters.

William let out a bored sigh, rolling his eyes. "Was there a particular reason for this meeting? Something of actual significance to discuss, or was it just to waste my time repeating facts I already know?"

The room cringed, the lot of us walking on eggshells with William, as if talking too loudly would suddenly make him explode. I briefly shut my eyes and took a deep breath. If William would simply focus and stop drinking for at least half an hour, he would be able to grasp what I had already deduced from the information they'd spread before us.

"We've been continuing to send troops across the Jidero, but we still haven't been able to figure out Brenden's strategy?" I asked.

Commander Dane shook his head. "Scouts have been patrolling our borders, venturing as close as they dare, but Brenden's army is very spread out. We still haven't been able to locate their central force, if it's even crossed the border yet, but as much military movement as we've been seeing from them, that seems highly unlikely. We should have been able to uncover it by now."

I inspected the map, taking note of where Brenden's troops were confirmed to be and where our own had been stationed. Brenden battalions were dispersing all along our border, but none were attacking.

"What of the towns and villages along the border? Do they have sufficient protection?" I asked.

The minister of war hesitated. "We sent additional troops, and they're barricading as best they can, but not every city and village has walls, leaving them the first ones vulnerable to attack."

A councilman piped up. "But we've also discussed if this is a plan to stretch our army thin, weaken us in any way they know how."

Whatever way we looked at it, the situation was bad. Brenden had ingenious military strategy, and I feared we wouldn't know their master plan until it was too late.

"You also have an issue with Algarar."

I turned my attention to where Darya sat at the end of the table.

William squinted, annoyance glinting in his eyes. He'd frowned at her when the council meeting started but refrained from commenting. Unlike now. "I'm sorry, who are you?"

Darya didn't miss a beat. "I'm the courier who carried Marco's letter for months while half the castle was off gallivanting in the wilderness doing who knows what. Finnigan would probably be ruling this country right now if it wasn't for me."

William gripped the edge of the table, knuckles turning bone-white. Unlike the rest of the kingdom, Darya knew the truth of what had lain in that letter, and William couldn't argue or even contradict her without condemning his mother for her actions. In truth, Darya was the one who had carried his mother's death sentence. I knew it. William knew it, and it was scrawled all over his face.

"She's proven herself a skilled courier and also possesses skill as a spy," I interjected before something horrible happened. "I trust her and want her included on the council meetings from now on."

In truth, she was far more valuable than that statement.

Once I'd finally had time to carry out an actual conversation with her, I learned she'd done more for Marco and Gharridan than I ever could've imagined, which was why I'd chosen to share almost everything with her.

"What is this news of Algarar?" I asked.

Darya brought her attention to me. She'd confided about incoming news from other spies and couriers that needed to be heard. "A messenger rode in from the north this morning stating that he spotted an encampment of Algarian troops heading toward the mountains."

"There were Algarian troops in Gapsvar." William's voice suddenly rang sober. "The letter—" He cut off. "The letter Taryn saw in Gapsvar also mentioned it."

"Do you think that Algarar and Brenden are in league?" a councilman asked.

I immediately shook my head. "Brenden is too proud, and Algarar is too monopolizing. It would take a natural disaster or last means of survival for them to work together. I think most of us know that Algarar will be attacking us for a completely different reason, and we don't know exactly how they plan to do this yet. I doubt Algarar will move until Gharridan and Brenden have decimated each other. They'll swoop in to take over the remnants."

William leaned back, staring at all the information laid out before him and mulling over his response. "Keep a close eye on the Algarian border, but I want our main focus to be Brenden."

We shuffled through a few more documents, more busywork than anything, before dismissing the meeting. I was more than ready to move on and leave, but William's voice stopped me.

"I need to speak with you, Vladimir."

I hid the dread rising up within me. I never knew what to expect from William anymore and therefore had no way to prepare. The others shuffled out of the room until only William and I were left. The close of the doors rang out in the abandoned quiet.

"I want her gone by morning."

I peered at him. "Want who gone?"

Darya definitely wasn't shy about giving her opinion, but I didn't think her quip had warranted this response.

"Taryn."

"*Taryn?*" The name shocked me. "Why?"

Finality hung in William's hardened eyes. "Because I want her gone."

I stared at him in confusion, trying to punch down my rising anger. "Did you miss the entire conversation we had where someone tried to assassinate Taryn? *Twice?* And they're still coming after her?"

William picked up his glass and took a lazy sip, shrugging. "She's never wanted anything to do with our government, so I fail to see how her protection is Gharridan's problem."

He'd never voice it, but I had sensed William hadn't wanted to see Taryn since what had transpired in the tower. I never imagined his hatred burned this deep.

"Make sure that she's escorted out," he added.

William turned as if to leave, but I wasn't done here. I stood my ground. "You two finally had it out, didn't you?"

"Whether we did or not is none of your business," William snapped.

I stepped closer to him. "When it concerns the safety of a

citizen of Gharridan, it does."

William let out a scornful laugh.

My jaw clicked shut. "Taryn doesn't leave this castle."

William set his glass down, whirling to face me. "Lest you've already forgotten, I must remind you that *I* am the king and the ruler of Gharridan."

"And *I* am the leader of the Kavari, tasked with keeping you from abusing that power. The power which was so graciously granted to you considering that you're just a half-blood with a conniving mother who tried to destroy this kingdom."

I shouldn't have been surprised by his sudden punch, but I was. Pain burst across the left side of my face. I twisted, ducking out of the way as his fist swung at me again.

"Don't forget I'm the one who allowed you to keep your position even after you tried to steal my throne," he spat.

He launched another blow, but he was intoxicated, and it was sloppy. My fist caught him in the jaw, the force sending a jolt through my arm. My face ached from where he'd struck.

William stumbled back, touching his lip, his callused fingers coming away with blood. "You know, you've been obsessed with Taryn since the first day she arrived here, always worried about her safety, going after her when she disappears." He cocked his head. "I'm starting to wonder if you have your own interests with her."

My next hit came before he had time to react, but he was ready for the third, and this time he found my jaw. My fist struck his gut and he doubled over in pain before springing out of reach.

"I swore an oath to her father, William," I snarled. "And it's my *job*. My duty. Something you wouldn't understand."

He ran forward. I rolled with the next punch, then drove my shoulder into his stomach, shoving him to the ground and pinning him with my forearm across his throat.

"Enough!" I yelled.

William struggled beneath me, but he was in no condition to gain the upper hand.

"Horrible things happened in that tower, William, things you will never be able to undo. You had everything you thought you knew ripped out from underneath you. That is no small event to endure, and I sympathize with your plight, but you were left with a kingdom to rule in the wake of its destruction. If you want to make it out of this, you are going to have to shove all of those hard things aside and become the king that this country needs you to be."

William continued to struggle, attempting to throw me off him, but when he realized that wasn't possible, he quit fighting and lay motionless on the floor.

"What is your plan as a ruler, William? Are you going to exile everyone who wrongs you? Disagrees with you? Would you like me to find you a scythe in place of a scepter?"

"No." Deadness saturated his voice.

"No?" I asked. "Then what in heaven's name is your reasoning for this madness?"

I let out a heavy breath, the barely controlled rage simmering within me.

"She hates me." His glassy eyes turned moist, the anger gone. "And I don't blame her, but every time I look at her, I see her pulling the knife out of my mother's gut, and I can't— I can't—"

His voice broke along with his will, and I closed my eyes.

That's exactly what I had been afraid of.

I stood up, pulling him to his feet and making sure he wouldn't fall apart then and there. He needed time to grieve. Time to process. Time to work through this upside-down mess of his life.

And it was time he would never get.

"You will have demons that will haunt you for the rest of your life, William," I said. "Demons that you will have to live with and face every single day. Most people aren't lucky enough to outrun them or escape them. So like those people, you have to learn how to deal with your demons. Because if you don't deal with them—they will destroy you."

He wiped at his bloody nose, splashes of crimson already tainting his skin. He was a mess. A mess I wasn't sure we'd ever be able to fix, but would have to endure for the rest of our lives—no matter how short they might be.

I strode toward the door. "Taryn stays."

He didn't argue, and the door slammed behind me.

Nic was waiting in the hall, his face lined with worry. Could there never be a moment of peace?

"What is it?" I asked.

"It's Taryn."

CHAPTER TWENTY-ONE

THE SMELL OF the leather glove covering my mouth haunted me. I could still feel the press of the dagger, the terror of the moment.

It's time for your first riddle.

I shuddered, wrapping my arms around myself as I paced, trying to figure out what had just happened. Trying to figure out *why* it had happened.

Vladimir barged into the room, and I jumped. He noticed my reaction and glanced around the space before bringing his eyes back to me.

"Did he hurt you?"

I shook my head.

"What were you even doing in there?" he asked.

Did he always have to start with an interrogation? "I had to pick up a few things. The door was open, Vladimir. I was in there for less than five minutes."

He studied me before asking the question everyone else had been wanting to ask. "Why are you still alive?"

I played the conversation back through my mind, still trying to make sense of it. "He wants to play a game of riddles. If I solve them, I have a chance of surviving. If not—" I cut off, but he took my meaning.

"What were the riddles?"

I shook my head again. "He only gave me one."

Vladimir stepped closer, filling my vision, but I couldn't meet his gaze even though the anticipation practically radiated off him. I took a deep breath.

"What is red as blood, bitter as wormwood, and holds the keys to both life and death?"

I'd been running it through my head, trying to make sense of it, but nothing had come of it. Was red actually referring to a color? Was bitterness actually referring to a taste? They could mean something completely different.

"Does it hold any meaning to you?" he asked.

"I haven't had much time to unravel it, but no."

I finally glanced up, surprised to see a lack of anger or frustration on his face. He just looked stunned. Defeated.

He rubbed his head, thinking. "If you do figure it out, how are you supposed to give him your answer?"

I shrugged. "He gave me no instruction, but if he was able to find me that easily …"

What would happen when he returned and I didn't have an answer? I shivered.

"He said I needed to answer them before my time ran out,

like if he didn't kill me, something else would."

Vladimir said nothing, and his perplexed expression frightened me.

He was never this quiet.

"Well," he finally said after a few minutes of silence. "I'll work on it, and if you come up with anything, let me know. I'll ask Katherine too."

He made as if to leave, still confusing me with his lack of comment, but paused when he turned the door handle.

"Do you feel safe enough to stay here tonight? I can have them move you somewhere else."

I wrapped my arms around myself.

No.

I didn't.

I didn't feel safe, and I didn't know that I ever would again. The assassin had made it very clear that if he wanted to get to me, he could.

"I'll be fine," I lied. "There's no window in here. He'd have to get through the guards first."

He'd already gotten a note past them last night, but neither of us voiced the obvious.

Vladimir nodded, seeming far away. "Let me know if you need anything."

"I will."

I didn't move for a long while after he left, working through the encounter with the assassin again and again, trying to figure out what bothered me so much about it. And what bothered me so much, I realized, was that I was still alive. The first two attacks, they'd given me no contact but simply gone straight in for the kill. The note, and the one tonight, those were different. Something had changed when Vladimir killed the other assassin, but I couldn't figure out what.

CHAPTER TWENTY-TWO

VLADIMIR

Pain lanced through my hand from where I'd struck William; a dull ache throbbed across my face and stung my ribs. I rubbed my jaw, knowing bruises were already forming, but at least I'd mustered the guts to stand up to William—for now.

I lay awake in bed that night, concern for everything threading through me. Concern for William about the volatile state of his mind. Was he stable? He was a dam cracking, on the verge of bursting at any moment. He'd nearly broken earlier, but just barely managed to hold himself back. If I pushed him, I was afraid that he would lash out even worse than he had tonight, and fragile as he was, we still needed him, because we didn't know what Brenden was doing. Didn't know what Algarar was doing.

Something was coming. Something big.

There was a captain continuing to cause trouble in the camps of soldiers outside the capital, asking questions about what really happened after the explosion at the gates and how the queen actually died, sticking his nose in places he wasn't supposed to. William and the council had built their fable on a lie, and it would eventually eat them from the inside out and come to fruition for all the world to see.

But most of all, I couldn't get the assassin and the riddle out of my head.

What is red as blood, bitter as wormwood, and holds the keys to both life and death?

There was no reason for him to drag this out through a game of riddles unless he was trying to toy with her, but even then, what was the point? They'd already tried to kill her, and thank heavens they hadn't, but why not just finish the job and be done?

Five minutes.

That part scared me the most. Four guards, a cleared room, an open door. Less than five minutes, and the whole ordeal had been over. Even less than that for him to get into the room with her—without her or anyone else noticing.

And the comment about her time running out.

The worries and doubts clawed at my mind, pushing away sleep. I rose in the darkness, pulling a shirt over my head and venturing out into the hall. I kept running the events of Taryn's poisoning through my mind over and over again, tried to piece together everything I'd ever heard about her mother's family from her. She'd shared so little, and all Michael had supplied me with was the family name of Illdalore. I knew that it wasn't from Gharridan, but where else? The skin tone, even of the assassin, didn't match that from Algarar or Brenden. But maybe it could be Gharridan, a family name from before. Gharridan was built from the scattered remnants of many small and different civilizations, a mesh of cultures. It could be possible. But was it?

I thought I'd been wandering aimlessly, but I found myself outside Taryn's door, wanting to question her again and to ask her about her family. Wanting to talk about the riddle. Surprise touched the guards' faces as they straightened their postures, and it brought me back to my senses. It was the middle of the night. Taryn was asleep. What was wrong with me? Just because I couldn't sleep didn't mean the others couldn't. I nodded to the guards without saying anything, continuing past her door.

A muffled but blood-curdling scream ripped from inside the room, reverberating off the halls like the dying wails of an angered ghost. Visions of Taryn's lifeless body on the bench and the black-clad assassin creeping toward her bed flooded my mind and I burst through the door before the soldiers even had time to react.

Silver moonlight illuminated the room through the skylight, revealing someone thrashing underneath the covers on the bed. My dagger was already in my hand as I scanned the room, but the space appeared void of any other life. I inspected the other side of the bed before sheathing the blade and unraveling a writhing Taryn from the twisted blankets.

She screamed again, leaving my ears ringing, and let out a whimpered sob.

"Taryn!" I said, grabbing her shoulders.

She struggled against me, arms swinging wildly into mine,

beating me back.

"Taryn!" I called again, tightening my grip as I tried to shake her awake. "TARYN!"

She jerked with a start, wild eyes flying open, desperate and ragged breaths heaving from her chest as she sat up, panic encompassing her face.

"It's me," I said. "It's Vladimir." I waited to release my grip until she calmed down. "You were dreaming."

She stilled, choking on a cry. "Vladimir?" She took in the room around her, settling but only slightly. "Was it really just a dream?"

I nodded my assurance.

She fell forward into my chest with a gasping sob, hands fisting into my tunic. I froze, stunned, and then wrapped my arms tightly around her, nodding to the guards shuffling awkwardly in the doorway that it was safe to leave. My mind raced, seeking a solution. I'd never seen her in such a state. Anyone in such a state. My shirt grew wet with her tears, sticking to my skin.

After a moment she seemed to calm down, then suddenly jerked away looking embarrassed, as if she realized what she'd just done, but the terror still reigned in her eyes. "I'm so—so sorry," she stuttered. "I don't know what came over me. I–I–"

She was still out of breath, her shift damp with sweat and clinging to her—

I cleared my throat. "Are you all right?"

She swiped at her eyes like she was trying to clear away memories and shook her head. "I've had nightmares before, but this? This was," She struggled with her words, the last three coming out in a whisper. "This was different."

Tears welled in her eyes, and I swept the hair out of her face, glancing around the room again, on high alert and paranoid I had missed an intruder. "Different how?"

She closed her eyes. "It was beyond real. I could see them. See the blood. Hear the screams, taste the pungent air, feel their fingers on my throat. I almost still can, like it's a memory …"

She lifted a hand to her throat, as if sensing imaginary fingers still gripping it.

I frowned. "What was it about?"

It took her a moment to respond. "Everything was red," she finally managed. "My parents, and Helvah, they were, they were—"

William had told me about Helvah, the little girl they'd left behind in Gapsvar, and I'd suspected that this continued to haunt Taryn.

She shuddered, eyes going wide. "I don't—I don't think I want to talk about it. Not right now at least."

"You don't have to," I said.

She looked traumatized.

She took a deep breath as if to calm herself and leaned back against the headboard. The silence swallowed us, leaving me unsure of where to go from here.

"I'll leave so you can go back to sleep," I said as I rose from the bed.

"No." Her hand shot out, grabbing my arm and stopping me.

"I'm sorry." She pulled her hand back reluctantly. "I just, I don't want to go to sleep again."

The fear that erupted in her at the thought of being alone caused me to drop back onto the mattress. This seemed like more than just a nightmare.

"I actually wanted to ask you about your parents, anyway," I said. "You've always spoken so little about your mother. Is there anything else you could tell me about her, anything that would make you think her family would want to harm you?"

The question distracted her like I'd intended.

Her brows drew together in concentration. "She hardly ever spoke of her family. I always sensed a deep hurt, a sadness. She did once mention she hoped that I could reconcile with them, but if they're trying to kill me, I guess that explains why our existence was always so secretive. They must have been looking for her all these years."

The thought troubled me. "But why wait until now?"

"What do you mean?"

I crossed my arms. "You've been in the capital for months, *well*, off and on. If they knew who you were, why wait until now to strike?"

The thought hadn't occurred to her. "That does seem rather strange. After waiting all this time, why choose now to strike?"

She looked up then studied my face, as if seeing it for the first time. Her lips pursed. "What happened?"

I lowered my brows in confusion, the pain of the motion reminding me that I had a fat lip, a bruised rib, and probably a very colorful eye.

"Ah," I said. "It's nothing."

She leaned closer, scrutinizing my forehead. "It doesn't look like nothing." Her cold fingers brushed across my temple, across the tender skin. She smelled like lilacs. With her this close, William's words swam in my mind.

You've been obsessed with Taryn ever since she came here. I can't help wondering if you have your own interests with her.

I pulled away from her touch, but her hand hovered in the air.

"It was William, wasn't it." It wasn't a question but a statement.

"We're good," I said, not liking where the topic of conversation led. "Don't worry, no one's throwing you out of the castle at dawn."

She set her jaw, still visibly upset over whatever had happened between them.

My gaze fell to her wrist, still lingering near my head as if afraid to move. I frowned, grabbing it and pulling it into a patch of moonlight.

"Taryn, what is this?"

She followed my concern to a black mark on her wrist, the line twisting in her skin to follow the path where her veins should be.

"I noticed a black dot on my skin this morning," she said. "But I didn't think much of it. This wasn't there when I went to bed. It—it looks like it's spreading."

I met her confused eyes.

I'd never seen anything like it before.

Taryn's face paled. "He told me. That's what he meant."

"Told you what?"

Heaviness filled her words. "You'll need to answer them before time runs out. Before *your* time runs out."

I swallowed. Maybe Katherine hadn't drawn that poison out of her after all.

CHAPTER TWENTY-THREE

I MUST HAVE drifted back off to sleep, because when I awoke in the morning, Vladimir was gone. The memory of the nightmare slammed into me and fear sparked deep within my gut. I'd had nightmares before, but *this* … this was unlike anything I had ever experienced.

I could still feel the heat of the flames licking at my skin, hear Helvah's screams as they penetrated my ears. I watched as the ricochet slit my father's throat over and over again, saw Zedekiah pierce his chest with the sword I carried in my hands, only then it wasn't Zedekiah murdering my father, it was my own hands that wielded the blade. The metallic scent of blood lingered in my nose. My father's face shifted between his and my mother's as I killed them over and over and *over* again. I tried to stop, but Zedekiah's hands circled my throat, forcing me to continue. It was an unbreakable time loop, an endless nightmare.

Vladimir's searching blue eyes in the moonlight were the only thing that had rooted me back to reality, convinced me that it was actually over, that it wasn't real. Embarrassment still pulsed through me over the way that I'd reacted, but he hadn't seemed to mind. Better him than one of the guards.

I felt like a child, craving someone else's presence because of a nightmare when our country was literally under attack. Vladimir had bigger things to worry about than my problems, but I was glad that he hadn't left. His presence always emitted a sense of security, that no matter how horrible a situation was, everything was going to be all right.

I stared at the black mark on my wrist, trying to keep the rising terror within me at bay. Maybe it was nothing. Maybe it was everything, but as I surveyed the strange lines simmering just beneath my skin, a chill crept up my spine—because it looked like I'd been marked for death.

I sorted through memories of my mother, trying to conjure memories of things she had said. She'd never warned me that they wanted us dead. Never insinuated that whatever drove the rift between them was this severe. If I'd found them on my own, charged into the midst of them with no warning—

But maybe something had changed since she left, and she didn't know how bad it had gotten.

I returned to my room after breakfast. I was already late. Vladimir had wanted Katherine to look at my wrist in the middle of the night, but I told him to wait. Katherine needed her rest, and I also wasn't sure if I even wanted to know what it was. That might be worse.

I brushed into the room, heading for the books stacked on the edge of the bookshelf, but the square of white resting in a patch of sunlight on the center of my bed stopped me in my tracks. I whipped out my dagger, frantically searching the room, but there was no one but me in here. I peeked under the bed before reaching for the parchment with a shaking hand. It was folded in fours, and I braced myself as I carefully uncreased it.

The words stilled the breath in my lungs.

CHAPTER TWENTY-FOUR

AN UNEASY FEELING slithered through me with each step that brought us closer to Taryn. Vladimir's description of what had happened planted a foulness in the pit of my stomach. Whispers from the nightmare I had walked through the night of the attack assaulted my ears, taunting me, and my body was taut as a bowstring.

I glanced down at the braided leather ring on my left hand, memories from last night flashing across my vision. The clear and dark blue sky spread above us with a blanket of endless stars like pinpricks in the darkness. Whispers of the night traveling along the wind as it trickled through my blood-red hair, elegantly half done up in a series of intricate braids with pearl pins threaded throughout the design. The swish of the emerald dress I'd worn as I walked, the white sash gleaming in the night like a ghost. A beacon.

I could still feel the warmth of Verone's dark hands threaded through mine. Our contrasting features seeming so different on the outside, but within there was no differentiation. Our souls burned the same. Complete. And we had knit them together.

We'd shared sacred words between the two of us.

Vowed.

Spoken in the presence of a bishop, the only other human witness to the union. But all of nature had been our witness. The branches of the trees creaked closer, the moon illuminating our forms. The grass bent to hear the promises that left our lips, the fealty that welled in our eyes.

It was not just a union.

It was a binding of souls.

A vow that could not be undone.

An infinite thread that tied the two of us together.

Broken only by death.

Ended only with unbearable sorrow that would crack two hearts and the hearts of those around them with a damage that could never be reversed.

I remembered the press of Verone's lips against mine, but it hadn't been like the kisses before. The ones stolen in secret alcoves, abandoned rooms, between assignments. It was a kiss of freedom. Of release. Release from the fears of the past, of all the things that could happen should anyone find out. The fear of rejection. The fear of lost hope.

But last night had sprung a new hope. One of beginning. One that would never end.

I eyed Vladimir walking beside me. I hadn't told him—or

anyone—yet. For now, I wanted to keep it just between our-selves. Especially with all of the extenuating circumstances sur-rounding us.

Vladimir and I pushed through the library doors, maneu-vering through the maze of shelves until finding Taryn hun-kered over a desk and rapidly flipping through the pages of a book, another crooked stack of volumes beside it.

I stopped before her, still uneasy, my nose crinkling in dis-taste.

Taryn slammed a note face up on the desk without looking at us. "It's the poison. It has to be."

Vladimir picked up the note, and I read over his shoulder.

"Where was this?" Vladimir asked.

I tuned out their conversation as I read the words again and again. Maybe it was the poison. Maybe it wasn't. If the assassin was close enough to Taryn to plant that note, he was close enough to know that she'd had a nightmare. He could just be trying to mess with her head.

I steeled myself, the strange feeling still swirling inside me.

"Let me see," I commanded.

From the look Taryn shot me, I could tell she sensed my apprehension. She came around the desk, lifting her left sleeve to expose her wrist.

I had to resist stepping back.

I'd known exactly where it would be before I even saw it. My body knew it was there, something *within* me knew that it was there. I swallowed. The strangeness walking here. Whatever this was, my body was *afraid of it*.

I took a deep breath, trying to calm myself. "It just ap-peared last night?"

"It appeared the morning after the attack, but it—" Taryn hesitated. "It seems to be spreading."

I examined the black mark without touching it. The lines did not appear to be on her skin, but rather in it, following the veins lining her wrist as if trapped inside.

"Can you draw it out of her?" Vladimir asked.

"No!" I snapped. The sharp word slipped out, sounding foreign.

Both glanced up at me in surprise.

I shook my head. "I'm sorry, I don't—"

My fingers trembled. Why was I acting so paranoid? What happened when I'd tried to draw out the poison had been a freak occurrence. It couldn't happen again.

"Sit down," I instructed, waving my hand.

Taryn sat cross-legged on the floor and I knelt in front of her, never taking my eyes from the mark. My skin recoiled from it, wanted nothing to do with it. Pain had memory, and perhaps my body remembered what it had experienced last time.

"Katherine."

Taryn stared at me, her green eyes etched with concern. For a moment, I could've sworn it was Michael looking at me, and I had to shake away the thought.

"If something feels wrong, you don't have to do this," she said.

I ignored her, grabbing her hand to flip her wrist up. I took a deep breath, closing my eyes as I brought my other hand up to touch the blackness.

At first, nothing.

Then.

It sucked me in.

The world around me crumbled into a ravaged wasteland. The shelves of the library still stood, cracked and decaying, their wood eaten by insects. The ripped-out pages of books drifted through the ashy air, the snapped spines and broken cases lying scattered across the split and shaking ground. Fires blazed in the distance, filling the sky with smoke and the world with an eerie light. The smell of war permeated the air.

Taryn still sat before me, face blurred, but the black mark glowed, the yellow lines I had seen before twisting up her arms in bigger, thicker roots, crisscrossing across her head and tightening around her throat.

"Taryn?"

She gave me no answer.

A chill drifted from behind me.

"I thought you would have learned by now there are things you shouldn't touch."

The flashes assaulted me again, the woman dying, Colleen's words echoing in my head—*It's called the touch of death*—and then there was the diamond, the lion, and the arrow shafts burrowing into William's chest. I saw his killer, saw him skulking beneath the shadows of his hood. The world ripped apart and I held the disintegrating pieces of it together.

I was the only one who could.

I tried to bring it back together while screams crawled their way out of my throat as the earth filled with blood and drowned me.

CHAPTER TWENTY-FIVE

T HE SECOND KATHERINE touched the blackness, it recalled within me every memory of pain I had ever experienced. I tried to open my mouth, tried to scream, but my voice had been snatched from me as the pain burned through my body. Katherine's eyes were closed, her lower lip quivering. Tears silently slid down my cheeks as my gaze locked on Katherine's hand on my wrist. I sensed Death's presence, but I couldn't see him. I feared he was coming for us. Coming for me.

Ringing filled my ears. Muffled shouting, but I couldn't escape the pain. I was frozen. Frozen until a hand shoved into my shoulder, pushing me back and breaking the contact with Katherine.

And then my eyes rolled back into my head.

"You know how dangerous that was!"

My mother's voice sounded far away. I lifted my lids, aware of my small child's body, of the fever wracking it. I was so, *so* sick. My head lolled sideways, trying to focus on the blurry forms of my arguing parents.

"And I don't care! She's dying, Evelyn! I've found no trace of any Radonaya in Gharridan. This was our only hope. You know they can't harm me. You know that they will hold to their word."

Tears invaded my mother's voice. "I know that they will, but that doesn't mean I trust every one of them to keep their word. My father *broke the oath*, Michael. They know I'm still alive, that you had something to do with it, and if they find *me*, they find *her*. I can't lose her. I can't lose you. I've already lost so much, and I can't, I can't—"

Her sobs were muffled by his chest, and within the memory I now recognized a trauma rooted deep within my mother, overtaking her, robbing her of a peaceful life. My vision flickered in and out, but I remembered the vibrance of the red flower, the sickly-sweet perfume of the petals' scent as my father crushed them, prepared them in a concoction that he trickled down my throat.

"TARYN!"

My eyes burst open.

Pale blue depths searched mine, their edges lined with fear, framed by a curtain of dark hair falling around them.

I blinked.

I was in the library.

Vladimir's hands left my face when I became alert, but the concern remained.

I looked to Katherine. She now huddled with her arms wrapped around her knees, rocking back and forth with horror encircling her face. Dizziness overwhelmed me as I sat up, and Vladimir put a steadying hand on my shoulder. My gaze fell to the black mark on my wrist, its lines now more prominent and defined. A low throb pulsed through my veins.

"What happened?" I managed.

Vladimir raked a hand through his hair, looking like he himself had gone through an ordeal. "You both fell into a—a trance and looked like you were in pain. You didn't respond so I broke you apart. Katherine came to first. You were out for longer. I don't know what they gave you, Taryn, but—"

"It's not her," Katherine cut in, shaking her head. "It's me."

Vladimir and I turned to her.

"There are things I never told you about what happened when we split up after Finnigan forced you to vie for the Crown," Katherine said. "I was attacked in a town. One of your men took two arrows for me, and I healed him, almost dying in the process, but there was a Radonaya there who saved me."

Vladimir scooted closer to her with bewilderment. "Why didn't you tell me? You've been looking for another as long as I've known you."

Katherine closed her eyes, shaking her head. "Because with everything else going on, there was never time. And there are things I learned about the Radonaya, reasons for the superstition around my people."

Vladimir leaned back, confused.

Katherine turned to me. "I possess something called the touch of death, Taryn. I don't know how to use it, I don't understand it, but I can't heal you, and I think that this may be affecting it. Whatever they gave you, whatever this mark is stemming from, I think that my power is only making it worse."

Katherine went into detail about what the woman, Colleen, had told her. The darkened hair. The City of Iso. How there was no way that Katherine could have killed the king. But I couldn't take my eyes from the mark on my wrist.

The memory of my sickness swam before me. A memory I'd forgotten about, buried deep within me.

My father broke the oath, Michael.

The words of their conversation haunted me, but even as I tried to decipher them, they weren't what I was primarily focused on. It was the vibrance of the red flower, the shape of the petals. The clarity of the memory that I'd never experienced in my previous encounter, and the knowledge with which it registered.

I rose to my feet, ignoring the strange stares of Vladimir and Katherine as I wandered over to where I'd left my father's books on herbology lying on the desk. I cracked open the cover of the top one, flipping through the pages of plants listed within and searching for what I had seen before. What was burned into my memory.

What is the deadliest plant?

Vladimir's words echoed in my mind, asked when he distrusted me after learning that I knew how to use a sword. Right after I'd nearly beaten William on the training fields. My answer had been instantaneous. Anyone's would have been. While an actual sighting of the plant was extremely rare, and some might even call it a fable, its dangerousness was drilled into everyone as a child. Don't mess with it. Don't even *touch* it.

My fingers stilled on the next page, eyes boring into a

sketched red flower, the text surrounding it filled with a plethora of warnings, poison markings, and death sentences. Uneasiness seeped deep into my bones as words the queen had spoken in the tower came back to my mind.

I strode back to them, cutting into the conversation without consideration. "I don't think this has anything to do with your touch of death, Katherine."

She frowned.

"Nor do I know why this is only happening now and you were able to heal me before. When the queen told me in the tower what she used to kill her husband, she said that she'd chosen it because the Radonayas' power doesn't work on that plant."

Katherine's eyes narrowed. "Mors Secunda? But what does Mors Secunda have to do with this?"

"I don't know," I shrugged. "But I do know, according to her at least, your healing won't work on it. But that's not the question here. Every time you've healed me, I've experienced some kind of memory. When you healed my back in the tower, it was like I was drowning in the Jidero river all over again. The first time you healed me, I experienced a brief flashback, one I haven't thought of since, but it's what I just saw now except with extreme clarity. These nightmares have also been triggering memories. Memories of a red flower. A red flower that I recognized from my father's herbology books. And I remember it now. I don't know how I ever forgot. When I was a child I nearly died with a fever sickness. I remember my father giving me some kind of medicine that came from that red flower."

"Taryn, I'm not following," Vladimir said.

"Mors Secunda is the deadliest plant we know of." I paused. "If that's true, then why did my father give it to me when I was on the verge of death?"

CHAPTER TWENTY-SIX

◆—◇—◆

TARYN

"THAT'S NOT POSSIBLE," Vladimir said. "It had to be the poison affecting you, messing with your mind. If your father had given you Mors Secunda, you would be dead."

I shook my head. "It sounds crazy, but I know what I saw, Vladimir. This was a memory, clear as day."

"I don't think you can count that as a memory, Taryn," Katherine said. "Whatever this is doing, it's messing with your head. With both our heads."

I snapped the book shut, slamming it down on the table. "I know what I saw!"

My voice sounded unreasonable to my own ears, but something within me said that this was an exact memory. It wasn't a trick of the imagination. I wouldn't be coerced into believing otherwise.

Vladimir and Katherine exchanged a glance before he stood to his feet, stepping toward me with apprehension. "I'm not saying you didn't see what you think you saw, Taryn. I'm saying that it probably is a real memory, but do you not think it's possible for the poison to have tampered with the memory? Inserted Mors Secunda in the place of whatever medicine your father used to heal you?"

I glared at him, seeing exactly where he was coming from but also how he was gently manipulating the conversation. "I see your point, but I assure you it is not. I stand by what I saw. I'm not asking you to believe me."

Skepticism littered Vladimir's eyes, but I ignored it.

That memory was stamped in my mind as real as the day it happened. My father had given me Mors Secunda, so how was I still alive?

And then it all connected.

"The riddle," I whispered, looking up at them. "What is red as blood, bitter as wormwood, and holds the keys to both life and death?"

I watched Vladimir try to dismiss the notion, but he couldn't. It fit too perfectly.

"Why would he tell you a riddle about Mors Secunda?" Katherine asked.

Why try to kill me only to then drag it out?

"I don't know," I said, trying to keep up with the possibilities bombarding me. "But I think that it's the answer, and I think that it's somehow connected to whatever happened between my mother and her family."

Vladimir's expression turned hard. "What if he's trying to

make you uncover what happened?"

"That still wouldn't make it make sense," Katherine said.

"Unless he wants to ensure suffering before taking his vengeance," I added. "I don't know." I turned to Katherine. "But you said this was also messing with your head. You still haven't told me. What did you see?"

Katherine stiffened at my question.

I stepped closer, all but smelling the fear on her. "What is it, Katherine?"

She avoided eye contact, her body turned slightly away from us. "Whatever they poisoned you with, my body—" She hesitated. "My body is afraid of it. I could sense it before I even entered the library. Every time I've touched you to draw it out I've seen, seen something."

She stopped speaking.

"A vision. I don't know what. It's like I touched or tapped into something I wasn't supposed to. Like I touched Death."

I knew Death all too well, and if she had seen him too—

"What did he show you?"

"Three arrow shafts protruding out of William's chest. I watched it happen, and there was nothing I could do to stop it." She finally met our eyes. "I think I'm being warned that William is going to die."

After much coaxing, Katherine briefly described her visions and nightmares to us, but it wasn't easy for her to get through them. I didn't doubt her words. I could sense the presence of Death from her descriptions, but if they were true it wouldn't even be a matter of winning the war. William had killed Brenden's king, and their people wouldn't stop coming for him until he'd been avenged. Keeping William alive was no small task. Especially when Gharridan was barely holding itself together. I swallowed. William and I weren't exactly—well I didn't know what, but the thought of him dying—

No. He wasn't going to die.

I flipped through more books in the library after they left, trying to trigger any other memories, but nothing came. I stared down at the strange black lines, willing them to give me an answer, but all they did was ask more questions.

I picked through Vladimir's account of his conversation with Finnigan and his conviction that he was hiding something important. I forced back my anger for the man, gathering my things before leaving the books behind.

As I descended into the dungeons, my mind continued to turn over the information. I was stuck with all the pieces but no way to put them together. Something was missing. Everything was missing. Katherine's vision. Her power. Mors Secunda. The poison. All of it had to connect somewhere.

I approached the guards and they crossed their spears to stop me. Heart pounding, I lifted my hand to reveal my father's golden ring. I wasn't actually sure if I was allowed down here, but I wouldn't be asking permission and I certainly wasn't taking no for an answer.

"I'm on official Kavari business, sent by Vladimir. He's held up with other matters," I said.

They glanced at each other for a moment as if unsure whether to question my authority, but it must not have been too serious because they opened the door for me.

I hid my smile.

Too easy.

Vladimir needed to hire better security.

One of the guards lit a torch and handed it to me before ushering me down to the steps below. I wasn't prepared for the darkness, and my insides clenched at the thought of being trapped in here, memories resurfacing. I could still feel the cold steel of Zedekiah's sword pressed against my throat, the fear of the unknown.

I squelched the flashbacks from my mind as I traversed down the damp steps, the flickering fire casting ghostly shapes along the wall that followed me, laughing at me. When the cell finally came into view, I hesitated, unsure of what to say, questioning why I had even come and if it was a waste of time, but the hesitation was quickly replaced by anger. I slammed the torch into an empty sconce, stalking closer to the rusted iron bars but keeping a good two feet of distance between them and me. I could just make out a dark form stretched lazily across the cot.

"Ah," a voice drawled out, feet swinging over the side of the bed. "The fierce Taryn Gallows come to tell me off? It appears the assassins weren't able to finish the job after all."

My chest heaved as fury rose within me, but I suppressed it, trying to keep my voice in check. "You know something."

Finnigan chuckled, sauntering up to the iron bars. "I know a *lot* of things."

His smug, condescending attitude made me sick. "You know something about the assassins."

"Knowledge is power. Power requires something in return." He smirked. "What is it that you would be willing to offer me?"

"What good could I do for you?" I scoffed.

A conniving smile lifted Finnigan's lips. "You got immunity for one man." He cocked his head. "Surely you can get it for another."

"I was just the messenger, I had nothing to do with procuring it. That came from you."

"You have resources." Finnigan leaned against the bars. "Use them."

I glared at him. "I would rather be murdered and learn nothing more about my mother's family than free you from here. Besides, I have no reason to trust you. For all I know I could use my 'resources' only for you to reveal you were bluffing and actually knew nothing of that which we speak."

"And what if I give you the information only for you to reveal you have no intention of helping me out of this prison cell?"

It felt like a sparring match, each of us darting in and out with our moves and counter attacks.

I shrugged. "I would say that we would just have to trust each other, but both of us know that is never going to happen."

We stared at each other, locked in a stalemate. I lifted my chin, trying for another tactic.

"You're a patriot, Finnigan, and your country is in danger. If you really care about Gharridan as much as you claim to, then you will help us with this."

He mulled over my words, making a show of it. He was bored. Had to be. Being in isolation must be driving him insane.

When he made no decision, I turned as if to leave, reaching for the torch.

"Wait."

I dropped my hand, turning back.

"I have no certain facts," he conceded. "Nor do I wish to help *you* all that much, but you are right on one account. I do love my country, and I am still a patriot whether behind bars or not. So mark my words, none of this is for your benefit."

I nodded. "Duly noted."

He shifted his weight, chewing at his lip. "Years ago, I made an acquaintance who spoke of a people and a very particular poison they used."

"Who's the acquaintance?" I asked.

He flashed a smile. "I can offer facts, but names cost."

"The information you just offered is completely unhelpful."

Finnigan made a tsking noise. "I wasn't finished yet. After the massacre in Algarar, your father completely disappeared for weeks without telling anyone. Gabriel, the leader of the Kavari, and King Roldan had no idea if Michael was even still alive, wondering if he'd been kidnapped or killed. He did eventually return and both parties were beyond angry. King Roldan even threatened to have him excommunicated from the Kavari, but he got over it quickly. Gabriel, however, did not. Something had shifted between Gabriel and your father before he disappeared. Before the massacre they were inseparable, operated as a unit and shared ultimate trust. Your father looked up to Gabriel in the same way that Vladimir looked up to Michael, but after the massacre, their relationship was never the same again."

I thought of the note stuffed between the binding on my father's book.

I have to go back for her.

He'd gone back for my mother, but if it wasn't Algarar, then where?

"That's still not very much information," I said. "All of it is speculation without fact. And what does any of that have to do with the assassins or the poison?"

Finnigan gave a shrug of indifference.

I stepped closer to the bars, aware that I stood close enough for him to reach out and grab me if he wanted. Vladimir would kill me if he could see my recklessness right now, but I needed more.

"You owe me," I said. "For the way you used me in your little game."

His expression implied otherwise.

I tilted my head. "Technically, I did everything that you asked on the day the queen died. It's not my fault that your plan was interrupted and sabotaged."

He laughed off my statement, stepping away from the bars.

I rolled my eyes in annoyance, but what I really felt was defeated. This was useless. I moved to make my way back up the stairs.

"How are the nightmares?"

His words stopped me in my tracks, and I turned back to face him. The look on my face was all the confirmation he needed to know he was right. That he'd hit the target. My brows lowered.

"What do you know about Mors Secunda?" I asked.

"Well it's red—"

"—as blood," I finished without thinking.

A smile crept up the side of his mouth. "Bitter as wormwood?"

Chills ran up and down my spine. "How do you know

that?"

"Like I said, I know a lot of things. One of which is that everyone always talks about Mors Secunda, how deadly it is, how imperative it is to stay away from it, but do you know of anyone who has ever actually seen it?"

"It grows—" I cut off.

I had no idea where it grew, where it came from. *What is the deadliest plant?* I'd seen drawings and paintings of it, but I'd never seen it in person, never heard of anyone who had run into a patch of it.

"No one seems to be able to verify its existence, but from what legends I have heard, have studied, it never makes for a good poison. It's far too detectable. Bitter as wormwood, dyes whatever it touches red as blood, and no matter what way it is mixed or concocted, its characteristics can't be erased."

Queen Adamara told me that she'd found a patch of Mors Secunda to poison her husband with, but how had she managed to give it to him without anyone ever knowing?

He stepped back up to the bars. "Vladimir said that the assassin who attacked you in your room looked like your mother. Where was she from?"

I doubted he would give me useful information, if he even actually knew any, but there was no way he could have known about the nightmares. Vladimir hadn't spoken with him since that attack, and he would have no other way of obtaining that information. Finnigan did know something. About my family. About the poison.

I selected which information to share with him very carefully. "My mother told me that she was from Dalendria."

I studied him closely, searching for any sign of recognition.

When I saw none, I continued, "But it doesn't seem to exist."

He ignored me, retreating to the cot and lying back on it, apparently done with our conversation.

I bit back my frustration and disappointment. We'd done nothing but run in circles around each other. He'd offered me nothing but more questions without answers, more confusion. This whole meeting had been pointless.

I stormed back up the stairs, but he spoke again before I'd made it up the first three steps.

"That's because you've been looking for it under the wrong name."

CHAPTER TWENTY-SEVEN

TARYN'S WORDS BOTHERED me all day.

I know what I saw.

But it wasn't possible. Maybe what she'd seen had been some kind of imitation, if she was convinced she knew what it was. If Michael had given her Mors Secunda, she wouldn't be with us right now. She would have died as a child. Yet something about the whole memory, the whole situation, didn't sit right with me. The thought that Katherine was unable to draw the poison out sickened me. Taryn was a ticking time bomb at this point. If we didn't find an antidote—

I clenched my jaw. What did the assassin have to prove by drawing it out like this? If he had the ability to strike whenever he pleased, as he stated, then why wasn't he? It made no logical sense. I had several covert soldiers scouring the city and everywhere within the castle to find a trace of this shadow man, but they'd found nothing. It was like he was invisible. Like he didn't exist and lingered in this world as a phantom, appearing where he wanted one second and disappearing the next.

Mixed in with all of those issues was Katherine's premonition that William was going to die. Obviously Brenden wouldn't stop until he was dead, but the chilling way in which she'd described the encounter, how she'd seen the same thing twice, the conviction in her words, led me to believe that something bigger at play was going on here.

And I had no idea how to decipher or stop it.

Nic clapped me on the shoulder, jerking me out of my thoughts. "You ready?"

I tightened Dante's girth, glaring down at the city. "Would it make any difference if I said no?"

"Probably not, but you could try if you wanted."

I frowned.

We mounted, making our way out of the castle courtyard and through the streets of the city toward the main gates.

"What are we looking at?" I asked.

I didn't like this. Any of it. But it had gotten out of hand enough that it needed to be addressed.

"It's escalated in the last few days," Nic stated. "The captains are having a hard time keeping it under control."

My jaw set. I didn't need one more thing pressing on me. One more cause for division. The unrest in squadrons of soldiers outside the city wasn't getting any better, which was to be expected considering the circumstances, but that didn't make it any easier to deal with.

The horses' hooves tapped against the cobblestones as they

trotted through the streets, people clearing out of the road as we passed by. I pulled at the collar of my jacket. The days were growing warmer, the sun's passing across the sky slowing down and lengthening the days.

War hovered around me like mist in the air, blurring the world and marring my thoughts. It whispered in my ear, planting seeds of doubt, trying to make me walk away from the battles that lay ahead. I shook away the voice, noting that significant progress had been made on the main gate. If everything went smoothly and they were able to gather enough of the correct supplies, it should be finished within a few days.

Trotting out of the city walls was like being released from a prison cell. I inhaled the damp twilight air, enjoying the moment of peace before reaching the storm that brewed ahead. The army outside had diminished. Multiple encampments still remained, but a great deal of the force had been dispatched to various locations along the western border in preparation for Brenden's invasion. Streaks of sunlight painted the edges of the horizon, the world nearly dark, and the soldiers mingled around the cook fires, ghostly shadows waving across their faces.

For this many people gathered, it was eerily quiet.

Until one voice rang out in the evening.

I dismounted, handing my reins to a soldier who started with surprise but dipped his head in recognition. Nic made as if to stay with the horses, but I ushered him forward, indicating for him to stay at my back. He handed his reins off as well, following a few paces behind. I kept my head low as I maneuvered my way through the throng encircling the flames, enraptured by the man speaking at their center who was holding a dripping mug of ale in his hand. No one else had noticed or recognized me yet. Good.

I prodded Nic forward. "Start asking questions."

He raised his eyebrow questioningly.

I responded likewise, whispering, "You're the one who never knows how to shut up. This should be easy for you."

He rolled his eyes in mock annoyance, but a coy smile played at his lips.

I knew he was up for this. There was no one better.

My gaze strayed back to the redheaded man. The center of attention. He had an ease about him, as if he were drinking with his friends around a table in a local tavern and not dividing the troops in a war camp. His tone sounded conversational and lacked hostility.

"All I'm saying," he said, "is I don't think we owe them anything else until we're given the truth."

Murmurs drifted through the men, some agreeing or disagreeing, but Nic's voice piped up above the rest. "The truth about what?"

The audience's attention drifted to Nic, as if they weren't used to people speaking out.

The man's gaze found Nic, taking him in and cocking an eyebrow. "You new here, boy?"

"Well, I think that's what my question implied," Nic said. He kept his arms at his sides, stance open.

I nodded, impressed at Nic's lack of reaction to the derogatory address.

The red-haired man chuckled humorlessly, stepping closer to Nic but still addressing the entire crowd. "Well, *new boy*, welcome to the conversation. To catch you up, someone is lying to us. We were told the Kavari were traitors, that the Radonaya killed the king of Brenden and started this war between our two countries, that Vladimir was in on it. But *now* we're told that the Kavari are pardoned, our queen is dead, her mess of a son now sits on the throne, and that one of the councilmen, Finnigan, was behind everything that transpired: the murder of Brenden's king, the severing of the Kavari, the death of Queen Adamara, this war placed upon us. We just lost Michael Gallows last year and learned that Zedekiah was a traitor. We're given facts with no explanations. Expected to go along with it and keep our mouths shut, discouraged from asking questions even when something is obviously wrong."

His statements and accusations hovered in the air, giving time for the words to sink into the men's minds and be pondered. He was voicing everything I'd been afraid of. Everything that I'd told William and the council would happen if they chose to lie to their people.

My eyes shot to Nic, willing him to speak.

Nic chewed on the inside of his lip, but even from a few feet away I could see the gears turning in his head, calculating his next answer. He shrugged. "There's lots of things we're never told as soldiers, and if I remember correctly it's our job to follow orders and not ask questions. If there's something that they haven't told us, I'm sure there's good reason for it."

The man shook his head, a look of disbelief marring his features. "Good reason? Because the higher powers in government always know best, right? They get to control the information we know, and our *lives*—all without letting us have any input."

"I'm sorry, are you saying that because you actually want to make it better for the people or because you've deemed yourself the best person to fill their positions?"

A jolt of shock shot down my spine at his words, but then I was trying to hide a smile. The man's rage was threatening to boil over, and he barely managed to control it.

"What's your name, boy?" The conversational tone disappeared from his voice.

"Alec." Nic didn't miss a beat, but inwardly I was shaking my head. Getting caught in a lie would only make matters worse in the end.

"Alec." The man stepped closer to Nic, surveying him up and down. "How long have you been in the army? Four months? Six?" He squinted. "I see some patches of fuzz, but you barely look old enough to even grow a beard."

One corner of Nic's mouth lifted. "What does that matter? I thought there were more important issues at hand, like your claim that our sovereigns are holding back information and lying to us?"

The man's lips thinned. "So you're content to just sit back and let the world pass you by without questioning anything? Accept the rules of your leaders simply because that's the way it's always been done and always should be done?"

Nic's face twitched. "No. The opposite, actually. I think you *should* question when something doesn't sit quite right, and dig to the bottom of it by going to the source of the problem. Not stirring dissension where there is none, causing division, and making everyone suspicious of their brethren. Doing that doesn't solve problems or answer questions. It creates them. It brings attention to the interloper and destroys any hope of unity."

His words had an effect on the crowd, which did not go

unnoticed by the main speaker. Or me. His words filled me with pride. Who was this kid?

"Yes," the man said. "The old adage. Go straight to the source? The only problem is that the source is too high and mighty to speak with you, and anyone below them is either too busy or refuses to speak with you, telling you to simply do as you're told, and declines any information or answers. The 'source' does not exist in our circles. I don't see any of them gathered among their brethren tonight, or any night."

If the man hit rock bottom, he would still keep digging.

"Then perhaps you should look harder." The soldiers turned at my voice, their faces holding instant recognition as they became aware of my presence. They shifted around me, stepping back and creating a pathway as I moseyed my way to the edge of the crowd.

The redheaded man sized me up, taking in the reaction of the people around him and surprising me by showing the tiniest bit of deference.

"Vladimir. How nice of you to join us tonight."

I glanced at the tense soldiers around me, working through the best way to handle the situation. It was like trying to walk barefoot on broken glass without getting cut. "Don't stop on my account. Please, continue. It sounded like you had some questions for me."

From the corner of my eye, I saw Nic morphing back into the crowd and slowly disappearing from view.

Smart kid.

"I actually do have some questions for you. I'm not sure how much of our discussion you heard, but we're being lied to, and we want to know why. What's going on up in that castle?

What's the Crown hiding from us?"

I held his gaze. "I would love to tell you all of the secrets we keep buried in the castle and all of the inner workings of the government, but you don't appear to be someone who knows when to hold his tongue, so that doesn't sound like it would be in Gharridan's best interest at the moment."

The deference disappeared from his face, the hot anger slipping through his calm exterior.

I swallowed while keeping my nerves in check. This was exactly why I had pressured the council to tell the truth about Adamara in the first place. The people of Gharridan deserved for us to be honest with them, to know the truth about a ruler they'd revered. They didn't deserve to be catered to or forced to believe a lie.

I circled to capture the attention of the group around me, meeting their gazes. "Believe me. I understand your frustrations. As your friend here has stated, Gharridan has been through much turmoil in the past year, and is headed for far more. There are always things in our past that could have been handled differently, situations that could have been avoided, but Gharridan is crumbling from within, and we are doing everything within our power to gather the pieces and meld it back together. All of you"—I thrust my arm out—"can either be a help to that, or a hindrance. Continuing to separate and divide in the midst of everything that is going on will only ensure that Gharridan will fall to its knees and never rise again. How you choose to move on from here is up to you. I'm not going to force you to do anything, but dismembering the country you love with one meeting like this at a time will do no good. More than anything, we need unity right now, and that's all I'm asking of you. All I need you to give. You took an oath to join this army. Remember that oath, hold to it, and remember why you love this country. Why you stand for it, and why it is worth saving."

I waited a moment, letting the following silence after my statement speak for itself and brand the words into the minds of the listeners.

"Unity and hope is all that I can offer you right now." I turned back the way I had come, the crowd parting before me, their eyes boring into my back. Whether out of respect or with the gaze of vultures, I wasn't sure. Murmurs and whispers traveled among them, commenting on everything that had been said, but the low voice of a man to my right stuck out, muffled in among the others.

"I still don't understand why *he* wasn't crowned as king."

My steps faltered, but I kept moving, joining Nic who was waiting by the horses where we swung into the saddles and guided them away, back toward the gate of the capital. I didn't speak at first, my thoughts brewing.

"Well done, Nic," I said. "Remind me to bring you to more arguments. That wasn't half bad."

Nic grinned. "Go ahead. Say you're proud of me."

I shook my head. "That might be too many compliments for one night. I need to hand those out sparingly."

He frowned, then rolled his shoulders. "So just like that, all of the discussion and unrest is going to disappear?"

I puffed out a breath. "Oh no. Redhead is far from done with his speeches and dissension, but silencing him through force would only make his ideas spread like wildfire."

The horses' hooves against the cobblestones ricocheted off

the buildings around us.

"What exactly was that supposed to do tonight then, if he's going to continue causing trouble?" Nic asked.

"Because now when he opens his conniving mouth to speak, I'm hoping that the people around him will think twice before listening."

CHAPTER TWENTY-EIGHT

OPENED BOOKS, SCATTERED pages, and hastily scribbled notes with blots of ink covered my floor. I had pulled every map, every book on herbology, anything I could possibly find of use in my digging, and spread it out in a massive semicircle around me.

That's because you've been looking for it under the wrong name.

Finnigan's words echoed in my head, his smug voice invading my thoughts over and over again. He knew where I was from, or at least suspected, but he refused to offer up any more information. As I stared at the chaos surrounding me, a feeling of stupidness overcame me for never having even considered it before. That's why I could never find it. Why no one had ever heard of Dalendria and didn't know where it was. Because the name I was looking for it under didn't even exist. Not in the memory of the people around me. It would have to go far back.

And I had.

I stared at the weathered map before me, looking at every marked country, every city, of the scattered remnants of ancient times that became the countries we inhabited now, from the burning sands of Brenden to the white beaches of Adellaia. I had maps of places beyond, of continents rumored to host enchanting balls and kingdoms dusted with magic, but something told me that my mother didn't come from across the sea. Or Gharridan either. With every scrap of information I had scrounged up, and after talking with Katherine about her encounter with Colleen, all the pieces pointed back to only one location. One possibility.

A knock came at the door, and I called for the visitor to enter, glancing up as Katherine swept inside.

She cocked an eyebrow at the chaotic mess that was the floor before shutting the door behind her.

"What's going on?" she asked.

"I went to see Finnigan," I said.

Her eyes bulged. "You what?"

"Vladimir said that he'd studied poisons. Finnigan was next to useless, but he knows more than he's telling us. When I told him my mother was from Dalendria and it didn't exist, he said it was because I was looking for it under the wrong name—and he was right. That explains why I've never been able to uncover anything about it, because no one here would know it by that name."

Katherine didn't look convinced. "But why would your mother give it to you underneath a false name?"

I shook my head, expanding one of the maps. "It wasn't a

false name. It was a name that would have been personal for her or her people, something that meant something to them, but that hardly anyone on the outside would have heard of."

I bit my lip and stared at the map. Not an ancient one, but a current one. "I think I know where she was from," I looked up. "And I think that the two of you have something in common."

It took Katherine a moment to follow me, but I saw the connection click in her eyes. "Taryn, are you saying—"

"Where did Colleen tell you the Radonaya were from?" I asked. "My mother spoke of her family *in the north*. What nation do we know next to nothing about that resides in the northernmost territory?"

Katherine cocked her head. "Iso. The City of Isolation."

I nodded in agreement. "I was looking through old maps, some written in the ancient tongue. It used to be known as *Flos Regni* which in Gharrideese translates to Dalendria."

She knelt on the floor beside me, studying the papers.

"Somehow this is all connected," I continued. "The Royal Massacre, the Radonaya, my mother. Her family was trying to kill her, and now they're trying to kill me. I found a note that my father had written, angry about something Gabriel had done, and he said that he had to go back for her. I'm assuming it was my mother he was speaking about. I don't understand why, but she did something—something connected to the massacre. Something worth trying to execute her for."

I looked up. "Do you think that my mother was a Radonaya who used the touch of death?"

Katherine shrugged. "I don't know, but Colleen said that a Radonaya's mother always dies in child birth."

I realized the implication of her words. Katherine would likely never be able to figure out who her mother was.

I stared at all the pages spread before me. "Then *what* is the connection?"

I jerked awake as I collided with the cold floor, the blankets twisted around my legs. My chest heaved, my skin slick with sweat. The moon stared back at me through the glass of the skylight, and I inhaled, trying to steady my breathing and calm my pounding heart.

The remnants of the nightmare assaulted my mind, and I mentally shoved them away, struggling to stand, bare feet stumbling on the rug. No guards pounded on the door, which meant I'd hopefully been left with the dignity of not screaming out this time. Blood flashed across my vision, images of the dagger buried in Queen Adamara's gut. I leaned against the side of the bed for support. I hadn't meant to fall asleep, but I remembered crawling to the bed in my exhaustion.

I lit a lamp, bringing the room to life, the light quelling some of my fears, before throwing on a dressing robe and slipping into my boots. I carried the wobbly candle with me as I left my room. The guards startled at my sudden appearance, but I just ducked past them, feeling strange as they followed a few steps behind me in the darkness. The last thing I wanted was to be trapped in my room, and the second last thing I wanted was to go back to sleep—which is what would inevitably happen if I stayed in there.

The eerie quiet of the castle made me want to move closer to the guards. It felt as if the shadows were watching me. I burst through the library door, anxious to be out of the corridors. Both I and the man inside startled at each other's sudden appearance.

Vladimir was plastered to one of the leather chairs, looking as if he'd dozed off and I'd just scared him awake.

"Sorry," I mumbled, hovering awkwardly in the doorway as I questioned whether to stay or go.

"Couldn't sleep?" He cocked an eyebrow.

I shook my head.

"Me either," he said, shifting in his chair and nodding at the one beside him.

I slid the door closed, leaving the guards outside as I placed the candle on a table beside me and plopped down into the cushions. No wonder he'd dozed off. These chairs might be more comfortable than my bed.

I peered over at Vladimir, who wore the same expression he always did, like the world was a riddle he couldn't figure out. A soot stain marred his tunic and his breeches were rumpled; dried mud caked his boots.

"What is it now?" I asked.

He threw me a confused look.

I shrugged. "I know you're exhausted, so whatever it is must be extremely strenuous to keep you up this late."

He didn't answer at first, still sorting out whatever was on his mind. "I think it would take less time to say what it isn't."

We sat in the quiet of night for a few moments, both content to not have to speak. I was still a little annoyed that he hadn't believed me earlier when I'd said I knew my father had given me Mors Secunda, but he couldn't be right about everything.

I stared at the rows of bookshelves. "I went to see Finnigan today."

That got his attention.

His jaw set hard. "Taryn—"

"And I think I figured out where my mother's family is from."

Whatever he'd been about to say, he stopped. "How?"

I talked through everything I'd discovered that day, including every detail of my conversations with both Katherine and Finnigan. I thought that sorting through it all again might trigger something, but I was still as stumped as before. Still no closer to a solution.

"*Flos Regni*," Vladimir repeated the old name of the country. "Something about Dalendria always lingered in the back of my mind, like something about it was familiar. That's why. Now that you're talking about it I remember a vague reference about it from when I was in history lessons."

"Can you tell me anything about it?" I asked, eager.

Vladimir shook his head. "There's not much to tell. Very little is known."

Which is the same answer everyone and everything seemed to have.

I dropped it, tired of talking in circles without finding answers. We spoke of other things, of his visit to the soldiers' camp and the disaster it possibly presented, of the blackness circling my wrist, the nightmare that had led me to the library.

Yet everything was continuously spinning out of control.

"What are we going to do, Vladimir?" I asked.

"About what?"

I let out a little laugh. "Everything. The assassin. The war.

The unrest. Katherine's conviction that William is going to die."

His looked lost. "I don't know. I don't know that I have any hope to give you. Even if by some miracle Gharridan is able to win this war, Brenden will still do anything within their power to make sure that William doesn't survive."

"I can't say I blame them," I admitted. "I felt the same way when it was my father. Honestly, I'm surprised that they haven't sent any of their assassins in yet to finish the job."

"I would like to say that the capital is too well guarded, but considering what happened at the coronation feast, I'm not sure of anything anymore."

The hopelessness in his voice nearly broke me. Vladimir always had some wisdom to offer, some breath of hope. But now even he had none. I curled up in the chair, pulling my legs against my chest and wrapping my arms around them.

"Vladimir—"

I cut the rest of my words before they could slip out. What was I going to say, that I was scared? Saying it wouldn't change anything, couldn't make anything better.

But I *was* scared.

I felt trapped like a caged animal, helpless as a flightless bird. It seemed no matter what I chose, no matter what I did, and no matter where I went, the only thing waiting for me was death. I couldn't escape my mother's past. Couldn't escape this poison. Couldn't escape this war.

"Taryn." His calm voice penetrated my mind, and my gaze flicked to his pale blue eyes, staring into mine. "I—"

He cut off, and I saw the war within his mind. He was trying to give me something to hold on to and had nothing. I swallowed, suddenly realizing that I had nothing to complain about.

My life was in danger, yes, but if I died, I died. That was my fate. No one was depending on me. Not really. Vladimir, however, had the weight of this entire kingdom on his back. The people were depending on him. More than his life was at stake, and I felt cowardly for the selfishness I'd displayed ever since I came here. Everyone looked to Vladimir for hope—but who offered it to him?

As he turned away, the defeated look on his face consumed me.

"Hey." I reached across the armrests to pull his face back to me, my hand resting on his rough cheek. "Don't give up, Vladimir. There is always hope, no matter how minimal. You can always find something to hold on to. Whether it's a drop of water in a drought, or a sliver of sunlight in complete darkness. You can always find a whisper of hope. If not for you, then for someone else. No matter how small, how quiet. It will always be there."

Vladimir stared back at me with a burning intensity, as if the words I spoke were life to a dying soul. I sensed the burdens weighing on him, the darkness of despair. Maybe we wouldn't make it out of this like we wanted, but that didn't mean we should stop trying or fighting to. His throat bobbed, gaze pinned to me. I waited a moment before removing my touch from his face, ensuring that my words had sunk in and taken root.

He jerked away as if only just realizing that I'd touched him.

"Promise me," I said, hunting for his eyes. "Promise me you won't give up hope."

He wouldn't meet my gaze. "Why?"

I leaned back. "Because you've given it to us on our darkest days, and I can't bear to see you live without it."

His jaw clenched, and I sensed my words had touched somewhere that no one else's had for a long time. He excused himself, giving in to the need for sleep, but I lingered in the library, not wanting to return to the dark world of my dreams. I chewed on my lip, absentmindedly thumbing through the pages of a dusty book to keep my hands occupied.

My father broke the oath, Michael.

My mother's haunting words circled my mind. My father had gone back, but for what?

You know they will hold to their word.

The question was who. Whoever it was, she'd been afraid of them. For me. He'd been seeking someone or something to heal me—but he'd returned with Mors Secunda.

Cold steel pressed against my neck.

My breath hitched in my throat. My fingers stilled on the brittle pages. I couldn't turn, could only move my eyes, which just barely caught the outline of a dark-clothed arm in my peripheral vision.

If I moved or screamed for help, they would cut my throat.

Assassin.

I hadn't heard or even sensed him approach. I should have been able to. It was like he'd materialized out of nothing. He made no sound, no movement, and I was painstakingly aware of the sharp blade barely restrained from slicing through my skin.

For a moment I heard nothing except the pounding in my ears, but then I felt hot breath against my ear, his inhalations barely audible.

"I've watched you searching."

His voice rumbled deep, but smooth and conniving. Goosebumps gathered on my skin as a chill passed through me.

"I have your answer," I said, trying to keep my voice from trembling.

"Then tell me, Taryn Gallows: *What is red as blood, bitter as wormwood, and holds the keys to both life and death?*"

"Mors Secunda."

He gave no reaction to my words, and I blurted out, "You know what the connection is, don't you?"

I don't know what insane courage possessed me to voice the words, but if I was going to ask for one thing before death, it was answers.

My heart slammed against my rib cage.

"Only death will bring you answers."

My hands trembled, overwhelming fear enveloping me.

"Then are you going to bring an end to the questions?"

I couldn't even swallow, afraid what the movement would cause.

His breath was still in my ear, tickling my skin. I wanted to scream at him for drawing it out. For not just doing it.

"No."

My eyes widened at his words, but he was so close I felt his lips brush against my ear as he whispered, "When it's time, you'll be so raving mad from the nightmares that you'll beg for death."

I sucked in a shuddering breath.

"Are you ready for your second riddle?" he asked.

I stayed silent, afraid to speak.

"Nothing can buy it, not secrets or wealth, but what valuable treasure can save all but itself?"

I gasped as the blade flicked across my skin then disappeared. My hand shot to my throat, but there was only a trickle of blood, no gushing. He'd only nicked me. I shot to my feet, running backward toward the door as I frantically scanned the shelves around me for the assassin, but it was like he had never been there.

I stumbled into the door frame, my sweaty hand sliding on the handle as I yanked it open and sagged against it, adrenaline pulsing through my veins.

"Assassin," I rasped.

With one glance at the blood seeping through the fingers at my neck, each of the guards drew their swords, one of them shoving me behind him as the others advanced into the library, doing a sweep of the room and trying to corner him.

But they wouldn't find him.

The realization made me weak.

The library only had one main entrance, but I knew there were others. Doors meant to stay locked, stairwells unused and long forgotten. If he didn't want to be found, he wouldn't be.

The guard was saying something to me, asking if I was all right. I nodded yes, briefly mumbling through what had happened as he handed me a handkerchief to press against the wound on my neck. Shouts rang out, a call for more guards, but I knew it was of no use. It was too late.

He was gone.

They led me back to my room as the search continued, but everything around me felt like a haze.

When it's time, you'll be so raving mad from the nightmares that you'll beg for death.

His words lashed themselves to my mind, playing over and

over. My eyes fell to the strange darkness creeping along my veins, and the only thing I knew with certainty was that I never wanted to sleep again.

CHAPTER TWENTY-NINE

❖

VLADIMIR

A BOTTLE KEPT company beside William. As always. I worried for him, wanted to intervene, but he wouldn't listen to me. Not right now at least. He hunched over the desk, scanning the documents before him. We'd yet to speak since nearly caving in each other's faces the other night. Not out of avoidance, but purely from the fact that our paths hadn't crossed.

I folded my arms across my chest, waiting for him to look up from the desk since he was the one who had summoned me.

He didn't.

I cleared my throat. "Is there something I can help you with, Your Majesty?"

"Don't patronize me, Vladimir."

"I'm not the king, William, you're the one who summoned

me here."

He dipped his quill in ink, scribbling his signature on the bottom of the document before looking up. "You failed to report on your visit to the military camp outside the city."

I frowned. William hadn't ever shown interest in such things.

"There's a rabble-rouser in the camp who is causing dissension among the men. It's gotten a bit out of hand. We paid a visit down there and tried to discourage it."

William nodded, but there was a strange glint in his eyes. His voice was too casual. "Did you arrest this man?"

"That would have made the issue ten times worse and proven to the people that we really do have something to hide."

"So you did nothing, essentially, except waggle your finger at them and say, 'No, no, none of this, now.'"

I frowned, pinning my gaze on him. "What exactly is this about, William?"

He slid a worn paper across the desk, turning it around to face me. "This arrived at the castle this morning."

I read the words scrawled on the page, my stomach sinking.

Amid several accusations and outrageous statements, one stood out among the rest.

We should have crowned Vladimir as king.

"Where did this come from?" I asked, flipping it over.

"It was sent by a courier from the encampments below the city. False name, false rank, and there is no means to trace it back to its creator. Apparently your little speech made quite the impression among the soldiers last night, or rather, some of them. I'm not sure what it is that you intended to accomplish."

"Someone who wants answers and rightfully so," I said,

anger rising within me. "Like I told you before, lying to the people and trying to pin all of this on Finnigan will only come back to haunt you. The pieces don't add up, and the people of Gharridan know it. They know something happened that they have not been made privy to. I went down to the encampments last night, having to lie to my fellow countrymen *again* to try to quell the unrest being spread among them. Something that I shouldn't even have to do if you knew how to rule this country right."

"Oh, so you're doing me a favor?" William shot back.

"That's enough, and I'm done arguing about this," I said. "If you think that I'm doing this for you, you're delusional. You are better than this. I know that you are. *You* know that you are, but I will not support you if you continue to act this way—so don't ever count me as doing you any favors. Count the favor as me turning my back and choosing to go along with and ignore everything that you have done. I do you no favors. I stay and put up with your antics because I love this country. I love Gharridan too much to allow it to crumble into ruin—not without a fight—and because I know what would happen to it if I were to leave it in your hands."

I watched the anger build behind William's eyes as he no doubt sifted his mind for the most perfect and scathing response.

It never came.

Someone pounded briefly on the doors before they swung open to reveal a page. "Your Majesty, Lord Vladimir," he gasped, glancing between us.

"What is it?" I reached for my sword instinctively.

"You're needed in the war council chamber immediately.

Urgent business."

Both William and I moved at the same time, wending our way through the castle without commenting on our previous conversation. I automatically began sorting through different scenarios in my head, wondering what could possibly have gone wrong. If the page was willing to burst into the room like that, unannounced, I wasn't sure that I wanted to know. Maybe they'd finally uncovered Brenden's main force or where they were going. Maybe there was a breakthrough on the western front.

The entire government was already gathered in the chamber. Katherine, Darya, and Taryn also occupied the room. At the sight of Taryn, my mind flashed to last night, but I quickly shook the image away. I tried to read the faces around me, but none of the people present betrayed anything. Most looked as confused as William and I. No one spoke, as if unsure of who was in charge.

"Would someone like to explain why we've all been summoned here?" William broke the silence. "Because as fun as it would be, I know we all have much better things to do than stare at each other."

William's lack of decorum really shouldn't surprise me by now.

"Our force on the other side of the Jidero intercepted two diplomats from Brenden," Verone spoke up. His gaze turned to William. "They requested an audience with the king."

My eyebrows shot up. "Did they specify what it was they wanted to meet about?"

Verone hesitated, not liking the direction of the conversation. "They said it was a matter for the king's ears only, that they had a proposition for him."

Nothing about this sounded right. "What does our perimeter look like?"

"I sent scouts out within the radius to check, but the current consensus is that there's no one else. It's just them."

I looked at William. "I smell a trap."

Everything about this was off. Brenden was conniving. They didn't send diplomats in for peace talks unless they had an ulterior motive. Had something else planned.

"I agree with Vladimir," Katherine said. "Brenden is powerful and cunning. Something else is going on here."

The council murmured their agreement, unease creeping through their ranks, but all of their attention was trained on William.

"What does the king say?" I asked.

For once, William looked serious. And the most sober I'd seen him in the last few weeks. "What are you proposing, then, that we send them away?"

Refusing an audience with diplomats who came in peace, or so they claimed, would not do us any favors. "I think it would be wise to hear them out," I said, "but not until we first uncover whatever it is they're planning."

"And how do you suggest we go about that?" a councilman asked. "There are only two of them. Verone already stated that there is no one else within our perimeter. If they had another plan, I think we would have seen or been alerted to something by now."

I cocked my head. "You mean like we anticipated and detected a Brenden sneaking into the coronation ball and nearly assassinating the king?"

The councilman frowned.

"We're going to have to meet with them one way or another," Verone said. "What do you propose is more advantageous for us, meeting them within or without the city gates?"

I leaned on the table, gripping the edges. "They're diplomats, not soldiers, and we're required to treat them as such even if we are at war. They can't be captured as prisoners." I took a moment to think. "Meeting them outside the city gates would be too public, and not being behind the walls of the city makes me nervous. Even if we can't see any Brendens, it doesn't mean that something isn't planned. I'd rather have the meeting in a controlled environment."

"Do you mean you want to bring them into the throne room?" Katherine pressed.

William shook his head. "Not the throne room. That would be too high an honor. I like the idea of the grand hall much better. It's an open space. We can have the room lined with soldiers, make sure that it's as safe as possible."

"Is that wise, Your Majesty?" a councilman asked.

"I believe that it's our best choice at the present moment."

I didn't like this, didn't like any of it. What we needed was for William to not be in the room at all, but if they were refusing to speak to anyone but him, we'd been left without a choice.

"I want to escort them in myself," I said. "Scout them out and ensure that they have no hidden weapons on them, nothing that could be used as a threat. I'd rather meet with them sooner rather than later."

"No," William cut in. "I think we should wait till morning and make them sweat it out. They need to be on our time and not on theirs."

"With all due respect," I objected, "I believe it would be wiser for us to hear them out immediately to uproot any plans they have established."

"And I," William rebutted, "do not believe in immediately granting the demands of other countries who show up on our doorstep unannounced. They are in our territory now. Not theirs."

"William—"

"My decision is final," he said.

I swallowed my next words. This was foolishness. It provided them with more time to plan whatever it was they intended to do.

"Then what time do you propose, Your Majesty?" I spit out the formal term like I'd tasted vinegar.

"Tomorrow. When the sun is at its peak." Finality rang in William's tone.

Verone began to draw up a security plan and distribution of troops as different scenarios were worked through among the council members. I input what I could, but I was distracted, not liking where the decision had gone.

Katherine pulled me aside when the meeting adjourned, fire in her eyes. "Something is not right here, Vladimir."

"I don't like it either," I said.

"Then why didn't you speak up more?"

"I did!" I sounded exasperated. "He's the king, Katherine."

"And you're the leader of the Kavari, *Vladimir*. Act like it." She pointed her finger at me and got in my face. "You have just as much authority as him, and you shouldn't let a matter like this go with little resistance, especially when you know that it's wrong!"

I threw my hands in the air. "He's the one they're trying to assassinate. If he wants to throw his life away, I can't stop him."

"Have you forgotten I had a vision about this very thing? About him *dying*?" Katherine shook her head. "This isn't you, Vladimir. I know you're trying to keep the peace and keep matters from getting out of hand, but with every meeting, you give him a little more power. And if you keep giving it to him a piece at a time, one day you won't have any left."

She stormed off, catching Verone who was waiting for her outside the door. My jaw clenched in irritation, her words digging deeper and truer than I liked, mixing with Nic's earlier warning to me.

One of you is going to have to assert dominance.

I couldn't win in everything against William.

Out of the corner of my eye I caught Taryn slinking from the room, no doubt trying to pretend like she hadn't heard any of our whispered but heated conversation. I remembered the brush of her fingers across my cheek, the hope she'd offered to me that I'd so desperately needed in my helplessness. Her head turned, revealing the edges of a bandage tucked beneath the high collar of her dress. I frowned, striding toward her.

"What happened?" I asked, reaching for it.

She flinched away and I pulled back, alarmed. "Taryn?"

She glanced around, but everyone had already left the room. "It's nothing."

"It doesn't look like nothing," I said.

She fidgeted.

She didn't want to tell me.

Worry creased my brow, running through a hundred scenarios I didn't want to think about.

She averted her gaze. "The assassin was in the library last night. After you left."

"What?" I raised my voice, not believing what I was hearing. Anger bubbled within me. "Why wasn't I informed about this?"

"Because you've had more pressing matters to deal with, and I'm telling you now anyway."

"What did he do?" I indicated her neck.

"He nicked it with a knife. Nothing more."

"Why didn't you ask Katherine to heal it?" I asked.

"It's nothing to worry about." Taryn brushed it off. "If it needs attention I'll ask her to heal it after the meeting tomorrow, but I'm really not worried about it."

"The assassin, did he …"

She shook her head. "There's no trace, and there never will be."

I pursed my lips. Maybe I should have stayed longer, encouraged her to go back to her room.

She read the look in my eyes, hand resting on my arm. "Quit blaming yourself. It's not your fault, Vladimir."

But that was the problem.

No matter what anyone said, it felt like everything was.

"Did you give him the answer?" I asked.

She nodded. "Yes, and he gave me the second riddle."

I crossed my arms. "What is it?"

"Nothing can buy it, not secrets or wealth, but what valuable treasure can save all but itself?"

I clenched my jaw. "The answers to that could be endless."

"But he's only looking for one," she said, and looked away. Something else was bothering her.

"Did he say anything else?" I asked.

Her steely gaze fixed on me. "When I asked him what the connection was, he said that only death would bring me answers. And that I would be so raving mad from the nightmares I would beg for death."

I'd hoped that maybe we were wrong about the nightmares, that there was another explanation, but this assassin knew exactly what was going on. Knew exactly what he was doing. Even if she did solve the riddles, nothing told me this game between her and the assassin would end well.

CHAPTER THIRTY

TARYN

I WOKE UP screaming that night.

One of the guards burst through the door, sword drawn and ready for an enemy, but I shooed him away, relenting that it was nothing more than a nightmare. I sank back into the mattress, shivering at the images that pervaded my mind. Vladimir and William crumpled on the floor, blood spilling from their bodies, surrounding them—

I leaned over the side of the bed and retched into a bowl that I'd learned to keep there. I'd moved back to my room since there was no point in trying to hide. No matter where I went, the assassin would always find me.

When I felt like I could stand, I rose to my feet and paced the room, heart racing even though I was exhausted. I slicked back the damp hair from my eyes, trying to bring myself into some semblance of control.

I would not let him win.

Would not let the nightmares drive me mad.

But I was afraid they already were.

It felt so real.

The chill of their bodies, the warmth of the blood seeping through my fingers. I shuddered. Death lingered. Somewhere in this room, or somewhere in the new day. I sensed the blackness, the taste of despair. The depravity of hope that swirled around his presence.

Something was wrong.

Everything in the world was wrong, but something about today was out of focus.

Something terrible.

Something that needed to be stopped.

CHAPTER THIRTY-ONE

I BARELY SLEPT that night, rising before the sun to prepare for the day. Unease swirled around me like mist, clouding my thoughts, marring my judgments. Brenden was using this meeting with William as a tactic, they were forming some kind of plan, some form of trickery. I needed to know what it was.

At first light I rode out to escort the Brendens into the city. Nic and three other soldiers flanked me as we approached the nearing squadron, the two foreigners walking in the center of the horses.

I didn't like the look of them.

Their lifted chins, haughty eyes, and gaudy dress. They walked like they owned the world and had nothing to fear, but most importantly, they were in a position to bargain—and they knew it.

No pleasantries were exchanged, only cold, hard stares.

If they'd arrived with weapons, they had already been surrendered, but I wasn't taking any chances. I ordered to have them stripped down to nothing, their skin inspected for anything unusual, but nothing besides dirt and tattoos could be found. I waited for them to protest our rudeness. They did no such thing.

When I was satisfied there was nothing they could hide, the men were given Gharridan clothing to wear. I wouldn't run the risk of their garb being tainted with poison or anything else harmful. Through the whole ordeal, they never spoke one word, even through the dishonor and disgrace displayed in our actions.

Courtesy did not concern me. Enemies stood before us. Not friends. They deserved no honor.

Everything within me protested as I reined Dante around, the diplomats marching in the center of our ring of horses as we plodded back to the gates of the capital. I considered blindfolding them until we reached the grand hall but threw the notion away. They needed to see our strength. Not sense our fear. As the horses' hooves clopped against the cobblestones, the entire scenario refused to sit right with me, and it nearly drove me mad trying to figure it out. The Brendens hid a purpose somewhere within this crazy mission.

When we reached the castle, I forced the men to walk in front of me, uncomfortable with the thought of them at my back for one moment longer. Twice as many soldiers milled about the castle, nearly everyone in the immediate squadron on duty. The only place we'd toned down the numbers was in the grand hall, deciding to limit the number of ears on our conversation.

I studied the two foreigners, trying to read them, looking for anything to tell me what was going on, but I found nothing. What if this really was nothing more than a diplomatic meeting and it was meant to make us go crazy trying to figure out what it was? It would definitely be a tactic to mess with us mentally.

When I crossed the threshold, I nodded imperceptibly at the two marksmen stationed within the room, and they nodded back, each having been tasked with watching the diplomat nearest to them, ready to take them out at the slightest hint of danger.

William stood in the center of the room, arrayed in his full royal uniform, the light filtering in through the windows glinting off the golden circlet and embellished jewels of his crown. To his right stood Katherine, Taryn just beyond her. To the left stood Verone and a handful of council members; the others were dispersed among the soldiers lining the walls. Apprehension marked their faces, and no doubt after the bloodbath they'd last endured at the hands of the queen.

My gaze drifted to the rafters, to the windows, the far end of the room, seeking out any threat that could hide. I moved nearer to Taryn, still somewhat between the two groups, which offered me a better vantage point.

William raised his chin, irritation in his eyes. He better not blow this.

"You stand in the presence of King William, ruler of Gharridan." My voice boomed throughout the room, bringing everyone to my attention. "What is your petition?"

The two diplomats took in everything around them before

folding their arms behind their backs in an easy stance, training their eyes on William. They had yet to betray whatever thoughts brewed behind their stoic masks.

"On behalf of the kingdom of Brenden, we have traveled here to petition for the surrender of Gharridan's king."

CHAPTER THIRTY-TWO

❖

KATHERINE

TENSION IMPRISONED THE room like that of a predator and its prey, both eyeing each other, one knowing it was about to die and the other preparing to go in for the kill. Both frozen in time, both waiting to see who would pounce or run first. The stalemate stretched between our two groups as we stared at one another, the Gharridans waiting for William's response.

When he finally did speak, William's voice held no emotion. "You're asking for me to surrender? To give myself up willingly to a foreign enemy?"

My gaze flicked back and forth between the men and William. Barging into our capital and demanding terms that would never be met held no tactical advantage for Brenden. So why were they here?

"Considering you killed our beloved king in cold blood, it seems the right and fitting thing to do. The easiest way to make amends and end this war before bringing further death."

"Is a soldier held responsible for each and every life he takes in war?" William asked. "Or is he simply following orders that he was given?"

William's words rang out, anger evident in his tone. "Gharridan does not surrender, nor does its king. If Brenden would like to submit a more plausible and agreeable option to cease the bloodshed between us, I am more than open to hearing it."

The Brendens exchanged a glance. I frowned at their calm amid the tension, wondering how they remained so composed.

The man on the right said, "Brenden offers no other terms of peace. The only standing offer to be accepted is for Your Majesty to surrender himself to our country."

William's eyes flit to Vladimir, and they seemed to communicate wordlessly.

"The offer is declined," William said forcefully.

Silence lingered in the aftermath of William's refusal until the man on the left cleared his throat, distaste hovering in his eyes. "I shall give you one last chance to save both your life and the life of your country, King William. Brenden is very gracious in offering this chance. Once it has been rejected, it will not be offered again." He dipped his head in deference, his gaze boring into William. "I ask your grace to *wisely* consider this offer one last time. Before it is too late."

Haughtiness filled the man's words, and I grew uneasy. It was off. The statements triggered something in my mind about him saying that this would be his *last* chance, his *only* chance. As if William would never have the opportunity, any kind of opportunity, to make a decision like this one again—like he was defending himself in a trial and awaiting execution.

William and the men continued to argue back and forth, but I tuned out their voices, training my focus on the man closest to me, taking in his Gharridan clothing, the baldness of his head, the close-shaved beard that covered the lower half of his face.

Black ink marked the side of his neck, and I shuffled slightly to get a better look. A familiarity pricked at the back of my mind at the design that wrapped around his neck. He turned to look at his companion, the motion revealing the tattoo to me in its entirety.

It was a lion.

Claws raised, tail flicked out, jaws bared.

The exact lion I had seen in my strange visions.

You're not supposed to be here.

My pounding heartbeat pulsed within my ears, the world growing fuzzy around me until my gaze fell on the floor, on the rug. The intricate designs woven around the diamond shapes.

Now you'll see things you were never supposed to see.

Fear lit within me, even though I didn't know what it meant. Verone's eyes caught mine, noticing my distraction, and my fingers subconsciously brushed across the leather ring on my left hand even as my mind was reeling.

Sweat dotted my brow. This was what I had seen, what Death had shown me, but I didn't know what it meant or how to stop it. I looked again at the tattoo, feeling as though the lion might come alive and leap out at me.

The designs of the rug swam before me, and I lifted my gaze to the ceiling as if searching for another sign or an answer.

My entire body froze.

One of the diplomats noticed my attention.

If I had been standing at any other point in the room, if I had chosen at any other time to look up, I might not have seen it, but I did, and the refracting light showed me exactly what I needed to see, even as the image of the arrow shafts in William's chest burned before my eyes.

I moved without thinking, without thought. There was no time to scream. No time to react. All I could process was the light glinting off the weapon in the rafters as I threw myself in front of William. My arms circled his neck even as the arrowhead broke the flesh of my back and lodged within me, the force shoving me against William's body and knocking the breath from my lungs. Black encompassed the edges of my vision as shock coursed through me. Then pain. And I found myself thinking, *how strange*. How fitting, but strange, for the healer to sacrifice her life to save another.

CHAPTER THIRTY-THREE

VLADIMIR

THE ROOM DELVED from peaceful talks to complete chaos within the blink of an eye. One moment the men were talking, the next Katherine jumped in front of William and arrows began raining down on us. I turned, shoving Taryn back toward the soldiers against the wall as I drew my sword, eyes searching for the source of the onslaught.

The two Brenden diplomats lay sprawled on the floor, two daggers in each of their backs, my marksmen having already taken them down. I ducked low as another arrow whizzed past my ear, so close the wind from it ruffled my hair as its feathers brushed across my cheek. My gaze shot to the rafters where two dark figures ran along the beams, raining a barrage of ricochets and arrows down upon us. I lurched toward the wall, ripping a bow and quiver from the hands of one of my archers and immediately firing back at the two strangers. Each shot I fired missed, finding its place in the wooden beams of the ceiling, anywhere but the actual intended target. The other archers fired as well, but the two invaders kept racing farther away, too high and awkward of an angle to get a decent shot.

Where were they running to?

My eyes locked on the far end of the room where light bled through the windows carved out of the stone.

"Nic!" I yelled, finding him already beside me. "Give me a lift!"

Adrenaline raced through my veins as I strung the bow across my back. Nic cupped his hands like a stirrup, and I stepped into it. He shoved me upward and I looped my fingers over a stretch of crown molding, pulling myself farther up the wall until I could reach the stones. My fingers and toes sought out each little ledge and grip, propelling me upward to the rafters. No fear of falling held me back; it was the fear of not reaching them before they disappeared that pervaded me.

My fingers brushed across the rough wood of the nearest beam, and I hoisted myself up until I was standing on it. The height was dizzying, but I cut my way across, jumping from beam to beam through the rafters toward where the assassins were clambering out the window. I hopped across at an alarming pace, giving no thought for missing a step and plunging to my death. Adrenaline drove me, spurred me on.

When I finally reached the window, I leapt through the frame, my boots slipping across the shingles. I grasped for traction, catching sight of the black-clad forms running away over the rooftop. In one swift motion, I pulled my bow free, nocking an arrow and letting it fly. It sliced through one man's calf, and he stumbled, grasping to catch himself on the shingles. I fired another arrow, which struck him in the back and sent him grasping for traction as he tumbled down the slanted roof, completely disappearing over the edge to an unknown death below.

I stumbled around the corner of the roof only to be met by a blade pressed against my jugular. I strained backward against the sharp edge, struggling to keep from slipping.

Bronze hair stuck out of a black hood, the man's brown eyes lined in black. He held the position, staring me down as if daring me to move.

"We didn't come here for you, Kavari." Indifference coated his voice.

He jumped back, removing the knife from my throat. In the same movement, I wrenched my own dagger from its sheath, extending it out to rake across his chest. An unknown armor kept it from penetrating to the skin. The hilt of his dagger flashed in my peripheral vision. I rolled my head as it struck me, lessening the impact. My weapon slashed across his thigh and came back dripping red, but he'd already gained the high ground.

He drove his shoulder into me, and I fell backward, sliding down the uneven shingles toward the edge. Panic flared within me as my body hit empty air. My hands grasped the edge of the roof, arms straining beneath my weight.

The bronze-haired man stared at me, shaking his head as if disappointed. "We gave your king a chance, and he rejected it. We will not rest until he is dead."

With those words, he hobbled away, disappearing around

the next corner of the roof. I roared both from frustration and pain, trying not to look at the ground below even as my head pounded at the blow from the dagger and my muscles screamed beneath my weight, my sweaty fingers slipping down the ledge.

Arms grasped mine, and my head snapped up to see Nic and another guard precariously pulling me back up the shingles even as they struggled to keep their footing themselves.

Once I was on my feet, I pointed and said, "He went that way."

But even as Nic and the other guard shot after him, I knew he was already gone. If he'd gotten this far without detection, he was near invisible and would stay that way. They'd be looking for a ghost.

"William," I mumbled, unable to stop the thought that he was dead as I staggered back inside the window and maneuvered my way down the wall with shaking hands. I scuttled down the stone, dropping the last several feet to the floor, the impact jarring my legs. A crowd had formed around something, someone. I tottered over, dread trying to hold me back.

"Is he ..."

I trailed off, inching closer past each body until the source of their attention stopped me in my tracks. William pressed a bloody bandage against his arm. He was kneeling on the ground beside Taryn, who was holding Katherine's pale hand.

Verone's hunched back blocked my view.

I stepped around him to see Katherine's form cradled in his arms. The world around me turned to ice, and everything within me went numb. Two black arrow shafts jutted out of her back, one dangerously close to her heart.

My knees buckled and I fell beside her shaking body. Blood

dripped from her mouth, over skin that had turned almost grey. She sucked in a breath, struggling to breathe, looking like a small child in her helplessness. Understanding of what was happening filled her face even as the blood pooled out around her.

"Did—did you get him?" Her voice shook, body overcome with shock.

"One of them," I assured her, masking the fear in my voice. "Nic is going to get the other one."

She gave a jerky nod, as if that was enough for her.

I watched the life draining from her. "What did you do, Katherine?" I whispered. "You're the healer, not a savior. You could have healed him."

A small smile touched her lips. "Protect the king at all costs. I just acted, didn't think."

A gurgled sound escaped her mouth and she coughed up blood.

I scooted closer, unable to keep my tears at bay.

Her eyes strayed to Verone, and she lifted a bloody hand to touch the tears pouring down Verone's stricken face.

"I love you," she whispered.

She looked back at me, barely able to lift her other hand as she indicated for me to take it. I squeezed it gently.

"I need you to promise me." Her voice was faint but firm. "Promise me that you and William will fix this. Don't let Gharridan fall. Make Michael proud. Do not let our sacrifices be in vain."

Tears spilled down my cheeks. "It's not a sacrifice that you had to make."

"But it was one I was glad to."

Katherine deserved more, deserved better than this. It

wasn't supposed to be her. It was never supposed to be her. She was the healer. She kept all of us together. Had been through almost every horror imaginable yet never complained. She'd served a country that hated her and never harbored any bitterness or resentment for it.

"I promise you," I whispered.

Katherine looked beyond me. "If I die for my country, I do not die in vain." She squeezed my hand. "It is my honor."

She met my eyes one last time.

"It is my duty. To serve this country. *I am bound to this country, and this country to me.*" Her voice wobbled. "I only wish I could have served it better."

Her eyes fell to my face, focusing on the knot I felt rising on the side of my head.

"You're hurt," she whispered, letting go of my hand as if to lift her own to heal it.

But she hadn't the strength and it fell back, limp in mine as the light left her eyes. A sob ripped out of me, denial cutting through me even as Verone pulled her bloody body against his chest, begging for her not to leave him, to come back. I stared at the face I knew so well, the one that kept me out of trouble, that wasn't afraid to call me out, the face I'd come to love as family. My shoulders shook as I waited for her to come back, for her body to somehow heal itself. But it didn't.

She was gone.

Katherine was gone.

And she would never be back.

CHAPTER THIRTY-FOUR

Taryn

L IFE.

It's not fair.

That was the one thing my mother instilled in me from a young age. Nothing in life is guaranteed. Nothing is promised. Treasure the time you are gifted with. Use it. Do not squander it on foolish pleasures, foolish trinkets of this life. Because one day, you may wake to find that everything you thought you had and loved is gone.

Just like today.

Crumbling tombstones surrounded us. William. Vladimir. Verone. Nic. Me. Above us hovered dark clouds threatening to burst with rain. Dirt clustered beneath my nails and coated my arms. We'd all dug the grave, deepening the hole one scoop at a time and finding a memory of Katherine tucked within each one. No one spoke. This ritual was ceremonial: the family dug the grave themselves, the last piece of care and devotion they could show to a loved one, to show how much they cared for them—even in death.

Tears silently slid down my cheeks as we dug deeper into the unforgiving earth, until the edges of the grave were over my head and those circled around us, watching, helped pull us out.

I dropped my shovel off to the side, wiping my hands on my dress as I stood beside Vladimir, unsure of how to bestow comfort when the pain was still destroying me inside. Still impossible to accept.

Vladimir wasn't going to make it.

His face was void of emotion, of thought. He hadn't been coherent since Katherine died, hadn't been able to process the events. He stood there, a shell of the man he once was, hollowed out by the unfairness of the world.

I lifted my gaze across the grave to where William stood, the stunned expression cemented to his face, also unable to process what was happening.

The soldiers approached with the coffin, and Vladimir threatened to crumble to his knees, the dam finally breaking in a trail of tears down his cheeks. I slipped an arm around him to support his mass of weight even as the tears fell from my own eyes.

I peered over the edge of the coffin, at her lifeless body within. Katherine's face and hair had been washed clean, and she wore a deep green dress. Her favorite. Her blood-red hair was spread out around her on the floor of the coffin, an array of hallow berries woven into the strands, matching the patch of flowers in Verone's chest pocket.

Her lids were closed, but even in death her face held a fair countenance, and I cried as I remembered the sly smile that would ghost her lips, indicating she knew about something that was going on around her when no one would expect her to. She'd been the most discerning, able to see past what others were hiding, perceive when something was wrong. She'd been the most sacrificial, trying to heal Vladimir of his wounds even as she was dying.

She'd deserved more.

I stared at the leather ring on her left hand, matching it to the identical one on Verone's and realizing what it had implied.

They placed the flat top on the coffin, nailing it in place before lowering her into the ground. Laying her at peace for the last time. I picked up my shovel, letting the tears flow freely as I scooped up a patch of the disturbed earth and poured it over the wooden box.

The bishop uttered words of comfort as droplets of rain began to fall from the sky, and then a woman sang a haunting melody. A melody full of memory and love, life and loss. It pulled against my broken heart strings to promise hope in the sorrow.

"And there in the meadow with life so fair
A bed of flowers they wove in her hair
And the air tasted fine and the water was sweet
And her cares fell away as she drifted to sleep
Do not weep, I am gone, but the memories will stay
Do not carve out your heart to have just one more day
For I lie in peace where the fireflies flash
In a field full of life where the beauty is vast
In the meadow of twilight beneath a star-swept sky
It's farewell for now, not forever goodbye.
Do not weep, I am gone, but the memories will stay
Do not carve out your heart to have just one more day
For I lie in peace where the fireflies flash
Surrounded forever by a beauty so vast
In the meadow of twilight beneath a star-swept sky
It's farewell for now—not forever goodbye.'"

CHAPTER THIRTY-FIVE

TARYN

BROKENNESS PERVADED THE castle like a sagging cloud of depression, pouring its deluge upon us, unable to bear the weight. War surrounded us, yet none of our leaders at the moment were capable of making a rational decision. Plans halted. Hope failed. Command dissipated. I thought as strong as Vladimir was, he would have already pulled himself together by now, but he was the most destroyed out of all of us, a ghostly frame of the man I once knew. Completely shattered.

Everything within me ached for Katherine, mourned her loss. The absence of her lingered like a song I loved but couldn't remember how to play, lost forever to the recesses of my mind but never forgotten. I didn't want to go on, didn't want to face the future, but I knew that I didn't have a choice.

That I had to.

The council had called several meetings, none of which Vladimir had shown up for, but they needed him. His country needed him. I needed him, which was why I braved approaching his door.

I stood, hand frozen in mid-air as I tried to hold myself together and appear strong. To my knowledge he hadn't spoken to anyone except Marco, and I had no idea what awaited me within the room. I knocked twice, waiting between each one. No one answered. I gathered myself before turning the handle and letting myself inside.

Grief encompassed the dim room. I paused in the doorway, letting my vision adjust before approaching Vladimir where he stood before the window. Rumpled black clothes hung on him, his hair was disheveled and unkempt, a scraggly beard gave him a wild appearance. His eyes were locked on the world outside, but they were unfocused and unseeing.

I eased next to him, entwining my hands in my skirt, unsure of how to speak.

So we didn't.

I waited in silence instead, but I didn't like the quiet. It left too much time for thought. Too much time to think on things I would rather forget.

After a while, Vladimir finally met my gaze. "She's really gone."

The words hovered somewhere between a question and a statement, denial amid an inevitable affirmation. I swallowed, nodding as I watched tears flood his eyes. I stepped forward, wrapping my arms around him and trying to keep the cracked pieces of him from shattering.

"It shouldn't have been her," he sobbed.

Tears streamed down my own face as I answered, "No. She deserved more."

His body wracked with grief, arms circling me for comfort, holding on to me as if the world around us were a raging sea and I was a piece of driftwood keeping him above the surface. We clung to each other for support, unable to stand on our own.

"I already thought that I'd lost her once. When William came back from Brenden. I thought it would nearly kill me then, but now, seeing it, seeing her leave this world, I can't—"

The crying kept him from going on, and I stroked his back. "I know," I said. I bit my lip, not wanting to say the next words, but knowing that they needed to be spoken. "But if Katherine were here, she wouldn't want us to go on this way. You made her a promise, Vladimir, and it's time to keep good on it. The council needs you. They need your guidance. You're still the leader of the Kavari, and you still have a country to protect and defend."

His hand fisted into my hair, face burying in my neck until his breathing steadily slowed and his emotions calmed. After a few minutes he pulled back, wiping the tears from his eyes with a new resolve in his face. A determination.

"I promised her," he said. "Katherine would chide me for responding like this."

I let out a sad laugh. "I can hear her saying it."

A small smile passed between us at the memory.

"I'm sorry." Vladimir met my eyes, and I knew he meant his previous demeanor. "But thank you."

I nodded to assure him that no apology was necessary. For

a moment we stood there, barely able to pull ourselves together.

"Is the council gathered?" His voice filled with distaste.

I nodded, wiping the tears from my eyes. "They've been waiting for you."

A flash of anger lit across his face. "It's time."

I looked up at him curiously. "Time for what?"

But he didn't answer. The vulnerable man who had sobbed against my shoulder only moments ago was suddenly gone, replaced by the one before me who now seemed to wear an impenetrable armor. He strode out of the room without even a glance back at me, as if he'd remembered what he needed to do and no one else would exist to him until he'd completed what he'd set out to accomplish.

CHAPTER THIRTY-SIX

VLADIMIR

FOCUS.

Anger bubbled within me as I approached the council room doors with Taryn trailing behind me. Katherine would've already scolded me like a child for my behavior, for dissociating like I had. We were at war. People died in war. Especially people who weren't supposed to—who didn't deserve to. Her death became a fact. I couldn't change it no matter how much I wanted to.

Taryn began, "I can stay outside if—"

I shook my head before she could finish. "No. I need you in there."

Everyone, including William and Verone, avoided eye contact as we entered the room. The tensions that used to rule our meetings had been replaced by uncertainty as everyone seemed to try to figure out an appropriate response.

"We're glad you could join us, Vladimir," Hart said. "Our condolences in light of everything that is going on. We're all devastated and broken—"

"Do not patronize me," I snapped, venom coating my words. "And don't you dare stand there and lie to my face. You hated Katherine, Hart. Most of you here did. So do not tell me you're broken or that you feel sorry for her death when all of you nearly put her there yourselves. You were so quick to judge when the queen laid out the accusations against her, so quick to condemn. Katherine would have bent over backward for anyone in this room, gone against her own good to smooth over contentions. She sacrificed her life for your king, for this country, and all any of you could ever do was sneer and look down at her, treat her like dirt, buy into the lies that the queen fed you, and I've had enough of it. Enough of *all* of it. Do not patronize me and mutter useless words that you wouldn't mean even under the threat of death."

They shrank back at my accusations, looking ashamed, but I knew they didn't care.

"Now, we have much to discuss," I continued. I turned to Verone, trying to keep my tone professional with him. "First and foremost, how in the blazing skies did two assassins subvert our entire security system, know exactly where we were going to meet, and position themselves in the rafters with an easy escape route without ever being detected?"

I internally recoiled from my cruel words. Verone had lost much, even more than me, and I knew that no one would be as hard on him as himself. But I had a job to do. I couldn't let friendship get in the way of words that needed to be said. This kingdom came first. Not empathy or friendship.

Verone gave no reaction to my anger. "It has been hard to deliver discipline when we're unable to pinpoint where the problem is. Nothing irregular was reported on any accounts. We have scoured the rooftops, questioned citizens in the city. We have no point of entry, no way of exit."

I lifted an eyebrow. "The tunnels?"

He shook his head.

"A mole?"

"I do not believe so, sir."

Verone was meticulous. He wouldn't have left any stone unturned, not in any case, and especially not in this one. "Then what"—I leaned forward—"*happened?*"

Katherine would have already had a solution for this, already known what was—

"They had to have been in the city days before the attack."

Taryn's voice caught me by surprise, and I turned. "What?"

She appeared unnerved by the sudden attention on her. "You're finding no point of entry. I've been researching, trying to find out anything about the Brenden assassins that I could over the past few days. I don't know much, but I do know that they're near invisible. They would have found a way in undetected or they wouldn't have come in at all. Everything would have been done at night. It would've been difficult for even a trained eye to spot them, because they're good. This is what they've been trained for. As far as where we were meeting, every soldier knew what was going on, where the meeting was going to be. It wouldn't have been difficult to overhear."

Mistakes upon mistakes.

"We have the body of the assassin you killed," Verone

added. "What was salvageable of him. The only identifying marker, besides his obvious Brenden appearance, was this mark stitched into the shoulder."

Verone produced a bloody jacket, revealing a circular symbol on the right shoulder.

"I've seen that symbol before. In Brenden." Taryn stared at it in shock. "The prince wore it."

I surveyed the symbol. Enlisting royals into a secret society wasn't a far stretch, and it gave them an inner knowledge of the dealings and loyalties within the assassins' ranks.

"Have we gathered any other information?" I pressed.

Wordless glances were exchanged throughout the room.

"So what you're saying is that it's not within our power to protect our own king?" I asked. "That's not acceptable." I looked down at the maps strewn across the table. "As soon as they find out William is still alive, they'll be back. Where are we at on the battlefront?"

The minister of war spoke up. "They overtook the city of Liera the day the diplomats arrived, and their main force has been located just beyond our western border."

I chewed on the inside of my lip. Not good. "How much time do we have?"

"We've been routing the soldiers to the villages farther out to fortify them, but I suggest we ourselves depart to join the soldiers as soon as possible." He sighed. "It's time."

I'd known we'd eventually have to meet the soldiers on the front, but I hadn't thought it would be this soon. We still had so much to do. So much to plan. It *was* time—but we didn't have enough of it.

"Then make sure the capital is sufficiently guarded, and

those who are left will leave with us to join the others."

William nodded his assent, but said nothing, and I noticed the glances being exchanged with everyone present except for me and Verone.

"There is another matter to discuss?" I prompted.

The room remained quiet, making unease coil in my gut. I thought I would have to pry the words from them.

"There's been discussion on the future of the Kavari," one of the lower councilmen began. "In light of recent and past events, we've been questioning if it's in the best interest of the country to continue the tradition, seeing as you're the only one left."

I stared at them, unsure if I had heard right. "In the wake of Katherine's death, in the middle of a war, at the brink of this country's civil unrest, you want to once again disband the Kavari? Completely undoing everything we've tried to rebuild in the past few weeks?"

No one spoke.

"All of you agreed to this?" I asked.

None of the council members would make eye contact, some of them looking ashamed. They were afraid, and nothing controlled people better than fear. By removing me from my position, they had a better chance at controlling William, and a better chance of coercing matters of government to go in their favor.

"You'll still have a position," William explained. "Nor do we need two warring men deciding the fate of the country."

From the look on his face, I could tell that he wasn't the one who had come up with the idea, but he hadn't shot it down either. The tiniest part of me whispered that this would be easier.

Maybe it was the answer—maybe it was time for the Kavari to discontinue.

But then Katherine's angry words filled my mind.

This isn't you, Vladimir. With every meeting, you give him a little more power. And if you keep giving it to him a piece at a time, one day you won't have any left.

She was right. Her dying face flashed before me, pale hand reaching for the wound on my forehead.

You're the leader of the Kavari, Vladimir. Act like it.

No more hiding. No more conceding to keep the peace.

"The death of Katherine does not end the Kavari," I stated. "The Kavari were created with a purpose. That purpose has not ended, therefore its existence does not change."

"With all due respect—" William began.

"With all due respect, *Your Majesty*," I cut him off. "If I go, you go with me. The whole castle can testify to your lack of sobriety since your mother's death. If you push *this*, I will push *that* matter, and I won't stop until you are removed from power, because no court will let you sit on a throne if you are found mentally unfit or unstable—and you've already proven that. You've ignored the advice of your council, ignored the advice of the Kavari. You threatened to exile the daughter of Michael Gallows. You've shown up intoxicated to official meetings and displayed a lack of respect to the subjects of this country.

"If we bring this to the courtroom, you will be removed from power, and once you are removed, I will name myself king regent since there is no other heir. All of which will bring us back to this exact moment here, except we'll have wasted precious, valuable time while our country is being decimated."

William opened his mouth in protest, his face red, ready to

argue. "You can't—"

I slammed my fist on the table. "You may be the king, William, but I am done going along with your antics to simply keep the peace. I am the leader of the Kavari, and I hold as much political power as you. This is a diarchy, *not* a monarchy, and it will operate as such. And if you take issue with that, I will have you removed from the throne. Is that clear?"

My eyes bore into him, around to the council, the audience too stunned to speak. This was what I should have done the first time William had overruled me, but I had been too much of a coward, too scared. I vowed to never be that man again.

"Are we clear?" My voice rumbled with the words.

Everyone looked to the king, who was still speechless, a plethora of emotions crossing his face. I stared him down, daring him to argue, preparing for him to. But he took me by surprise when his face fell in defeat, the fight leaving his eyes.

"I will concede."

I let out a relieved breath and raked my hands through my disheveled hair.

"But only if you instate another Kavari before we leave."

I stilled at his words.

William watched for my reaction. Instating a new Kavari was pointless and provided no advantage. I knew this. He knew this, but he lifted his chin. He was offering me a compromise. I'd just walked all over the king and defied his sovereignty. It needed to happen, and I had every right to, but I also realized the reality of the matter. William couldn't just agree or concede to me. He still had to display his own power. He would give me what I wanted, but only because I was willing to give him something in return. Instating another Kavari was for appearance's sake.

"Agreed," I said.

Hart looked at me with a glint in his eye. "Who do you have in mind for the position?"

I took a moment to respond, wishing that the one I knew needed to become one would speak up behind me, but she had no interest in taking the oath. She never would.

"I've had someone in mind for a while," I admitted. It was true, but it was too soon. He was too young.

"And while we're on the subject," I added, wanting to push the knife in as far as I could, "I will not push for it in the midst of this war unless it becomes absolutely necessary, but Gharridan needs to know the truth about the queen. About what really happened in that tower. Dissension still lingers among the people over whether or not Katherine killed the king, and I do not want her memory tainted. All of you thought that a lie was the best option, but we're having issues among the ranks. People aren't buying it, and it will end up causing more trouble than good. If you won't tell them the truth one day, then I will."

William studied me as if trying to decipher what was going on inside my head. "We will discuss it in the future, but there are more pressing matters at the moment."

I nodded.

The rest of the meeting went on without incident, and even though so many things were still up in the air, I'd felt like I'd just won the war when the battle had only just begun.

CHAPTER THIRTY-SEVEN

◆◇◆

TARYN

I ONLY LISTENED as the council finished their meeting, but mentally I was sifting through everything that was being discussed. An underlying anger drove Vladimir as he asserted his authority, and rightly so. He needed to—I just hoped that their temporary agreements would last. I thought William would have balked, put up a fight or thrown Vladimir out, but he just stood there and took it. I noticed the lack of a bottle in his hand and couldn't recall seeing one there since Katherine's death. The dullness in his eyes suggested something was going on inside him.

Vladimir's temper was still brewing after the meeting.

"I think you did the right thing in there," I said.

"I know I did."

His words felt like a slap.

"I'm sorry." He rubbed his face, looking apologetic. "I have a lot going on right now, and I can barely think straight."

One discussion from the meeting hung at the forefront of my mind, and I lingered between leaving and staying. I went for it.

"Do you actually have someone else in mind, or was that just to appease the council?"

He paused at my words. I could read it in his body language. See it in his face. He wanted to ask me, but he wouldn't because he already knew what my answer would be.

"I do, but I don't want to name them without first offering the position."

I nodded, then excused myself to leave it at that. Who he had in mind, I couldn't tell, and part of me considered the fact that there really wasn't someone in mind and he was only delaying the inevitable. Guilt writhed within me, had been writhing in me since hearing her last words. Since the funeral. Katherine's patriotism had lit a spark, called me to action, but I couldn't help thinking about my mother's family. I knew she was from Dalendria, and Katherine was connected to Dalendria somehow as well. If I sacrificed myself like Katherine, I might never know. What would honor their memories better? Serving Gharridan, or finding out where my mother's family was from? I went back and forth in my mind, questioning how to move forward, but came no closer to a solution.

Everything had shifted in Katherine's absence. I hadn't had a place before, but Katherine had become my friend. Now even she was gone. Pressure from all sides bore down on Vladimir, and I didn't want to waste his time with my insecurities.

It was strange. I'd spent so long on my own, but in the time since I'd left home, I'd grown used to others' company, used to having someone to talk to, to share things with. Now that it was gone, I didn't know what to do with myself.

I wandered down to the kitchens, finding Nic and Darya around one of the tables. I sat down with them, unsure of how to approach conversation.

"Nic," I stated.

He dipped his head, dark curly hair spilling forward as he rolled his eyes and indicated Darya across from him. "I told her this was my table, but she wouldn't leave."

Darya ignored Nic as she inspected the penmanship on the paper before her, not caring enough to even acknowledge him.

I hid a smile. I liked Nic. He possessed a good heart and a kind soul, and he definitely kept Vladimir on his toes.

Ink stained Darya's fingertips, her thick, curly hair pinned up on her head in a messy knot.

"How are you, blood vier?" she asked.

I shrugged. "I'm alive."

She cocked her head, still not looking at either of us. "I guess that's a good thing."

I made a face. "I would hope so."

"Have you been to visit Marco?" Her words cut right to the bone.

"Not since—" The words died in my throat, grief flooding through me again.

Darya didn't miss a beat. "He's doing well, far better than he has been in the past." A smile touched her lips. "He even remembered my name."

"That's a wonderful improvement," I said. I'd tried to continue visiting Marco, but in light of everything happening, it had fallen somewhat by the wayside.

"Do you think he'll ever completely …" I trailed off.

Darya placed the quill in its cradle before taking a sip of her tea. "Not completely. Not enough to function on his own. They did too much damage to his mind, but I think … I think he'll continue to get better—even if he'll never be the man he once was."

And perhaps that was why I was holding back, because I knew that becoming a Kavari could possibly mean sacrificing everything. That's what it had meant for my father, for Marco, and now Katherine.

I stared down at the black lines pervading my skin, shivered at the memories of the nightmares from last night. I might already be sacrificing everything.

"How did you become a messenger, Darya?" I asked, changing the subject.

"Her mouth probably got her kicked out of every other job she tried for," Nic muttered.

The muffled sound of a boot connecting with a shin came from beneath the table.

"Ouch!" Nic jerked in his seat, leaning down to rub his leg.

"You're just like my younger brother, only twenty times more annoying and not nearly as fun."

Darya scowled at him before turning her attention back to me. "Marco knew my family and had connections that we wouldn't have been able to find otherwise. My eldest brother presides over a town in the southern border, and my other two are enlisted in the army. I don't like people. Or swords. Or following orders. So I took this job. Originally he found me a position as a scribe, and while I do enjoy writing, it wasn't nearly as exciting for me."

"How many years have you been doing it for?" I asked.

She shrugged. "Since I was about twelve."

"Is there really enough correspondence to keep you busy?"

Something flicked across her eyes, but it disappeared just as quickly, making me question if I had seen it at all.

"It's not always the job you want, but it keeps my back warm and my belly full."

Vladimir trusted her completely, which meant Darya was more than she claimed to be.

She was hiding something.

"So Nic really is twenty times more annoying than your brother?"

Darya scrunched her face. "Did I say twenty? I meant thirty."

CHAPTER THIRTY-EIGHT

VLADIMIR

THE FOG MARRED my vision as I made my way down to the training fields where the morning sessions were already in full swing. The clash of steel and shouted orders filled the air, their sources invisible to my eyes. Within two days, these training fields would lie silent and all but empty, filled only by the skeletal force left behind to defend the city.

I maneuvered through the mist, visiting ring after ring and getting close enough that I could observe them. The soldiers were doing well. They'd trained. They were ready. But would it be good enough?

As I watched them work, I studied each of their faces, wondering which ones would never return, never see their families again. War feasted on lives like Death feasted on souls, its battle drums always beating within my ears, winding down the clock to decimation.

I finally found who I was looking for, my gaze landing on Nic finishing up one of the group exercises.

I signaled for him to join me.

"What's up, boss?" he asked, out of breath.

I jerked my head away from the others. "Private lesson?"

He grinned, jogging away to drink a swig of water before following me.

We ventured far enough away that the noise of the morning routines faded in the distance before drawing our swords.

I kept up an easy manner of conversation as we circled one another.

"The troops look like they're doing well," I observed. "Ready for battle."

Nic shrugged with indifference. "As well as usual."

I swung with a blow that he quickly parried.

"Has there been any more dissent among the soldiers?"

He jabbed at me, but I intercepted the blade, sparks flying off the metal.

"It's better. Not eradicated, but not as bad as it once was."

He struck again.

"Remind me how many years you've been in the military?"

Nic's face implied he didn't know whether I was insulting him or praising him. "I became a squire at age twelve, like all the other boys."

I nodded. He definitely had training, but he was still so young.

A smile crept across his face. "If I'm not mistaken, that means I started younger than you."

I cocked an eyebrow. "You've heard some interesting rumors."

We caught each other in a quick succession of blows before breaking apart again.

He *was* younger than I had been, albeit probably by only a few months, but he also had a family that he could go home to when he was off duty. Most soldiers did.

I pushed the thought away.

"Do you see a career in this?" I asked. "In the military?"

He thought about my question for a moment before shrugging again. "Most likely. There haven't exactly been many other options opening up, and hey, depending on how this war goes, I may not even get that far."

His words killed the hope inside me, bringing me back to the reality of our situation. No regret hung in his eyes; the statement was indifferent to him. His impending death was simply a fact. The fact that I couldn't save him or anyone else from if we didn't find a way to win this war or stop it entirely.

We sparred for a few minutes longer, forgetting the talking. Some of his choices took me by surprise and impressed me. He'd definitely improved. A lot.

"You've been practicing," I observed as I sheathed my sword. "Was military always the path you wanted to go?"

"Dad was military," he said, a little out of breath. "So were my brothers. I was the youngest and expected to follow in all of their footsteps. Personally, I thought something in the court or politics would be more my style, but my mother squashed it, saying I didn't know when to shut up and keep my tongue, which would most likely make people despise me, thus resulting in me getting killed at a young age."

I smiled. "Well, I can't say that she was wrong."

Nic rolled his eyes. "I can learn." A mischievous glint flashed in his eyes. "I might even have to go after your job one day, become a Kavari."

I kept myself from betraying any emotions. I couldn't have directed the conversation better myself. "You think you have what it takes to be a Kavari?"

He gave me a knowing look. "Not yet—I'm barely eighteen. I see what you have to deal with and I have no desire for that kind of pressure. I'm happy to be the man in the background. I don't want to have to argue with the Crown and council." He pointed a finger at me. "But one day, if we survive this war, I bet that you're going to be begging me to become one."

If he only knew.

"But then I would have to listen to you talk even more than I do now. I don't think I could handle that. I don't think anyone could handle that."

Nic scowled. "Well if you weren't so sullen, quiet, and brooding all the time, I wouldn't have to fill the empty air, now, would I?"

The humor dissolved from my face.

Are you just going to sit here brooding all night?

I'm not brooding.

The definition of the word would beg to differ.

Katherine's voice from the night of the feast filled my mind, shattering the already broken pieces of me. What I wouldn't give to hear her voice here beside me. To receive even one more word of her wisdom.

"I'm sorry, boss, I meant no disrespect."

Nic turned uneasy, noticing the visible shift in my disposition. It took me a second to compose myself before I clapped him on the shoulder.

"None taken. You just reminded me of someone. That's all."

CHAPTER THIRTY-NINE

TARYN

THE STUDY DOORS hung wide, the bright sunlight from the windows spilling out into the corridor. I shielded my eyes, frowning as I peered inside. William lounged in a leather chair, twirling an empty glass in his hand.

No guards stood outside the door. I frowned.

"William?" I crossed the threshold and made my way across the wooden floor.

He didn't acknowledge my presence, face turned away from me.

My hand reached to where it knew a dagger was strapped to my thigh. If he was drunk, I didn't want to stick around for his scathing comments, but I also worried about why he was by himself. Thoughts of the assassins filled my mind. Verone would have the soldiers' hides for this.

"William," I said again as I made my way around the chair to face him.

His gaze was distant, somewhere else, leaving his face unreadable.

"Are you all right?" I asked. "Where are your guards?"

I squinted, the sunlight harsher than I remembered.

"Why did you kill her, Taryn?" Deadness hung in his voice, like he'd been drained of all emotion.

I stiffened at the question, apprehension rising within me.

"I—"

"You know what I think?" He grinned, finally meeting my eyes. Where his voice lacked emotion, his face did not. He spit the words like venom. "I think that you wanted to."

I shook my head, taking a step back. "You've been drinking. I think it's best if I leave."

He lurched to his feet, grabbing my wrist before I could flee and pulling me against him. "None of these deaths started happening before you came here. Beva, my mother, and now Katherine."

My jaw fell open.

The stench of alcohol radiating from his breath overwhelmed me. His grip tightened on my arm, and the blinding light from the windows made me nauseous, dizzy.

"William, this isn't you—"

"Isn't it?" He raised his voice. "Or is this who you've driven me to become?"

"Let go, William," I demanded. I tried to pull away, but his grip was like an iron shackle.

"You never wanted any of this." He leaned closer, his lips nearly brushing mine. "Never wanted me."

A strangled sound escaped my throat as I found myself unable to move, unable to escape.

"But here you are, still in the middle of it. Still causing problems."

His hazel eyes turned menacing. "If I hadn't turned back for you in the wilderness, sought you out in that blizzard, you would have frozen to death, and I can't help but wonder if that was the biggest mistake I ever made."

Something within me broke.

"That, however," he whispered in my ear, "is one mistake I won't make twice."

Pain split open my back, and I gasped, looking down to see the sharp tip of a bloody dagger sticking out of my gut. I couldn't move, just stared in shock at the red permeating the white of my dress, the world turning a million colors around me before blackening. The chill of Death hovered around me, and I looked up at William, betrayed, but it was no longer William that stood before me.

It was Katherine. Staring back at me with the eyes of Death and—

My eyes shot open as the scream ripped out of my throat like a strangled animal. I flew up in the bed. The door to my room burst open, the guards stumbling in then stopping in shock. My body shook, fingers trembling, lips quaking. I reached behind me to touch the place where the dagger had penetrated, the memory of the pain seared into my mind, William's heartless eyes boring into me.

"Miss Gallows?" Hesitance hung in the guard's voice.

"I'm fine," I croaked. "Sorry to disturb you. It was just a dream."

When they finally backed away and shut the door, I stumbled out of bed to the desk and lit a candle. I jumped at a sudden noise only to see that one of the pillows had fallen off the mess of a bed. The light flickered in the darkness, and I searched the shadowed corners, feeling vulnerable, like hungry and menacing eyes were watching me, waiting for me to turn my back so they could strike. I told myself it wasn't real. No one had stabbed me in the back. Death hadn't taken me. I leaned my forehead against the cool stone walls, taking deep breaths to calm myself.

You'll be so raving mad from the nightmares that you'll beg for death.

I inspected the black on my wrist. It had spread. Tiny lines were also forming on my other wrist. My arms trembled as I stared at them. How much time did I have?

I exchanged my fear for anger. Anger at this impending death, this impending war, at these assassins we couldn't trap, these attacks that we couldn't stop. Anger at what I knew I needed to do. I belted on an overdress and wandered out into the hall with no wish to return to the land of dreams.

Once again, I found myself outside the library, where light was seeping through the cracks in the door. I pushed it open without thought, unsurprised to see Vladimir sitting inside. He looked angry too. Angry like me. I strode in, choosing a chair with a wall at its back and eyeing the one the assassin had snuck up on me in.

"Did Nic say yes or no?" I asked.

Annoyance flicked across Vladimir's face.

I shrugged. "He was the only viable candidate I could come up with."

"I didn't ask him."

Didn't was different from hadn't. "And?"

"I'm not going to."

I cocked an eyebrow. "Why not?"

I could tell I pushed him, but I wasn't in a caring mood. I wanted something to distract me. Something to take my mind off the nightmare. The glare of the light from the dreams still made me want to squint. I could still feel William's lips nearly brush against mine, still feel the pain of the dagger as it split open my back.

"He's not ready, and it's too much to ask of him. Besides, the council would laugh the nomination out of the room."

I failed to see how this solved anything. "Won't they disband the Kavari if you don't find another one?"

Hardness set across his face. "I won't allow that to happen."

"I don't think they're going to give you a choice," I said.

"I'd like to see them try," he growled.

"Well then it sounds like we'll have plenty of entertainment tomorrow along with everything else."

"This isn't a joke, Taryn."

"I never said it was."

"Making light of it is the same thing."

"Well making light of it is the only way I know how to deal with it, otherwise I'd drown in the depression of it all. Even you can't deny that every chaotic event in the past few months has been playing out like a comedic stage drama that gets more bizarre with every act."

He grimaced.

It didn't feel like everything that had happened could be real, but it was. We'd lived it.

The next words fell unbidden from my lips. "If something

does happen, to William, who becomes the new ruler?"

Vladimir met my eyes, aware of the implications of my words. "There are things I'd rather not think about right now."

The anger resurfaced within me at the injustice of it all. The inability to escape our circumstances or do essentially anything about them. How trapped I felt. I no longer had purpose here but to slowly wither away as the nightmares consumed me. Vladimir needed a Kavari. I was the only choice. I didn't want to be one, and I hated the guilt rolling through me over wanting nothing to do with this. I hated feeling obligated to do something against my will, and also hated myself that I wasn't even willing to consider it.

Katherine would have, and that only made the guilt double within me. I knew why. It was because I was selfish. I didn't want to be tied to this, didn't want to be held down by a life I never asked for, but did I really even have a choice anymore? That was where the anger stemmed from. It wasn't the prospect of joining the Kavari. It was the prospect of not being given the choice. I craved the choice. I'd controlled very little of my life, and completely losing what freedom I had left went against everything within me. Rebelled.

I rose to my feet, eyeing the rack of swords on the wall. They might be important or antique, but at the moment, I didn't really care. I pulled one of them free then indicated Vladimir's sword belt resting beside his chair. "Then don't think."

I moved to the open space in the center of the room and took the leather-wrapped hilt of the sword in both of my hands, planting my feet apart.

"Taryn, what are you doing?" He sounded more confused

than annoyed, which was a good start.

I rolled my shoulders. "You need to not think, and I need practice." I tested the sword's weight. "And I also need to hit something or I'm going to go crazy."

Vladimir didn't move. "It's the middle of the night."

I cocked an eyebrow. "I'm sorry, do you have something better to do?"

He just sat there staring at me as if warring against the decision, but in the end he took up the challenge, unsheathing his sword and venturing closer.

For a moment I second-guessed myself. The last time I'd sparred was before the bloodbath in the throne room with Zedekiah. The last time I'd fought was against Zedekiah in the snowy woods. I wasn't exactly in practice, but I shoved the unease away.

I darted in first to take Vladimir by surprise, but he parried the blow, and I jumped back. We circled a few steps before I moved in again, but he easily flicked my blade aside. I frowned. He guessed my next move, and the next. What I'd meant as a distraction began to frustrate me. Sparks flew from where our blades collided, the clash of the metal echoing out in the stillness of the night.

"You keep looking exactly where you're going to go." Vladimir shot in for a blow, which I parried. "Don't. And stand up straight."

The critique took me by surprise, but I quickly applied the feedback.

I'd gotten sloppy.

I swung again, but next I knew, the edge of his sword found my throat. "Dead."

I stepped back, flustered. "Again."

Vladimir shrugged his shoulders as if disinterested.

Heat flared within me. "I'm sorry, am I not a worthy opponent?"

I caught the smirk on Vladimir's face before he turned, which made me unleash and attack with a new ferocity. He must have eyes in the back of his head, because he saw it coming, warding me off with each and every blow. I hadn't expected to defeat him, but nor had I expected to feel this helpless. He was by far the best swordsman I had ever seen or dueled. He beat me again and again until sweat littered my brow, and my arms ached from the weight of the sword. He didn't even look like he was trying. The anger bubbling within me intensified, manifesting itself in each of my movements.

It didn't go unnoticed.

Vladimir took a step back. "What are you so angry at, Taryn?"

I gritted my teeth, charging in again only to be pushed away.

"I think that's enough," Vladimir said.

But I wasn't done.

I came at him again, refusing to back down as all of my emotions struggled within me.

He won again.

"I said that's enough."

A noise at the door distracted Vladimir, and that was all I needed to finally gain the upper hand. I came in from his left side, feinted to the right as he realized what I was doing, and then tripped him off his feet. He sprawled onto his back on the floor, and I placed the tip of the sword against his neck. "Dead."

I barely had time to appreciate the triumph within me before his foot swept underneath me. The world spun until I was flat on my back with Vladimir hovering over me, the edge of a dagger pressed against my throat.

"Dead," he growled. "Don't ever let your guard down too quickly."

I briefly squeezed my eyes shut at my stupidness, at my inability to get the upper hand even once, but the frustration and anger dissipated as we panted, exhausted from both exertion and the lack of sleep. Vladimir stared at me, an unreadable expression in his gaze. We didn't move. We were two broken people, struggling with things that neither us nor others could ever relate to, and I suddenly saw Vladimir for all he was, all he was dealing with. Everything that he had sacrificed. Why had I never seen it before?

"I didn't let my guard down," I said. "You were already dead."

He barely shook his head, his dark hair hanging over his forehead. "I don't give up that easily."

I waited for him to move, but he didn't. We stared at each other, eyes locked, still trying to catch our breath, and our close proximity unlocked a thought that had lodged in the back of my mind from the first moment I'd met him, sitting across the fire, the shadows dancing across his face. Tears pricked at the corners of my vision at the intense realization of it, the understanding. All he was to me. All he had ever been. I wondered if the thought had also lodged in him as well, buried so deep that it could never be uncovered, but then I didn't have to wonder, because I recognized the look in his eyes, the same look I had seen in William's in the dungeon and in the tower.

Here, in the middle of the darkness lit only by a few candles, it was like all the dirt fell away. Vladimir had hidden whatever he was feeling well, but my mind backtracked over the past few months, finding the confirmation in his actions. His worry. His care. He had never said anything, and knowing that *something* had happened between William and me, I doubted he ever would. That was just his nature. Always putting others before himself. Why had I never seen him this way before, seen him for who he really was?

His head dipped lower, so close, less than a mere handsbreadth away from changing everything forever. I heard my breath catch in my throat, scared and uncertain, still trapped beneath him. His face hovered inches from mine, hesitating, searching, his hot breath scalding my cheeks, and then his eyes filled with restraint.

"It's late," he whispered, and his weight was suddenly gone.

He offered me a hand up, gaze locking with mine, and an emotion I couldn't place trailed across it. "Your father wanted you to become a Kavari, wanted you to be here."

He said the words as if trying to reassure himself.

I stiffened. "What do you mean?"

He hesitated, as if only just realizing he'd said the words out loud. He shook his head, backing away. "I'm sorry, it's— I don't know what I'm saying."

He moved to the chair, strapping on his sword belt and sheathing his weapon before leaving the room.

But I wasn't a fool.

He knew something.

And Vladimir knew exactly what he was saying.

CHAPTER FORTY

Taryn

*Y*OUR *FATHER WANTED you to become a Kavari, wanted you to be here.*

Vladimir's words haunted me, hitting deeper and harder than he could have ever imagined. And they unlocked a mystery I'd always known. They were the key I'd been searching for, but even though it was now unlocked, I still couldn't figure out how to open the door.

Vladimir had acted like it was nothing, but I knew that it was everything, and I'd been stewing over all the truths I knew for hours, because Vladimir was right. I knew it deep within my heart—my father had been preparing me to join the Kavari.

The sparring. The tracking. The riding. My mother had never agreed with it, never liked all the things my father was teaching me. I'd never understood why. My mother's iron grip on my life had never let me venture alone into the village, never let me trust anyone. It wasn't until after her passing that I'd branched out, gotten to know some of the people in Navarre. Their kindness and the widow Lidia were what kept me going after she was gone because my father hadn't been there at all for me.

I'd kept up my sparring with the other children in the village, hunted for my own food, practiced everything my father had taught me. Considering how much I'd hated him, I never understood why, but in those early years, I'd been hopeful that one day he would come riding up the path, and I would want him to know that I wasn't a disappointment. That I was still worthy of his love. That he could be proud of me and have a reason to keep coming back.

I even suspected that he had wanted me in the capital after his death, although I had no idea why.

My father had wanted me to become a Kavari.

My mother hadn't.

Their argument circled in my mind.

My father broke the oath, Michael.

Something changed *after* her death. Something changed *before* his death. And whatever it was, whatever he was trying to accomplish, me becoming a Kavari had been a necessary requirement to fulfill it.

You could belong here. If you wanted to. In fact, you have the very birthright to belong here. To serve a purpose.

Tears blurred my vision at the memory of Katherine's words. She had given everything, would have given more, and I was balking at the idea of giving anything. Even one minute. One day.

I inhaled sharply.

I was a coward.

I had always been a coward.

My father hadn't been.

Beva hadn't been.

Katherine hadn't been.

And it was time that I stopped being one.

Maybe it wasn't about having a choice. Maybe it was about doing the right thing. Maybe it was about taking up the mantle where Katherine had dropped it, and doing for this country what she'd strived to do herself.

Maybe it was time—no, it *was* time.

Time to take the oath.

CHAPTER FORTY-ONE

VLADIMIR

THOUGHTS OF THE previous night clouded my mind as I prepared travel arrangements the next day. I never should have indulged in the duel, but Taryn had been angry, and I'd been frustrated. Both of us had needed a distraction, and it had worked. For a short time anyway. Neither of us were completely in our right minds. One of us could have ended up with an actual injury, and it had only ended when I'd pinned her beneath me, but that brief moment had shaken all sense from me. Shaken *every last piece* of sense from me as I'd stared down at her look of defeat, her exhausted face still breathtaking, making me forget myself. Forget that a desire that should never have been planted had done more than just take root within me. Forget it was a hope I could never wish for. And in that moment of forgetfulness when everything was about to change, I'd seen it in her eyes. The idea. The realization. The curiosity, but she couldn't know that it went both ways. She never could, because it could never even be a possibility. Michael made me promise to protect her, not—

I squeezed my eyes shut, forcing my brain to focus. There could not be a worse time for an unnecessary distraction. More important things were at stake, but even as I tried to ignore it, I was angry at myself for pretending like it had never appeared. I had always known that it existed, in the back of my mind, and these unyielding circumstances had brought it to the forefront, but whatever had happened or was going on with her and William ruled out the thought.

I had a kingdom to protect and a war to win.

And a branch of the government to uphold.

War laughed at me, a constant press against my mind, its greedy fingers reaching to take everything I'd ever loved or called home. We needed to find a way to end this war before the war ended us.

Much as it pained me, I didn't go back on my decision to not ask Nic. I'd done the right thing. He wasn't ready. He was too young, and I refused to instate a Kavari for appearance alone. I didn't know how I would persuade William and the council to agree to keeping the Kavari with just me, but I refused to let its legacy dissipate into nothing. They needed to wait until after the war was over. At least. If only one man could represent the Crown, then only one man could represent the Kavari.

Conflict twisted around the room like tendrils of smoke, weaving in between the council, Crown, and Kavari. Testing where our allegiances lay, questioning the intent of our actions. What was decided in the room today would either make Gharridan—or break it.

The fate of the Kavari rested on my shoulders.

My fate hung in the balance.

And it seemed Queen Adamara was getting exactly what she'd wanted.

She'd undermined the foundation of this country. Murdered Michael. All but ruined Marco. Katherine was gone on account of the consequences stemming from the actions she'd ordered of her son. And now I was the only person left in the way of her plan. I was a fading piece of the last remnant of the Kavari of Gharridan—and now that part of me was about to disappear. But perhaps it wouldn't matter if the Kavari were discontinued and forgotten, because there may not be any Kavari to return from this war.

The meeting started off discussing travel plans, troop coordinates, arrangements that needed to be made. The next few weeks would be passing in a blur. Everything needed to be planned meticulously, and every backup plan needed another backup.

"What of our news from Algarar?" I asked.

The minister of war consulted his documents. "We've yet to nail down an understanding of what they're trying to accomplish. There has been some movement within their military, but nothing threatening. Nothing large enough that we could justify sending more of our troops to the southern border instead of the western."

I shook my head, frustrated with our lack of intel. "That's probably all for the best. I don't think Algarar means to move against us until both Gharridan's and Brenden's armies are so weak they won't even be able to put up a fighting chance."

I kept my focus on the matters at hand, trying to ignore the question I knew would eventually come, and trying to block out the fights and arguments that would inevitably ensue. Every matter of concern was exhausted before the question finally came, as if the entire room were dreading it.

Well, all except one.

"Who have you chosen to join the Kavari alongside you, Vladimir?" Hart asked.

He lounged in his chair wearing a knowing smile, like he owned the entire court. My hand curled into a fist, wanting to punch it off his face. I knew he was waiting to shoot me down, waiting to rip the Kavari away from me and all of my authority with it.

William and the council turned to me with expectation. Some faces held hope. Some held consolation, and others, like Hart, wore smug expressions.

Stand your ground.

But what could I do with no ground to stand on?

"I—" I began, but the words died in my throat as defeat washed over me.

The doors burst open with unnecessary force, smacking against the walls. I spun in alarm, my sword halfway out of its sheath.

Taryn stood in the hallway, looking just as stunned as the guards at her spectacle, but the surprise vanished. I immediately recognized the determined look plastered to her face, the confidence in her step as she strode into the room, shoulders back, head high, ready for a fight.

My throat bobbed.

This couldn't be good.

"This is a private meeting, *Miss Gallows*," Hart sneered.

She took in each of our faces. "I would apologize for being late, but it seems like Vladimir has yet to inform you."

"Inform us of what?" the minister of war asked.

Taryn locked eyes with me. "That I'm to be the next Kavari."

I searched her face for any semblance of a lie or a joke, but there was none. If she really intended to take the oath of Kavari, then something had happened. Something had changed.

William threw me an incredulous look. "Vladimir, is this true?"

I opened my mouth, then shut it again. If she was doing this for the wrong reasons—

"Please excuse us for a moment," I said. "We'll reconvene upon our return."

I placed a hand on Taryn's shoulder and propelled her out of the room, almost dragging her to one of the balconies and locking the doors. If anyone was in the gardens below, they shouldn't be able to overhear us, but I still peered over the railing before wheeling on Taryn.

"What is this about?" I demanded. "Do you have any idea what you're doing?"

"Exactly what I just stated in there," Taryn said. "You need a Kavari, and I'm the most viable candidate. I want to take the oath."

I shook my head. "You've been running from this ever since that first day in the throne room. What changed?"

"What do you think changed?" Her eyes grew moist, but she held the tears back. "Katherine sacrificed her life, gave up everything. This is bigger than whatever I want right now. You yourself said that my father wanted me to join the Kavari."

Something I should have never let slip past my lips. I'd suspected it ever since I'd first seen her on the training fields, but I'd never mentioned it before. Because I couldn't make it fit. I couldn't make it make sense. It still didn't.

"This is a serious decision, Taryn." My voice turned grave as I stepped closer, watching to make sure my words got through to her, that she completely understood. "We're all grieving, but you can't be operating on an emotional high."

Her eyes filled with annoyance before flitting away, distracted. "This is not an emotional decision, Vladimir. I've made up my mind, and this is what I want."

She was hiding something.

"What aren't you telling me?" I asked.

She threw her hands in the air. "I'm telling you everything. This is what I want."

I couldn't deny that she would be a better choice than Nic. She possessed the fortitude to be a Kavari, she'd just never had the determination or the drive. There was, however, one thing that I didn't think she had ever considered.

"If you take the oath of Kavari, it is for life," I stated.

She looked at me like I was stupid. "I know."

I hesitated, unsure of how to phrase my next statement. "I'm not assuming or prying, but if you—if there was ever anything between you and William, and you join the Kavari, there never can be again. We're meant to be two separate entities to balance the other out. Something like that would be considered a conflict of interest."

From the look that shadowed her face, she hadn't thought of that. She grew quiet for a moment, gaze drifting to the gardens as if weighing her decision as the wind pulled at her hair.

"There's nothing between us." She brought her attention back to me. "And there never will be."

The words rang with finality, and a tenseness hung in her tone. Her expression held no remorse, no regret. Something had once been between them, but whatever it was, it was apparently gone. Lost. Forever.

"Are you certain?" I asked.

"I'm not sure how many ways I can say yes to get the point across, Vladimir."

When we reentered the room, the council members and William watched us expectantly.

"I present Taryn Gallows as a candidate for the Kavari. If any are opposed, please speak now."

I waited for objections, but none came. My gaze drifted to William, who was staring at Taryn. He would be aware of what this meant, the implications, but I couldn't read what was playing across his face.

"The Crown and council are in agreement," he said at last. "She will take the oath at dawn."

CHAPTER FORTY-TWO

TARYN

BLOOD TRICKLED THROUGH my fingers as I plunged the dagger into the queen. Again. Her dead eyes stared vacantly at me, the floor turning into a sea of blood that lapped at my ankles. Bile rose in my throat, but I couldn't vomit, and the world around me turned dark as I splashed into the waves around me but couldn't feel the wetness. Cold steel pressed against the pulse of my throat. One small movement would end my life—

But something was wrong.

I wasn't on the floor.

I was in a bed.

My bed.

My eyes were open. A dark shape hovered over me, and that was what held the dagger to my neck. Was I still dreaming? A draft filtered into the room from the window that hung ajar. No. This was very much real. My vision adjusted enough to define the shape as a black-clad figure, but I couldn't see their eyes in the darkness. If I screamed or moved even an inch, I would be dead. He'd caught me off guard, and I wasn't prepared.

I thought panic might course through me, but it didn't.

Nor did dread sink into me.

I was about to die, and it was simply a fact.

"It's time to answer your riddle, Taryn Gallows," he said. "Nothing can buy it, not secrets or wealth, but what valuable treasure can save all but itself?"

I'd played the words over and over in my mind, pulling at different theories, but everything seemed either too obvious or too obscure. It wasn't until that moment I realized how cruel he was, even if he had no way of knowing.

"A Radonaya," I whispered.

Tears flooded my eyes at her memory. At her sacrifice.

"Very good." The assassin almost sounded impressed. "You've only one left to answer, but I've tired of our game and will have to cut it short."

I almost swallowed, then thought better of it. "Get it over with, then."

I knew it was the assassin from before, from my family. I only wished I'd learned the reason why, uncovered the answers before the end, but perhaps death would bring the answers I sought. I lay there, waiting for the feel of the blade slicing into my neck, but it didn't come.

The assassin stayed frozen above me, arm locked in place, the pressure of the dagger remaining consistently even. What was holding him back? The quiet curled around us like smoke.

"You sound just like her."

The statement confused me until I pieced together what he meant.

My mother. He was referring to my mother's voice.

Wisdom told me to keep my mouth shut. Curiosity screamed for answers.

"Before you kill me," I said, "could you at least tell me what she did, and why you came here to assassinate me?"

He remained still. "I swore to never speak about it again and was instructed to not give you direct answers."

I waited a moment before adding, "And I'm sure you were also instructed to assassinate me without hesitation."

Something like regret tainted his words. "I don't agree with what I have to do, but if I don't complete this job, someone else will. I'm sorry."

His apology stunned me.

If he really didn't want to kill me, he had a funny way of showing it. Especially with all the mind games he'd put me through during the past few weeks.

"How did you know my mother?" I asked.

I was amazed at how he never flinched, how his arm never seemed to shake, and how he remained perfectly still while the weapon never broke contact with my skin. He stood like a statue, making me question his humanity.

"We were friends," he finally relinquished. "Long ago. She wouldn't approve of this, but she made her choice. She didn't choose honor, and her choices affected all of those around her."

His statements made no sense, and I couldn't wrap my head around it.

"If you don't agree, then why are you going through with it?" I asked. "Why do you have to be the one to do it?"

It took him a moment to answer me. "Because unlike her, *I* don't have a choice."

The words I'd once told William echoed in my mind.

You always have a choice.

"I don't see anyone here forcing you to do it," I said.

"Not everything in this world is tangible or visible. You may not be able to see pressure, but you can feel it. Someone doesn't have to voice a threat in order for it to be real."

"Then why the mind games?"

He chuckled. "So many questions."

"You're an assassin. Surely the thrill is in the kill and not the hunt, why haven't you chosen to kill me yet?"

"You're a blood vier. Surely you have no greater opportunities available, why haven't you chosen to join the Kavari yet?"

Goosebumps prickled up my arm, and fear struck for the first time. Suspicion rose within me, but there was nothing hostile in his question. It held more curiosity and had almost a *hinting* tone to it. He was still playing his game, whatever it may be.

My eyes narrowed as I debated how to answer. "Why would you care?"

"Because I've been harvesting information from this castle for weeks, and I find your lack of position very interesting. I'll ask again. Why haven't you joined the Kavari? With the Radonaya passing from this world into the next it seems you're needed more than ever."

How deeply had he infiltrated the castle?

"I'm taking the oath at dawn."

I expected a laugh, a reaction of some sort, but he said

nothing. And his lack of response frightened me more.

"Well," he said. "Isn't this a twist in the story. Perhaps I won't kill you."

The chill of the blade vanished, the pressure gone, and in one phantomlike movement the assassin was suddenly at the window.

"Wait," I called out, sitting up in the bed. "Are you just going to let the poison finish me off?"

He turned his hooded face back toward me. "I have no cure for it."

I suppressed a laugh. "If there isn't a cure, then why don't you just kill me now?"

"Because it won't kill you *yet*. And I said that *I* had no cure for it. Not that there wasn't a cure. I cannot undo what has been done."

Hope bloomed within me.

I stared at his dark form outlined by the moonlight. "It's with your people. Isn't it? All my life, I've wanted to know what happened between my mother and her family. If they can cure me of this poison, why can't I just come with you?"

"If I take you with me right now, they will kill you."

He moved to go out the window, but I called out again. "So death is my only hope?"

I heard the despair in my voice, the hurt.

He paused before answering, "What's rarer than silver and diamonds and gems, but when given as gifts, unites the kingdoms of men?"

He'd said that he was done with riddles.

"One day, *after* you've taken the oath of Kavari," he continued. "If you choose to visit Dalendria, you may come, but only if you come in white. And you are to never speak of this con-versation."

Like a wraith, he was gone, and for a few fleeting moments with the world so still and quiet, I wondered if maybe all of it hadn't simply been a dream. After all this time, he hadn't killed me. He'd decided to let me live, but only after learning that I would join the Kavari. He and my father both wanted some-thing for me that my mother hadn't.

CHAPTER FORTY-THREE

A S THE OATH of the Kavari fell from my lips, binding my life and fate to that of Gharridan, I expected to feel like my soul was being sucked away, like invisible shackles were being welded around my wrists, but I didn't. Instead, a sense of finality washed over me as a feeling of purpose flooded through me. A hope that I'd never possessed before. I'd never been more sure of anything in my life.

Partly because Katherine's death had driven me to this moment.

Partly because I knew that if I didn't choose this path, I would be assassinated.

Could possibly still be assassinated.

I will protect
And I will defend.
I will stand my ground—I will not give in.
Till I draw my last breath
Or stars fall from the sky
I will sacrifice all—Even unto my life.
I am bound to this country
And this country to me.
I take the oath of Kavari—I pledge me to thee.

I kept my attention on Vladimir, ignoring the people gathered before us as he recited the oath and I repeated it. Last night he'd given me a copy to look over, as if offering me one last chance to back out, but I had already decided. I'd already made up my mind. Not that I'd had much of a choice. He'd also brought up the discussion of a ring, but I had asked to keep my father's. I wore his sword belted at my waist, the foreign weight feeling both awkward and reassuring. Elaborate braids woven into my hair by Darya were piled atop my head, the rest of it flowing freely down my back.

No fancy feast or grand event followed the ceremony. No training. Vladimir simply swore me in and that was the end of it. We were leaving. Headed for war.

"You're good with people," Vladimir said as the room emptied. "I suggested to the council that you work in foreign affairs as Marco did, and serve the people as Katherine did."

I nodded. The only place I'd ever been outside of Gharridan was Brenden, but I was willing to learn. Willing to do whatever it took.

"One day, if there's time …" He trailed off.

If we survive this war was what he didn't say. And he left the conversation at that.

There wasn't time for training, wasn't time for discussion, and we left at first light the following day.

They'd been exercising Stryder when I couldn't make it down to the stables, but he'd regained what weight he lost and then some. I gave him the eye as I tightened the girth two notches larger than I used to. We were down to only a few battalions. Shouting soldiers, creaking wagons, and stomping hooves surrounded me as I double-checked to make sure that I had everything I needed.

All appeared to be good.

Vladimir had briefly tried to force me to stay, but I quickly shut him up by saying I thought I was supposed to be an ambassador, and wouldn't this entangle into foreign affairs?

The plan was for William and Othello to start out at the head of the company, then quickly shed his royal cloak and fall to the center of the group, blending in with all the other soldiers. Vladimir knew the Brenden assassins would be back, and he didn't want it to be easy for them to pick William out.

Getting the rest of the military ready and finally leaving took longer than I expected, but once we were finally moving, I knew we wouldn't stop until nightfall. A sense of uneasiness settled over me as I realized that I would be one of the only women in the camp. It quickly vanished when Darya rode up beside me.

"What are you doing here?" I asked.

She threw me an incredulous look. "I'm a courier. How do you think they get messages between the regiments back so quickly when they can't use falcons?"

"I thought maybe you'd retired after your last mission."

She scrunched up her nose. "Yes it was long, and yes it was unpleasant, but I don't like staying in one place for too long. I would make a terrible housewife, and the men in my life know that. I still have to eat somehow."

I let out a little laugh. She was always so straightforward, so brash. Not afraid to say what she thought or of what others might think of her.

"What about you?" she asked.

"Me?"

She glanced around. "I don't see anyone else being a part of this conversation. You took the oath of Kavari. That's no small thing. Did you do it because you wanted to do it or because you felt like you needed to do it?"

My immediate thought was because I wanted to do it, but that wasn't the whole truth. "Honestly?" I said. "Both."

She accepted my answer.

"I'm sorry, is this woman bothering you, Miss *Kavari?*"

Nic trotted up beside us, a mischievous glint in his eyes.

"If you move your horse one foot closer, we will only be fifteen feet apart. I warned you that if you came within fifteen feet of me again—"

"I already told you that it was an *accident,* Darya. I didn't know you were standing there, and I'd already swung the pitchfork—"

"Did you know that was my favorite dress?" She glared at Nic. "I had to leave it behind because it still smelled like—"

"I'm sorry it was your favorite, but I'm sure you have plenty of—"

"My mother made it for me, spent precious money on the fabric, and—"

Nic let out a sigh. "How would you like me to make it up to you, Darya?"

She turned her head, and I caught her trying to hide a smirk. "I suppose if you brought me fresh water to wash my face with every morning, I *might* consider forgetting about the incident. Mind that I said *might*. There's no promises."

Nic shot her a glare in return. "Anything else her royal highness would require in a *battle camp*?"

Darya lifted her chin. "Now that you mention it—"

"No," Nic cut in. "I'll make sure you have fresh water. That's the only deal I'm making you." He turned to me. "Taryn, congratulations. We're so honored for you to join the ranks of the Kavari, although I do apologize for some of the company you're forced to keep. Most of us have far better manners."

He'd grinned and reined his horse away before Darya could fire something back at him.

She shook her head. "I think he and my brother were twins separated at birth."

I watched him ride out of earshot before peering at Darya. "That wasn't your favorite dress, was it?"

She scoffed. "Heavens no. I hated that thing. It was so scratchy and itchy. I was more than glad to have a reason to be rid of it. What person in their right mind would wear their favorite dress to the *stable* of all places?"

I couldn't hide my smile.

"Nic's ignorance just earned me an extra ten minutes of sleep every morning. I couldn't have worked it out better myself."

CHAPTER FORTY-FOUR

VLADIMIR

TRAVELING WITH THE army nearly made me go crazy. There were too many people, too many logistics, too much baggage to carry. I could make the distance by myself in half the time. More than that, I craved the subtlety one could get away with by traveling alone. You could easily miss one person slipping through the woods. You couldn't miss an entire army.

I positioned scouts in every direction. There were enough men to keep our security at the highest standards.

Multiple times I found myself turning to look for Katherine, wanting to ask her opinion or run something by her, but then with the sinking feeling of loss, I realized that she was gone, and I would never be able to speak with her again. The crushing grief threatened to drown me, and I was barely able to keep it at bay.

Every worry pressed down upon me, but the greatest was war, looming before me like an angry storm awaiting to unleash its wrath upon the world.

I found myself glancing at Taryn as we rode. I'd come up beside her a few times, and we spoke in low voices about certain matters of government, but other than that I had kept my distance. Originally, I'd planned for her to stay behind in the castle, but she'd quickly outsmarted that. Assassins would be back for her, not that city walls had protected her or William much since the attempts, but there was something far more open out here, even surrounded by a massive army. I worried it would be far too easy for them to slip through and infiltrate our ranks. Taryn hadn't seemed concerned when I'd brought it up, and I'd been mulling that over ever since. Before, she'd been anxious about the assassins. I'd seen her try to hide it, but now all of that was gone. She brushed it off when mentioned.

Something had changed. Or she knew something, but she wasn't telling me what.

"Don't look too cheerful now, boss. Someone might think you're in danger of smiling."

I frowned at Nic. Why did everyone always think I looked grumpy?

"I'm sure you're also having the time of your life, Nic," I said.

He grinned. "It may be slow, but I find this far more entertaining than being stuck at the palace like sitting ducks. I know we're probably all marching to our deaths, but it's not winter, and there's campfires every night. Food could be better, but it's not too shabby for war camp food—"

I shook my head, unable to suppress the grin spreading across my face as Nic droned on and on. I hoped he would stay this way. Keep his optimistic perspective before the horrors of the world tried to strip him of it. We needed more people like him.

"Nic?" I said when he finally paused for breath.

"Yes, boss?"

I glanced around, making sure we wouldn't be overheard. "I want you to be my eyes and ears in this camp. Be nosy and figure out what's going on. Anything happens, anything odd, anything of note, I want to hear about it."

He nodded, giving me a knowing look. "So I'll kind of be like your personal spy?"

"You're way too obvious to be a spy, Nic, but you're good with people and changing the tone in a room."

"You don't think I could be a spy?" He threw me an offended look.

I deadpanned. "I know you can't."

He scowled. "I'll take that as a challenge."

Despite the worries that nagged at me, everything progressed smoothly.

Until the third night.

I awoke to screams that sent the entire camp into an uproar.

Grogginess masked my eyes as I stumbled from my tent, strapping on my sword belt. Soldiers emerged from between the canvas flaps of their tents with drawn swords and strung bows, just as confused as I was but still looking for a fight. It took me a moment to figure out that the screams were consolidated—and that they were coming from Taryn's tent.

I stumbled over, throwing a look at the guards just standing there, noting that they'd been her guards in the palace as well.

"It's normal, boss," one said.

I motioned for them to dismiss those who had been awakened and pushed into the tent, fumbling through the darkness and running into the edge of the cot. I muttered under my breath, watching as Taryn thrashed beneath the blanket, crying out—

"KATHERINE!"

The name stilled me, enveloped me in a trance, those moments when I had watched the life slip away from her. I shook myself out of it, grabbing Taryn's arms and trying to keep her from hurting herself. She fought against me, and I called her name over and over again to draw her attention, louder each time until she finally startled awake in a fit of tears.

Ragged gasps escaped her throat as she took in her surroundings before relaxing and trying to calm down.

"I'm okay," she managed, and tried to push me away.

"Taryn—"

"I'm okay," she said, more as a way of assuring herself, embarrassment flashing across her face. "Please go. I'll be fine."

I hesitated.

She thought she was fine, but I knew better. This wasn't normal. And it wasn't getting better anytime soon.

"Vladimir," she pleaded. "Please. Go."

So I did.

But I'd seen the lines on her wrist, multiplying and growing darker. She was in denial, but I knew it was only a matter of time.

CHAPTER FORTY-FIVE

WELL.

Isn't this a twist in the story.

Perhaps I won't *kill you.*

The assassin's words ghosted through my mind, chilling me. Riding with the army provided plenty of time for analyzing and thinking. Sorting out all the pieces of the puzzle.

Even for his apology, I knew that he would have done it. Would have ended me right there.

But he didn't.

Not because he didn't want to.

He'd made peace with assassinating me—until he learned I was to be a Kavari.

Could it be the missing piece? Why my father could always live openly, but my mother and I were hidden away. Why he'd wanted me to join him, trained me to. My mother's family, whatever they were, could not touch me as a Kavari.

But that still raised the question, Why the poison?

Unless, because I hadn't been a Kavari yet, that skirted around whatever moral rule or vow that held them back.

My father broke the oath, Michael.

Her family held to something, some strong form of conviction.

When I'd asked him about the poison, he'd said that *he* didn't have a cure, not that there *wasn't* a cure, and that if I ever came to Dalendria, I was to come in white.

It was either the answer to all of my problems, or a lure to a bigger trap. Wandering in blindly sounded like a death sentence, but as I stared down at the insides of my wrist, at the black lines twisting beneath the surface, I knew that I might not have a choice. Not if I wanted to live beyond this war. It wasn't going to go away or get better on its own.

"If you think any harder, you'll think yourself into unconsciousness." Darya rode beside me on her palomino.

"You're just jealous because you're bored."

She shrugged. "Maybe I can help you work it out. You look like the stable master just gave you a pile of tangled tack to sort."

I chewed on my lip. Katherine was who I'd talked about this with. I wasn't sure I was ready to open up about it to someone else, but I'd been drawn to Darya these past few days. We'd taken solace in one another, both required to be here but neither sure what to do.

"Do you know anything about the City of Iso?" I asked.

She laughed. "It may not look like it, but I know a *lot* of things, Taryn. Even about Dalendria. What would you like to know?"

She even knew the correct term for it. She was definitely hiding something. Whatever she claimed, she was far more than a simple courier or messenger. She acted like no one, but she knew everyone. A far higher intelligence hid behind her brown eyes. She spoke brashly, but she was always listening. Always calculating.

"For starters, they're sealed off from the world. How?"

She threw me an incredulous look. "You don't know anything if you don't know that."

I rolled my eyes.

"I can't say much for its earlier history, since they've been sealed off for more than a hundred years. Any rumors left are legend, but what is known is that they decided to shut their gates from the outside world and vowed to never open them again. Anyone who has ever attempted has been killed on sight."

"Why not give a warning?"

"I think the field of bones is warning enough."

I looked sharply at her.

She arched an eyebrow. "The city is surrounded by a wall two times the height of Gharridan's. The archers are never seen, but anyone who breaks the tree line and ventures toward the impenetrable gates loses their life to an arrow."

My throat went dry. How in the world was I supposed to visit Dalendria if that was what awaited me? If that *was* where my father had gone back to, then there had to be another way in. But that could take weeks, months even, assuming that I wasn't killed in the process.

"Do you know anything about their people?" I asked.

"That's where my knowledge ends. I can tell you most anything about the outside of it, but next to nothing about the inside."

"I thought you said you *knew a lot of things*, as you put it," I mimicked her words.

She tossed her hair over her shoulder. "That *is* a lot about the City of Iso. Most don't even have that knowledge."

I caught sight of Vladimir up ahead in the company. He'd spoken to me a few times, but other than that all but ignored me. Perhaps becoming a Kavari would change the dynamic between us. Except for the other night, when I'd woken half the camp with my screaming. I swallowed. It was only going to get worse from here.

CHAPTER FORTY-SIX

VLADIMIR

NEW SHOOTS OF bright green grass sprang up on the ground around us as we made our way across the landscape, the world giving way to spring. At least we wouldn't have to worry about freezing to death or crunching through snow. We'd reach the military outpost within a week. What we'd do from there, I wasn't sure.

I strode through the tents, making my way to the command tent. I'd only received the summons moments ago, the squire stating that a messenger had ridden into the camp. I ducked beneath the tent flap, finding the other military leaders already gathered inside. Taryn stood just beyond the table as if afraid to approach. She'd have to change that. Have to be more confident.

Ever since disturbing the camp in the night, she'd distanced herself from almost everyone, even me. I figured she thought people were afraid of her, but they weren't. They were worried for her, and like me no doubt felt helpless by not knowing how to help her.

"What news?" I asked.

The messenger was still panting, face flushed as he tried to stay upright. "Brenden took Fenville and Rainar. Many fled, but they are both under Brenden control. Both along the border."

Two cities.

I stared at the weathered map splayed before us on the table, my heart dropping.

"Those were two of the cities we sent extra reinforcements. How quickly did they fall?"

The messenger grimaced. "Too quickly. There were many casualties. They have weaponry, Vladimir, battle contraptions that I have never seen before. Their explosives are ten times the size of ours, and they have hooks, means of getting over walls, in quiet, stealthy ways."

My gaze met William's.

The continent had been at peace for over twenty years, but that also provided over twenty years to invent new weaponry. We would have no way of knowing what they had developed until we met in battle.

"What of their main force?" I asked.

The messenger swallowed. "We just received word that it crossed the border yesterday."

The last bit of hope within me deflated. We were behind. Late. We should have already been there, should've been there to prevent them from crossing the border.

"Casualties?" I kept my head low.

It took the messenger a moment to answer. "Total count unknown, but many, and many more wounded."

We were about to lose this war without ever meeting on the battlefield. If we couldn't defend our borders and keep them from conquering our towns and villages—

"What does the king say?" I asked.

William looked just as lost as I. Neither of us had ever faced war like this. Faced anything like this.

"Minister?" William asked.

"You want to avoid a head-on collision at all costs," the minister of war said. "Taking back those cities is essential, but if Brenden already has control, they have the upper hand of defense, which makes our job ten times harder. We need to win those cities back. Fenville especially is crucial with the major water supply running through it, and their fortified wall. That's our biggest loss of the two—or of any that we could have lost."

I chewed on my lip. "How far is it from here?"

"Four days' march."

"Do you think—" I turned to my left, seeking the familiar advice. The words died on my tongue when I found empty space.

I cleared my throat, trying to regain my thoughts. "I say we lay siege to the city at night. Take them by surprise. Are there any hidden entrances, any weak points that we could gain access through?"

The minister of war frowned. "No. Well, technically there is one, a very public one that I'm sure not even the Brendens would touch."

Repulsion coursed through me as I grimaced. "Well, if there's no other way."

CHAPTER FORTY-SEVEN

KATHERINE STARED AT me, blood dripping from her eyes like tears. I gripped the bow in my hand as my trembling fingers nocked an arrow and released it. Then another. I couldn't stop. Even though I cried. Even though I begged for mercy, my hand drew another arrow over and over again and again. Only it wasn't just Katherine. The face transformed.

It was Queen Adamara.

It was William.

Vladimir.

My parents.

Beva.

It was Helvah.

My arm reached for another arrow and stopped as if held

in place. The pain was agonizing. I had to nock the arrow, but I couldn't. And then I saw Death staring at me. The horrors I glimpsed in his depths made me scream, made me want to die to get away from them.

Someone called my name from far away, trying to get my attention, but I was stuck. I couldn't leave. Couldn't breathe. Something slapped me across the cheek, and my eyes burst open.

Vladimir bent over me in the darkness, worry creasing his brow.

No. Not darkness. Moonlight.

My vision focused on the world beyond him. I was outside of my tent. On the ground, with a crowd of soldiers around me. Every single one of them stared at me. My hands trembled. I must have woken half the camp. Heat rushed to my cheeks as I filled with embarrassment. Shame.

Vladimir whispered something to me, but I blocked it out and squirmed from his grasp, running. I didn't know where, I just knew that I needed to get away. Away from the scene, away from the looks on their faces—and away from the pictures in my mind as the arrow struck each person I loved again and again.

My feet fell to the earth like bricks of lead as they pounded against the ground. Bare feet. Something halfway between a laugh and a sob escaped my chest. I wasn't even wearing boots. At least I had a thin day dress over my shift, sparing me any more embarrassment.

By the time I made it to the edge of camp, I could barely breathe. I gasped, choking down sobs as I tried to control myself, but I kept falling back into hysterics. It felt like the life was being squeezed out of me. I couldn't draw enough air.

A hand rested on my shoulder, and I jerked away, but its grip remained.

"You need to take deep breaths, Taryn."

I wanted to obey, but I couldn't. Their faces stared at me.

"You're panicking, Taryn. Listen to my voice. I want you to breathe in as deeply as you can. Breathe in."

I tried to listen, to steady my breathing. Katherine's lifeless body swam before me as the arrow struck her again.

"Now breathe out."

Vladimir kept repeating the words, and as the minutes passed I slowly brought my breathing and my heartbeat back down to a normal speed, a sense of calm washing over me as I finally managed control of the visions.

We sat down in the shadows just outside the edge of camp with a blanket of stars spread above us. The wind tousled my hair and I ran a hand through it, trying to understand what had just come over me.

"I'm okay," I said, but I knew the words were only to reassure myself. "I'm okay. I'll be okay."

Vladimir watched me with those piercing blue eyes as if assessing the situation. Assessing me. "You're not okay, Taryn." He scooted closer. "And it's okay to not be."

The tears came then, breaking the dam. "I can still see Katherine, Vladimir. I don't—I know I took the oath, but the nightmares are getting worse, difficult to separate from reality. I don't know if you want me to do this. I don't know if I *can* do this."

"I don't think *I* can do this, and I'm not even the one having nightmares."

His words took me aback, and I searched his face but only found raw honesty. "But you're so good at it. So confident."

"Not always."

"What keeps you going?" I asked.

He gazed off into the night. "Knowing that it's the right thing to do. That if I don't do it no one else will, and if I don't do everything in my power to protect this country, people are going to get hurt. I know there are better people for the job. I know Michael could've found a better apprentice, but I'm the one he chose, and I'm the one who took the oath. And it's my responsibility to give my all, even if I fail, even if I could have been better."

"He would've been proud of you," I said. Even if I didn't know my father well, it was a fact that lodged deep in my gut. My father chose well. "And no matter what anyone says, you're not a failure. I'd like to see them do a better job in these uncharted waters. No one knows what to do."

Vladimir dipped his head, and I cocked mine. "Where did he find you, anyway? I don't think you've ever told me."

The stillness of the night assaulted me, and Vladimir's silence sent me questioning if I'd gone too far. I knew he wasn't originally from the capital, but he'd never spoken of it before.

No one had.

Vladimir's voice came out low and uncertain. "I was—"

He cut off, whether he was searching for the words or they were just too painful to speak, I couldn't tell. "When he found me, I was on trial for murder. He told me I could either train under him or hang."

I blinked, unconsciously stiffening as I stared at him, questioning everything I thought I'd known about him, but it couldn't be true. My father wouldn't have brought a murderer into the Kavari. Yet he didn't take back his words, didn't change them. He refused to meet my gaze as I sat there, waiting for him to continue.

"My father ..." Vladimir trailed off, moonlight displaying the indecision warring on his face over whether or not to continue. "I can't conjure any memory of him where he wasn't holding a flask or a bottle in his hands. He shielded his eyes from the sun with them as he stumbled to work late every morning, visited the tavern after, and when he was good and wasted, good and angry, he'd come barging back through our door with a swinging fist and a bellowing voice."

Vladimir paused, his voice falling quieter. "My mother would always stuff me beneath the bed when she heard him coming, shove anything and everything in front of me so that he wouldn't find me. So that he wouldn't hurt me. He never did, but he still looked. And I could hear—" He swallowed. "*I could hear everything.*"

He stopped. I didn't move. Couldn't move.

"I've tried to remember a day without seeing the bruises, but I can't. I praised the light of day and hated the darkness. Because the darkness meant fear. Darkness meant pain, and it never went away until the light returned in the morning. The reek of alcohol always infiltrated my nose, filled my senses. The smell meant betrayal and hurt. To this day I can barely look at it without envisioning its scars on my mother, can't pass a drunk man without wanting to vomit at the memories they conjure.

"There was one time, when I was eight, I plucked up enough courage to scurry from my hiding spot and try to stop him. I had just wanted it to stop, wanted to help her. My entire face was swollen the next day. My mother made me swear that I would never *ever* leave my hiding spot again, that I would never interfere, saying that she could endure the pain, but she could not endure seeing me in pain.

"There were times when I asked her why we couldn't leave, hide, go somewhere else, but she simply confided in me that he was all she ever had. She didn't have anyone, anything else, and she didn't know how to leave, how to feed and take care of us if she did, even though I begged her repeatedly. For her own sake."

I swallowed, unable to imagine being so alone that you had no way out of a situation so horrible. Vladimir's face betrayed no emotions, but they clustered in his voice and in his pauses between words.

"Once I was old enough, I started making my own plans and found my own way to a job, to get her out of there. I had it all worked out, a job for both her and I, and a small room to live in. It was little more than a closet and we'd have to leave everything, but I didn't care. I just wanted her out. I was twelve. I told her my plan, and after much persuasion and assurance I got her to agree to it. She said to give her that night, and she would be ready to leave the next morning. I hugged her tightly—"

Vladimir's voice cracked, and my chest constricted.

"And I left, to tie up a few loose ends, to make sure everything was secure and in place. I wasn't gone but for an hour or two and when I—" He struggled to get the words out. "When I … when I got back, the house was turned inside out. All of the furniture was smashed, and amid the devastation, I found her, found—"

Tears rolled down my cheeks as his broken voice continued.

"She had told him. I knew she had. Why, I'm not sure. She had to have known how he would react, but nevertheless she had given it away. Maybe he'd seen her packing. I don't know."

He trailed off, staring at the ground, anger replacing the pain that had been there only moments ago. "I left the house, rage controlling me, and I swore that I wouldn't come back for her body until he was dead. Until I had killed him. When I arrived at the tavern, I found him in a room upstairs entangled with someone else. I ripped him off, tried to do to him what he had done to her, but he was bigger. Stronger. I didn't stand a chance, except for the anger that burned within me. We crashed into the hall, fists flying. He broke three of my ribs, cracked my jaw, but there was one moment when I managed to shove him off. And the stairs were there. I watched. Watched as he fell back, head over feet, down the stairs, all the way to the bottom where he snapped his neck."

Vladimir stopped, as if reliving the memory, as if trying to make sense of it.

"As I watched him fall, I've never been filled with such a satisfaction in my entire life, but it was quickly replaced by guilt. Because I knew that my mother would have been disappointed in me. She would have chided me for allowing the hate to control me like it had controlled my father, and in that moment, I didn't care anymore. Technically, it was an accident. I hadn't realized how close to the stairs we were, but my father's drinking buddies pinned the murder on me, and when they discovered my mother's body, they blamed me for that too.

"I wouldn't talk to anyone, wouldn't speak. I was given an unfair trial, and then another because I didn't defend myself in the first. After they convicted me and I was sitting in a prison cell awaiting my execution, Michael, your father, walked in. He'd somehow gotten wind of the boy who murdered both of his parents. Michael had an intuition for things that just weren't quite right.

"He postponed the hanging, and came to talk with me every day. I didn't want him there. I was ready for the gallows, ready for it all to be over with, but he wouldn't let it go. He—" Vladimir swallowed. "He got me in a way that nobody else ever had, and he somehow pried the truth from my lips. I thought I would be in trouble, that it would do absolutely nothing, but he gave me a choice. He said I could either go to the gallows, let all of it be over with, or I could return to the capital with him and train to become a Kavari."

Empathy rushed through me as I understood Vladimir in a way I thought I never could.

"I tell you all that not for pity, but to say I felt completely inadequate the entire time I was training. Michael always saw something in me, but I never could. I let my circumstances and my past dictate how far I could go in life, but the truth is, Taryn …" He met my eyes. "I will never be adequate. None of us ever will be, but we were tasked with the job of protecting Gharridan, of protecting its people, and it's up to us to do the best with what we've been given."

I nodded, trying to find the key in his words. I wanted to say I was sorry, but that didn't seem right. So instead I curled my arms around my knees, looking out into the darkness.

"Thank you for sharing that with me, Vladimir," I said.

How horrible of a person I must have seemed to Vladimir when I first met him. While the relationship wasn't without issues and things I still didn't understand, I was blessed with a father I knew had loved me. Had cared for me, and I'd nearly thrown it all away, wanted nothing to do with him, whereas Vladimir had grown up with nothing of the sort. He'd been raised in fear. Raised in a situation that no child should ever have to experience, let alone live through.

He moved as if to rise, but I laid a hand on his arm, stopping him. "Please don't go. Not yet."

So he stayed.

I didn't want to sleep, and he looked too preoccupied to, so I asked him about my father, about the good memories he made later in life. Somewhere in the conversation, I started sharing my memories too, and for a few moments it was as if the rest of the world and all of its problems disappeared. I found myself gravitating toward him in the chill until our shoulders were brushing. He relinquished a small smile as he spoke, his blue eyes catching mine. The openness surprised me, but also brought comfort, and my mind strayed back to the night in the library when he'd pinned me with his dagger, the look that had crossed his face. He would have kissed me, but the restraint pulled him back, and I wondered if I would have let him. I entertained the thought as we spoke, let it pool through me, but I couldn't say that was what I wanted.

And it didn't matter, because as dawn began to wake the world and the camp started stirring behind us, I was reminded that it didn't matter what I wanted in life, because after this war, I might not even have one to live.

CHAPTER FORTY-EIGHT

VLADIMIR

ARKNESS CLOAKED OUR force from foreign eyes as we approached Fenville. The dead of night hung around us like a mighty shield, but I feared the threat of dawn that lingered only a few hours away. I studied the city, working through our plan in my mind. Woods surrounded Fenville on every side, making hiding our army easy among the close-packed trees. If we could sneak past the guards and get into the sewer system without being detected, we might have a chance, but getting that far would mean riding on little more than a hope and a prayer. *If* we managed to get the gates open, our success depended on keeping them open long enough for our soldiers to pass through without getting cut down—but those moments of getting to the gates and getting through them were crucial. Lights burned along the city's walls, but I couldn't make out any patrolling guards from this distance.

I glanced at the men behind me, both disappointed and relieved with my options. I'd ordered William to stay at the camp, leaving him behind in a cloud of anger and frustration, but I wouldn't risk him being recognized in battle. Not yet. I wanted a better idea of what we were up against first. The main camp could offer him more protection than our battalion, especially with the assassins still chasing after him.

I'd ordered Nic to stay behind as well, which left me feeling like I was missing my right arm, but I needed someone I trusted to keep watch within the camp, someone who could get into the inner workings, and I trusted no one more than him.

"When are we going in?"

I frowned at Taryn's voice next to me. Getting her to stay behind had proved too large of a challenge.

"*We're* not going anywhere," I whispered. "You already argued your way this far. I don't like us all clumped together if we don't have to be, especially when we still don't know Brenden's master plan, which is why William is back at the camp."

I sensed a retort rising in her, but it never came. What did come was the memories of the other night flooding my mind. I don't know why I'd brought up my parents. I'd only ever shared that part of me with Michael and Katherine—and Katherine hadn't even known the entirety of it—but something about Taryn released words and parts of me that were always meant to stay hidden. Always meant to stay stored in a dark hovel within me no one could ever find. But those perceptive green eyes and discerning voice reached farther than they should. Farther than I ever should have allowed them to.

"Besides," I continued, "I need you to be my eyes and ears up here for anything that goes wrong, and if this goes south"—I turned to her—"you fly back to camp to tell William what happened. And you don't look back."

Defiance sparked in her eyes, but I admired it. I wouldn't like the idea of leaving us behind either.

"I need you to promise that you will."

She looked away. "You know I'm good for it."

Actually, I didn't. She was stubborn as a mule, never listened, and tended to act without taking her head along with her. It drove me insane, but maybe that was because I tended to think with my head *too* much, which was why even though she made me want to pull my hair out sometimes, her resilience was one of the things I liked about her.

I walked away from the thought, concerned by how her presence was becoming a distraction to me.

I motioned to the four soldiers I'd previously picked, then whispered instructions to the commanders, verifying that everything was ready to go. Our chances of failure were much higher than success, but none of us voiced the reality of the situation. Either we would make it out, or we wouldn't.

We crept away from our hidden battalion, the five of us moving like wraiths in the night. We knew the prints of the city, had spent hours studying them last night, knew exactly where the sewage came out, where it joined with the creek that flowed to the river.

If any guards patrolled the wall, it would be difficult to see us with the burning lights. I doubted they would have that high of security; the city was theirs. As far as they knew, no Gharridan army was in sight, but we had to prepare for everything.

We lingered at the tree line, surveying our options before stepping out into the open. Clouds cloaked the moon, leaving our world darker than normal and aiding us in our operation, but we were still sitting ducks. Our footfalls whispered through the grass as we sprinted toward the wall, but no shout came from above, no arrows flew to impale us.

One step down.

When we reached the shadow of the wall and I saw how small the entrance was, I shook my head and begged for mercy. We'd be on hands and knees. The distasteful reality flashed across each of our features as we exchanged glances, and then I finally gave the nod, grimacing in apology before hunkering down to crawl into the hole. At the first splash, the first sensation of substances, I forced my mind somewhere else, forced it to not think of what I was crawling through even as I gagged. I somehow managed to retain the contents of my stomach, though I heard two of the men behind me lose theirs.

With each agonizing shuffle forward, the tunnel seemed like it stretched for miles, even though I knew it didn't. After about twenty feet, it expanded enough to where we could walk hunched over instead of crawling. The smells assaulting me were so strong and foul I wondered if I would ever smell right again.

I slowed, seeing the entrance of the sewage drain that would be our exit. The group halted behind me, and we waited. I counted several breaths before inching close enough to get my first glimpse into the streets, searching and listening for anything that could hinder us, harm us. All stood quiet. From my vantage point I saw no lights in the houses or on the streets. The city slept, but I was surprised the occupation appeared to have left it so peaceful.

When I found no reason to delay any longer, we crawled our way out into the street one at a time, smelling like rotten flesh and feces, the odor clinging to us like death.

Two steps down.

We became one with the shadows in the alleyways, the cool night air touching our wet skin, sending shivers down our spines. With each street conquered, hope rose within me. We might actually have a chance. I kept glancing around, unnerved at the lack of lights or people. The Gharridans wouldn't have let the Brendens overtake the city without a fight, without a battle, but I saw no evidence of such a thing.

We continued maneuvering through the city until we turned a corner and the gatehouse came into view.

Three steps down.

One Brenden guarded the gate levers, and I frowned at the lack of security. Were they really that confident? I signaled one of the men and they slunk around until they were in a position to knock the man out. The Brenden crumpled to the ground, but it didn't trigger any other guards. Unease crept into my gut even as we moved closer to our goal.

Four steps down.

Movement caught my eye along the wall, and I held the men back, afraid we'd been spotted, but whatever it was had disappeared. Being this close, we couldn't afford to hold off any longer.

"Quickly," I whispered.

Two kept watch with drawn swords while three of us pulled the crank on the gate. A loud, screeching groan reverberated off the walls, drawing shouts from above as the gates slowly swung open.

Come on. Come on.

The dark cloud of the Gharridan army flew toward us from outside the gates, and I allowed myself a small smile.

Five steps down.

One more to go.

We were actually going to pull this off.

The once-quiet city exploded to life around us with the scrape of swords against leather sheaths and the clank of armor as troops rushed down stairs, but we had the advantage. They weren't prepared. Torches drifted down from the outer wall, the Brendens gathering together. I drew my sword as the first line of Gharridans poured through the gate while letting out a wild bellow as they charged into the city.

So much for the element of surprise, but they'd been expecting to immediately meet swords. The Brendens who'd begun to gather turned tail and ran, delving farther into the city as our men chased after them, ready to take back what was ours. My gaze darted to the rooftops, searching for archers, for an ambush, but there was none.

No military strategist in their right mind would have left a besieged city this vulnerable. I moved with the men, strangely aware that something was wrong. No faces peeked out of windows, no lanterns were lit beneath the doors at the sudden commotion. All was silent, and even the Brendens we were chasing seemed to be vanishing into thin air.

Something was *wrong*.

Something was *very* wrong.

I caught sight of a Brenden, racing after him only to watch as he lurched toward a rope swinging down from the outer wall, scrambling up it before both he and the rope disappeared over the other side. What was going on? I scanned the alleyway to investigate and froze, my eyes landing on a dark-clad man standing in torchlight, his gaze fixed on me.

Black lined his eyes, his features difficult to make out in the dark, but I would have recognized him anywhere. Every thought in my mind disintegrated as I let the anger unfurl within me, and I lunged forward, sword arced at the assassin responsible for Katherine's death.

CHAPTER FORTY-NINE

TARYN

I HATED WAITING.

I also hated being told what to do, even if I saw the logic in Vladimir's thinking.

I started out on Stryder, but dismounted after only a few minutes, unable to sit still. I paced beside him, biting at my nails. A small irritation pulsed through me at being sequestered to the hillside, but secretly I wasn't disappointed. I had no desire to trudge through the excrement they were in.

I just *also* hated being out of the loop.

While I tried not to think of it, I knew how skeptical Vladimir was about this mission, even if he didn't show it. I even knew how big of a gamble it was. We just didn't have another choice. Around me, the soldiers stood ready with their swords drawn, waiting to run for it at the first sign of movement from the gates.

But nothing happened.

The minutes stretched on until I wondered if it had been hours. Though my eyes were completely adjusted to the darkness, it was still difficult to see, so I didn't know if they'd crossed to the sewage drain yet. My heart pounded. They could've been caught. Could already be dead.

I placed a hand on the hilt of my father's sword hanging at my side. The last thing I wanted to do was have to turn and run if this entire operation failed.

The massive gates let out a groan, creaking outward, and the men to the left of me rushed forward without hesitation, racing softly across the grass like a herd of bounding deer and getting louder as they picked up speed the closer they got. Within a minute, they were pouring into the city with battle cries, surging forward into whatever lay beyond the gates.

I let out a deep breath, allowing myself a tiny twinge of relief as I watched by myself from the hillside.

But it didn't last.

I stepped closer.

It was quiet.

Too quiet.

There should be the clash of steel against steel, the rage of battle, but all I continued to hear was the roar of the men and the fading pounding of their feet.

A rustle came from the right of me and I whipped out my sword, searching the darkness in alarm. I squinted into the forest. It could have been an animal, but we surely would have scared them off by—

Something—someone—stepped out from the trees with

trembling hands. My fear spiked, but then they moved closer. It was a girl, no older than fourteen, with a wild look in her eyes, arms raised in surrender. It looked like she'd rolled in the mud, grass and dirt clinging to her like sweat. The hem of her dress was shredded, her plated hair falling out of its braid and frizzing around her face.

"Who are you?" I demanded. "What are you doing here?"

"They shouldn't be going in there," she said, fear lacing her words. She spoke Gharridan with no hint of a Brenden accent.

"Why?" I asked. I debated taking my eyes off her before throwing a quick glance at the city, catching sight of shapes and shadows shimmying down the walls and bounding away from the city, heading for the woods. Confusion washed over me.

"Because the men are in the woods," she said, stepping closer. "I've been hiding in the trees for days, was up high enough that I saw your army approaching earlier. I would've come sooner, but I only just managed to work my way around them."

Fear roiled in the pit of my stomach. "Got around who? Which men are in the trees?"

"The Brendens." She turned urgent, speaking faster. "The men who attacked our city. I climbed a tree and watched it happen. They marched everyone out and took them somewhere. I was too scared to move, so I watched them and saw the Brendens retreat into the woods earlier in the night."

My fear struck face swung back to the city and I involuntarily took a few steps forward. Questioning. Wondering. My mind shot to Vladimir, who was unaware that this was all a trap. That was why there was no sound of weapons. The Brendens had their own plan. They had known we were coming. But how? And why had they moved the people?

Two heartbeats later, my answer came.

CHAPTER FIFTY

VLADIMIR

REASON LEFT ME. Left me with nothing but rage as I charged toward the man, followed him deeper into the city, past shuttered windows and up and down dark alleys. I'd lost him once. I wouldn't lose him again. His face was branded into my mind. The face of the man who took Katherine from this world. The memory of her death flashed before me, her skin pale, dress drenched in blood, hand lifted to heal the injury on my face.

Did—did you get him?

I couldn't see anything, couldn't think anything other than that this man needed to die. Needed to pay for what he had done. The rage took control, driving me forward.

I only wish I could have served it better.

I rounded a corner and the assassin spun with unnatural

speed, shooting a knife toward me that I easily dodged. He drew another, backing out of my reach.

"Your king," he said. "Is he here?"

I shook my head, blood boiling. "No, but I am."

I swung at him, and he contorted around my blade. He held no weapon of his own besides the knives in his hands that easily parried my blows, sparks flying off the metal. The clash of steel ricocheted off the walls. I forced him backward, coming at him again and again, but he was always just out of reach, just far enough away from the sharp edges and tip of my sword. His knives deflected my blade, scraped down its sides, forcing it away, forcing me into defeat.

You're the leader of the Kavari, Vladimir. Act like it.

Frustration overcame me as Katherine's voice echoed in my head, pushing me harder, but then sense started to pool in my mind, warning me that this was off. Something wasn't right. I focused on the fight, trying to take control of the rage, trying to calm my mind. I studied him, tried to guess his thoughts and intentions.

I misstepped.

Panic jolted through me, but he made no move. Didn't even react.

He could have easily struck a fatal blow or thrown one of his knives into my jugular with what I'd just left exposed, but he hadn't. He'd let it happen, then acted like it never did.

I lurched back, my chest heaving with exertion, my weapon heavy in my hands.

He was *playing* with me.

"You're stalling," I called him out.

A smile turned up one corner of his mouth but never

reached his eyes. "That's because it's not time."

Goosebumps traveled up my arms like a disease, the hair on the back of my neck prickling.

We'd misjudged this. Whatever was going on, he was multiple steps ahead. I tentatively glanced around, wary of what Brenden had planned.

"Time for what?" I asked.

He glanced up at the wall before pulling a missive from his pocket and throwing it at me. "When you return to your king, we have another proposal for him. I predict he'll be much more willing to speak with us after tonight."

After tonight?

Without ever taking my eyes from him, I picked up the folded missive and tucked it into my jerkin.

"A proposition for what?"

A rope flew into my peripheral vision, falling down along the wall. Without missing a beat, the assassin jumped for it, propelling himself up the stone wall even as the rope was lifted from the other side. I raced forward but could only stare in shock before searching for a way up myself, but there was none.

I whirled.

Why was the city empty?

Why were the Brendens disappearing over the walls of a city they'd besieged?

I took a step toward the alleyway, and the world around me exploded with flames and smoke, the force ripping me off my feet and sending my back and head crashing against the stones of the wall. Then I descended into darkness.

CHAPTER FIFTY-ONE

TARYN

THE GROUND TREMBLED beneath me, and I stumbled backward, trying to keep my balance. The heat rushed toward us. Stryder and Dante reared in fright, the whites of their eyes reflecting off the light of the fire. I lurched for the reins, grasping them and digging my heels into the dirt as the strength and fear of the two horses nearly lifted me off my feet. I barely kept them under control as they tried to bolt with the other horses.

"Easy," I crooned, but I couldn't hide my fear from them.

I finally got them back to all fours, trying to keep them in place as they pranced beside me, still wanting to flee.

My wide eyes stared at the city in horror as buildings collapsed within themselves, fire engulfing the remnants of the town as a mixture of smoke, ash, and dust billowed into the air like an ominous cloud. The darkness from the rubble blacked out almost the entire sky.

Tears collected in my eyes, shock holding my body hostage.

Brenden soldiers flooded out of the woods, surrounding the city on all sides and cutting down any of the Gharridan soldiers that managed to escape the carnage within.

I tried to wrap my head around it, tried to comprehend what had just happened, but I couldn't.

All I could do was gape.

Vladimir.

My chest ached, the pain threatening to split it open.

And then the Brendens spotted us, running toward us, the flames now illuminating us in what had once been shadows.

"Here!" I thrust Dante's reins into the girl's hands and helped her swing up into the saddle.

Both horses still jittered, and I jammed my foot into the stirrup, Stryder circling around me as I hopped on one foot, following him before I had enough leverage to swing onto his back. I gathered the leather reins in my hands, shooting one last look at the burning city behind us.

Vladimir's face filled my mind, a million moments, a million questions, but there was nothing I could do. No way I could get to him. No way I could save him even on the slim hope that he was still alive.

I need you to promise that you will.

I had to return to William. The king. Return to the army, to tell them what happened. To tell them that their comrades were dead. To warn them Brenden was a far more cunning enemy than we had ever imagined. To sever their hope.

"Hold on tight and follow me," I instructed the girl.

I dug my heels into Stryder's sides, sending him flying forward into the night and leaving everyone and everything except my shattered heart behind.

Every time I glanced at the girl beside me, she was hunkered low on Dante's back, hands threaded into his mane while her wobbly legs clutched too far back on his sides. She'd clearly not had much experience with horses and was doing everything possible to keep from tumbling off his back. I don't know what I would do if she did, because the Brenden soldiers pursued us farther than I thought they would.

I veered the horses north, searching for the small stream we'd passed that I knew ran nearby. It wasn't much, but it might confuse them enough to let us get away or encourage them to just give up. We found the river, and Stryder's hooves pounding through the surface sent a spray of water splashing around us. The rising sun sent streaks of color spreading across the sky, lighting our way but also making us easy to spot from a distance now. At least the landscape in this area was fairly wooded.

Once a ways up stream, we left the water and I questioned which way to go. I'd been drilled on the way to get back to the main camp, but I also knew where we had planned for stragglers to rendezvous if something went wrong. I warred with myself, knowing I should rush back and alert the main force, but if there was any chance—

I swallowed the lump in my throat, trying to deny the possibility that Vladimir—that he was—

I urged Stryder forward, making up my mind. If I didn't see

anyone by tomorrow morning, then I would go back.

The taste and smell of smoke still clung to my tongue and lingered in my nose.

All those people.

People I had known.

Dead.

I pushed the thoughts from my mind, trying to stay numb to the truth. I glanced at the girl beside me, debating what we were even going to do with her once we got back. She couldn't reside in the midst of a war camp, she was barely older than a child. But we couldn't send her off on her own and risk leaving her to the mercy of the Brendens either.

We made it to the outcrop by midday, and I spent the next few hours searching every direction for any sign of life or danger. Once evening fell, I retreated under the cover of the rock face, trying to keep the rising panic at bay. I split a few wrapped pieces of meat I had with the girl and questioned her about what had happened.

Her eyes darted around as she spoke, arms crossed tightly across her chest. She was like a wounded animal, cornered and controlled by fear. She'd been out picking berries when the Brendens attacked the city. She'd ended up stuck in a ditch in the trees, hiding from the Brenden scouts patrolling the woods.

"I couldn't escape," she said. "I was too afraid of being caught. Two days later they were marching the people south, out of the city, and I knew something was terribly wrong. I scurried up a tree and hid there for a while as I decided whether or not to make a run for it. The soldiers disappeared up the trees too, and when I saw your army coming, saw the Gharridan flag, I knew that I had to warn you."

I wrapped my tired arms around my legs, my mind racing. Brenden knew we were coming. They'd planned this. Planned from the beginning to ultimately destroy our army with no mercy. I knew it was war, knew that war was cruel, but it was one thing to know that in your head and another thing entirely to see it lived out in front of you. I sifted through the faces of the soldiers I remembered, trying to recall which ones had gone on the mission and which ones had stayed behind. Courage had radiated from our force in the face of death, but none of us could have imagined what it would look like. If this was what we were up against, then for all of our good spirits and hope, we didn't stand a chance.

I closed my eyes, only to have visions of Vladimir's charred body assault my mind. The light gone from his pale blue eyes.

No one came that afternoon or evening, not even when the world descended into night, but the horrors of what lay behind us in the city assaulted my mind. Both awake and both in dreams when I finally slipped off to sleep.

My dreams took me to the center of Fenville, where I was surrounded by hundreds of burning and screaming Gharridans, all of them asking me why. Why I had left. Why I hadn't helped them. The black lines on my wrists transformed into shackles that held me in place and wouldn't let me leave. Wouldn't let me help.

I startled awake, the girl shaking my shoulder, terror filling her moonlit eyes.

"I'm sorry," I said, and then I apologized again. "It was just a nightmare. I'm sorry if I scared you."

She held a finger to her lips, shaking her head and glancing off into the distance.

That jolted me out of my panic, and I snatched the dagger from my boot, questioning the distance to my sword lying across the saddle bags. I peered out into the night, trying to pick out what she had seen, and then I heard the hoofbeats of a horse.

We were not alone.

CHAPTER FIFTY-TWO

VLADIMIR

EVERYTHING IN MY body ached like I'd tumbled off the edge of a cliff and landed in a sea of sharp rocks. Maybe I had. Maybe every bone in my body was broken. My hearing was muffled, overrun by a constant ringing that made my head spin and wouldn't go away.

And I was moving.

Rough gravel scraped across my back as someone or something dragged me away.

Grit stuck in my mouth, heat flared all around me, screams reverberated off the walls, smoke polluted the air. The sensation of being hauled like a dead animal stopped, but dizziness still swarmed me like I was lost in a roiling sea. Nausea rose within me. I might puke. Loud voices perforated the muffled ringing, making me grimace in pain. My side and back screamed with the pain.

I forced my eyes open, immediately disoriented as I struggled to get my bearings, my vision fuzzy at first. Dark monstrous shapes surrounded me, circling like vultures as they moved in and out of my peripheral vision. Spears. Flashes of red and gold. Sabers.

Soldiers.

Brendens.

Enemies.

"You smell like—"

A tsunami of water dumped over my head, drowning out the rest of the Brenden's words. I rolled onto my side, grimacing at the pain as I sputtered to get the water out of my throat and eyes.

I know, I wanted to say in reply.

I tottered to my feet, suddenly aware of the weight of my weapon still sheathed in my sword belt. Somewhere close by a horse whinnied. I reached for the hilt but a hand stopped me. I looked up, barely staying on my feet through the pain and confusion. Black-outlined eyes filled my vision. No emotion swam within their depths.

The ringing in my ears faded, but I could hardly hear out of my right one. The assassin gripped my collar, his other hand patting the top of my chest. I should push him away, kill him, but I couldn't focus. Couldn't think.

"You have a job to do. Take the proposal to your king, and then give us your answer."

Proposal?

I recalled the missive I'd stuffed into my jerkin just before the explosion.

The explosion.

Taryn.

The men, had they—

"You now know what we're capable of," he continued. "I suggest your king consider wisely before refusing."

He shoved me away into a horse coated in soot.

"Now go, Kavari, and don't look back."

My foot reached for the stirrup, but I had no balance and nearly fell beneath the horse's hooves. Someone prodded me from behind and shoved me up into the saddle, forcing the reins into my hands. They were just going to let me leave. What in the world was this proposal? I heard a smack on the horse's rump and gripped his sides with my legs as the animal took off with me. Clarity returned one fragment at a time, and I turned to see where fire and smoke and ash still billowed behind me.

Everything came back, the weight of it heavy enough to flatten a mountain as the events that transpired—the deaths, the implications—crashed down on me.

CHAPTER FIFTY-THREE

TARYN

BOTH FEAR AND hope rose within me, and I indicated for the girl to stay put as I crept around the rock, trying to get a closer look and also deciphering the fastest way out of this.

I couldn't see the horse's breath in the night, it was too warm, but there was a rider on him. The horse abruptly stopped, letting out a sigh. I heard it chewing around the bit in the following silence.

"Taryn?"

My heart skipped in my chest, the faintest flicker of possibility awakening the dormant hope within me. I took a step forward, thinking it was a trick of the night, just ghosts playing with my mind.

"Vladimir?" I called out. It couldn't be possible. I'd seen the explosions, seen the Brendens surrounding the city. He shouldn't have been able to escape it. Yet I'd come here, anyway, hadn't I?

The saddle creaked as the rider dismounted, leaning heavily against the horse for support. I rushed forward, recognizing Vladimir's form in the darkness.

He's alive. He's alive. He's alive.

I crushed him in a hug, immediately regretting it as he winced and his stench overwhelmed me. I barely managed to hold in a gag.

"You're alive, and you—" I took a step back, trying to get away from the stink.

He bent over slightly and clutched a hand to his side.

I scrunched up my nose, wanting to be close to him but at the same time very far away. "Are you okay?" I asked. "Because you don't smell okay."

"What?" He turned his other ear toward me.

I repeated the question and he shook his head. "Smell is from the sewer, pain is from the blast that threw me into a wall. I don't think any of my ribs are broken, but they're definitely bruised."

I surveyed the night-filled landscape, looking for anyone that could have followed him before leading him up to where the girl still huddled by the outcrop.

"How did you get out?" I asked.

Soot and ash covered his skin and clothes, and each step he took brought a grimace of pain. I noticed a glossy patch of hair that looked like dried blood.

He's alive.

"The Brendens dragged me out."

"What?" I spun toward him, thinking I'd misheard. "They just let you walk away?"

Vladimir settled his exhausted body on the ground, stretching out his legs. I pulled out the water canteen and offered it to him, and he took several large gulps before handing it back.

"When I was in the city, before it—" He cut off, the thought marring his features. "I saw the assassin, chased after him, but he was luring me away the whole time, from the main blast." Vladimir patted his pocket. "He gave me a proposal for the king. After the explosion they dragged me out, put me on a horse, and sent me to deliver it to him."

I stared at where his hand touched the lump in his jacket. "What is in the proposal?"

He shook his head. "I don't know yet. I want it to be opened by William."

Why would they leave Vladimir in the explosion only to pull him out? Could they not have just sent us the proposal? Whatever it was, it couldn't be good.

"Vladimir why would they …" I trailed off, unable to give voice to the reality.

Defeat weighed down on him. He dropped his head in his hands, his voice laden with emotion. "All of those men, Taryn, I led them into a trap, led them to their deaths."

I shook my head, fighting back tears. "You didn't know, Vladimir."

His hands slid to the back of his head where they fisted in his hair. Tears glossed his eyes. "But I should have known. I'm their leader. I should have died in that explosion. It's not fair, not right, that they're all dead and I'm still here alive. They trusted me. Depended on me. And I led them to their death."

The tears slipped from my eyes, leaving narrow trails through the dirt on my cheeks. I wasn't in his position, couldn't even fathom what he was going through. He knew those soldiers more personally than anyone. I'd seen him invest in them, care for them as he asked a man about his pregnant wife back home, told an older soldier of a new remedy he'd heard of for stiff joints. I'd watched him join them by the fire and take an interest in their lives, what they were most looking forward to after the war. They were his blood not by birthright but by choice, and they were the closest thing he had to family. There were no words I could offer that could take away the pain, no comfort to ease the loss. This tragedy would haunt him for the rest of his life.

I took his hand and squeezed it, not having anything else to offer. We shared the silence, the unspoken respect and admiration for those who lost their lives. Who laid down their lives, claimed by an early and unnecessary grave. Who charged into battle, taken down by the power of a monster they couldn't even defend themselves against.

"Vladimir?" I asked softly.

His pale blue eyes met mine in the darkness.

I swallowed. "I don't know what I would do if you hadn't made it out."

I'd thought he'd been dead, thought he was lost forever, but fate apparently had a way of bringing him back to me. His piercing gaze never left mine, a sea of raw emotions and vulnerability laid bare crashing within it. Maybe I'd said the wrong thing, and I almost wished that I could take it back, but I'd meant it. I'd feared losing him, and now I knew that I couldn't lose him. And I knew he saw that truth written across my face.

"Thank you," he finally said.

"For what?" I whispered.

"For leaving. For doing what needed to be done. I don't know what I would have done if you hadn't made it out either."

He held my gaze for a long while, the implication of his words rooting in me, stirring dormant feelings that never should have been disturbed and awakening possibilities that never should have been conjured. If he made me promise to leave him again, I wouldn't be able to keep it, and I would break that promise over and over again.

CHAPTER FIFTY-FOUR

TIME WAS OF the essence, but I could barely stand the smell clinging to my body and neither could anyone else. We traversed to the river, where I dunked below the surface, scrubbing as much from my skin and uniform as I possibly could. I tried to scrub away the flashes of the explosion, the screams of the men, but those stayed with me. Nothing would ever be able to remove the stains they'd left upon me.

When I returned to the girls and the horses, my clothes still dripping, their noses didn't scrunch up as much as before so at least it was better, but I could still taste it on my tongue, whether it was my imagination or not. I couldn't wait to burn my current clothes and put on a fresh set.

The smell of the fire that night filled my lungs and I nearly stumbled, haunted by the lives of the men I'd led to their deaths. Even if there had been survivors, Brenden would've wiped out any remnants.

There had been five hundred men in that battalion.

Five hundred.

All dead.

Gone.

For most, I hoped they had gone quickly, sent to the next life without realizing that they'd even left the first, and wished that none were in agony, that few had endured death by the Brendens ready to meet them at the gates. Hope for their swift deaths was all I could offer, because I'd failed them in everything else.

The scouts saw us before we reached the main camp. One rode out to meet us, and I told him to ride back, to have the king summon the war council and arrange a meeting. My gaze wandered to the young girl tagging along with us. What in the world were we going to do with her?

My side screamed with pain as I dismounted, and I winced. Each step sent a jolt of lightning through my ribs. Soldiers stared as we passed, eyes flitting behind us, looking for an army that would never return.

A grim mood overwhelmed the stuffy command tent as we entered. No one spoke. It took me a moment to open my mouth and relay what had happened. The words caused momentary shock, then uproar. I pulled the missive out of my jerkin, handing it to William.

He took it with apprehension, unfurling the crisp edges to

read what was written inside. His eyes passed over the words, halted on something he saw. He swallowed, refolded it, and placed it on the table.

"What is the proposition?" I asked.

William pushed the parchment across the table to me. I unfurled it and read the words aloud, the room falling quiet.

You have seen our power. What we are capable of. Our quarrel is with your king—but Brenden is merciful. If King William, son of King Roldan, will surrender himself to Brenden, the people and armies of Gharridan will be spared, and Brenden will retreat behind its own borders.

That was why they'd blown up the city. To demonstrate their power and to try to force our hand. If we didn't give in to their demands, they would annihilate Gharridan into nonexistence.

I looked up and watched William carefully, trying to figure out what was going on inside his head. He kept his emotions hidden well, but the gears of his mind were still turning.

I shifted my weight to the other foot, immediately regretting the movement.

"The answer is no," I stated.

"I haven't given my opinion yet," William countered.

"No, but they just offered to spare all of Gharridan in exchange for your life. Any good king would be considering it."

"And what if I'm not a good king?"

"Even if you weren't a good king, you still know that you and your mother were responsible for this war."

William's gaze darted away. "It's a reasonable offer."

"It's a trick," I retorted, "and a jab of humiliation. Do you really think that Brenden will honor their word? If they kill our king, that's a sign of utter defeat. They have won. There would be nothing left to stop them."

William shrugged. "What am I supposed to do then, Vladimir? Watch them kill my people one by one until we get to the same point? Them executing me for my crimes?"

The minister of war cleared his throat. "While it seems to make sense, I have to agree with Vladimir on this one. We cannot give in to demands, nor can we trust Brenden's word on this."

"Then what are we supposed to do?" William roared, slamming his fist on the table. "We just lost an entire battalion to an ambush that we never saw coming. How many more are they going to take? The only way this ends is with them sending each and every one of us to the slaughter, and then leaving Gharridan burning in their wake. They've already infiltrated us."

A vein pulsed in William's temple.

"What do you mean?" I asked.

William's glare shot across to Verone, who had remained silent through the discussion.

"While you were gone, one of our soldiers was found dead in the center of camp with his throat slit, a Brenden mark on his body."

I stared at him. "Nobody caught this?"

Fury simmered behind Verone's eyes. He shook his head.

Anger roiled within me, but it didn't make sense. "Why mess with us? Why kill a random soldier and not go straight for William, like they've been doing before?"

"That's the problem," Verone said. "I don't know. I can't make sense of it. Not unless it's another scare tactic to force us to surrender William to them."

I ground my teeth together, wracking my brain for a solution.

"Maybe there's another way around this," William said.

If there was one, I didn't see it.

"They made their own demands," he continued. "I think we need to make ours."

I shook my head. "Brenden isn't going to give in to any demands. They're technically in the right, so they don't have to."

"I'm not talking about demands," William said, and I saw that worrisome mischievous twinkle in his eye. "I'm talking about another opportunity. A compromise. Something that provides both of us opportunities to show strength and not straight-up humiliation."

I shook my head. "I'm listening, but I can't say that I'm following."

"I say that I challenge Brenden's king to a duel. If I win, they have to walk away, go back to Palazaar, but if he wins, they get the satisfaction of killing me. If I'm dead, maybe Brenden will leave Gharridan alone."

A duel.

A battle of equal opportunity.

And one they couldn't refuse without appearing weak or afraid.

"I don't like it," the minister of war said. "That's a risky gamble running on chance and honor. You need luck. You have to be honorable enough to keep your end of the bargain."

I chewed on my lip. William was an excellent swordsman, but fighting a Gharridan in a practice ring was different from a full onslaught with a Brenden he'd never sparred with before. High stress. Everything to lose. Everything to gain. Yet he wouldn't have the same drive that Brenden's king had. William had murdered his father. There were a lot of things he could beat, but I didn't know if pure revenge and passion was one of them.

"I think Brenden would go for it," I put in. "They like the chance to show off, to prove that they're the best, the greatest. They like competition, and they like high stakes. It's a chance to prove their worth. Far better than a straight-up surrender, because this would show Gharridan's utter defeat."

"But if William loses?" Verone asked.

"Like he said, he's who they're after. I'm not sure they would continue sacrificing soldiers when they've already gotten what they wanted. They evacuated the town before blowing it up, which tells me they're not fond of killing innocents for the fun of it, which is one thing that I can give them credit for."

"And if William wins?" Taryn spoke up for the first time. "That leaves Brenden not getting what they wanted. Do you really think they'll hold to their word?"

"It's a gamble," William said. "But this entire war is."

I turned my attention to William. "Do you have the confidence that you can do this? That you can beat him?"

"You know what I'm capable of, Vladimir, and the fate of the entire kingdom will be riding on my back. I won't be unprepared or give less than my all, if that's what you're implying. I know exactly what I'm getting myself into, and I think that it's the best way."

The war council discussed it among themselves, but I was studying William. I realized what was different. I hadn't seen him this sober in weeks, and he was confident. Not cocky confident as I had always seen, but sure confident, like he was willing to do whatever it took to save the people of his country.

Something had prompted him to change.

Logistics were discussed, terms, contracts, but I kept rounding back to the two possible outcomes of the duel. Playing out the different endings.

"Are we agreed?" William asked.

The gathered room nodded their affirmation.

It was the best chance we'd had since the start of this war, but we still stood with nothing to gain and everything to lose.

"And Vladimir?" William said.

I turned back to him.

"Get out, and don't come within ten feet of anyone until you've had a bath."

CHAPTER FIFTY-FIVE

❖

THE SCRIBES HAD the proposition written up an hour after our agreement and sent the messenger on his way to the Brendens. If everything went according to plan, we would meet them in three days' time at our designated meeting place to discuss the terms and hammer out a contract with half of our army behind us.

But I still didn't know how I felt about the entire thing.

In one way, it offered hope, but only if we won. If we lost, William would be dead, and even though we'd faced death countless times before, this felt different. It felt dooming. Intentional.

I scuffed the toe of my boot against the ground, knowing I should try to get some sleep, but not wanting to. Darya had taken in the girl from Fenville, relieving that burden from the rest of our shoulders, but I still worried about her. A war zone was no place for a child. My gaze wandered to exactly where I knew I shouldn't go, where my thoughts had been wandering all day and distracting me, yet before I realized it, I was already heading that way.

I don't know what drew me to William's tent, but I slipped inside the canvas, finding him poring over a battle map inside. His windblown hair was perched in a state of disarray, and stress lines marked his face.

He must have sensed my presence because he looked up, catching my eyes, but then immediately dropped his gaze again.

"You know, I don't think I've ever met anyone else with the same affinity for a death sentence as you," he muttered.

"It's kind of hard to lose that affinity when death keeps seeking you out," I said.

William cocked an eyebrow. "In my experience with you, it's actually been the other way around."

This would get us nowhere.

I took in the vacancy of the tent, the strange lack of advisers that always surrounded him, and I realized that he really didn't have anyone. Even before he'd become king, I'd never heard him make mention of friends. He may have been close with some of his fellow soldiers, but his rank would always distinguish him from everyone else. He wasn't like them. Would never be like them. And he'd lost his entire family, lost everyone who could relate to or understand what he was going through. He was completely alone.

"Was there a reason you came barging into my tent unannounced?"

I'd hardly call it barging, but I was still trying to figure out the same question. Vladimir was working out the logistics of the army, Darya was busy with the girl, and in my loneliness I guess I had sought out the only person I knew to be just as lonely as me. Even after everything, I missed my conversations with him, missed the way he had made me laugh, missed the way it used to be.

"If they accept our terms for the duel, will you be ready?" I asked.

"I'm always ready to fight to the death every day of my life, Taryn. If only someone had challenged me sooner, I could have already proven myself a champion. I don't know that I'll be able to sleep for the excitement."

"I'm being serious, William."

"As am I. I made a mistake and now I must die to correct it."

"You're not a martyr."

"Aren't I?" His eyes flashed up to meet mine. "It seems my death is the only way to end this war and save my people from total annihilation. My death solves everything. If I were already dead, we might have completely moved on from this. My own mother—"

He cut off, and I sensed the anger and grief entangled within him and his internal conflict over how to deal with and respond to it. He had every right to be angry. His mother's selfish decisions and failed schemes was what put him in this precarious situation, but it warred against the fact that she had still been his mother, had still been the woman who raised him, the mother he'd loved.

"You know how I feel about your choices, but I also know that throwing yourself on a sword isn't the answer to all of our problems."

"Why not?" His voice came out mocking. "Katherine did it."

I stiffened, the air in the room seeming to chill and fill with despair.

"The amount of sarcasm spewing from your mouth implies your reluctance to speak of something. Is that what this is about? What all of it is about? Katherine?"

I waited, thinking he might never answer me, but considering our tumultuous relationship, I was surprised I'd even managed to get this much out of him.

"It should've been me."

He stared at the wood of the table without seeing, his mind transported somewhere else. "Vladimir wishes it would have been me. I can see it every time he looks at me. He wishes that I had died and Katherine had lived."

This was what had been plaguing him.

"Given the chance, do you really think he would have been able to choose between the two of you?"

William smiled humorlessly. "That's the thing, Taryn. Vladimir has to do what is right, do his job. If he was given the choice, he would still pick me. He would pick me because it was what he had to do, not because it was what he wanted to do."

Even though I wanted to, I couldn't find an argument against his words—because he was right.

I read the struggle in his eyes. "You can let it out. I'll still listen."

Emotions warred across his face. Maybe I had overstepped my bounds. We were barely on speaking terms after all. The minutes stretched between us, both of us lost to our own internal horrors. Both hurting and unsure of how to cope, and I found it strange. Where once easy conversation had passed between us, we'd been left with stunted words that led to nowhere. Circles hung beneath William's green eyes; his posture looked broken. I no longer saw the king who'd tried to banish me from the city, who'd turned into someone I no longer recognized. Instead, I saw a boy with responsibility thrust upon him. I saw his shoulders sagging beneath the weight of this duty, beneath the weight of the crown. A boy who had lost everything he ever had and gained everything he never wanted.

He squeezed his eyes shut and relinquished the confession. "I treated her so horribly for all those years, thinking she killed my father. Even after learning the truth, it was hard to look at her differently. I agreed to let her take the fall for the king's death. I pushed her around, I—" He cut off, as if holding back tears. "She didn't hesitate. She knew what was coming. Even after everything, she willingly sacrificed her life for mine, and I just— I can't—"

I knew the pain. The pain of regret. The pain of never being able to ask for forgiveness, of never having the chance to say the things that you should've said. Things that you needed to say.

I placed a hand on his arm. "None of us deserved her, William, and if she was standing here with us today, I know that she'd forgive you. But if you want that forgiveness, you will first have to forgive yourself."

And that was one of the hardest things of all.

"I have a lot that I need to forgive myself for, some things that I'll never be able to." His eyes met mine. "But one day I hope that you can forgive me too."

I waited for his words to stir the feelings buried somewhere deep within me, but they didn't. Whatever I had once felt for him was gone. I knew I would always care for William, but not in the way I once had, and I was grateful. Grateful for learning things I would rather have learned now rather than years later when it was too late to back out, but I was also fooling myself if I thought that it would have ever gone that far. William had been a prince, and now he was a king. Kings did not marry women with no title and rank, with no experience or advantages to bring to the table. His duty to his country would always have to come first, even if his heart lay elsewhere, and even if by some chance we'd been able to overcome all the obstacles, I'd forever severed that hope by joining the Kavari.

"I do forgive you," I said. "But only if you forgive yourself."

"You know, if I had surrendered, not been so quick to assert my authority, maybe she would still be alive."

I thought back to the moment, the way the two Brendens had said this was William's last chance.

"You're the king, William. You can't surrender. You'd be relinquishing Gharridan to their control." I hesitated. "And even if you did surrender, they wouldn't have let you live. They might have taken you back to execute you, but they would *never* let you live. What they wanted seemed almost ceremonial, and I can't help but think if giving you the chance to confess has something to do with how they honor and appease their gods. You may have had that moment of relief, but those assassins would still have fired at you."

The truth of the statement hung between us, the only comfort in our strained conversation.

"Thank you, Taryn."

The sincerity of his words gave me hope. Hope that we might eventually be okay—if both of us survived that long—and hope that the William I once knew and cared for still resided somewhere within him, and if coaxed free, would mold him into the king that Gharridan so desperately needed.

CHAPTER FIFTY-SIX

Vladimir

VULNERABILITY CREPT INSIDE me at the reality of being out in the open.

I didn't like it.

Even though half of Gharridan's army stood at my back, I craved a wall to defend us. Especially when we didn't know what was coming, what the enemy was thinking, or how they would go about their plan of attack should they choose to. Anything was better than this naked feeling before the rest of the world.

We stood assembled in the field we'd deemed no-man's-land, waiting for the arrival of the Brendens. If they chose to come, we would be ready, but uncertainty still collected deep within me. They could arrive here just to slaughter us, without even listening to the terms of the treaty.

William, Captain Verone, and the minister of war all stood to my left, Taryn to my right. More than once I found myself turning to look for Katherine.

A roughly constructed table sat ten feet in front of us with several pieces of parchment held down by a rock, a quill and ink atop it. The furious glare of the sun beat down on us, growing warmer by the hour as we continued to wait with rattling nerves and shuffling feet.

The scouts had circled back ten minutes ago, letting us know that the Brenden army had been spotted moving our way from the west. My eyes roamed the peaks of the distant hills, waiting for their army to top it, while my hand rested on the pommel of my sword, ready to draw at a moment's notice. Behind us, our soldiers stood armored and ready for war. We had no guarantee the Brendens would honor our request. They could take our counteroffer as an insult and simply ride in to destroy us.

I straightened when the first line of Brenden soldiers crested the hill, my stomach dropping as their numbers continued to grow even though I knew our army would look just as formidable. Their vibrant red and gold uniforms shone in the sunlight. I didn't like this, and I didn't trust them. Their army stopped as far back as ours, equal distance to where we stood at the table, then parted ranks as five men rode up between them, dismounted, and strode forward on foot. I peered at them, trying to judge their faces.

"King Jeshenai is in the center," Taryn narrated beside me. "He was the eldest son of King Arguis. On his left with the bronze hair, dressed in black, that's another son, Prince Tristan."

I recognized him before the words left her mouth, anger billowing within me. No black lined his eyes, but even at a distance, I knew exactly who he was.

"Prince Tristan"—I spoke the name like a curse—"is the assassin who murdered Katherine."

The memory of kneeling beside her on the bloodstained floor as she struggled to draw breath berated me.

You're hurt.

Taryn bristled. "Are you sure?"

"I've been in close combat with him. Twice," I said. "Yes. I'm sure."

"His daughter isn't here," she observed. "I recognize the other three, but not by name."

"One is their minister of war," William filled in. "The other two are a general and the battle master."

I studied each of their faces, lingering the longest on the bronze-haired prince's, unable to forget what he'd done to Katherine. We quieted as they came within earshot. They came to a stop, leaving the same amount of distance we had left between us and the table. Our gazes locked, the breeze ruffling through our hair and toying with our uniforms. The fate of our nations hung between us.

"I see that our request was denied," the king of Brenden said. "Were it not for the great honor of our army getting to witness the death of your murderous king, we would have counted it as an insult, but to avoid further bloodshed, as you have pointed out, we have come to discuss the terms of a duel."

Brendens were more arrogant than a herd of train-rattling peacocks.

"What terms have you brought before us today?" William

asked, stepping forward.

"We do not make deals with murderers." The king didn't even acknowledge William. "Let us have them written out."

If they were already this blatant with their disrespect, this meeting wasn't going to end well.

Tristan's beady eyes surveyed our line, stopping on my right. "Taryn Gallows will write them out."

Not good.

Taryn stiffened beside me, but when I turned, no emotion passed across her face. She hesitated for a moment, as if waiting for a rebuttal, then stepped up to the table, sliding a swathe of parchment from the rock holding it in place.

My grip tightened on the pommel of my sword, eyes flicking from Tristan to Taryn. She reached for a quill. Why her?

She dipped the tip in ink, head bent, waiting for instruction.

Brenden's minister of war spoke. "King Jeshenai of Brenden and King William of Gharridan shall engage in a duel of blades, a fight to the death, after first light on the morrow. If Gharridan triumphs, Brenden will retreat from their lands and forgo any warfare over the matter of the death of King Arguis. If Brenden triumphs, Gharridan will fully surrender to Brenden control with no opposition."

My gaze shot to William. He kept his face impassive. This was a high gamble. "Gharridan agrees to these terms."

Brenden's minister lifted his chin. "In addition, should Gharridan fail, Brenden shall be given possession of the Kavari Taryn Gallows."

Taryn's head had jerked up. I couldn't see her expression as she stared at King Jeshenai and Prince Tristan.

"If this term is denied," the minister continued, "the duel

and contract are void."

The world fell dead quiet, the tension stretching between our two groups. I felt like the wind had been knocked from my lungs, the demand so unexpected that it took me a moment to process it.

Taryn's head bent back down to the paper. "Done."

"Not done," William and I responded in unison, but Taryn was already writing.

I stepped forward in protest, and Captain Verone shot out an arm, warning me. A strained look encompassed William's face.

"If we don't agree to it," Verone said, barely moving his lips, "this field becomes a war zone."

The quill scratched against the parchment, the bottle clinking as Taryn dipped it back in each time to replenish with ink. When it was finished, she set the quill in its holster and retreated. I swallowed. What did Brenden want with Taryn? Did they think that she too was responsible for their king's death? But she'd been certain they'd known it was William in the end, and why would they have only requested William's surrender and not hers if they'd believed that?

King Jeshenai inclined his head. "Gharridan shall sign first."

I stepped forward with William as he moved to sign the agreement. Nothing within me trusted the assassin to not attack William while he was vulnerable as his back bent to sign. The Brendens' gazes roved over us as William swirled his signature on the agreement, and I never took my eyes from them.

William finished, and we stepped back. The Brenden king then moved forward to sign, his assassin brother stepping with him. My jaw clenched, the hand on my sword wishing to betray the need for honor.

"We shall meet here after dawn, with our armies gathered round to watch," King Jeshenai said. "May he who is most worthy prevail."

He backed away, waiting until he'd reached the others before turning around. His entourage retreated to their army and our group followed suit, except I never completely turned my back on them. I kept them within my sights, waiting for them to go back on their word.

When we reached the line of tents, William walked off without saying anything. Taryn moved to follow, but I blocked her path.

"You can't just agree to terms without your sovereign's permission, *especially* not after he verbally overruled it," I said.

She threw me an exasperated look. "What else was I supposed to do? Would you rather be crossing blades with them right now as their army destroyed us? He said the agreement was void without that term. They didn't give us a choice, Vladimir, didn't give *me* a choice. It was our only option."

"It doesn't matter if there wasn't another option," I argued. "You cannot agree to terms without discussion, Taryn. This involves the entire country of Gharridan. Not just you."

"I know it involves the entire country, which was why I was willing to say yes to whatever they demanded of me."

"And what if William loses?" I shot back. "Have you thought about what that would mean for you? What that would mean for Gharridan? Who knows what Brenden actually wants with you."

"If William loses then it won't matter either way."

"You're not a pawn anymore, Taryn. You're a Kavari. You have to operate as part of a unit. You can't just go off on your own making decisions without others' input."

"You mean like you do?" She threw my own words back in my face. "Because that's all I've ever seen you do since I arrived here."

"That's different—"

"Oh, is it really?" She cut me off. "Katherine may have sided with you on nearly everything, Vladimir, but I will not."

Her words cut deep, and some of the anger dissipated from her face. "When I took the oath of the Kavari, I promised to do what was best for Gharridan. And if doing what's best for Gharridan means putting myself in danger or arguing against the leader of the Kavari, then so help me I will do it."

She stormed away, and my fists clenched at my sides as I inhaled slowly, trying to regain my composure. Maybe inviting her into the Kavari had been a mistake.

Someone made a noise a few feet away from me, and I turned to find Nic standing there, surely having overheard the whole thing.

He gave me a sardonic smile. "You know what they say about women and warfare."

I scowled, marching away. "Shut up, Nic."

"Whatever happens, personally my money is on her."

CHAPTER FIFTY-SEVEN

TARYN

MAYBE MY IMMEDIATE acceptance of the treaty terms was stupid, but it was looking like I was possibly about to die no matter who won the duel. I huffed to the other side of camp, finding Darya sitting at a table, mending the leather of a bridle. I plopped into the chair next to her, picking up a piece of tack to work on as well.

"Did the meeting not go well?" she asked.

"No," I grumbled. "It went fine."

"Then why do you look like you're about to punch something?"

I glared at her. "Because everything I do is always criticized. Brenden brought me into the agreement. I don't know why, and I don't care, but Vladimir about lost his mind over what I did."

"Well, should he have?"

I threw my hands up in the air. "I don't know! When I first came here I wanted nothing to do with any of this, and then I stayed because Gharridan was in such shambles. I wanted to leave, but then my mother's family was trying to assassinate me, and then Katherine—" I sucked in a breath. "That drove me to the Kavari, but I still don't feel like I'm making a difference or hold any kind of authority. It's just a name and … and—"

"And to find meaning, by surrendering yourself to the Brendens you feel that it gives you purpose."

Her words hit like a slap to the face. Was that why I was doing this? Forcing myself into all of these situations because I felt like they gave me some kind of purpose?

"I can guarantee you, Taryn, that a death wish will never find you any purpose in life."

Maybe that's what I'd been seeking all this time.

"We didn't have another option, Darya."

"I believe you. Brenden has the upper hand, which is why they're calling all the shots, and if Brenden brought you into it with no context, I'm sure that Vladimir is probably a little freaked out."

"We're all freaked out," I muttered.

Darya scrutinized me. "I wouldn't push Vladimir, Taryn. I don't know much, but I've observed enough that if something happened to you it would break him."

I held to my denial. "You'd be surprised."

"I think you would too."

My hands trembled as they held the leather. The meeting had shaken me, but I was already shaken. Shaken from everything that had transpired since I left Navarre, and still recently shaken by the idea that Vladimir had almost died. I didn't mean to argue, didn't mean to act without consideration, but I also didn't know how to deal with everything that was crashing down around me, didn't know how to fight it. Simply pushing everyone else away from me and keeping my distance seemed the easiest solution at the moment. Especially when the sands of my life were running out. The black marks on my skin caught my attention, their strange shimmer vining up my arm. I'd woken the camp again last night and no doubt would again tonight.

Maybe that's why I'd been so quick to forfeit my life, because I knew that whatever Brenden wanted from me, they wouldn't have me for long.

CHAPTER FIFTY-EIGHT

VLADIMIR

I KEPT MYSELF busy all afternoon, drawing up plans of escape should the Brendens trick us, including having the horses saddled and ready to go, the camp ready to be left behind. Irritation bled from me like sweat, and I snapped at those I shouldn't, unable to keep my focus as I stormed from one task to another throughout the day. Anger wasn't the problem. Fear was, but I couldn't show fear and therefore covered it up with anger.

I met with Captain Verone, and in hushed whispers we went over our plan of action should Brenden not hold to their end of the bargain. If it came to open battle, we had enough soldiers to have a fighting chance against the Brendens to defend our land. The men were positioned accordingly. It shouldn't be a problem.

The battle master entered and they continued the discussion as I stepped outside for a moment of brief reprieve and fresh air. Everyone had gathered around the fires for dinner, quiet chatter drifting around as they consumed their stew.

A cascade of dark brown hair among them caught my attention. The firelight reflected in Taryn's green eyes, flashing like emeralds. She laughed at something one of the men said, head tilted back, soft lips curled up in a smile. Part of her hair fell forward over her shoulder, brushing against her cheek and collarbone.

My throat bobbed.

Her rash decisions were maddening, her arguing tongue infuriating, but her determination was inspiring, her passion captivating—and when she was near, for a moment, nothing else existed. When she was near, I could no longer look away.

Her gaze lifted, catching mine, as if sensing me there in the darkness.

Shouts erupted from the edge of camp, drawing our attention. Verone emerged from the tent, and we trotted through the camp to reach the source of the commotion, passing startled soldiers along the way. Flames devoured one of the tents, licking at the canvas. Several people had gathered blankets, trying to put it out before it had the chance to spread.

I grabbed one of the soldier's arms. "What happened here?"

"It just came up out of nowhere. A spark lit in the darkness and then it was on fire."

It was nowhere near one of the cook fires, and it was right at the edge of camp. The dead body they'd found while we were gone flashed before my mind.

"William," I breathed.

I bolted back to the other side of the camp, racing to get to him.

I flung open his entrance flap and burst inside. He was mid-gulp drinking water. He turned, mouth still pressed to his canteen to give me a disapproving stare.

"Can I help you?"

"There was a fire at the edge of camp," I said.

He cocked an eyebrow. "Could you please clarify how that concerns me? I don't deny to be many things, but I also don't believe that expert fire extinguisher was on my resume when I was sworn into office."

I scowled. William could be so—

I marched into the bedchamber sectioned off from the rest of his quarters, searching every inch to make sure that something wasn't off or not where it was supposed to be.

"It's Brenden, William. They were behind that dead body, and they were behind this fire. They're messing with us, and I don't trust them to hold to their word."

"What would you have me do? Call off the duel because Brenden decided to be shady?"

Frustration roiled within me, knowing that something was wrong, but not being able to figure out what. I shook my finger at him. "I need you to be careful, William, and I need you to watch your back. I know that you'll do everything within your power to win tomorrow, but I'm still not convinced that this is going to be a level playing field. Gharridan has already lost one monarch, and I don't know that the people would be able to handle losing another."

My words sobered him. "I know what this could cost us,

Vladimir, and I trust your judgment if you think that something is off, but I still have to go through with this. I will, however, watch my back." He stood. "Since you're here anyway, I had a meeting with the war council earlier, and we drafted this document."

He handed me a rolled-up piece of parchment, and I threw him a quizzical glance before unfurling it. I glanced over the text, faltering when I realized what it implicated.

"No, William, I never asked for this, and I don't want it—"

William shooed my words away with his hand. "You can argue with the council members if I die. I haven't been in the right headspace. Even if I survive this duel, I might not make it back to the capital alive, and Gharridan needs to have confidence in who the next leader is going to be. You may not want to be king, but I need you to at least be king regent if something happens to me until you can put a more viable person on the throne."

He wiped a sheen of sweat from his brow, and I noticed a slight tremor in his hand. William had changed. Not enough, but enough to get us through this war. I knew it stemmed from Katherine's death, knew that her sacrifice had affected him indefinitely.

I nodded my acceptance, and he clapped me on the shoulder. "But be well aware that if you try to steal my throne before I'm actually dead"—he leaned in closer—"I'll kick your backside so hard you'll fly all the way to Covel Sea—and I won't be sending a ship to rescue you."

A smile twitched at my lips amid the serious nature of the joke. "Understood, Your Majesty."

CHAPTER FIFTY-NINE

✦◇✦

TARYN

I WATCHED THE soldiers put out the fire, chewing on my lip. A sinister feeling overwhelmed me, and I stared into the darkness beyond the camp, unnerved that something might come charging out of it at any minute. The glow from Brenden's fires still shone from their side of the field, but the nagging sensation wouldn't leave me alone.

I didn't want to go to sleep, not yet. I could almost feel the black lines pressing into my skin, waiting for the moment they could claim me with their nightmares. Nor did I want tomorrow to come. It whispered a promise of change, and I wasn't prepared for that. Not yet.

I found Vladimir sitting on a crate outside his tent and sharpening his sword. His dark hair fell forward, shadowing his face, his uniform looking rumpled from the day. I'd seen him staring at me from across the fire, the look burning a hole straight through me, but anger wasn't what I had seen in his eyes. What I'd seen had made me question everything.

I grabbed a stool and pulled it up next to him. He glanced at my presence before returning to his work. I expected him to say something, but he didn't, and I suddenly found myself at a loss for words. I didn't like this petty arguing, this misunderstanding between us.

"Do you have any leads on the fire?" I asked.

"No."

I pursed my lips. This was going to be harder than I thought.

"Do you think William's ready for tomorrow?"

He grunted, and I crossed my arms.

"Oh look, there's Nic, flying through the sky right now. He's convinced that it's going to crash down on us in the morning."

He nearly cut his hand as his whetstone slipped off the blade. He shook his head in irritation, jaw clenching.

"Well, at least that got a reaction out of you," I said.

"It has been a *very* long day, Taryn."

"I'm well aware," I snapped. "Or did you think you were the only one affected?"

"I think you need to go back to your tent."

He still hadn't looked at me. "I didn't come here to argue."

"Then why did you come here?"

"I'm sorry that I overruled you and William today, but Vladimir, is that not exactly what you would have done if you had been in my place?"

He said nothing, and my hope deflated. I must have read him wrong, read everything wrong. I'd come here to try to fix things between us, but as usual I kept making everything worse.

"I shouldn't have been so upset with you," he said softly. "And you're right, I would have done exactly as you had if I'd been in your place. What happened scared me, and I covered it up with anger. I'm sorry. I shouldn't have taken that out on you. Or anyone else."

I swallowed. "This, everything going on, is a lot, and I don't know how much more I can take."

He shook his head. "Neither do I."

It was too much.

"I'm not cut out for this," I whispered. "Not for war or for the Kavari."

"No one is cut out for war." He finally looked up at me, meeting my eyes. "But as for the Kavari, I grew up with this, Taryn. You didn't."

I let out a sad laugh. "Are you saying it gets easier?"

"Nothing ever gets easier, you just learn how to handle it better. Sometimes. Sometimes it's just as hard as the first time. And sometimes you adapt to deal with it better, differently."

He set aside his whetstone, inspecting the metal of the blade. He stood to sheath it, and I stood with him, stepping into the shadow of the tent away from prying eyes.

"Promise me that you're going to survive tomorrow, Vladimir."

His startled eyes met mine, and I held nothing back.

"I promised back in Fenville that I would leave you, and I did, and now I need you to promise me that you'll make it through tomorrow."

He stared at me, the same look I'd seen earlier enveloping his eyes. His throat bobbed. "Why?"

A lump lodged in my throat. I should close my mouth, walk away, but the confession came spilling out. "Because I thought you were dead. I thought you were dead, and I had to turn and run without any hope, without even knowing for sure. My mother, my father, Beva, Katherine, now possibly William. In that moment I thought I'd lost you, and I realized that I—I can't lose you too."

I'd stepped too close, but now I couldn't step back and I was staring into his pale depths, aware of the raw emotion plastered across my face, what I was feeling completely laid bare before him. I don't know what possessed me, don't know what reason had left my mind since we were in the middle of a war, but every time I closed my eyes, the fear of his charred body haunted my mind, and the fear of losing him overcame me.

Something flickered across his features, a kindling of hope, a breath of want, but then a shadow overcame everything within him and he took a step back.

"Taryn, I can't—"

Heat flooded my face, and I immediately averted my gaze, throwing my guard up.

"I'm sorry," I said, too forcefully. "The last few days have left me completely out of sorts, and I don't know—"

"It's not—"

"It's late," I said, turning away. "I'll see you in the morning."

My pace quickened with each step, but instead of pain, I just felt numb. I flew into my tent and dropped onto the cot, trying to pull myself together. Something had been there between us at one point, but whatever wall he'd built had no intention of coming down. I put my head in my hands. Why had I said anything? I told myself it was the stress of the last few days, the emotional turmoil with so many dead, with the low prospect of our survival, but even as I fed myself the lies, I knew the only thing those circumstances had done was confirm it.

I shouldn't have gone there, but it didn't matter anyway. If William lost the duel, tomorrow would be the last sunrise any of us would ever see.

CHAPTER SIXTY

VLADIMIR

I STORMED TO the edge of camp, seething.

I knew better.

I knew what Taryn meant to me, what she'd meant to me for a long time, but I'd told myself it didn't matter, that it wasn't real. Yet the way she'd looked at me tonight—

I forced my eyes shut, knowing I'd unconsciously wished for that, and I hated myself for it. For a moment, everything else had disappeared, all sense had left me, but then Michael's voice echoed in my mind.

I have a daughter in Navarre, Vladimir. I need you to swear to me you won't let anything happen to her, that you'll protect her, keep her safe.

I was doing a fine job.

And he hadn't meant this.

He'd never meant this.

She was a Kavari. I was the leader of the Kavari. War surrounded us while death hovered near. It didn't matter what I did or didn't want, because Gharridan came first. Gharridan would always come first. Katherine proved that by giving her life. It wasn't fair to allow myself to dwell or entertain such ideas, especially not right now.

I need you to promise me, Vladimir.

She'd asked for a promise I wasn't able to keep.

I knew better. I could *do* better.

It couldn't happen, and it ended here.

And even though I wanted nothing more than to go find Taryn, to tell her I was sorry, to pull her against me and kiss her until the rest of the world and its problems faded around us, I didn't.

Instead, I strode back to my tent and embraced everything that came with being the leader of the Kavari.

CHAPTER SIXTY-ONE

◆◇◆

TARYN

DEATH HUNG ON the horizon when I rose the next morning. A sinister presence rifled through the breeze in the air. Dark storm clouds, angry as a frothy, roiling sea, gathered around us threateningly. The promise of rain rolled in like a curse. The heavens grumbled with a great bout of thunder that shook the earth, like the world itself was angry about this turn of events. The wind around me strengthened, whipping my long dark hair around my face.

A deluge was coming.

I pushed against the wind as I made my way to William's tent. The king's tent. Uncertainty hung over the entirety of the camp. Many of the soldiers had already taken their places in the field, preparing to watch the duel. Hoping for their king to win. For their king to end the war.

A sprinkle of rain splattered against my skin as I walked, warning of a far heavier rain to come. The guards curled back the canvas flaps for me, and I entered. William stood in full battle armor, his sword already belted to his side, holding his helmet in one hand as a squire finished buckling the last of the pieces into place. I'd never seen him wear full armor before. He looked menacing. Daunting.

He looked like he had the potential to win.

Vladimir stood off to the side but paid me no attention. I paid him none as well.

William caught my gaze. "Come to wish me luck?"

"I don't need to," I said. "I know you've already wished yourself luck."

"Took the words right out of my mouth."

That brought a faint smile to his face, but like always, he used the humor to quell his nerves.

Outside, the rain picked up, pattering against the canvas and running down the sides like tears.

"Time to go," Vladimir said.

His movements were stiff, formal. His jaw clenched.

I caught William's arm before he could leave. We'd been through so much together, we would always have a connection, an understanding between us.

"Go do what you have to do," I said.

He nodded his thanks before stepping out into the rain, and I followed behind, pulling my cloak tight around my shoulders to ward off the rain. Our procession walked to the small dip in the field where we had met the day before. The Brendens, arrayed in full armor, camped out on the other side of the ridge, their attention riveted on us as we descended to where King

Jeshenai was waiting. This battleground gave the impression of an amphitheater, and it suddenly felt very clogged and full with the two armies looming over us, waiting to see what would happen.

Apprehension overwhelmed me as I understood that I could very well be about to watch William die.

I glanced over at the enemy. Tristan stood by his brother, throwing glances our way as they conversed in low voices, no doubt discussing last minute tactics. The Brenden king was arrayed in full armor as well. It added a lot of weight, wore them down more, but it could very well save their life from a death blow.

I took my place beside Vladimir with the other head leaders, and an official from each kingdom gathered at the meeting grounds to read off the rules of the duel. The winnings. My eyes flit to the army.

Would they really abide by the agreement if William won and just let the man who killed their king walk away? Unease twisted within me.

Once the official business was out of the way, both William and King Jeshenai fit their helms into place and pulled their face shields down before drawing the swords from their scabbards. The curve of the Brenden king's sword drew my eye, and I found myself inching closer, wanting to know what happened the moment that it did.

With nothing but the sound of pelting rain, they circled for what felt like minutes, neither wanting to give away their plan of attack to the other, but eventually one of them would have to cave. William said something in a low voice to the king, indiscernible to everyone else, and they exchanged a few words.

Suddenly, William dove forward, weapon slicing through the air toward his opponent's side. The Brenden king brought his curved blade up to meet William's, knocking his sword aside and immediately doubling back with another blow. The king was a risk-taker, but so was William. Sparks flew as the king's blade scraped down William's vambrace.

I wanted to tear my eyes away, to not watch, to know the outcome only once it was over, but I was forced to watch. To wait for the fateful death blow.

William didn't give anything about his fighting style away. He kept the king on his toes, moving in and out of the deadly dance, trying to stay one step ahead in the game. In and out, blow after blow came down. The armor weighed their movements and slowed them.

I crossed my arms, riveted on the battle.

William feinted left, doubling back and sneaking a blow beneath the armor, but it was so thick I didn't know if it did much damage. My stomach dropped, knowing what would have to happen in order for this to end.

And both of them realized it too.

Both simultaneously stepped away, calling for a respite.

"We can't do this in full armor," William called out. "Not if you want a quick and easy death." He pulled off his helm.

King Jeshenai did the same. "Well, it's a good thing I never planned on dying today."

I crowded in as William came back, sweat pouring down his brow as he gulped down the saucer of water offered to him.

"Help me." He nodded to us.

Vladimir and I began unstrapping the armor, working as quickly as our fingers would allow, the rain sending them slipping across the buckles.

"This is going to get messy, William," Vladimir said through gritted teeth.

"I know," he agreed. "But we can't keep doing this forever. Eventually it will have to end."

Within a few moments all of William's armor was stacked in a heap on the muddy ground.

"Round two should be fun," William joked, striding away.

The rain thickened, pouring down on us, the mass of water making it difficult to see. The ground was about to become very, very soft and slippery.

King Jeshenai wasn't much older than William and looked far younger now, without his armor to intimidate.

Mud splashed around William's boots and clung to the fabric of his trousers. His golden hair was plastered to his face.

A flash of lightning lit the entire sky in a jagged streak, followed a moment later by a great crack of thunder that rattled my rib cage.

The dull clash of steel rang out again, muted by the rain but still audible. The blows came fiercer this time, angrier. Cheers rose from both sides, depending on which opponent appeared to have the upper hand in the moment.

Darya came up beside me, the hood of her cloak pulled up, water running down the sides and back.

"Well, he's not dead yet."

I wasn't sure which king she was referring to.

King Jeshenai swiped at William's leg, causing him to stumble backward and leaving him no time to recover. The king was nearly on top of him. William pitched forward in a roll away from the king, his hand sliding along the ground, fingers digging into the earth as he turned back and flung the mud into the king's face.

The king stumbled back, clawing at his eyes, trying to wipe his vision clean. William was back on his feet, coming at him again. A cut across the arm, a nick on the cheek. The king contorted this way and that as he tried to regain his bearings.

But while the mud had once been William's friend, it now became his enemy. He swung back around, but the mud betrayed him, and he slipped onto the ground. The king took the advantage, raining a death blow down on him. William barely managed to maneuver his sword up to block the attack, but the king drove his weight against the force of the blade, driving it closer to the pulse at William's throat.

The sheets of rain intensified along with the fight, and I took a step closer, horror clutching at my gut. William's leg shot up, striking the man in the crotch. The king bent over as he backed away in pain, but William stumbled to his knees, his sword coming round to sink into the side of his flesh. The yell the king emitted reverberated through the air as a bolt of lightning burst overhead, deep thunder rolling across the landscape. William wrenched his sword free, swinging it around for the final blow when he suddenly staggered backward, and I squinted to see what I'd missed. His blow faltered, and he kicked the king to his knees, bringing the tip of the sword to the king's throat. He was an inch away from death.

The cheers of the men died down, the plink of the rain and the roar of the thunder the only sound as we all stared, waiting for William to deliver the final blow.

The tip of the sword rested above his throat. I watched William's lips move, but couldn't hear what he was saying above the pounding of the rain.

Then William stepped back, toward our side.

"I will grant you the mercy of your life if you will concede," William bellowed above the storm.

The king heaved in ragged gasps, clutching at his wounded side.

He would not give in.

And William didn't want to kill him.

The king lifted his hand in defeat.

A roar erupted from our side, going above the storm. The cheer of victory. Of the enemy's defeat.

William stumbled backward.

But it was too easy.

And that was when I saw Death, lurking in the trees.

My eyes shot to Tristan, his hand inside his jacket, pulling something out with uncanny speed, but then his attention focused on his blood and mud-soaked brother, the Brendens helping their king out of the dueling circle.

Who had Death come for?

Fear seized me as William limped away. I hadn't seem him take a hit in his leg, but blood now soaked his trousers.

Vladimir tried to shoulder William, but he pushed away from him, turning to his men and pumping his fist in the air. As Darya and I moved closer, I could see the pain branded into his face, the blood pooling from his wounds and intermingling with the mud. His already fair skin had grown several shades paler, and I could see the fear etched on Vladimir's face as well.

"Get him to the command tent, quickly," Vladimir ordered. "Get the healers."

Two of the soldiers helped William make his way back to

the command tent and we followed close behind. Once inside the security of the tent, William collapsed into a chair with a grimace and one of the soldiers tied his belt above the wound to still the bleeding.

"Did you really think that was going to work?" Vladimir demanded, no doubt referring to his mercy on the king.

He groaned as the soldier ripped his trouser leg apart, revealing a deep and nasty wound underneath. "He had a concealed dagger in his boot and stabbed me."

I sucked in a breath. The rules explicitly stated no weapons were to be used except for their swords. If the king had cheated—

The wound caught my attention. It was already festering, not as a normal wound should, and one word filled my mind.

Poison.

"No, I didn't think it was going to work. It was a fight to the death." William let out a humorless laugh, staring down at it. "But now it looks like it's going to depend on who dies from their wounds first."

CHAPTER SIXTY-TWO

I STARED AT the nasty wound, blood still gushing from its center. The rain was a chorus on the tent, the only steady thing about this situation.

"Vladimir." Nic bustled into the tent, stopping at the sight of William. "Uh …"

"What is it?" I asked, still distracted by Brenden's complete lack of decorum.

"The Brenden army hasn't moved. All of the soldiers are still standing out there, armed for war and watching us. They've made no sign of leaving."

"That's a direct breach of the treaty." William grimaced as the healer once again applied pressure to the wound.

"And they know we can't do anything about it," I grumbled. "They know we can't afford to attack, which was why they cheated with the dagger. We should be retaliating, but we can't because we know that we'll lose."

Thinking Brenden was honorable enough to uphold their end of the bargain was foolish.

"Are they just going to attack us?" Taryn asked. Her face looked stricken.

I shook my head. "No. They're going to wait until our king dies first, and then they're going to decimate us."

"Then what even was the point of all this?" she hissed.

"They needed to demonstrate their power," William said, "prove how formidable they really are."

Nic's voice came from the door of the tent. "Can I talk with you a moment, boss?"

Warning flashed in Nic's eyes. Not good. I sighed, pulling my hood up as I stepped back out into the rain. This blasted downpour wasn't helping anything.

"What is it?" I snapped. What Nic considered pressing information didn't always pan out to be.

He looked over both shoulders. "Scouts found something suspicious in the trees, a hastily abandoned campsite. On our side, not Brenden's."

"How is this important right now?"

He hesitated. "Because there was an Algarian uniform left behind. This isn't Brenden, Vladimir. Someone from Algarar is here, and I think you should see it."

Algarian interference was the last thing we needed right now. It was the worst time to leave William, but I needed to make sure this threat wasn't valid. I ground my teeth, shooting a glance at the Brendens. They hadn't attacked, but they also hadn't moved. It was only a matter of time before something happened. I informed one of the guards that we'd return shortly, then turned back to Nic. "Show me."

The small abandoned campsite was situated just inside the trees, close enough to see into the field but far enough in to not be easily detected. The rain had washed one of the uniforms out from underneath a little hovel in the bushes, otherwise I doubted the scouts would have ever noticed anything.

It was four Algarian uniforms.

I leaned closer.

What looked like fragments of Brenden armor stuck half-way out of the mud, a Brenden dagger and arrow also not far away. My mind spun, trying to piece together why there would be four Algarian uniforms here and recalling the strange fire.

"Nic," I said. "The fire last night. Was anything missing from the tent?"

"I believe the soldier lost one of his uniforms and a few weapons."

"What about the dead man they found in camp a few days ago?"

"We buried him just over the ridge."

Nothing else of use remained here. Whoever had camped here, they'd left, and in a hurry. A hunch unfurled within me, one I hoped wasn't true.

"Can you show me where?" I asked.

We remounted, and I followed Nic through the trees to where the grave was, the horses struggling in the muddy hillside. Nic pointed, and I pulled up Dante. My stomach plummeted. The rain had washed away the shallow grave, but it looked like it had been disturbed beforehand, and the revealed body had been completely stripped of its uniform.

"What is it?" Nic asked, stepping closer.

The pieces swirled in my mind, fitting together. Only one answer made sense, explained all of this away. "Queen Adamara wanted Brenden to wipe us out before they moved in. The Algarians must have been sent to scout us, watch us, make sure that the battle was unfolding as it should, but watching wouldn't be enough. Algarar would want to ensure warfare. They no doubt saw how the duel fared, that neither of us are moving."

What would be their next move?

The pieces clicked together.

My head snapped up. "I think they're impersonating people from each of our armies. This rain would offer them enough coverage to sneak inside without suspicion."

I wheeled Dante back toward camp, Nic on my heels.

"Boss?"

"William and King Jeshenai are in danger," I called to him. "I think they're going to try to sabotage our armies to make sure we go to war, whether we're responsible for it or not."

Dante's hooves smacked against the muddy ground as he carried me back to camp, my thoughts reeling. The impersonating soldiers would look just like us, and if he got too close to William, or Taryn—

I prodded Dante with my heels, urging him to go faster. Precious time slipped through our fingers, too many strides still separating us from the war camps. I shook my head. We'd barely managed to end a war and Algarar was about to start it again.

CHAPTER SIXTY-THREE

TARYN

I WATCHED WHILE the healers inspected William's leg and tried to determine what the poison was. They argued among themselves, leafing through the many vials and ointments in their bag, but none of them were sure. If they couldn't figure out what it was—

I peered out of the tent, searching for Vladimir, but he was nowhere to be seen. Eventually I asked one of the guards and he informed me that he had left with Nic.

I frowned. What was bad enough to draw him away at a time like this?

I pulled up my hood and slipped from the tent, my boots squishing into the soft earth. Brenden's army still stood ominously on the other side of the valley. Ready. At attention. If they started to charge, they would reach us within a minute. We didn't have adequate time to prepare, but nor could we retreat first as that would come across as a sign of defeat.

I waited in what had become a drizzle, my mind at war within me. The Brenden command tent Prince Tristan had disappeared into with his brother drew my attention, as if calling out to me. Whispering my name above the storm. No one had come out since they'd entered, but several people had gone in. The attack would be issued from there. Brenden would not retreat. Whatever honor we'd imagined them to hold did not exist among their ranks. As soon as their king gave the order, they would attack. We had no hope.

Or … an idea popped into my mind.

We only had one hope. One thing left to try.

The idea promised no success, but if we were out of options—

I set out across the soggy landscape, the bottom of my dress and boots coated in mud and weighing down my legs. No one paid me any mind as I passed them, heading to the spot where the duel had taken place. It may not even work, but I had to try. Blood intermingled with the standing water and mud caking the ground, abrasions and deep boot-printed holes gouging the earth.

I went as far as I dared to the invisible barrier separating our armies, staring out at the enemy for a moment before sliding my hood back and waiting for them to approach me. To get *who* I wanted to approach me. My eyes bored through the hazy mist, the water soaking into my hair and trailing down my back, dampening my clothes. I pulled the clasp of my cloak tighter around my neck, trying to keep the rain from sneaking in.

No one from the Brenden or Gharridan armies approached

me or even moved. William was indisposed, meaning Vladimir would be the only one with enough authority to call me back and stop me, but he wasn't here, and I hoped he wouldn't return until I finished what I'd set out to do.

A figure materialized in the rain like a phantom, making their way down to where I stood.

Prince Tristan.

He wore black battle armor, a dark cloak thrown around the back of his shoulders to ward off the cold and rain.

"Our dealings with your kingdom are done."

"Then why are you still here?" I asked.

Tristan lifted his chin. "The terms of the agreement were that the battle was to the death. Both kings are still alive, making the treaty both unfulfilled and void."

I refrained from shaking my head, stunned at the admission even though I hadn't expected any different. "Your kingdom already broke the terms of the treaty when your brother brought a knife into the fight."

"Just as William brought death to our father," Tristan snarled.

"So you were going to kill him either way."

"You did the same thing for your father's murderer, did you not?" Tristan asked. "Brenden is willing to let Gharridan go, but we will never let William go. He has to die."

"How bad is your brother?" I asked.

Tristan's stared at me with his brown eyes flanked by thick dark lashes, as if trying to discern whether or not my question was a battle tactic. "He's alive. For now."

Both kings might die as a result of this duel, and it would do nothing to end the bloodshed. I swallowed my fear and hesitance, preparing to lay it all on the line. Telling him the truth was dangerous. It would make Gharridan appear weak and broken, but it also could be the only chance to keep our kingdom from being destroyed.

"William regrets what happened in your father's study every day," I began. "I've seen it slowly destroy him, but he had no other choice. He was given orders, and he had to follow them."

"Orders sent by your country!" Tristan spat.

I took a deep breath at his flare in emotions, the constant dampness on my face chilling me.

"Do you remember the Royal Massacre?" I asked. I watched closely for any recognition.

His face once again turned to stone. "How could I forget? Gharridan possesses a specialty for assassinating the rulers of other kingdoms. You consider us to be merciless, but perhaps Gharridan itself is the monster."

"King Dorjan was spared to rule the kingdom, but there was another Algarian royal who survived."

He shook his head. "You are mistaken. The entire family line was wiped out except for him."

"That's what we thought too, but there *was* a daughter who survived, Princess Djara, and they kept that secret from the rest of the world, claiming she also perished in the massacre."

"Why would they keep her a secret, and what is the relevance to our present circumstances?" he asked, growing impatient.

"Because for years," I continued, "she and her brother plotted the revenge of their family. Planning it all out. They sent her to Gharridan, where she claimed to be from a fallen kingdom and drew the eye of King Roldan, who married her. She established herself as the Gharridan queen before later assassinating her husband with the poisonous plant known as Mors Secunda. Once he was out of the way, she went after the Kavari."

Tears sprang to my eyes and mixed with the drops of water on my skin. "She murdered my father and tried to pin it on Brenden. To make sure her plan was carried out, she dispatched her son to Brenden to kill your king under the ploy that Brenden had attacked our kingdom first. That woman was Queen Adamara, and she's been scheming and plotting for years to enact her revenge on Gharridan."

Tristan stared at me with the same stone-cold expression. "You weave quite a fable, Miss Gallows. Especially for one who tried to kill my father herself."

"That was when I thought he was guilty of murdering my father. I backed off when I saw the truth in his eyes. I only ever wanted the truth, Tristan."

"Why are you telling me this now?" Skepticism rang in his voice. "Lying to try and save your skin because you know Gharridan doesn't have the means to defend itself?"

"Because before, no one thought that you would believe us. But the truth is this: Queen Adamara is enacting her revenge on Gharridan even from the grave. She planned to start the war with Brenden by having Gharridan murder your king, enticing you into conflict so that we could both completely destroy each other and Algarar could rise above the ashes to rule both of us."

"Brenden would never fall to an Algarian rule," Tristan said.

"Are you sure?" I asked, cocking an eyebrow. "Because how able is your army going to be when a brand new, massive, and fresh army is ready and waiting to go to war with them after a full-out war with Gharridan?"

He hesitated at my words. "So you want us to what, turn our backs like your country didn't assassinate our king, treasonous queen or no treasonous queen?"

"I'm not excusing William's actions," I said, "but he was following orders. I know what you are. Don't tell me that you've never had to fulfill orders that you didn't want to."

He was quiet for a moment, the falling drizzle around us lightening just enough to expand our eyesight. I couldn't read his expression, could only guess at what he was thinking.

"If you want to convince me of this, convince my country of it, we will not engage in warfare with you, but I will need something in return."

My mouth went try.

Gharridan had nothing to bargain with.

"What do you want?" I ventured.

"You know that the alliance between our countries was a shaky one. Did your father ever tell you how he secured it?"

I shook my head, and Tristan stepped closer, water dripping from his chin and nose.

"He brought us a healing plant that could cure any ailment. Two doses. One was used to save my mother years ago from a fatal sickness. The other after my sister was born, when she was deathly ill. There was not a third dose to save my mother again. Or a fourth to save my father. If you want us to reinstate our alliance, you will bring me as many doses of this plant as you can find, and quickly. I fear that my brother will perish to infection without it. I would ask for Katherine, but I know she's dead."

I knew nothing of healing plants, knew nothing of what he

spoke, but the assassin's words filled my mind. The third riddle I hadn't answered.

What's rarer than silver and diamonds and gems, but when given as gifts unites the kingdoms of men?

Rare indeed.

"I've never heard of this healing plant you speak of, or where it comes from," I said.

"Your father obtained the healing plant from the City of Iso."

His words halted the world around me. That was where my mother was from, where Katherine's people were from, where the assassins sent to kill me were from. Anticipation rose within me, searching for answers.

"Anyone who tries to enter is killed," I said.

"I know," Tristan shrugged. "We lost several men trying. No matter what we did or however peacefully we approached, we couldn't get in. Couldn't even get acknowledgment, but Michael did. If he found a way in, then surely you can too, and if you want to keep us from going to war with your kingdom, those are my terms."

What he asked was impossible. Or was it? My mind flashed back to my conversation with the Dalendrian assassin. He'd told me I could visit Dalendria—after I'd taken the oath of Kavari, and only if I came in white. Maybe it was possible.

"I will do what I can," I said. "But I can't guarantee it, and I don't know that it can be done quickly."

"I understand, and we will wait for Algarar to make their move to see if what you speak is true, but I want that healing plant before the end of the war."

If his brother did develop an infection, he would be dead

before I could even reach the city. He wanted the plant for something else. The prince could even be lying, and as soon as I stepped away they could launch us into full-scale war, but I had nothing else to go on and had to blindly put my trust in him.

I nodded. "Are we agreed then?"

He hesitated before dipping his head. "We are agreed."

With that assurance, I turned to leave, but when he said my name I looked back sharply.

Something struck my shoulder, and I jerked at the impact, stumbling on the slippery ground. I looked down. An arrow shaft protruded from my shoulder, the head embedded deep in my flesh. Blood poured down the front of my cloak, merging with the rain. That arrow had been meant for my neck, and that single twisted movement saved my life. If Tristan hadn't called my name—

Two more jolts of slicing pressure struck me, searing my body with a burning pain that paralyzed me. Comprehension left me as I stared at the protruding arrows, the bright red blood.

And then I was tipping backward as if falling into a dream, into a trance, staring up at the sky, rain pelting my skin like daggers as a bolt of lightning shattered across the heavens with an explosion of thunder, and when the lightning receded, so did the light.

CHAPTER SIXTY-FOUR

VLADIMIR

THE CLASH OF steel and the roar of battle rose to meet our ears before we ever saw it. Panic exploded within me, and it took all of my self-restraint to keep it at bay. Dante broke the tree line, galloping into the damp valley, and the sight before me sent a jolt through my system. No-man's-land no longer existed. Gharridans and Brendens blurred together in a bloody battle. Men littered the ground. Some dead, some screaming in pain.

The desolation of Fenville assaulted my mind, my eyes, all of my senses. Bodies burning. Soldiers, who were never given a chance to defend themselves, dying. Pleading. Soldiers I should have been able to save, but couldn't.

My throat felt raw as I stared at the scene before me.

Taryn.

William.

"Find Taryn!" I yelled at Nic.

I skirted Dante around the fighting, trying to get to the command tent. Our soldiers had held the line, leaving the main front contained to the center of the field, but it wouldn't take long for the Brendens to breach it. The command tent loomed before me, and I kicked my feet from the stirrups, throwing my right leg over the front of the saddle before hitting the ground running. I crashed through the entrance.

"William!"

He looked up, perspiration dotting his brow, his injured leg stretched out before him as he tried to buckle on his sword belt. Behind him stood a soldier I didn't recognize. The soot on his uniform instantly drew my attention. I ripped my sword form its sheath, advancing forward and forcing him into a corner.

"Step away from the king," I commanded.

"Vlad—"

I ignored William, inspecting the man closer while resting the tip of my blade against his neck, drawing a bead of blood.

"You're not Gharridan," I said. "Why are you here?"

The impostor displayed no fear, only triumph.

He smiled. "For chaos."

A dagger appeared in his left hand, arcing toward me, but my sword was already in his neck. I pulled it back out, his body crumpling to the ground. He'd gotten too close. I ducked my head out of the tent, yelling at several men for horses.

"What instigated the fighting?" I asked.

I slipped an arm beneath William's shoulders, helping him rise to his feet. His face blanched white at the pain.

"I don't know." He shook his head. "One of the soldiers

called Captain Verone out, saying that Taryn was speaking with the Brendens on the field."

"What?" I nearly roared.

"The next thing I heard was them charging into battle." He stumbled, groaning in pain. "Funny how I'm the king and no one thought to inform me."

And no one had stayed to guard him. If I'd gotten here any later William might already be dead. We slipped out of the tent and I searched for Taryn, but the rain and chaos made it impossible to see anything. Three soldiers approached leading a quartet of horses.

"Get the king to safety," I ordered. "Take him to the main camp."

William leaned against one of the horses for support. "I'm the king, I can't—"

One of the soldiers helped me shove William up onto the horse, no doubt destroying whatever work the healers had done on his leg.

"Right now your only concern is staying alive," I said. "Hold on tight and don't you dare pass out."

The other soldiers mounted, and I nodded at them, grabbing my sword and turning toward the battle without waiting to watch him leave. I charged toward the front lines, assaulted by the smell of blood and sweat, opened flesh, the cries of pain and the clash of steel ringing in my ears.

"Who attacked first?" I yelled at a soldier.

"We did!" His blade arced into a Brenden. "They fired at Gallows' daughter during a peace treaty."

My beating heart stilled, the gut-churning sounds around me muffling in my ears. I pushed forward. Searching. One foot in front of the other. Charging Brendens. My sword raised, ready to meet them. Parry. Strike. Feint left. Slam hilt into the head.

I passed body after body, fighting my way toward the front to get a better view, to see. The ground gave way beneath my feet, the penetrable surface slowing me down. Brenden. Strike. Dead. I had to see if she was there, if there was any hope, if she was still alive.

What was she doing talking with the Brendens?

Protect her.

One request. That's all he'd made.

And after last night, I'd alienated her.

The world grew thick with blades, the space around me clogged with soldiers. Some friend. Some foe, but soon the Brendens outnumbered us, drove us back. I never reached the center of the field, never caught sight of anyone. We'd been so close. So close to avoiding all of this, avoiding bloodshed. Avoiding war. But still, the death bringer had come.

War laughed as he circled me, sent my soldiers to their deaths, held me in his clutches and vowed to never let me go. He breathed scalding air down my neck as he destroyed the world around me and battled against hope—and nothing was strong enough to keep hope from crumbling to its knees.

CHAPTER SIXTY-FIVE

WE CALLED THE retreat.

And everything within me died.

We held the Brendens off as long as we could, ushering the wounded to the back as we tried to hold the line, but Brenden pushed forward, breaking past the first line of our tents. We could hold no longer.

The rain pelted us, laughed at us, chased us. Pandemonium broke out and chaos erupted as we all turned at once and ran. Ran to get away from the curved blades of the Brendens as they snapped at our heels like ravenous wolves.

The men had saddled the horses this morning, having everything prepared in case something went wrong. But the Brendens didn't have horses. Not this close. They would have to go back for them first.

Mud flew around us like water as Dante pushed farther and farther ahead. It was madness, but we ran. We ran and we didn't stop. The Brendens would be close behind, but our only hope of survival would be getting back to the main camp.

The healers were already prepared when the first line of cavalry thundered past the outer line of tents in the main camp. Many of the soldiers had ridden double with the wounded, while others who were injured and managed to ride a horse on their own now collapsed out of the saddles to the ground.

Not many men surrounded me.

Not many men had made it back.

I searched the way we had come, thinking I must be mistaken, that there was another line of Gharridans returning, but this was it. This was all we'd returned with. My head spun, trying to process everything as I stumbled through our broken remnants. Somewhere in the fray, I managed to find Captain Verone.

"I want scouts posted over that ridge to alert us when they're coming, and news the second they hear or see the smallest sign," I ordered.

I glanced behind him, seeking out a familiar face. My mouth went dry as I swallowed, afraid to ask the question.

"Nic?"

Verone trudged on. "I haven't seen him yet."

I nodded, following him through the camp, helping with the wounded, watching the outlying lands, looking for any sign of stragglers.

Any sign of a certain straggler.

But there was no sign.

Every muscle in my body ached as we worked. My hands

shook, sweat intermixing with the mud and the rain drizzling down on us. I was near soaked through, but I barely noticed. I found William in a tent, one of the healers changing his bandages. No doubt the ride had reopened whatever had clotted in the wound and possibly ripped the stitches. The healer lathered an ointment across the wound before wrapping it closed with a clean bandage.

"Are you all right?" I asked.

William grimaced. "Did you go blind in battle? Because any seeing man would know that was a terribly stupid question."

He would be just fine.

For now.

"Would someone like to explain to me what happened?" I circled the tent, taking in both William and Verone. "And why Taryn was in the middle of that field in the first place? Why she's still missing?" Anger raged in my voice, but it cracked on the last sentence, the fear trying to overpower me. I held back the emotions begging to war their way out of my body.

"I don't know what she was thinking," Verone said, "but when I came back out of the tent, she was standing in the middle of no-man's-land. The other side had already seen her, and I couldn't approach without appearing threatening or letting on that we had no idea what was happening. After a minute, that assassin came out to talk with her. None of us could hear anything that they were saying. Not with the distance and the rain, but she was trying to convince him of something, and it looked like it was working. And then that's when they fired the arrows."

William stiffened.

I froze.

"The arrows?" I asked.

"She ..." Verone seemed to realize he knew something we didn't. "She— Right as she turned to leave, she was struck with three arrows."

I gripped the chair for support.

Three arrows.

"Is she ..."

I couldn't even say the words.

"When the Brendens fired at her, we sounded the charge. I saw her fall. I never caught sight of her again after the fighting started."

Three arrows.

She'd fallen.

And no one had been there.

No had had been there to stop the bleeding,

We'd left her out there on that field that was now crawling with Brendens and littered with the dead.

I should have been there, should have—

But if I had been there, I wouldn't have uncovered the Algarians' plans.

I pressed my fists against my temples, trying to process what was happening. "It wasn't Brenden."

Both of them stared at me before shaking their heads.

"You weren't here," Verone said. "The arrows came from their troops."

"I know that's what it looked like, but it wasn't a Brenden underneath that uniform," I said. "It was an Algarian. They had two impostors planted on each side."

I explained to them what Nic and I had found. The conclusions I'd drawn. "That still leaves one man unaccounted for. William, I want all of the soldiers escorting you to be someone that we know well. He may have already left. I don't think he'd blend in well on a normal day, but I'm not taking any chances."

We discussed possible tactics, if the Algarian was still here, what he might be trying to plan, but none of our ideas seemed viable. None of this seemed viable. It had all unraveled so quickly.

What are you here for? I'd asked the impostor.

For chaos.

William's face turned grave. "How many men did we lose?"

I tried to keep my emotions in check as my soul broke within me. "I don't know, but not many of us returned."

William swallowed, trying to keep himself in check as well. "Verone … do we have any chance of winning this war?"

Verone didn't give an immediate answer. "I know that I should offer you hope, but I'm afraid I can't seem to find any at this moment, Your Majesty."

"Then you need to tell me what to do," William said, "because I don't know how to give people hope where there is none."

I knew the answer, but I didn't want to voice it.

Taryn's words came back to me unbidden.

You can always find a whisper of hope.

She'd been wrong.

"We need to retreat," I finally said. "They're going to destroy us if we're out in the open like this. Ervonne is the closest big city, they'll head there next. If we have a city wall to shield us, that's our best chance. If they take that city, we retreat to the capital, and we defend it the best that we possibly can. I have no hope to offer beyond that other than we cannot give up." I pointed at William. "And I want you out of here by first light tomorrow. I can't lead a war if I'm constantly having to sacrifice soldiers to protect you."

"You want me to tuck tail and run?" he asked.

"You're in no condition to fight, and you're the one they want dead. And you're not *running*, you're going ahead of us. You can tell the city to prepare for our entry. You have the evening to rest up, but then I want you gone."

The tent flaps flew open, and Darya stormed inside. "Brenden hasn't advanced yet. They're taking their sweet time."

"It's not going to last," I said. "They're going to pack their gear, take what we left behind, and then come for us. Their main force will probably be close behind. Darya, I want you to go with William. I trust you as a courier, and if there's something imperative we need to know before reaching the city, ride back out to us."

Darya looked slightly shocked and annoyed by the orders, but she dipped her head in acknowledgment before stepping outside.

"Taryn," William began, closing his eyes against the thought. "Is she …"

"I don't know," Verone said.

My jaw clenched.

I left the tent as well, making my way through the camp and seeing where I could be of use, but eventually I had to step away. I strode to the edge of camp, feeling dead inside, my cold body unable to even summon tears. Not even the heat of my anger warmed the chill within. And I crumpled to my knees, jerking forward as I retched onto the ground.

Death.

Death surrounded me.

What was she thinking? Going out on that field. Meeting with the Brendens.

I wretched again, sick at our situation, sick at everything.

I fisted my eyes. Dead. Everyone I'd ever loved was dead. There was no one left.

I was alone.

And I had no time to grieve.

I had a country to direct, to instill faith within where there was none.

I gasped for breath, the moist air flowing into my lungs as I stumbled to my feet.

There was much to do.

I held meetings with the soldiers, gave out orders, made plans where there were none so that we would be ready to leave in the dead of night if need be or at first light in the morning. The men's eyes were empty, lifeless, devoid of hope. They'd already marched through hell and we were about to go back again.

I had nothing to offer them.

Those with fatal injuries hadn't made it out with us. Many of the remaining soldiers would recover, but getting them to safety with limited wagon space when they needed rest would be difficult. Everything from here on out would be difficult. I walked to the edge of camp again, eyes heavy, limbs wary.

My eyes wandered to the tree line, and I saw a scout escorting a single rider with a figure slumped in front of him. I froze, unable to do anything but stare, not wanting to let myself even dare to hope, dare to think, but then my feet pounded against the pliant earth as I ran out to meet them. The hope rose unbidden when I picked out Nic and Taryn's features in the darkness, but then my heart slowed. Taryn's face was ashen grey.

Blood stained nearly every part of Nic, his face exhausted. "She's still alive, but barely."

I reached up to take her from his arms. Her entire dress was shredded, the fabric wrapped tightly around her calf, hips, shoulder. Blood drenched the garment. Only a few pieces of the blue fabric could still be seen underneath. Her body felt lifeless, and I lifted my arm to support her lolling head. An arrow shaft still jutted out from her shoulder and hip around the bandages.

Alive?

Alive.

But barely.

I ran to the camp with her dead weight in my arms.

"Get me a healer," I bellowed. "NOW!"

Two soldiers bolted out of my way, clearing a tent and pulling a table away from the wall. I gently laid her on top of it, her blood-soaked hair splaying out around her in a tangled mess. I pushed it away from her forehead, the strands crusty beneath my fingers. The grey pallor of her skin struck a chord of fear deep within me. *Was* she still alive?

But then the faintest rise of her chest, the barest movement of hope.

Nic was talking behind me. "Once we were far away enough from the fighting, I got back off because she never would have made it if I didn't stop the bleeding. So I did my best. The horse pulled up lame about two miles out, so we had to walk very slowly back. That's why we weren't here sooner."

Three healers started working on Taryn.

They worked one wound at a time, starting with the shoulder. The healer pulled off the bandage and then ripped the dress open, revealing the nasty wound the arrow had made.

"I think it's embedded in the bone," she said. "We're going to have to cut it out."

I swallowed. Chances of surviving the infection this would bring were minimal. I held her down as they heated the knife and then cut open the flesh to yank the arrowhead out, but Taryn never moved, as if she were dead already. Even when they placed the hot iron over the wound to cauterize it, she remained limp and still. I needed something, a sign to show that she was still alive, but there was nothing other than the tiny breaths her chest revealed.

The arrow to her hip had only hit skin and flesh, and they pushed it all the way through. Still no movement. The smell of burning flesh was sickening, enough to nearly make all of us puke. The last wound had no arrow; only half of it had swiped across her calf, but it looked like it had severed the muscle. When they were finally done after washing out the wound with water and alcohol, applying ointment and salves, I was left alone with her. They'd moved her to the bed, and I had a million responsibilities, but I sat beside her, holding on to her hand, running off the warmth still in her fingertips.

Begging for a miracle.

Begging for anything.

FOUR DAYS LATER

CHAPTER SIXTY-SIX

TARYN

FIRE SEARED MY skin and licked at my wounds, ate at every aching inch of my body. I wanted to scream, wanted to end the torment, but I couldn't move, couldn't speak. The pain trapped me in a dark and lonely cell with no reprieve, no release. The nightmares held me prisoner, poking at me and prying the tears from my eyes as they played my worst fears before me.

I just wanted it to end.

No escape.

There's no escape.

You'll never escape.

A crack in the darkness let in the faintest sliver of light, lifting me away from the nightmares.

I remembered the rough jolt of a wagon beneath me, each jerk feeling like someone was snapping my bones and ripping my body from the inside out, and then the sensation of being carried, the comfort of a deep and warm voice centering me, drawing me away from the other worlds and into this one.

But the pain was too much.

I didn't want to stay.

The darkness beckoned to me, promising release if I would only just give in—and release was all I wanted.

But every time I reached for it, let myself succumb to the darkness swirling around me, that voice pulled me back.

Don't you dare leave me, Taryn.

I wanted to leave. I wanted it to end.

Keep fighting.

What if I didn't want to?

I'm so sorry.

Sorry for what?

Taryn.

My eyelids fluttered open, feeling like they weighed a million pounds. The world spun, and dizziness overwhelmed me. I rolled over, crying out at the pain that rippled through me. Vomit poured out of my mouth. I blinked back tears, needing the spinning to stop. Someone's face swam before my vision.

Vladimir.

He held a bucket in one hand, his other pulling the hair away from my face.

I vomited again but had nothing more than bile. I squeezed my eyes shut, aware of the throbbing pain pulsing throughout my body.

"Can you—" I coughed, dryness cracking my throat. "Can you help me sit up?"

"I don't think—"

"Please," I begged. "Just a little."

I heard him move about the room, stepping back and piling something on the bed before slipping an arm beneath me. I leaned against him as my body tilted. Immediately I wondered if it had been the wrong decision, but I pushed through it. I'm not sure if I blacked out again, but whenever I opened my eyes, the world had stopped spinning.

I found Vladimir sitting on a low stool beside me, his worried eyes searching mine.

"Where are we?" I croaked.

He hesitated. "Back with the main camp. We're heading for Ervonne."

I stilled at his words. We weren't supposed to be at the main camp. We were supposed to be—

Fear and confusion wafted over me as I struggled to understand. I glanced down at my body, unable to see beneath the blankets and afraid of what I might find.

"Do you remember what happened?"

I searched through the dim memories, desperately trying to remember. "I—I was struck by an arrow."

I peered down at my left shoulder.

"You were shot by three," Vladimir clarified. "Once in the shoulder, once in the hip, and thankfully the last arrow only grazed your calf. You're lucky to be alive."

I shook my head. "That doesn't explain why we're here. Tristan agreed to help stop the war." I could feel the tears brewing behind my eyes from both emotion and pain. "Why did they shoot me?"

Vladimir bowed his head, not meeting my gaze as he relayed everything that had transpired. The battle. The retreat. The lives lost and left behind. The impostors.

My mind reeled, still clouded by a thick fog I tried to navigate and find my way out of.

"What do you mean that Tristan agreed to help stop the war?" Vladimir asked.

"The flower ..." I trailed off, then explained the conversation to him. "If it wasn't actually Brenden that tried to kill me, then Tristan's offer is still on the table. If we can get into Dalendria, convince them to give it to us, we might be able to end this war."

The possibility swirled before me even as the state of my body tarnished my hope, because I couldn't go. We'd already lost so much, but if there was even the slightest chance that Tristan would still honor the agreement—

"I can't risk the lives of any more men. We're stretched thin as it is, and I don't want to throw their lives away on the empty promises of an assassin prince. The entrance to that city is a graveyard."

"My father found a way in," I mumbled. I wanted to fight but didn't even have the strength to raise my voice.

"And we don't have time to uncover his secrets on a false hope," he said.

I rolled my eyes. "Vladimir—"

He stood to his feet. "Now is not the time to argue. You can barely keep your eyes open. I think you need to rest."

What I needed was to get out of this bed. Several quips zipped through my mind to throw at him, but I never got to say them, because just as my lips began to move, sleep was already taking me.

I didn't remember much until the next day, when Vladimir carried me back into the cart. His presence brought comfort. Something warm, something solid to hold on to. I brought up Dalendria again that night, and he immediately cut me off. I pursed my lips, realizing I would get nowhere with him, at least not while I was incapable of even walking on my own. Maybe Vladimir was right. Or maybe it was too much for him, to have hope dangled in front of him that he didn't even know was true. It was possible that Tristan could have lied, and doubtful even if he had spoken the truth that he would hold to it after the battle. Brenden wouldn't have known of the impostors. So I let it drop for the next few days as Vladimir escorted me from my tent, to the healer and to the cart.

In a way, I missed the blissful nature of unconsciousness, but I had time to think this way. Especially since I had nothing better to do than lie in the cart as we made our way to Ervonne. I watched the sky pass by above me as I sipped from my water canteen and nibbled at dry strips of meat, my mind working the entire time.

Stiffness overwhelmed me the next morning when I finally stood in the healer's tent after Vladimir had dropped me off. By now I could maneuver my way around on my own, but not very far and only with excruciating pain.

"Let's take a look, shall we?"

The older woman helped me unlace my dress, and I realized it was the white one I had left in my tent. No doubt the other was completely ruined, although this one now appeared more tan since it was coated in the dust of the road. I grimaced as she slipped my elbow out of the sleeve then watched with trepidation as she began to unwind my bandage, which was moist with blood where the wound had soaked through. I fisted my right hand at the sight. I didn't have a good angle, but I could see enough.

She studied the raw wound, and while she tried to hide it, I caught the flash of fear and disappointment that crossed her face.

"How bad is it?" I asked.

"We'll get some salve in there and some fresh bandages."

I stepped back when she tried to apply the salve, shaking my head. "Don't lie to me. Tell me how bad it is."

She screwed up her face, uncomfortable with the turn in conversation. This was the first time Vladimir had left me in the healer's tent alone.

"Did he tell you to lie to me?" I asked.

She sighed. "He doesn't want you to worry, and if I'm honest, I haven't given him the full truth either. I'm doing everything I can to keep his spirits up right now."

If Vladimir didn't want me to know, if he'd been trying to keep it from me—

I bit my lip. "Please tell me. I need to know."

She gently applied the salve to my wound, and I winced at the deep pain her touch brought. "You're lucky to be alive, Miss Gallows. It's a miracle, considering all the times that you've tempted fate, but I think you may have gone too far this time. I'm doing everything I can to prevent infection, but with how long the wound went without treatment—I'm simply amazed it hasn't set in yet."

I swallowed, digesting her words and coming to a full understanding of what she meant. "How long do I have?"

She put the salve away, pulling out a clean bandage as she met my eyes. "If infection sets in, at best I would give you a few weeks. At worst? A few days."

The blue sky passed above me as I rode in the cart later that day.

I was going to die.

The knowledge seemed strange this time, given in advance as it was and being faced with something possibly far away instead of the imminent death that had been so brazenly laid before me in the past. Strange that I was even still alive. It was too much luck for one person. I closed my eyes, the heat of the sun beating down on my skin. Infection would come, she feared it had already started, and when it did there was no Katherine to save me, no Katherine to make the most horrible of wounds close up and disappear. If I made it to the city, that would already be too much mercy granted me.

But if the infection didn't kill me, the nightmares would. The black lines twisted around my arms like vines. Thicker. Fuller. I understood, more than knew, that they were preparing to strangle me. That my time was almost up. In that moment, I wished for death, wished for it to come swiftly, not billow slowly like a rising storm, visible in the distance but not yet within reach. All I could do was wait for it to reach for me, to take me.

And in the maddening calmness of the acceptance of my death, I realized what I had to do. What I needed to do. Perhaps, even in my brokenness, I had one thing left to offer. We were only a few days out from Ervonne. It had to be before then, because once we were there, my chance would be gone.

CHAPTER SIXTY-SEVEN

VLADIMIR

THE ONLY THING that kept me going, from losing every last shred of my sanity, was the fact that Taryn was alive. I kept as close to her wagon as I could all day while not neglecting my duties. I tried not to hover, but I couldn't help it. Scouts rode in, keeping us updated on the advancement of the Brenden army. We lost at least one of the severely wounded every day. Usually more. I didn't have time to take care of Taryn, but I didn't care. I wasn't going to let her out of my sight.

Nic offered to step in for me and I nearly bit his head off, then hastily apologized. It was anger that controlled me. It was fear. Fear that everything was about to be ripped away from me, and I was holding on with every ounce of strength to not lose what precious little I still had.

And even that was slipping away.

I knew the healer was trying to keep it from me, knew that Taryn's wound wasn't healing right. I knew what spawned from that. Knew what Taryn was in for. If infection set in, it would be gruesome, and I could only pray that it would take her swiftly instead of gradually dragging it out before death finally came for her, but mostly I prayed that it wouldn't come for her at all. I pushed the troops hard, harder than they should have been pushed, but we needed to get out of the open, and I hoped that Ervonne might offer some remedy that our healers could not.

But we had to get there before it was too late.

CHAPTER SIXTY-EIGHT

◆◇◆

TARYN

I CAREFULLY SLUNG the bag over my right shoulder, dreading the distance that it would take to get back to my tent. I'd set everything into place, scared that someone would figure out what I was doing, but as far as I could tell, I was still in the clear. I started limping toward my tent at the other end of the camp one excruciating step at a time. The slice on my calf and the wound through my hip smarted with the smallest movements and screamed with the shortest steps. Sweat pebbled my brow. There was no way I would make it, no way I could pull this off, but I had to try.

"What are you *doing?*" Disbelief coated Vladimir's voice as I turned to find him staring at me. "Did you walk all the way over here?"

"Hobble would probably be a better word," I mumbled.

He sighed before striding over and, being mindful of my wounds, scooped me up, to which I gave a little yelp of surprise.

"I can walk," I protested.

"As you said, you can hobble," he muttered. "But that would take you two hours, and I don't have time for that right now."

I relented, not having the energy to argue with him.

I leaned my head against his chest, grateful for the moment to relax even as guilt crept in over knowing what was coming. I pushed the thought away.

"Thank you," I breathed into his shirt.

I don't know what I would do without him.

He tensed when we reached the side of my tent before setting me down in the shadows. I still grimaced at the pain despite his carefulness. He clenched his jaw, a tormented expression in his eyes as I watched the weight of everything bear down on him. He'd been working himself tirelessly, pushing his body and mental sanity to the limits. If he kept going this recklessly, he was going to break.

My advances might not have been welcome, but in that moment, I didn't care. I placed my hand on his rough cheek, drawing his attention.

"It's going to be okay, Vladimir," I said, the words nearly sticking in my throat. "We're going to get through this. There's always a flicker of hope somewhere, somehow."

He leaned into my touch. "You don't know that."

I shook my head. "But if I want to survive, I have to believe it."

He placed his hand over mine, cupping it to his cheek. "How are you doing?"

I swallowed. "Still the same. Although I'm not sure how honest the healer has been with me."

No accusation filled my tone, but he was aware that I knew. He hung his head, breaking eye contact. He held back for a moment, as if warring over a decision, then made up his mind.

"I—I'm sorry," he said, stepping closer. "I thought you were dead, and I can't—" He tried to hold the emotion back. "I'm ripping at the seams, Taryn, and I can't lose you right now." He brought his eyes back to mine, the vulnerability painted in them almost enough to break me. "I can't— I can't lose you either."

I can't lose you.

The same words I'd confessed to him before the duel, when he'd walked away from me. Made me think I'd read him wrong even though I was certain he'd felt the same way. My throat constricted as I tried not to wonder, to hope.

He leaned closer, his hand brushing against mine, interweaving our fingers together, stroking against them. I held his piercing gaze, questioning whether pulling away or staying would be more painful. For both of us.

He swallowed, the intensity of his pale blue eyes burning straight to my core. "Taryn, I—" He tilted his head toward me, our faces so close. "Do you think ..."

My breath hitched in my throat, heart pounding. His low voice consumed me. The hope was written all over his face, the desire apparent. "One day, when all of this is over ..."

The unanswered question lingered between us, the power of what happened next firmly within my grasp. To protect this feeling, or shatter it.

I tilted my chin up in answer as longing filled my whispered words, conveyed all the emotions coursing through me. "One day."

He dipped his head, lips brushing against mine with a feather-light touch, asking, searching. I kissed him back, asking for more, and he reciprocated. Shivers raced up my spine as his fingers trailed down my back, mindful of where my injuries lay. His other hand curled around my neck, slipping into my hair and tilting my face up closer to him. My cheeks burned and pulse pounded with the intense unfamiliarity of his lips, his touch, and my mobile arm hooked around the back of his neck to keep him as close as possible, because in this moment, I never wanted to be parted from him again.

Something drew me to Vladimir in a way that I couldn't explain, and like the pull of the tide dragging me out to sea, I could never escape it. And I didn't want to. Being with him was security, being with him was infuriating, but knowing him was understanding, it was learning all the secret joys of life that only revealed themselves to those who truly admired it.

Where everything else in life had been unstable, Vladimir had been my rock. He'd pulled me back from the edge so many times, saved my life on countless occasions, and as memories flickered through my mind and his arms tightened around me, hands gentle where his lips were not, I was overwhelmed at his presence, at his unyielding ability to always be there.

When I'd first laid eyes on him as he sat across the fire from me, when I'd been a bitter brat with no feeling for her father, he hadn't given up on me. He'd helped me through the loss of my father, assuring me it wasn't my fault, had helped me understand how he had always been there. Danced with me at the coronation ball, stayed with me after the poisoning. He didn't force me to take the oath of Kavari, had never forced me to do anything, and had left the decision up to me even though it hadn't felt like I'd had a decision at the time. In the face of death, in the promise of insecurity, he had selflessly given of himself to everyone, never putting himself above the lives of others.

And I had to let him go.

I knew I had to, but I couldn't. I needed him. Needed him like the world needed a sunrise, like blossoms needed rain. I needed him like the air in my lungs because in the darkness of despair he was the one who breathed me back to life. I wanted to fold his hand in mine and never let him go, but I knew that I had to.

I pulled back slightly, both of us breathless.

"Vladimir," I whispered, tears stinging my eyes.

His forehead pressed against mine, eyes squeezed shut. "One day?"

I held on to the moment, held on to everything I ever wanted and everything I could never have.

"One day," I whispered back.

A chill crept in where he had once warmed me, because I knew it was not a whisper of assurance.

It was a whisper of goodbye.

Because it was too late for one day.

One day had been stolen, and whether both or only one of us knew it—one day would never come.

CHAPTER SIXTY-NINE

❖

VLADIMIR

I WRESTLED WITH myself all night, the darkness trapping me within my own thoughts. I knew I shouldn't have said anything, knew that I should have walked away, but I couldn't. Not after thinking she was dead, not after enduring these tense days, wondering if she was going to make it. She had to know, at least once, and now the one thing crowding out everything else in my mind was the memory of her lips against mine, the feel of her beneath my hands.

I rolled over, unsuccessfully trying to redirect my thoughts.

I'd suspected she felt the same toward me, first guessed it during our sparring match in the library. But when she'd approached me the other night, I'd denied it to keep myself at bay, to not let myself dare to imagine it, and now we'd both promised.

One day.

But since not even tomorrow was promised, one day might never come.

Sleep still pressed against me when the sun rose the next morning, but I forced myself to rise. The soldiers were already breaking camp. I took a step toward the command tent, knowing that I needed to meet with Verone, but instead my feet carried me to Taryn's tent unbidden.

"Taryn?" I asked through the canvas, checking to see if she was awake.

I hesitated a moment, but when I heard no answer or movement from inside, I eased back the flap, peering inside. It was empty. I frowned. She must have already gone to the healer. As I turned, my eyes caught on a scrap of paper lying near the head of the bed.

Trepidation slithered through me as I slowly stepped inside the tent to pick it up, my gaze roving over the three words.

Please forgive me.

I stared at it in shock, the breath stilling in my lungs.

Where would she—

Our conversation about the bargain Tristan had offered flashed through my mind, but she couldn't be stupid enough to attempt that on her own. She'd never make it.

I exited the tent to find Nic striding toward me, the possibility of it working its way out. Taryn was beyond determined and stubborn, but this?

"Get me Dante," I ordered before sweeping past him, marching toward the command tent where I knew Verone would be waiting. Panic rose within me even as I tried to keep it at bay. I picked up my pace. If she had really left for the City of Iso, she wasn't going to make it that far. Not with her wounds. She was barely going to make it traveling with us.

Verone was engaged in a conversation with a messenger who had just ridden up, and he turned at my approach. "Vladimir, I'm glad you're here, I—"

"Taryn's gone," I said, looking around for Nic. "I have to go bring her back."

"She can barely move. Gone where?"

I raked a hand through my hair, pulling at the strands. "I told you what Tristan said, and I think she's trying to get into the City of Iso."

He stared at me for a moment before something registered within his expression, and the sadness and acceptance that filled his gaze cut right through me.

Nic came trotting up with Dante, and I reached for the reins, but Verone put a hand out to stop me.

"You can't leave, Vladimir."

I jerked back, pointing my finger to the north. "Would you have me leave her to die out there?"

I circled to Dante's left side, reaching for the stirrup.

"She didn't tell you, did she?"

I stilled at the dead tone of his voice. "Tell me what?"

Our argument had caught the attention of the soldiers, and Verone stepped closer to keep them from overhearing.

"The healer spoke with me last night," Verone said.

I wanted to clamp my hands over my ears and block out the rest of the world, go back to this morning when everything had been normal, when everything had been right, because I knew what he was about to say, and the moment he said it, it would become true.

"It's infected."

I closed my eyes at his words. "That's why I have to go bring her back, Verone. If we can get her to Ervonne, get her treatment—"

"She knew that she was going to die, Vladimir. If not from the infection, then from the poison that wrought the nightmares. That's why she went, no doubt to spare the both of you, and to try to do one last thing with her life, heavens bless her. She made her choice, and you cannot rob her of that."

"Then we need to make sure she gets there, make sure—"

"You're needed here, Vladimir, with your men. More than ever." Verone grasped my arm. "Look around you, do you not see the fear in their eyes at the prospect of you leaving?"

My gaze drifted to the idling circle of men around us, the apprehension and the worry blatant in their faces.

"If you leave now, it's going to destroy any hope that they have left."

The world split around me, within me.

"She made her choice to give herself to this kingdom up until the very end, and now I need you to make yours. And before you suggest sending someone else in your stead, are you really willing to send more men to their death on a false hope?"

I looked north, recalling last night with the shadows dancing around us, the words falling from her lips. She hadn't been giving me a promise. She'd been telling me goodbye. Moisture gathered at the corners of my eyes, threatening to break free.

"Now, are you going to stay?" he asked.

I nodded reluctantly, having to shut down everything within me to keep from falling apart.

"I know exactly what you're going through, and I know

how hard it is going to be, but I need you mentally focused, Vladimir. The messenger has something important to tell us."

I turned to the soldier, who still looked out of breath, the dust only now starting to settle around his mount's hooves.

"Sir." He dipped his head. "I've just come from the south. Algarar has crossed the border. They've already taken two of the southern cities."

Shouts ricocheted through the camp before he'd even finished speaking, another messenger flying into view. The horses' hooves pounded against the ground, sliding to a halt in front of us. Panic was plastered all over his face.

"Report," I ordered, bracing myself for whatever horrible thing was coming next.

He struggled to catch his breath, his hollow gaze boring into mine. "Sir, it's—it's the king."

CHAPTER SEVENTY

I'D BRIBED A squire to bring me Stryder saddled with provisions, telling him I'd been tasked with a secret mission that no one must know about. He'd believed me, and he'd been a fool. I wasn't even sure if I could get in the saddle at first. I'd had the boy lead Stryder up to a cart that I struggled to climb up, and then clambered onto Stryder's back from there. Spreading my legs across his back pulled at the stitches on my hip, and I nearly blacked out at the pain. When Stryder started walking, the movement made it ten times worse. I had to bite my tongue to keep from crying out, from screaming.

I don't know how I made it through that first night.

That second day.

I'd asked the squire to use the lightest saddle they had, but it still felt like a bag of rocks when I pulled it from Stryder's back. I had no idea how I was going to get it back on, because it was too far of a stretch on the stitches to try to deadlift it with one arm. In the end, I coaxed Stryder to lie down, grateful for the silly tricks I'd taught him back in Navarre, and slid it up onto his back. Tightening and buckling the cinch with one hand was another story. When it came time for the bridle, Stryder was too sweet, lowering his head so I could easily slip it over his ears.

The days passed.

Three. Four. Five. Six.

And then, on the seventh day—the fever found me.

The days held no memories. Only pain. Maybe I wasn't even going in the right direction, but I was still moving toward the two giant mountains jutting out in the distance. Tristan said it was wedged between them, and so that was where I headed.

Sometimes, the delirium tried to take me, but I wouldn't let it.

Not yet.

I forced myself to keep going, to make it a little farther.

Because it was the only hope for Gharridan.

I didn't have much to offer, but if I could succeed at this, if I could get there in enough time, maybe it would be the last good thing that I could do.

I wasn't going to survive anyway, and I didn't have long.

The smell from the wound in my shoulder was nauseating.

Colors leaked through the bandage.

The mountains loomed before us, stretched higher into the air. The world around me had dropped in temperature, but I didn't have the strength to pull my cloak around my shoulders, so it was draped across my lap. Tristan said I couldn't miss it, but maybe I was hallucinating, maybe I was going in circles—but then we crested a ridge and broke out of the tree line. Sunlight accosted me, and I weakly shielded my eyes from the harsh light that had moments ago been hidden by the canopy of trees. Through my fever and delirium, my breath caught in my throat at what spread before me.

The ridge dipped down into a low valley spread between two jagged mountaintops rising up on either side. Encased in the center was a massive stone wall, reaching up toward the sky, as tall as the highest spire of the castle at the capital. It ran in both directions, to the left as far as the eye could see and disappearing into the forest on the right, leaving it impenetrable to any entrance. It had to be two if not three times the size of the wall of Gharridan. A massive, solid iron gate was set into the center of the structure, the only break in the intimidating structure.

My gaze fell to the valley below, my throat constricting.

Corpses and bones littered the field full of lush green grass and vibrant spring wildflowers. It was a graveyard, but a graveyard adorned in all the glory of heaven. Or maybe none of what lay before me was real, and I was simply entering into the gateway of heaven myself.

I slowed my breathing, taking in everything about me as it

might be the last time, then with eyes pinned on the gates, I urged Stryder forward into a canter.

I will protect

And I will defend.

I will stand my ground—I will not give in.

Stryder's gate was smooth, but it still jolted my body, and I gritted my teeth as tears sprung to my eyes from the rocking motion. The corners of my vision threatened to go black, but I pushed against the darkness, if only for a moment longer. My dirty hair flowed behind me, the skirts of my ruined dress flapping around my legs. Arrows protruded from the corpses on the ground, and I waited for arrows to fly from the wall. Waited for them to strike me. We were nearly within firing range.

My eyes slid closed, waiting for the end, for the last strike of pain. I hoped that Stryder would be spared, that he might find his way back home.

Till I draw my last breath

Or stars fall from the sky

I will sacrifice all—Even unto my life.

The sun beat upon my closed eyelids, the last taste of it I would ever have. Unconsciousness tore at me, wanting to take me away. Shadows passed across my eyelids, and I opened my eyes for what I thought was the last time. Stryder slowed to a trot, then a walk before stopping in the shadow of the wall, his nostrils flaring in and out.

And I couldn't go on anymore. Death waited, and the darkness was there. I could no longer tell it no.

I am bound to this country

And this country to me.

I take the oath of Kavari—I pledge me to thee.

As I fell, I heard the sound of groaning gears and screeching hinges, and I knew, even though I never saw it.

The gates.

Opened.

END OF BOOK THREE

EPILOGUE

BITTER GLADES OF grass and soft dirt mixed in the man's mouth, his body crumpled facedown on the ground. Blood stained his trousers and seeped through the bandages on his leg, but pain pulsed through his entire body, aching like it had been slammed against a wall. Blackness coated his vision. He'd hit his head.

His fingers brushed against the wet grass, the dampness of the ground he was sprawled upon. Confusion wafted through him. Faint memories of riding a horse and heading for a city drifted through his mind, but failed to connect to why. Until his hearing came back.

Moans echoed around him, the cries of dying men. Hoofbeats pounded around his body, shouts, battle cries, and then— then he remembered.

Ambush.

The weak man rolled his face out of the dirt, turning to

reach for his sword hilt that was digging into his ribs, answering the question of why the pain was more excruciating than it should have been. Through his bleary vision, he watched weapons clash, watched soldiers—his soldiers—fight and then fall around him.

He knew that he had to get to them, had to help them.

With wobbly legs, he struggled to his feet only to make it a few stumbling steps as he grimaced with pain before a boot swept beneath him, sending him to his knees. The tip of a sword gleaming with blood hovered over the wild pulse at his throat, holding the power of life and death over him.

The man wanted to curse the enemy, but his disoriented mind couldn't even place their faces, couldn't distinguish which kingdom they served. He wondered if the rest of his army had already been defeated, or if the enemy had come straight for him. Come to finish the job. Perhaps it was the assassin prince who held the blade.

A dirty hand grabbed a fistful of his blond hair, yanking his head back and keeping his body rooted in place. The kneeling man wanted to throw out a sarcastic comment, but it was diffi-cult to conjure amid the pain, making him think he'd hit his head harder than he originally thought.

Bodies of his Gharridan comrades lay strewn across the ground. Lifeless.

"If you're going to kill me," he croaked out, "then get it over with."

"Don't worry, we're not here to kill you yet. *Will.*"

The familiar voice sent a violent shiver crawling down William's spine and froze his blood to ice, making him question if he could really be *that* unlucky.

The man who had spoken stepped into his field of vision, a sardonic smile plastered across his face.

"Do you even remember me? It's been a while, but not that long. You may be a king now, but I know that I haven't forgotten you or that accursed child of Michael Gallows."

A limp plagued the man's gait as he strode over to his horse. "We have a long journey ahead of us, and I'm rather ready to be home and rid of you."

William let out a bitter laugh. "I will not be your prisoner. If you want all of your men to make it back alive, then I suggest you kill me now."

The captain hesitated before shrugging with indifference and motioning to one of his men.

A scream pierced the night as a soldier dragged a woman forward by her thick curly hair. He shoved her to the ground where she cowered before the king, her scared brown eyes locking with his.

Fear lit within him.

"I had a hunch you might not come willingly." The captain brandished a dagger. "So I found some leverage. I highly doubt that she's *just* a courier." He pressed the edge of the dagger against the woman's neck, cutting into her dark skin and drawing a trickle of blood. "Either you come with us willingly, or we start leaving her behind." He cocked an eyebrow. "One piece at a time."

The woman couldn't shake her head no, but she told the king with her eyes to not accept the deal. To let her die—but he could not. It was unfeasible to admit defeat for the life of one person, but death already circled the king like a cloud of angry vultures, displayed on the dead soldiers surrounding him. No.

Blast leverage. Keeping the woman alive for as long as possible gave her the best chance of escape, because right now, there was none.

"Are we agreed?" the captain asked.

The king shot another look at the woman who pleaded for him to not accept, but he could not sacrifice another life.

"As long as she is left unharmed, we are agreed."

The captain chuckled, removing the blade from her neck and leaving a thin cut behind. "I thought that might talk some sense into you. It got your tongue working last time. Let's go."

The soldier behind the king dragged him to his feet, William unable to support himself, while another soldier stepped behind him to bind his hands, the rough rope scratching against his skin.

"And where is it exactly that we're going?" he asked.

A knowing look glinted in Captain Dugal's eyes, sending William's skin crawling with fear.

"Why to see King Dorjan, of course." He smiled. "After all, he's been so looking forward to finally meeting his nephew."

ACKNOWLEDGMENTS

This series would really be nothing without my mom, who is the first person to always read my books (practically tries to rip them from my hands before they're done) and reads every book multiple times, always telling me they were just as good the fourth or fifth or eighth time through. She has single-handedly backed this series more than anyone, and I couldn't do it without her.

A retraction is in order as my dad, who I said would never read these books (ahem, the dedication for The King Slayer), but actually DID read them and loved them. I didn't believe my mom when she first told me he was reading them. But not only did he read them, he now recommends them to people as much as my mom does. Both of my parents are amazing marketers and recommenders of this series. Thank you, and I love you guys.

My sister Donna, who this book is dedicated to, is my book buddy although we have wildly different tastes in genres. She puts up with a million texts or phone calls regarding writing or books or authoring, basically everything under the sun, and still answers all of them. Thank you so much for having my back and being the best supporter (and sister) you possibly can be.

To Caitlan Honer who is like—super awesome—and also doesn't bat an eye when I'm like "can I run these thirty-seven questions and concerns past you really fast?" or lets me blow up her phone with eighty million messages. You're such a great friend and writing friend, and I have no idea how I would do this without you.

Thank you to my Aunt Debbie for reading an early copy and for all of the valuable feedback. (sorry for making you cry!)

Thank you to my friend Courtney for answering my medical questions regarding infection after giving her some pretty vague and wild scenarios.

Thanks also to my brother for helping me with my crazy battle tactic questions.

To my cover designer Franziska Stern, you KILLED this cover and I am so in love with it!!

Shout out to my awesome editor, Rachel Oestreich, for working her wizardly editor magic on both The Death Bringer and The King Slayer, thank you!

If you've stuck with me this far into The Blood Vier series, thank you so much for your continuous love for these characters and this story. Readers like you are why these books happen, and us authors couldn't do it without your support. Also, thank you for still loving me after the massive cliffhanger I just left you on.

Finally, *Thanks be unto God for his unspeakable gift* and for the joy of having the privilege to write these stories.

LEAVE A REVIEW

If you enjoyed reading *The Death Bringer*, please consider leaving a review on Amazon, Goodreads, or Barnes and Noble. Reviews help authors find more readers like you.

CHRISTY R. HARRILL is the book-loving and anything medieval fantasy obsessing author of the *Blood Vier* series. She lives in Oklahoma where she enjoys hiking with her dog Hank and devouring every book she possibly has time for. Christy loves winter, and still hopes to attain the dream of getting snowed in with four feet of snow one day. She thinks that the only good thing about summer is wearing sandals, and has a weakness for buying pretty notebooks— even though she already owns far too many blank ones at home.

For more information, please visit Christy at
christyrharrill.com
Or follow her on Instagram and TikTok

DON'T MISS THE FIRST TWO BOOKS IN CHRISTY R. HARRILL'S *BLOOD VIER* QUARTET!